PRAISE FOR
THE MOON SHIFTER SERIES

Mating Instinct

"Katie Reus creates a vivid world filled with sexy shifters, explosive danger, and enough sexual tension to set the pages on fire. A fabulous paranormal romance!"
—Alexandra Ivy, *New York Times* bestselling author of *Fear the Darkness*

"*Mating Instinct*'s romance is taut and passionate. Add to that a fast-paced suspense plot and a deftly built paranormal world, and Katie Reus's newest installment in her Moon Shifter series will leave readers breathless!"
—Stephanie Tyler, national bestselling author of *Unbreakable*

"I could not put this book down.... Let me be clear that I am not saying that this was a good book *for a* paranormal genre; it was an excellent romance read, *period*." —All About Romance

"Once again, Reus delivers another clever page-turner." —*RT Book Reviews*

"A sexy, well-crafted paranormal romance that succeeds with smart characters and creative world building." —*Kirkus Reviews*

"This series keeps getting better and better."
—Joyfully Reviewed

continued . . .

Primal Possession

"Reus has definitely hit a home run with this series. . . . This book has mystery, suspense, and a heart-pounding romance that will leave you wanting more."
—Nocturne Romance Reads

"Reus's world building is incredibly powerful as she seamlessly blends various elements of legend and myth. . . . But the romance between a shifter and human is the real highlight—it's lusty, heartfelt, and shows love can conquer all." —RT Book Reviews

"[Primal Possession] has all the right ingredients: a hot couple, evil villains, and a killer action-filled plot. . . . [The] Moon Shifter series is what I call Grade-A entertainment!" —Joyfully Reviewed

"If you like your romance hot with plenty of buildup and a plot that sucks you right in, Primal Possession is simply a must read." —A Book Obsession

"Impossible to put down. . . . Ms. Reus bangs out a top-quality story." —Fresh Fiction

Alpha Instinct

"You'll look forward to visiting this world again soon!"
—RT Book Reviews

"Reus has an instinct for what wows in this perfect blend of shifter, suspense, and sexiness. Sexy alphas, kick-ass heroines, and twisted villains will keep you turning the pages in this new shifter series. Alpha Instinct is a winner."

—Caridad Piñeiro, New York Times
bestselling author of The Claimed

"Alpha Instinct is a wild, hot ride for readers. The story grabs you and doesn't let go."
—Cynthia Eden, New York Times bestselling
author of Angel in Chains

"Reus crafts a fast-paced action story. . . . *Alpha Instinct* is awesome: an engrossing page-turner that I enjoyed in one sitting. Reus offers all the ingredients I love in a paranormal romance."   —Book Lovers Inc.

"Prepare yourself for the start of a great new series! . . . I'm excited about reading more about this great group of characters."   —Fresh Fiction

"A well-plotted, excellently delivered emotional and sensual ride that grabs hold and doesn't let go! . . . Ms. Reus delivers mystery, suspense, and a romance nothing short of heart pounding!"   —Night Owl Reviews

"A strong book full of mystery, intrigue, and a new world to explore. . . . I thoroughly enjoyed this one as I suspect lovers of the paranormal romance genres will do as well!"   —Ramblings from a Chaotic Mind

"If you're looking for a new shifter romance to sink your teeth in, then look no further. *Alpha Instinct* is action-packed with a solid romance that will keep the reader on the edge of [her] toes! . . . Highly recommended for fans of Rachel Vincent's Werecat series."
            —Nocturne Romance Reads

PRAISE FOR
THE DEADLY OPS SERIES

Targeted

"Fast-paced romantic suspense that will keep you on the edge of your seat!"   —Cynthia Eden

"Sexy suspense at its finest."
            —Laura Wright, *New York Times*
            bestselling author of *Eternal Sin*

"Reus strikes just the right balance of steamy sexual tension and nail-biting action. . . . This romantic thriller reliably hits every note that fans of the genre will expect."   —*Publishers Weekly*

Also by Katie Reus

The Moon Shifter Novels
Alpha Instinct
Lover's Instinct
(A Penguin Special from Signet Eclipse)
Primal Possession
Mating Instinct
His Untamed Desire
(A Penguin Special from Signet Eclipse)

The Deadly Ops Novels
Targeted

Other Titles
Enemy Mine
(A Penguin Special from Signet Eclipse)

AVENGER'S HEAT

A Moon Shifter Novel

KATIE REUS

A SIGNET ECLIPSE BOOK

SIGNET ECLIPSE
Published by the Penguin Group
Penguin Group (USA) LLC, 375 Hudson Street,
New York, New York 10014

USA | Canada | UK | Ireland | Australia | New Zealand | India | South Africa | China
penguin.com
A Penguin Random House Company

First published by Signet Eclipse, an imprint of New American Library,
a division of Penguin Group (USA) LLC

First Printing, February 2014

ISBN 978-0-451-41795-4

Printed in the United States of America
10 9 8 7 6 5 4 3 2 1

For my sister. Thank you for always being there for me no matter what. The world is a beautiful place because you're in it.

Chapter 1

Erin Flynn shot the tall male shifter next to her a quick glance as yet another female they passed on the street gave him an assessing, purely sexual look. Since they'd arrived in New Orleans an hour ago it had been the same reaction from practically every woman they'd come across. A few men too. Not that she blamed any of them, even if she did have a sudden urge to claw their eyes out.

Simply put, Noah Campbell was smoking hot. Tall, broad shoulders, sharp cheekbones, inky black hair a woman could easily imagine running her fingers through, and perfect olive coloring that showed off his Greek heritage on his mother's side. Didn't matter that it was an icy January day, he looked like he'd just stepped off a Mediterranean beach, all toned and tan. He definitely evoked thoughts of sex, sin, and sultry summer nights.

They passed a woman dressed in jeans that might as well have been painted on, a bright red coat belted around her tiny waist and five-inch knee-high boots. When she practically undressed Noah with her eyes, Erin frowned at her friend. "Are you being intention-ally oblivious?" No way could he have missed how people were looking at him.

Noah's guarded dark eyes flicked her way once be-fore he continued scanning the nearly deserted cobble-stone streets. They'd parked outside the long and narrow shotgun-style house they were staying in with another shifter and fae warrior, both of whom had decided to hang back while she and Noah scoped out the city. And the tension hadn't left his body since the moment they'd stepped out of that pastel blue and pink house with peeling yellow shutters.

"Not oblivious, just not interested." A curt answer so typical of him when he was annoyed or stressed. Right now she thought he might be a bit of both. He didn't look at her again, but she could practically feel the heat of his dark eyes searing her. Knew what she'd see if he looked her way again. Lust and need.

Some days she wished he'd find a woman. A sweet beta female who would be perfect for him. It would slice up her insides to know that someone else would be touching what she considered hers, waking up ev-ery morning next to him . . . but at least he'd be happy. Maybe she'd finally be able to move on from this con-stant state of wanting him but knowing she could never have him.

God, she was so fucked up.

Instinctively she patted the front of her thick coat, needing to feel the two short blades strapped to her chest beneath it. She didn't go anywhere without them.

Even slept with one under her pillow. "Did you finally call your father?" she asked.

"Nope."

Resisting the urge to growl at him, she shoved her hands in her jacket pockets.

Just great.

As the newest enforcer-in-training for the North American Council of lupine shifters, Erin was on her first mission by herself. Technically she wasn't in training anymore but she still thought of herself that way. Her mentor, Jayce, had told her that she was ready to go out on her own investigation so here she was. He'd sent Noah along, but it wasn't so Noah could look out for her—that would have pissed her off. New Orleans was Noah's father's territory and the situation right now had the potential to be volatile.

Noah's father shared the city with vamps, feline shifters, and fae, and she was pretty sure a few demons made their home here too. The old city just appealed to them. New Orleans was the one place in the United States paranormal beings had agreed to share. It was either that or endure a bloodbath fighting over it.

Not worth it when they were practically under a microscope by the humans they'd revealed themselves to two decades ago. Erin still thought that was a stupid decision on the Council's part but it was over and done with. Not much anyone could do about it now.

The one thing she'd asked Noah to do was make contact with his father before they'd arrived. It irked her that he hadn't, but in the past year and some odd months since she'd been friends with Noah, he hadn't said more than a handful of sentences about the powerful Alpha and she hadn't pushed. She didn't like talking about her past so she understood his need for privacy. Still, his father was Alpha of this territory and deserved the respect of a freaking phone call.

"Damn it, Noah," she muttered, but didn't continue as they rounded another street corner. The difference from the quiet one they'd just come from was vivid.

A variety of scents and noises accosted them. Tobacco, liquor, a mix of cheap and expensive perfumes, raw sex, and some kind of spicy food tickled her nose. Sometimes she cursed her extrasensory abilities. A few bars blasted music, but a steady, low-key stream of tunes flowed out from the Full Moon Bar as they neared it.

Even if she hadn't scented all the paranormal beings inside, the lower level of music was the first giveaway that the place catered to people like her. Paranormal beings had extrasensory everything, something humans seemed to usually forget. And something she was thankful for because it had the potential to make her job as enforcer easier.

"I talked to my mom earlier and she told me my father would be here tonight," Noah said quietly.

Erin knew Noah talked to his mother practically every week, but hadn't spoken to his father in years. She might not know everything about his family dynamics, but she knew enough. And this had disaster written all over it. She pulled her cell phone out of her pocket, ready to dial the number of Angus Campbell she'd received from Jayce before she and Noah had left North Carolina.

She should have just taken care of this herself but she'd wanted to let Noah do it. Even if she was on

Council business she was still entering another Alpha's territory and he deserved a heads-up. Noah knew the protocol well. No doubt he was just showing up unannounced to piss his old man off. Not the way she wanted to start this investigation.

Scrolling to the number as they crossed the street, her head snapped up at a crashing sound. A giant female jaguar tumbled out of the bar they were on their way to, her fangs and claws extended. Definitely a shifter. The animal let out a loud snarl then rushed back in through a splintered blue door.

Erin's eyes widened as a shot of adrenaline punched through her.

"Shit," Noah muttered, moving into action.

Unzipping her jacket as she ran, she unsheathed her short blades from their protective casings. They weren't quite two feet long, pure silver, and her best defense in close combat. Which was the type of fighting she preferred.

She respected the hell out of snipers, but this was her game. As a shifter she was unique because she preferred to fight in her human form. Just like the other enforcers across the globe. It wasn't because she was stronger in human form—though she was strong and fast—it was because once she let her beast out, it was difficult to rein her wolf back in. For Erin, keeping the balance between her animal and human side was a bitch.

After the long drive cooped up in a car with Noah and too much sexual frustration—that she'd been battling for months—she needed to let off some steam and this was the way to do it.

To her annoyance Noah rushed into the dimly lit bar first, but she was right behind him. The gorgeous black jaguar with a faint orange background and dark spots was rolling around on the floor with a male vampire. They were slicing each other to ribbons, though Erin knew the big cat was holding back. Jaguars—regular or shifter—had powerful jaws and this one wasn't biting.

There were about two dozen people there, but no one was intervening. What the hell?

A few humans, a handful of tall ethereal-looking fae, vampires, and lupine and feline shifters in human form all lounged around the bar staring at the two in open amusement. How was this remotely funny?

Screw that. "I'm taking the male down. Stay out of it," she murmured to Noah, hoping he'd listen. Sometimes he was overprotective of her and she had no problem taking care of herself.

Without waiting for a response, she jumped into the fray. She was young for a shifter, but incredibly quick and knew one day—if she lived long enough—she'd have a better grasp on the strange power she could feel growing inside her every day.

Lightning fast, she sliced at the feline's shoulder, earning a surprised cry. The big cat immediately jumped off the vamp and backed away.

The vamp lunged at Erin and even though she could sense the power rippling off him in waves, she dodged to the side and sliced her blade across his chest as he sailed past her. Blood spurted everywhere but it wasn't even close to a killing blow. The sweet scent that filled the air was different from the normal coppery scent of human and shifter blood.

The dark-skinned vamp turned, a look of surprise on his face. She didn't know if it was because of her speed, her sex, or her apparent youth. She also didn't care. His fangs flashed, claws unsheathed as those hostile dark eyes narrowed at her. She heard Noah growl behind her.

"I've got this, Noah!" They'd fought side by side before and while he might hate her fighting, he better at least respect her enough to handle herself.

Out of the corner of her eye she realized the feline shifter was crouching, ready to pounce—on her!

What the hell is going on? She'd been trying to help the shifter out. Before Erin could move to defend herself an eerie growl and the sound of bones breaking ripped through the slight murmur of voices and low music. A flash of dark fur she recognized as Noah flew through the air at the cat.

Annoyed he'd intervened, but having no doubt he could take care of himself, she didn't lose her momentum as she raced at the vamp. Right now all she cared about was subduing this guy as fast as possible. She didn't have time to sing and dance with him. That meant going on the offensive.

Using a barstool as leverage, she jumped on it, then a table before hurtling through the air. Raising a blade with her right hand, she brought it down as if to stab him through the chest. Calculating his attempt to swivel away to the left, she swept up with her left hand, slicing him through the gut.

It wouldn't kill him, but silver burned vamps and shifters something fierce. His skin sizzled as he cried out under her blow. She didn't stop there. As he instinctively attempted to grapple with the blade, she brought the other one down on his forearm, pinning him to the floor.

Blood pooled everywhere, creating a dark river around them. The sickly sweet scent wafted up. "I'm not going to kill you if you stop struggling," she bit out, flashing her canines in a show of aggression.

Immediately the vampire went limp, but the rage in his eyes didn't diminish. "What the hell is wrong with you?" He wheezed out the words.

Before she could respond she heard a feminine cry behind her. "Don't hurt him! He's my mate!"

Instead of turning around, she quickly glanced at one of the mirrors in front of her displaying a full blue moon and advertising a new beer. In the reflection she saw a naked woman likely of South American descent being restrained by a very naked Noah, since his clothes had shredded during his change. Something sharp and deadly rose up inside Erin at seeing him tangled together with a female, but she forced it back down and focused on the crazy situation in front of her. She narrowed her gaze at the vamp still shooting her daggers with his eyes. "That's your mate?"

He nodded, his lips pulled into a thin line. "We were just having a bit of an argument. Nothing serious."

It had looked pretty damn serious to her. That's when she scented the feline on him. No, not just on him, but practically *in* him, living under his skin. Yeah, no doubt they were mated. Sure had a weird way of acting like it. Glancing around, Erin noted that everyone had given her and Noah a wide berth and had congregated at the back of the bar.

"Attack me or him"—she tilted her head in Noah's direction without taking her gaze off the vamp—"and I'll cut off your head." Without waiting for his response, she withdrew her blades and put a good ten feet between them in a split second. The instant she'd cleared the vamp, Noah let the female go. Erin didn't sheathe her weapons though. She wasn't worried about herself, but the thought of anyone hurting Noah . . . it brought out something dark inside her. Some days she hated that feeling because he wasn't hers. It was like this constant battle waging inside her.

Ignoring everyone and uncaring about her nudity, the feline knelt by the vamp, cupping his cheek and stroking a hand down his chest. Blood pooled around him but he was already practically healed. "Are you hurt, baby?"

"For the love of . . ." Erin turned toward Noah and using strength she didn't realize she had, kept her eyes way above his belt line and steady on his face. "What the hell kind of place is this?"

Before he could answer, a booming male voice silenced the room. Even the music shut off. "Martina, Razi, get the hell out of here and don't show your faces on this street for a month."

The vamp and feline—still freaking naked—practically ran from the bar, bleeding all over the place and cursing a blue streak. But not before shooting Erin a murderous glare.

Once they were gone her attention was drawn to the back of the bar where a big male who looked like an older version of Noah, minus the dark hair, was walking through the sudden gap between the onlookers.

Definitely Noah's father. Beside her, Noah tensed. It was subtle, something she noticed only because she knew him so well.

And you'd like to know him a whole lot better, wouldn't you?

The big lupine strode right toward them, stopping only a foot away after he'd given them both assessing looks. "You'll have to excuse Martina and Razi—that's just foreplay to them."

"They were fighting like animals," she said, though she had no reason to defend her actions.

"We *are* animals." His dark eyes looked so much like Noah's it rattled her, but she didn't let it show.

Instead Erin shrugged. "I take it you're Angus Campbell."

"And you are Erin Flynn, newest enforcer in North America. Jayce called to let me know you would be here soon, though I *expected* a call from you." His head swiveled to Noah and his dark eyes turned hard.

They were the same height so the two men just glared at each other. She could practically see the flood of testosterone rolling off them. Despite the differences in their appearances, because Noah had certainly been blessed with his mother's features too, the tall broad-shouldered Scottish shifter was obviously Noah's father. It was stamped in the harsh, defined facial features.

Angus looked to be about forty by human standards but Erin knew he was at least three hundred. Very old for a shifter and *very* powerful. He'd have to be to control New Orleans for as long as he had, which had been since the Jazz Age. Almost a century ago and long before most humans had known of the existence of paranormal beings.

Clearing her throat and drawing the big shifter's attention back to her, she took a subtle step forward placing herself in between father and son. One of Noah's hands settled on her shoulder in a way she knew he meant to be proprietary, something his father didn't miss. The feel of Noah touching her like that should have annoyed her. Instead, it soothed her inner wolf in a way she decided to ignore. Angus's eyes flicked to Noah's hand, then back to her face so quickly she would have missed the speculative look if she hadn't been watching him closely. Let the old Alpha make of it what he wanted.

When it was clear Noah didn't plan to respond to his father's statement, Erin continued. "We need to talk about what's going on. Unless you approve of what's happening in your city." It wasn't a question because no one in their right mind would want things to continue the way they were in New Orleans. But she wanted to gauge his reaction.

Those dark eyes flashed with raw anger and for a moment she saw the wolf lurking beneath the man's surface. "Six pregnant female shifters missing . . ." His jaw clenched once and she could feel his power radiating for an instant. There was a reason he was an Alpha. "Whoever is responsible will pay." As he spoke, she heard the animal, not the human talking to her.

And he was right. Someone would pay. But not by his hand. It would be by an enforcer. *Her.*

Erin's eyes narrowed. When she got her hands on

the culprit or culprits, they'd be judged. And they'd sure as hell suffer for their crimes. Preying on a pregnant female, regardless of species, was the lowest of the low. All the women had been taken while alone. Two from their homes, one from a park, one right outside her real estate office, one from a grocery store parking lot, and one from a restaurant while her mate was in the vicinity. The two homes had been disturbed, but no serious damage. And the others taken had left behind purses and keys at their abduction sites. It was the only reason anyone had any idea exactly where they'd been kidnapped from.

Meli was the last shifter who had been taken and she was the only one linked directly to Angus's pack. The only lupine. It was the main reason the Council had sent her here. Angus was a powerful Alpha. The other five missing shifters were all feline with no pack or political pull. Erin had memorized their basic information and seen photographs of each woman.

The feline grabbed right before Meli was so *young*. Her name was Ciara. At twenty-five years old, newly mated for a scant six months, she was two months pregnant and the only redhead in the bunch. Her appearance didn't matter to Erin but when she'd looked at the girl's picture it had jarred her straight to her bones.

Something heavy settled on Erin's chest. Hurting a woman in that state when she was weaker, defenseless . . . it was just so wrong on every level. The heaviness seemed to grow inside her, pressing down until it was hard to breathe. The women must have been so terrified.

Noah had been silent, but his hand flexed once on her shoulder and she didn't miss the soft growl he let out. He wanted blood as much as she did. The feel of his fingers clenching around her pulled her from her thoughts and back to reality.

She was going to hunt whoever was behind this like the monsters they were. But first she had to figure out who was responsible for the disappearances and why. She just hoped Noah let her handle this investigation her way.

Chapter 2

"If I remember right the last time you were in a bar fight, a female was also involved." Noah's father didn't look at him as he spoke.

Next to him Erin stiffened. *Interesting.* Noah shrugged in response, not willing to talk more than he had to at the moment. His skin felt too tight for his body and now wasn't the time to lose his cool. Even if he was itching for a fight. Anything to expend all the energy barely leashed inside him. Since sex was off the table—until Erin finally admitted she wanted him—fighting would have to do it.

Noah kept stride with Erin as they walked out of the bar with his father. Thankfully there had been extra clothes behind the bar for him to change into—not surprising since this was a shifter-run bar. His father hadn't said where they were going, just told them he had a private place to discuss things that was completely soundproofed. But Noah knew exactly where they were headed. The Alpha owned a town house a block down from the bar. Or he had about a decade ago.

That was just the way New Orleans was set up. In the French Quarter, sometimes a home and bar were separated by only a stone's throw. Of course the old wolf had a few homes in the Garden District too. That was where the majority of the pack and Noah's mother lived most of the time. Angus spent his nights with Noah's mother, but the Alpha liked staying in the Quarter, liked keeping a pulse on what was happening in the city. Made sense for his position, especially since he had a lot of businesses there.

Noah took in the ornate wrought iron trim on the fences lining the old buildings as they passed, careful not to look at his father. He hadn't expected to see him so soon after arriving, though he probably should have. It was hard to look at the old man and not see his dead, younger sister staring back at him. Fiona had looked so much like Angus it shredded Noah's insides to see him after so many years of estrangement.

Clenching his jaw and forcing those thoughts away, he used his peripheral vision to watch Erin. The petite, very lean redhead had been driving him insane since they'd left North Carolina. Well, longer than that. With ivory, flawless skin and a smattering of freckles across her nose and cheeks she almost looked like a young, innocent college kid. But he'd seen her in action enough recently to know she could handle herself.

She tried to pretend the scorching kisses they'd shared over the past few weeks meant nothing. That she didn't want him. But every time she turned those mercurial gray eyes—that had an almost imperceptible ring of amber around them—in his direction, he felt her heat and need for him. Hell, he could smell her lust sometimes too. A sweet magnolia scent that had the ability to bring him to his knees. If she'd just admit what she wanted it would make life a hell of a lot easier. Women were fucking complicated though.

In typical Erin fashion she'd braided her shoulder-length red hair tight against her head and wore all black. Black cargo pants and a black T-shirt that molded to her like a second skin. She also had a black cap tucked in her jacket pocket with a tiny white skull and crossbones stitched on the front. A gift from Jayce before they'd left. If Jayce wasn't so unbelievably happily mated, Noah would have wanted to slice him up for giving Erin any gift. Her thick jacket covered her tight shirt and her blades, taking away the nice view he'd gotten earlier of the outline of her nipples.

Gritting his teeth, Noah shoved that image out of his head too. Thinking about Erin in any sort of state of undress would only short-circuit his brain.

Not that it mattered. The woman *never* left his thoughts. Seeing her jump into the middle of that fight had taken all his control not to attack that male. But he hadn't wanted to distract her. Didn't matter that all his biological urges had been clawing at him, telling him to kick that vamp's ass. If he'd gotten in her way it would have undermined her position in town. As enforcer—something he fucking hated, even while he respected it—people had to know she could handle her own. Especially since she was completely untried.

As they reached the brick town house he wasn't surprised to see not much had changed. A wrought iron balcony covered in an excess of lacy ferns looped around the second story and a fleur-de-lis the size of his fist that he guessed might have been made out of real gold adorned the bright turquoise door. Definitely his mother's influence. She liked color even if it was just a splash. His father didn't give a shit about any of that. Before they'd taken two steps up the short set of stairs, his father looked at his cell phone and cursed.

"One of the pregnant females has been found. From my pack." His father's voice sounded more animal than human and Noah understood why. As Alpha it was up to him to protect his pack. Even one missing was too much.

"Alive?" Erin asked, hope threading that single word and searing right through Noah's chest. She might be an adept warrior—hell, more than adept, she was a skilled fighter especially for her young age—but she had a big heart and hated seeing anyone suffering.

"Barely." Noah's father shoved his cell phone at Noah. "She's in the house off Coliseum. You remember which—"

"Yes. Go, now." Noah might have issues with his father, but the man cared about those in his charge and he'd be able to get there a lot faster on his own.

Before he'd even finished speaking, his father had shifted right in the middle of the street. Fur streaked with browns and reds replaced skin as human became animal. Then he was gone in such a blur, Noah didn't even see when he rounded the corner of the street. His clothes and shoes were in shreds, his keys on the sidewalk. Noah scooped them up, knowing his father had meant for him to retrieve his belongings.

Erin breathed in awe, but only for a millisecond. "How are we getting there?"

They could shift and run in animal form, but she wasn't familiar with the streets and he didn't want to be hassled by law enforcement. He thought about running back to where they'd parked her car, but knew it would take too much time. Noah nodded back toward the direction they'd come from. "Saw a bike parked out front of the bar."

The run back took them mere seconds. They only passed one human couple on the street. He belatedly heard them gasp after they'd flown by using their supernatural speed. He and Erin jerked to a halt in front of the bar. "I'll be back in a sec," he said to Erin before hurrying through the busted-up door where he dumped the ruined clothes. The bar quieted the moment he stepped in. "I'm Angus Campbell's son and I need to borrow that Ducati out there. I'll—"

The bartender tossed him a key ring with a single key on it. "You wreck it, you pay for it."

Noah nodded at the tall dark-haired feline shifter, surprised his father had a feline working for him, but it was New Orleans, the melting pot for supernatural beings.

He found Erin outside, already sitting on the back of the bike. Sliding on in front of her, he hated himself just a little for the way his body flared to life as she curled her arms around his waist. He must be a masochist. Didn't matter that she'd made it abundantly clear friendship was all he was getting from her, he still enjoyed the feel and scent of her wrapping around his body.

Gunning the engine, he took off, driving at break-neck speed through the narrow streets, until he was free of the cramped Quarter. He zoomed around cars, stopping at red lights only if other vehicles were coming. He'd broken about a dozen traffic laws by the time he made it into the lush Garden District.

Flashes of beads hanging in a few oak trees caught his eye as he sped down a cobblestone road. They were either leftovers from the last Mardi Gras or someone was getting ready for the upcoming celebration next month. A mesh of well-kept antebellum, Victorian, Greek Revival, and other various styles of homes flew by them in a blur until he pulled up to one of his father's mansions.

The ornate black wrought iron gate was open so he weaved in between the double line of cars along the winding driveway. Looked like the house was full tonight.

Erin was off the bike before he'd stopped and pushed out the kickstand. He missed the feel of her immediately. Magnolia trees dotted the yard, guiding their way to the stately mansion as they silently strode up the rest of the walk together.

The moment they reached the raised porch the front door flew open. A younger female he vaguely recognized nodded at them and motioned for them to follow. Hurrying inside and up a winding staircase, they stopped in front of the first door at the top.

The dark-haired girl knocked softly as she opened it. A second later his father, mother, and another male shifter he guessed was the pregnant female's mate by the agony on the guy's face, strode out.

"I want to be in there with her," the male said to Angus, his voice more of an animalistic growl.

"She's stable and so is the baby. Let Erin talk to her." For such an intimidating Alpha, Noah's father had a soothing voice that could put anyone at ease when he wanted to.

"But—"

"Imelda might be more willing to talk without you around. She doesn't want to hurt you; I saw it in her eyes, Evan. She knows hearing about her pain will make you suffer. Let this woman do her job. Let her investigate and find the bastards who took Imelda. Then you'll have your vengeance."

Noah looked down as something sharp pierced him and realized his unsheathed claws were digging into his palms. The thought of Erin being taken from him, while pregnant no less, brought his beast to the surface. He hadn't lost control since he was a cub, but even thinking about Erin in danger . . . he couldn't go there. Not even in his imagination.

The shifter named Evan didn't respond. Just shifted to his wolf form on a loud growl and raced down the stairs, bits of clothing trailing after him.

"Her name is Imelda?" Erin asked quietly.

His father nodded. "According to our doctor she and the baby both have a stable heartbeat, but . . ." His jaw clenched and he shook his head, as if pushing away an unwanted vision or memory. "She said she's okay to talk to you."

Noah knew the only reason his father was even letting Erin in that room was because she was an enforcer. Not an enforcer-in-training, but full-fledged. She had the backing of the entire Council and more important, Jayce Kazan. And she was in charge of the investigation. It still surprised him that his father wasn't being a bigger dick, trying to take over, but maybe the Alpha had changed.

When Noah went to follow Erin his father raised a hand, as if to stop him. Noah knew he should show him more respect, especially since he was in Angus's house, but his canines descended and he bared his teeth in a blatant show of aggression. It had nothing to do with their estrangement and everything to do with Erin.

Raw fury flashed in his father's eyes, but his mother placed her hand on his forearm, instantly stilling the powerful Alpha. Without another glance at either of them, he followed Erin, shutting the door behind them.

He went where she went. End of story. Even if she didn't seem to think she needed him.

Eventually he knew he and Erin would come to blows over his need to be with her, to keep her close, but that was just too damn bad. He *wanted* to have it out with her, to understand why she kept pushing him away.

The mating ache grew inside him hungry and painful with no outlet. Her continual rejection of him was only making it worse.

As his gaze landed on the bed, he froze. "Meli?" For some reason it hadn't registered that Imelda was his childhood friend, *Meli*. *Fuck.*

Erin had pored over the files Jayce had given her, memorizing everything about the missing women on their drive here. But Noah had driven, letting her prep for her first investigation without his interference. Now he wished he'd at least looked at the list of names. He'd known one woman was from his father's pack, but the rest were felines. He hadn't thought he'd actually know any of them. Not after being gone for so many years.

The tall, long-legged shifter with dark hair pulled up in a messy bun gave him a small, tired smile. "It's been a long time, Noah." Her voice was raspy, hoarse, and the shadows under her eyes made her look almost ghostly.

He crossed the room in seconds, pulling up a high-backed chair on her left side, across from the place Erin had chosen. "I didn't realize you'd been taken."

Meli swallowed hard, tears pooling in her eyes, but she didn't respond. One of her hands rested protectively over her big belly.

Noah watched as Erin gently took the woman's free hand in her own and lightly squeezed. Meli turned, a look of surprise crossing her face, but didn't pull away. "I'm Imelda, but you can call me Meli, especially if you're a friend of Noah's."

Erin smiled faintly and glanced at Meli's large belly. "I'm glad your baby is safe."

"Me too," she said on a broken whisper.

Something dark and haunted passed over Erin's features. It was so painful it sliced right through Noah's soul. He'd seen that same expression the day they'd found her behind that Dumpster, broken, bleeding, so close to death he hadn't even been able to hear her heartbeat. . . . But not once since then had he seen that *look*. Up until a couple of months ago she'd been so quiet and reserved, but she'd eventually come out of that shell fighting. The look in her eyes now threw him off-kilter, reminded him how much she still kept from him. How vulnerable she could actually be when she let her guard down. But it was gone before he'd blinked, her mask firmly back in place.

"Can you tell us about who took you?" Erin asked softly, her mere presence seeming to soothe Meli. He also noticed she hadn't taken off her jacket, probably so her blades wouldn't frighten the wounded shifter.

Meli shook her head, a stray tear rolling down her pale cheek. "I never saw their faces. I know there were at least two of them, but they caught me from behind when I was coming home from the grocery store. It all happened so fast. I—" She broke off and quietly began to sob.

Outside and very near the window of the room, Noah heard an eerie howl. Likely Meli's mate, who would be sensing her anguish. Pain for the male he didn't know settled in Noah's chest.

He may not understand exactly what the mate was going through, but Noah had been helpless before to stop the pain of those he cared about. His sister and then Erin. Hell, even before he'd known Erin's name, he'd wanted to shoulder all the pain that had emanated from her the day they'd found her. Being unable to do so was like silver fucking daggers burning through him. Sharp and jagged.

Erin murmured soothing sounds, the action so at odds with the fighter he'd just witnessed less than an hour ago. It was one of the reasons she'd make a perfect enforcer. So many people thought their job was simply to crack down on lawbreakers. Though that was part of it, enforcers needed patience. She had that in spades.

Not to mention empathy and kindness. It wasn't a side of her everyone got to see, but he had and it made him care for her even more.

He was sorry Meli was in pain and hurting but part of him wanted to demand answers, ask more questions so they could get to the business of hunting down whoever had taken her. Not Erin. She sat patiently holding on to this stranger's hand as if she had all the time in the world.

Eventually Meli looked at Erin, her eyes bright with more tears. "I'm sorry. I know you have questions."

Erin shook her head. "You have nothing to be sorry for. Whatever happened to you, it wasn't your fault. Just take all the time you need." Another hard swallow, the ghosts of her past rising for a heartbeat in those clear gray eyes.

Meli frowned for a moment, then shook her head briefly. "They didn't sexually assault me or anything like that. They kept me drugged up and in a dark cell. I was fed three times a day and the only time anyone came into my cell was to take my blood. Over and over. They nearly drained me dry each time until I was almost dead." She shuddered.

"Why?" Noah asked, unable to stop from interrupting.

Her frail shoulders lifted. "I don't know. But . . . it was our kind who did this to me. Lupine shifters. There was a human there too, but he worked for the shifters. That much was clear. I know there were other females nearby that they'd taken. I could hear some women crying, some begging to be set free, but they were all felines, I'm almost sure of it. Their scents are so different from ours."

"Did your captors ever talk to you? Ever give you a hint of why they were taking your blood?" Erin asked.

She shook her head. "They didn't say much, kept me blindfolded if they came into my cell. I got the feeling they didn't care about me one way or another. I was . . . a job to them."

"How many do you remember?"

"Three, I think. Two shifters and one human. I . . ." She frowned as she trailed off.

"What is it?" Erin pushed when Meli didn't continue.

"One of the shifters who came by right before they decided to dump me was so angry. Maybe a few hours ago or it could have been a day or two. It was dark where they kept us so I lost track of time. He was angry about something, wanted them to 'get rid' of their problems but I couldn't understand what they were saying at the time. Later I realized they were talking about me. Their voices were so muffled and I was fighting a bad fever then. It sounded like one of the others was angry about something but that's all I could make out."

From the looks of it she was still fighting a fever considering the flush in her cheeks. She withdrew her hand from Erin's and clasped both her hands over her stomach.

"Did you see any distinguishing markings in your cell or even on your captors? Like a tattoo maybe? I know you said you were blindfolded but maybe you saw something?" Erin sat perfectly still, her lack of movement likely designed to keep the other female at ease.

"The cell was empty other than a cot and a bucket for me to . . . uh, anyway, no, I didn't see anything else. Or I don't think I did. If I remember I'll let you know."

"You're doing really great, Meli. Would you mind if I took a few pictures of your wounds? I'd like them for our records and I'd like to do some cross-referencing. If this isn't the first time they've taken pregnant shifters I want to know." Erin's face was strained as she spoke, her gray eyes turning to almost black.

Meli nodded and held out both her arms straight while Erin snapped shots using her cell phone. Whoever had done this to her hadn't been gentle. They'd drawn blood so many times, obviously from the same veins over and over. As a pregnant shifter, Meli was almost as weak as a human, her ability to heal and overall strength on the lowest level possible for a shifter. It was why pregnant shifters were taken care of, looked after so carefully. Noah hadn't realized he'd growled until Meli jerked her arms back to wrap around herself and Erin shot him a sharp look that told him to get under control.

"Why do you think they let you go?" Erin asked as she looked back at Meli.

"They didn't *let* me go. They thought I was dead. My heartbeat was so faint I could barely hear it and my baby"—her voice broke again, but she shook her head once and continued—"I thought my baby was dead too. I just lay on the cot, limp. The human was the one who eventually got rid of me. He was in a hurry when he dumped me into the back of some kind of vehicle, an SUV I think. There was another body in there with me, a feline shifter. A tall black woman. She was . . . dead." Her voice cracked on the last word.

"You're sure she was dead?"

Nodding, Meli rushed on quickly, as if she needed to get it all out. "Unfortunately, yes. I don't know how long we drove around but it felt like hours. I thought for sure the human would discover I was still alive, but he never did. Just tossed me in a shallow grave and hurried off."

Noah looked at Erin and was alarmed to see how pale she was. But her expression was intent as she listened to Meli. "This is really good information. Do you remember anything else about your captors or surroundings?"

Meli shook her head. "No. As soon as I was alone . . ." A shudder racked her and now tears fell in abandon. "Oh God, I thought I was dead. I thought maybe it was all a sick joke. Once I was coherent enough I tapped into my psychic link with my mate—I'd been too drugged before, they kept me that way constantly—and then he was there, saving me and our baby. Oh my God, I thought—" Her voice broke again and this time she sobbed. Before either of them could react the door flew open and a shirtless Evan strode into the room.

"Get the fuck out," he growled at them.

Noah was surprised the male had held out this long. If he were in his place, Noah wasn't sure he could have. Wordlessly he and Erin stood and headed for the door. As they pulled it shut behind them Meli's strained voice called out. "Wait, Erin—I remember seeing a ring on one of the men. It was a wolf, probably white gold or maybe platinum. My blindfold had inched up a little and I remember seeing the flash of metal. The eyes were bloodred. I remember thinking it was creepy because it reminded me so much of a feral wolf I didn't understand why anyone would want to wear it."

Erin nodded once. "Thank you."

"Honey, you need to rest." Evan was slipping into the bed next to his mate and pulling her tight against his chest as Noah shut the door behind them.

For a single brief moment he was actually jealous of the couple. They'd been through hell yet they had each other. Evan was free to hold the woman he so obviously loved and she curled right into his arms.

Forcing his selfish thoughts down, Noah focused on Erin. He wanted to pull her into his arms, hold her delicate, lean body close to him, but knew she wouldn't welcome it. "Are you all right? You look a little shaken."

She nodded, but he didn't miss the stress lines around her mouth. "Fine. I need to send these pictures to Ryan. Now that we know these shifters aren't being taken for sexual purposes, I want him to cross-reference this with old police files. Maybe the humans know something we don't. I'm going to contact the Council, see if they have reports of dead bodies showing up with similar markings."

Ryan, resident computer genius at the Armstrong-Cordona ranch, could hack into practically any system he wanted. And the Council no doubt had a vast array of resources. Right now he didn't care about any of that. "Erin, you sure you're okay?" She'd looked so damn pale in that room. If she needed an outlet, he wanted to be a sounding board for her.

Her gray eyes turned cold, stony. "I'm *fine*. I don't need you getting all worried or possessive. Pregnant women are being abused for God only knows what purposes. *That* is what's important right now. Not"—she waved a hand at him—"your sexual frustration or whatever is going on with you."

Trying to turn it around on him made him only more frustrated. She wasn't fine. She was just too fucking stubborn to admit it because she'd view it as a weakness. Didn't she understand he'd do anything to erase the pain he'd seen lurking in her eyes?

His claws automatically unsheathed, anger lancing through him at her words. "You think this is sexual frustration talking? Because I care about your well-being?" Right now he was so edgy he took a step back, not waiting for her answer. Not really wanting one.

She wasn't going to let him in. Never had except for a few brief stolen kisses, but deep down he realized she may never let him get closer than what they had with each other now. It drove him insane. He needed space to run, to expend all his energy before he lashed out and said something he couldn't take back.

Erin fought to pull air into her lungs as she hurried down the stairs and out the front door. All protocol dictated that she stay and speak with Angus, but she couldn't.

Not now.

She needed space to breathe and wouldn't find it

here. Not with Noah hovering so close. Seeing so *much* with those dark eyes. When Jayce had assigned her to this case she'd known it would be hard to deal with, but she also knew she could do it. She was stronger than her past. But Noah made her feel vulnerable, made her want to let her guard down and she hated how well he sensed her moods. She'd hidden her discomfort from him, she was almost sure of it. Well, clearly not, no matter how much she wanted to convince herself.

Somehow that wolf *always* knew what she was feeling.

The thought of him knowing what had happened to her, what she'd lost . . . rubbing a hand in the middle of her chest, she tried to make that near-constant ache go away. As if it was a physical thing. She carried the emotional pain everywhere she went. Like fifty pounds of invisible baggage. She almost snorted out loud. It might as well be physical.

As she stepped out onto the front porch she saw Noah's discarded clothes. He was obviously out running. She knew he was upset with her and she hated that. Hated the fact that she could ever hurt someone as special as him. But it seemed she did more often than not without even trying. He just wanted so much more from her than she'd ever be able to give. Something she'd told him so many times. That knowledge was the only thing that slightly assuaged her guilt. It wasn't like she was leading him on. She'd been up front from the beginning about what she could and, more important, could *not* give to him.

Without stopping to think about whether it was a good idea or not, she snagged the key to the motorcycle from the pile of fabric and got on the bike.

Riding without a helmet gave her the perfect sense of freedom she desperately needed at the moment. She thought she heard someone shout after her, but she ignored it. Ignored everything as she tore down the narrow cobblestone street. Noah would be fine without her. He was at his family's house. *Someone* would give him a ride back to the Quarter. If he even came back to the place where they were staying tonight.

Getting away from Noah and the *stupid* need she had to open up to him was the only thing that mattered.

She zipped along, passing streetcars, a big part of public transportation in New Orleans, and other vehicles. Working this case was going to drive her insane if she let it. And she refused to. She was going to channel her nightmares and fear and make them work for her. No matter what, she would find out who was taking pregnant shifters and bring them to justice.

They'd been taking Meli's blood, draining her until she was almost dry. Which was really odd. Why would anyone want shifter blood?

Vamp blood she could understand. It got humans high as freaking kites, gave them super strength, and made them totally unpredictable. But shifter blood? What was the point? Obviously there was a reason behind it and she had a lot of research to do if she wanted to get a good grasp on this case. The pictures of the shifter women who'd been taken were seared into her mind and she was determined to help them. Especially now that she'd met Meli. It still blew her mind that anyone could target a female when they were at their weakest. That took a certain kind of monster; one she'd gladly rip to shreds.

The ache in her chest grew as memories clawed at her, pulsing through her in vicious waves until she felt practically numb.

Dealing with this case might end up bringing all her history out into the open for Noah to see and that terrified her. It was bad enough he'd noticed that she'd been affected by simply talking to Meli. If he pushed her hard enough she knew that she'd eventually crack and tell him her secrets. Some days she just wanted to curl into his embrace and let him hold her. Like the day that he'd found her so close to death. So damn close her would-be murderers had thought she was just that. Too bad for them she was a hell of lot harder to kill than they thought.

Noah and the rest of her current pack had found her when they'd been on a trip down South for . . . something. She couldn't remember even though he'd told her later. Hell, she didn't remember much from that day, just that Noah had draped his coat around her and snarled at anyone who got too near, including his own Alpha. He'd wanted to take her to a hospital but she'd refused. Her body had already started knitting itself back together and she hadn't wanted to face more people, especially humans. So Noah had transported her back to Connor's former ranch in upstate New York.

Shaking herself, she tried to bury thoughts of Noah and his constant gentleness. Right now wasn't the time.

The drive back to the Quarter didn't take long. Not on a motorcycle. She weaved in and out of cars, ignoring the honks and middle fingers she got. The way people drove in this city was crazy. She was just joining in. Getting off this bike, then calling Ryan was her number one priority. And she couldn't ask Ryan what she needed with Noah hovering, *listening*.

Not surprised the space from earlier was taken, she drove down a block and parked the bike in between two midsize cars along the curb. The moment she stepped off the vehicle she felt the vise around her chest loosen a fraction.

She was in control. She could do this investigation well. Now that she knew these pregnant women were being taken, not killed right away, she *had* to find them. Even though the case rattled her on too many levels, she pushed aside her personal issues. There was no room for that crap right now. The past was over, and she would not let it affect her anymore.

As she hurried down the sidewalk, she ignored a few appreciative stares and whistles from a group of drunk frat boys and skirted past them, keeping her stride purposeful. The sound of the zydeco-style music got louder the closer she got to the bar. The mixture of blues and Cajun music—and the only reason she knew that was because Noah listened to it all the time— would have made her want to dance under different circumstances. Hearing a fiddle always did that anyway. Probably something to do with her Irish roots. That or the fact that her mother had played.

The soulful sound of the fiddle combined with an accordion, drums, and bass guitar was too much not to make her smile just a little. New Orleans had an energy all its own.

The Full Moon Bar was packed when she stepped inside for the second time that day. There was a beefy security guy checking IDs but he glanced at her and didn't move as she stepped past him. There were a lot more humans there this time. Nice blend of all the species in fact. Before she'd taken two steps the bartender made eye contact with her, motioned for her to wait, then stepped out from behind the three-deep bar.

There were a few grumbles but the tall, dark-haired feline didn't seem to notice. More likely he didn't care.

"You got my key?" he rumbled, holding out a hand.

Okay, she didn't have to look far for the owner. She nodded, handing it to him. "Thanks for the ride." She started to leave when he stopped her.

"You here to investigate the missing shifters?" he asked so quietly she barely heard him above the din of patrons and music.

She shrugged, her eyes narrowing at him. "Why? Do you know something?"

His expression darkened and for a moment, the animal stared back at her, not the man. His green eyes went complete cat, then flashed back in a blink. "No. My sister is one of the missing."

She racked her brain, seeing the faces of all the missing women from the photos Jayce had given her. There were four Hispanic women and she couldn't tell which one he was related to, though she remembered all their names. "I'm sorry," she said, meaning it. To *not know* what happened to someone you loved was more than anyone should have to bear. At least with a body you could find a semblance of closure.

"I'm just grateful someone other than their families and Campbell is looking for them." He let out a harsh curse and for a brief moment the bar quieted except the music.

Just as quickly the talking started up again. "Why isn't your Council doing anything?" she asked the bartender. From what she knew, her Council of lupine shifters were the only ones taking an interest in this case. Something told her it was because Angus Campbell was the shifter in charge of New Orleans and he held a lot of clout.

"There isn't a feline Alpha here. To them we're just mongrels living among wolves and vamps. No political pull, you know?" So much bitterness laced those words.

She nodded once. "I get it."

"So . . . how's Imelda? I'm friends with her mate but didn't want to call right now." The worry in his eyes was genuine.

Damn, word traveled fast. Guess it didn't matter if there was a species difference, shifters were known for being huge gossips. Pack life and all. "She's got her mate to support her so she'll recover." The tall, leggy shifter had been strong. The fact that she'd talked to Erin at all with such clarity right after her rescue told Erin that.

"Why did they take her? What did they . . . do to her?" There was a desperation in his voice and in his eyes that tore at Erin's insides.

Looked like not everything had been spread through the grapevine. And Erin had a feeling it would stay that way if Angus Campbell had anything to say about it. If this shifter found out that other shifters had been draining Meli's blood, he wasn't going to get the information from her. "Hell, I don't even know your name—"

"Can we get a fucking drink over here?" A broad-shouldered lupine shifter with spiky blond hair shouted from the bar, cutting her off.

She briefly eyed him. It was difficult to distinguish all the scents in this crowded bar but if she had to guess she'd say he was alpha in nature, but definitely not Alpha—not like her own leader, Connor, or Angus. And he didn't look big enough to be a warrior. Erin was surprised it had taken this long for someone to get annoyed. The feline in front of her didn't flinch at the interruption so she continued. "I can't tell you anything, but I might have some questions for you tomorrow when you've got time. You're a bartender, you hear things you might not even realize are important." Plus he'd be motivated to find whoever had taken these women. She needed all the contacts and friends she could make. Something Jayce had taught her.

He nodded even though he looked dejected. "All right. My name's Hector, by the way."

A name and face immediately popped into Erin's head. "Your sister is Leta."

His dark eyebrows raised a fraction as he nodded. "Yeah. She's an artist."

"She sells her paintings in Jackson Square on weekends, but a few local shops showcase her work." Erin had read the files front to back over and over until she'd memorized everything. Leta was twenty-four, young by shifter standards. She'd moved to New Orleans almost a decade ago with her brother after their father died, then had gotten mated to another feline artist two years ago. And she was three months pregnant.

Hector pushed out a long, tired breath. "Yeah."

Erin should leave. She told herself to keep her mouth shut, but the pain on the guy's face was too much. Taking a step forward she dropped her voice so only he could hear her. "The women are being kept alive and they're not being assaulted . . . sexually. Do *not* tell anyone." Before she'd come to the city Jayce and the Council had told her they were worried the women were being taken for some sick purposes—which they were, but at least it wasn't for what they'd originally feared.

His features relaxed slightly. Not much, but Erin hadn't expected it. The male nodded and reached into his back pocket. After scribbling two numbers on a card for the bar, he handed it to her. "I get off here at two. Call anytime, day or night. If I don't answer my cell, call the other number. It's my mate's and she'll answer. She and Leta are best friends and . . ." He shook his head. "Some days I feel like I shouldn't even be here working while she's gone. I just . . . fuck, I want my sister back." Jaw clenched, he quickly turned and headed back for the bar.

Erin slid the card into her jacket pocket then left. More careful of her surroundings than normal, she navigated her way through various streets until she made it to Chartres Street and headed east.

The few remaining artists' displays she'd seen earlier with Noah as they'd cut through Jackson Square were now gone. Young Leta should be home with her mate after a long day at the Square, not locked up and scared.

People milled about, loud and raucous and likely

drunk. Erin weaved in and out of the humans and other paranormal beings until she reached a much quieter part of Chartres. Gaslight lamps flickered, creating shadows off the older buildings and adding to the magical air of the city.

As she passed two males on the cracked sidewalk, one covertly nudged the other. She could guess why. She'd done enough research of The Crescent City that she knew this wasn't a dangerous area, but if she'd been human, she wouldn't have been walking alone at night. It was too deserted, too far away from the restaurants on the west side of the long street. In case they had thoughts of attempting to rob her, she flashed her canines. Spikes of fear so potent it nearly smothered her senses shot off both men and they quickly crossed to the other side of the street.

During the rest of the walk she only ran into one older black man closing up an international-style market before she hit the residential area where she was staying. The elongated and narrow house was divided so that it was almost like two separate residences. She figured it had probably been apartments or rented out as a bed and breakfast at one time. The front half of the house had two bedrooms, a living room, kitchen, and office. The back had four bedrooms that were all connected by a main area that was a combined kitchen and living room. She imagined it was how a dorm living area would look.

After opening the modern wooden privacy fence, she didn't bother relocking it. She'd scent anyone coming. Though it was dark, the near-full moon illuminated all the surprisingly lush green plants of the backyard.

There weren't many flowers blooming though, not in this cold weather.

Once inside she headed straight for the second bedroom on the left. Turning on her laptop, she collapsed on the queen-size bed and called Ryan.

He answered on the second ring. "Hey, short stuff."

She allowed herself a brief smile at the nickname. "Hey. I need you to look some stuff up for me. I'm going to be doing research too, but I need all the extra help I can get." She didn't bother with small talk. Not when her time was limited.

"No prob."

"I need you to do some research on blood rituals for shifters. Specifically blood taken from pregnant shifters. Look up blood rituals related to vamps and fae too," she added. Might as well be thorough. "But focus on anything to do with pregnant shifters and blood, whether it's ritual shit or . . . whatever." She couldn't figure out what the effect of shifter blood was, so wanted to investigate a ritual angle. Maybe this was somehow related to witches. Lord, who knew at this point.

"That's fucking weird."

"Tell me about it."

"What's going on down there?"

She gave him a brief rundown of what she'd discussed with Meli, then sent him the photos she'd taken of the shifter's small wounds and asked him to search for dead and pregnant missing shifters drained of blood. He'd done some searches before she'd left North Carolina, but now they had more information. The blood thing was a new angle. A strange one, but new was good. She'd been on this case only a couple of days but felt like she was already so far behind.

She wanted a national search done. The Feds had ViCAP and she knew Ryan would either hack into their system or call in a favor and have someone search records for him. The man was older than their Alpha and had a lot of contacts.

Not to mention she had some Council resources. Their database probably wasn't as updated as it should be, but the enforcers around the globe added any horrific crimes or assaults involving shifters, vamps or other supernatural creatures to it. Since they didn't report even fifteen percent of attacks or grievances between supernatural species to the humans, they needed to keep track of things somehow.

Surprisingly the humans were fine with it. They preferred to let shifters and vamps self-govern themselves, and as long as humans weren't injured or there was no spillover violence into the human world, no problem.

Once they disconnected, she set up the corkboard on the easel she'd requested be waiting here for her and put up the pictures of the missing women, except for Imelda. She kept all her notes in her laptop and had a feeling she'd do most of her research electronically, but she wanted to see the faces of the missing women.

To remind her of what was at stake. These women deserved everything she could give them. They deserved the rescue she'd never had.

Chapter 3

Erin smelled him before she opened her eyes. That earthy, piney scent that made her think of lying naked on a soft patch of grass in the middle of the forest with Noah right next to her. The natural instinct she normally had to reach for her hidden weapons wasn't there. Not with him around. Even her inner wolf trusted him. She couldn't decide if she loved or hated that.

She took a long moment, pretending she was still asleep so she could savor his presence without him knowing. After a few seconds she opened her eyes to find Noah near the entrance to the bathroom. From his position he was blocking the floor lamp by the desk. It illuminated him, making him look even larger than he really was. At six feet four inches, that was pretty damn big. His inky dark hair was wet and slicked back. It looked even darker, almost a blue-black because of the wetness.

And oh Lord, his shirt was *off*. All those taut lines

and perfect muscular striations. No fat anywhere. The man was absolute perfection. She blinked a couple of times, trying to keep her physical reaction from showing while completely expecting a reaming for leaving him at his father's mansion. Unfortunately her nipples tightened anyway as she imagined what it would be like to look down and see his dark head between her legs as he brought her to climax with his mouth. She barely bit back a groan at the sudden erotic image.

"Hey," he said softly. "Didn't know you were sleeping."

Pushing up from her half-sitting, half-lying position against the headboard, she moved her laptop that had long since gone to sleep off her thighs. Even though she'd asked Ryan to help out with research, she'd immersed herself in searching any database she could until she'd gone cross-eyed. "It's fine," she murmured, wishing she could get that hot image out of her head. Kinda hard when he was standing half dressed in front of her. Glancing at the clock on the nightstand she saw it was one in the morning and frowned. "You just got in?"

He nodded and scrubbed a hand over his jaw, which had more than just a shadow of stubble. "Yeah. I was gonna borrow a razor if you have one. I must have left mine."

Not liking the foreign feeling of jealousy that welled up inside her as she wondered why he'd been out so late, she nodded at the attached bathroom. "Look in the black bag on the counter. I've got a couple extra."

"Thanks." He came back into her room carrying a

purple razor. Turning the antique chair at the desk around, he straddled it and folded his arms over the top. His arms flexed, those damn muscles tightening, teasing her. "You fall asleep working?"

She nodded again, wondering why he didn't seem mad about her leaving him. Granted he'd run off first, but she shouldn't have just left him there. "Just trying to figure out what, if anything, other than being pregnant these six women have in common. If their lives intersected somewhere. From what Meli said it sounds like her captors wanted to make room for more shifters." If she could figure out how the women were being picked other than the pregnancy angle maybe she could find out who was doing this and why. And stop more from being taken.

"You need help with anything?" His voice was utterly sincere. Not a hint of annoyance at her.

She looked at the dark screen of her laptop and for a brief moment thought about turning it back on and working. Instead she shook her head. "Not tonight." There wasn't much more she could do and after so many hours of traveling she knew she needed sleep. Without a clear head she'd be useless to everyone.

"So what's the plan for tomorrow?" he asked.

"I want to question the families and mates of the missing women. The reports Jayce gave me were pretty slim. Maybe by talking to some of them I'll learn more." She also wanted to scour the city, get a feel for it, try to make contacts with anyone who might be helpful.

He nodded once as he stood, showing off all that naked expanse of skin. "I talked to Angelo on the way in. He and Brianna are going to talk to some of her contacts tomorrow. She knows some vamps through her family connections."

Erin had almost forgotten about them. The warrior shifter and warrior fae were staying in the front of the house. Angelo was one of her packmates, though she didn't know him as well as Noah, and Brianna was pretty cool as far as fae went. Erin wasn't sure what the deal was with those two, but had a feeling that before they left New Orleans, they'd be a couple. If they weren't already. "I didn't even hear them when I got in."

Noah shrugged, his expression completely unreadable. "Thanks for the razor. See you in the morning." Then he was gone, like a damn ghost. Her door shut so quietly behind him she didn't even hear the snick of it moving into place. *What the hell?* Was he messing with her?

Staring at the door, she didn't know what to do. Or how she was supposed to feel. He'd just left and she wasn't sure what that meant. Why hadn't he yelled at her for leaving him?

Feeling unsettled, she stripped off the rest of her clothes, took a quick shower and brushed her teeth. But even that didn't help. An edginess swam through her, raging and unsteady. She knew what it was.

Sexual freaking frustration.

A low growl built in her throat but she pushed it back down. After changing into purple-and-white polka-dotted pajama pants and a long-sleeved purple shirt, she went out into the common area. Pausing only for a moment, she marched across to his room and didn't bother knocking. He had to be screwing with her head and she wanted to know if he was.

She found him lounging on the bed reading a book, still wearing a pair of jeans and nothing else. The quilted blue and brown comforter similar to the one in her room was thrown back so that he was stretched out on the sheets. Bright oil paintings of gas lamps and silhouettes of men playing saxophones hung above the bed but all she could focus on was Noah.

He raised an eyebrow at her, almost mocking, but she couldn't be sure. "Everything okay?" He sounded so casual she felt a little stupid.

Instead of leaving, though everything in her being told her to, she said, "Aren't you mad at me for leaving you? Don't you want to yell at me or something?"

He set the paperback down on the nightstand. "Do you want me to yell at you?"

She crossed her arms over her chest. "No."

"Then why are you here?" His face was so unreadable. Not even a hint of what he might be thinking. Normally he didn't shut her out like this and she found it unnerving.

Erin bit her bottom lip and decided to go for honesty even though it killed her. "I don't know. I don't like the thought of you angry at me, and I thought you might be screwing around with me. I don't care what most people think but . . ." She trailed off, unwilling to go down that path. She cared way too much what Noah thought and it scared her. "I'm sorry I left you and . . . I just want to make sure we're okay."

His expression softened a fraction. "I'm not mad. We

both needed space." His voice was soothing, the sound of it wrapping around her in a silky embrace.

"So where were you tonight? Why were you out so late?" Crap, was that jealousy in her voice?

Now something dangerous flashed in those dark eyes. It was almost predatory, but then it was gone so quickly she couldn't be sure. "You care who I'm spending my time with?"

Yes. "No." The answer was automatic even if it was bullshit. She cared more than she wanted to admit to herself.

He didn't respond and she couldn't find any words. Feeling a little pathetic, she turned to leave. Before she'd taken a step Noah had crossed the room and was in front of her, toe to toe. *He moved fast.*

"What do you want from me?" he asked on a soft growl.

She looked at his lips. She couldn't help it. When he talked, she just wanted to stare at his mouth. Well, she wanted to do more than stare. How many times had she imagined that mouth on hers? On *her*? Just as many times as she'd told herself what a stupid idea it was. After they'd kissed not too long ago, it had been harder and harder to quell those fantasies. They'd never gotten super intimate but now that she knew what he tasted like, it was almost impossible to not do what her body practically demanded.

A man like Noah wouldn't settle down with someone like her. He would want a mate and children. The whole package. Just like all shifters. Family was so damn important to her kind.

But she wasn't whole. Could never give him everything he deserved. One day he'd realize that. Still, being so close to him like this, sometimes it felt like they were the only two people in the world. She could pretend there weren't monsters out there and that they could have a total cherry pie life.

If only.

Noah looked at her, his dark eyes searching for something. What, she didn't know. His piney, earthy scent intensified and she could practically feel the heat coming off him. More than anything she wanted to feel that heat covering her, taking her, filling her with pleasure.

Then his mouth was on hers, stroking and teasing and *taking*. One hand cupped her face and the other threaded through her damp hair. He gripped the back of her head as their tongues and bodies melded together.

It was impossible to think straight when her body was on fire. She burned from the inside, wanting to strip their clothes off and just *be* with him. Damn the consequences and what would happen after her heart had been shattered. She knew without a doubt that it eventually would be once they crossed this line. Because what she felt for him was more than lust, even though the word also started with an "L".

Losing herself with him, giving him pleasure, taking it—she desperately wanted that. She tried to convince herself that it would just be a physical thing. Lord, it had been so long since she'd been with anyone. Her body ached for that connection. But it was more than physical with Noah. She knew it even if she wouldn't admit it. And if Noah was eventually going to realize she wasn't the woman for him, she'd take from him now.

Barely thinking, just feeling, she reached between their bodies and grasped his jeans button. She could have him naked in seconds. Could be riding him and—

It took a moment for it to register that he was holding her wrists in a firm grip and stopping her.

Breathing hard, he took a step back from her. She saw a flash of his canines but he'd controlled his inner wolf by the time she'd blinked. "Why are you stopping?" *Wasn't this what he wanted? What he'd been after for over a year?* Right now she wanted to chase away dark memories, make a few precious ones with Noah. More than anything, she wanted to have this with him. Have a piece of him to hold on to later.

He shook his head, his jaw tightening. "I'm not doing this with you. Not like this." The words came out a deep growl.

"Like . . . what?" *Didn't he want her?*

"I'm not going to be just some physical outlet for you. Something you'll regret in a few hours after you've gotten some sleep. If you want me, you're going to give me *everything*."

Something about his voice changed when he said that word. It made her take a step back. There was a dark, primal note that shocked her to her core. It wasn't the Noah she knew. Not exactly. The man in front of her looked hungry in a way she'd never seen. "Everything?" The question came out as a whisper.

His eyes darkened until she saw both the wolf and man staring back at her. He looked as if he wanted to completely possess her. Finally he spoke and his order surprised her. "Go."

She blinked. "What?"

"Go to your room. Now. If you stay, you're giving me everything I want." A soft order that sent a thrill up her spine even as it scared her.

Knowing she was being a coward, she didn't respond. She couldn't. Hell, she could barely catch her breath.

Backtracking, she left the way she'd come and let herself breathe only once she'd closed her door behind her. Sagging against it, she raked a shaky hand through her almost dry hair. What the hell had just happened?

Staring at the closed door for a moment after she left, Noah stripped off his jeans. He'd seen such vulnerability in Erin's eyes. She'd finally let her guard down with him, but not enough to give him what he wanted. What they deserved.

He wanted to take Erin so damn bad right now, but the only outlet available was to let his wolf take over, to calm him down. As his bones broke, shifted, and realigned back into place, an immediate calming followed the sharp pain that was always part of the change to animal form. It somewhat eased the painful ache he always carried for her.

He'd felt that heat from her and he'd wanted to take her right up against the door. Hell, it didn't matter where.

But he'd come to a decision earlier while running free on his father's land. Erin was ready for him now, even if she didn't realize it. Ready for a relationship.

She hadn't been a year ago and maybe not even months ago when they'd shared that first kiss. She was now.

She'd come out of that broken state they'd found her in when she'd decided to pick up her blades and start fighting again. When she'd taken on some of their old neighbor Taggart's wolves in her animal form, ripping them to shreds for attacking their land. More so when she'd agreed to train as an enforcer.

Noah still had nightmares about finding her naked, bleeding, and bruised, dumped in the garbage. Her gorgeous red hair had been matted around her face and she'd been covered in purple bruises. He still didn't understand how someone had been able to hurt her so bad. Not with her strength.

Erin was young for a shifter at fifty years old, but she was faster and more lethal than some he'd seen twice her age. And that strength would only grow until she'd be on the same level as Jayce. Something that absolutely awed Noah. On his most primal level, he hated watching her fight, but another part of him loved seeing all that grace and agility. She was a beautiful sight to see in that mode.

Right now, in this city, without their pack around them, he was going to change things between them. The dynamic of their relationship had shifted tonight and he was pretty sure she realized it. If she hadn't, she wouldn't have run back to her room. She wanted him, of that he had no doubt. So he was going to capitalize on it. He'd made the decision earlier tonight and he wasn't going to stop until she was his. He felt that mating hunger to claim her and he wasn't going to deny it anymore.

He'd take a little, give a little, make her want him so bad she ached the way he constantly did. But he wouldn't give her the release she wanted. Oh, he planned to pleasure her all right, but he wouldn't give her everything he knew she needed. Not until she admitted what was really between them and told him completely about her past.

It killed him that she didn't trust him enough to tell him who'd hurt her. If he had names, they'd be dead. And he would make them suffer. Death was a part of life for shifters and he didn't relish the idea of killing anyone. Sometimes it was necessary, but for whoever had hurt Erin, he'd take pleasure in killing them. With no guilt.

Sighing, he jumped onto the bed and laid his head on his forepaws. Sleep in his wolf form was always the best. Right now he needed to be on his game. He was going to help Erin find the fuckers taking pregnant women and he was going to convince her they were meant to be together. As he let himself succumb, sleep quickly pulled him under.

Erin cracked her eyes open and tried to move. Raw agony splintered through her body as she attempted to sit up. Where was she and why was she in so much pain? It was like tiny knives had burrowed their way under her skin everywhere. She tried to drag in a breath, but her lungs ached with the effort.

Everything came flooding back as she remembered what had happened. How she'd ended up . . . She rolled her head to the side and grimaced at the torture that followed from the slight movement. She could see an empty beer bottle tipped over on its side next to an open to-go food container. A rat had its face buried in the box and was chomping away.

As if it sensed her watching, it lifted its head and made a squeaking sound before resuming eating.

A new wave of pain flooded her as she became more aware of her surroundings. Which was good and bad. She needed to figure out where she was, but the aching was getting worse and making her woozy.

Or maybe that was the stench surrounding her. Old, rotting food and . . . shit, she was behind a Dumpster. Her vision became more acute and she could make out the sharp edges of the big green metal container. Those fuckers had tried to kill her—likely thought they had—and left her as if she was actual garbage.

Moving against the pavement, she tried to call on her wolf to comfort her, to change into her lupine form, but she didn't have the strength. The concrete was rough against her naked back as she tried to push up. She couldn't though. Crying out, she bit back the sound quickly as she realized her arm was broken. She had no clue if they were still nearby and she couldn't risk anyone noticing her until she'd regained some of her strength.

She could hear the sound of cars zooming by in the distance; then she heard a shuffling sound. Like feet. Then male voices.

Oh God. Had they realized they'd made a mistake? That she wasn't really dead? She was covered in so much blood and her heartbeat was so faint she could barely hear it herself. They'd already taken everything from her. Now they just wanted to finish the job.

Though she hated the weakness, fear spiked inside her as she tried to scoot away, to find a place to hide. She was in no shape to fight and wasn't stupid enough to think she could take anyone on right now. Erin just wanted to survive. She'd get her revenge later, but she couldn't do that if she was dead.

As her palms pressed against the concrete, she let out a whimpering sound when a broad-shouldered, hulking form appeared around the corner of the Dumpster.

It wasn't her attackers, but the male was a shifter. Jet-black hair touched his shoulders, or maybe it wasn't actually that dark. She couldn't tell the exact color because of the setting sun behind him and her vision was starting to fade again.

He cursed and took a step toward her and she couldn't help it. She whimpered again. God, she couldn't take any more abuse.

The big male froze, looked at her with sympathy, then stripped off his coat and gently covered her with it as he made soothing nonsensical sounds. Realization dawned that he was going to help her. She shouldn't depend on a stranger. Doing so was beyond stupid, but she had no choice.

And this stranger smelled so damn good. Like . . . safety. Even if he did look terrifying. Like an avenging angel. A really beautiful one. She wanted to bury her face against his chest and soak up all that strength, which just sounded stupid, even in her head. Holding on to the ludicrous thought, she finally succumbed to the darkness edging her vision. . . .

Erin's eyes flew open, her heart beating wildly as she took in her surroundings of the guest room in the New Orleans home where she was staying. She wasn't near death behind a shitty Dumpster. Belatedly she realized she clutched her blade in her hand. Sighing, she slid it back under one of her pillows, then punched the other one in frustration.

She needed sleep and her stupid dreams weren't helping any. How the hell was she supposed to get anything done if she kept dwelling on the past? She hadn't had a dream like that in months. Working on this case was already messing with her head.

Sighing, she curled on her side and closed her eyes. She was stronger than her past. Maybe if she said it enough, she'd actually believe it.

Noah wasn't sure how much time passed until an annoying buzzing sound cut through the quiet room. His eyes instantly opened and his ears perked up. Looking at the nightstand, he saw his cell phone vibrating against it.

Bracing himself for the pain, he shifted. The covers tangled underneath him as he returned to his human form. The antique clock on the wall above the nightstand said three. Two hours of sleep. Just great.

Grabbing his phone he tensed at the sight of his father's number. This was definitely not good. "Yeah?"

"You remember the Colby house?" No preamble or hello.

Yep, this was going to be bad. "Yeah."

"Meet me there with Erin as soon as you can. Someone found a body and called me. Her name's Kaigen. Erin should have the file on her."

Noah started to respond but was talking to dead air. Figured. He and his father had gotten into an argument before he'd left the mansion a few hours ago. It was always the same. Time and space hadn't done a damn thing to diminish the tension between them. Of course his mother had tried to defuse the situation and he hated that she felt she had to do that.

Sighing, he pulled on a fresh pair of jeans, a black sweater, and black boots. After quickly brushing his teeth he headed across the common area to Erin's room. He knocked and opened only when she mumbled, "Come in."

Curled up on her side with her laptop next to her and that damn corkboard in her line of sight—he hated that she was torturing herself with their faces—she gave him a bleary-eyed look. "What's wrong?" she asked in a raspy voice he found sexy as hell.

"Got a call from my father. They found another body."

Erin's shoulders stiffened. "Does he know who?"

He glanced at the corkboard, a vise tightening around his chest. Erin had the names of the missing women underneath each photo. Three of the women had Spanish roots, one was black, and the last white. He touched the photo of the woman named Kaigen. "It's her."

"I was hoping Meli was wrong when she said the woman with her was dead," Erin said quietly. "She has two kids."

Shit. He turned around to find Erin already out of bed, half-naked, dressed only in a sports bra and boyshort panties, crouched in front of her open suitcase. Under normal circumstances the sight of her would get him hot, but now he felt only a sense of sadness for the dead woman's mate and family. "I'll meet you out front. Gonna tell Angelo and Brianna what we're doing."

"Okay." She didn't look up as she pulled out a pair of cargo pants and a long-sleeved T-shirt.

The way the house was set up was a little weird. He figured it must have been two separate places at one time. Heading through the utility room with a brand-new–looking washer and dryer, he opened the door that connected to the front part of the house and stepped into another kitchen.

A small light was on above the sink, illuminating the stainless steel. Though it was three in the morning he heard movement. By the time he made it to the hallway Angelo was already standing half-in, half-out of one of the bedrooms, looking only partially awake but ready to move into action if necessary.

"What's up?" Angelo asked, his voice gravelly with sleep.

"Just wanted to let you know we found another body. Erin and I are headed out now. One of us will call you later with details." Technically they didn't owe a call to either of them, but Angelo was his packmate and Noah respected that. He knew Erin did too, even if she was here on assignment from the Council.

Noah still wasn't sure why Angelo was here at all. Brianna had helped out their pack very recently with information gathering and she'd killed one of the bastards who'd targeted and hurt his pack. When her leaders learned about what was going on here, they'd wanted her to check things out too. As a member of the Fianna, legendary fae warriors, Brianna might be slight and almost ethereal looking, but she could hold her own against anyone. He'd heard from Erin how she'd killed a member of the Antiparanormal League by harnessing some kind of lightninglike energy with her hands. Angelo had practically insisted to Connor that he be allowed to come with Brianna, which surprised Noah since the blond female didn't seem to even like him.

When her head popped out from behind the doorway Angelo was standing in, Noah's eyebrows raised. Okay, maybe she did like him. She ducked under the arm Angelo had braced against the frame. "What body? Do you know who it is? How was she killed?"

Noah shook his head. "I have no details right now other than a body was discovered." Well, he knew the name of the deceased but it wasn't his place to tell either of them.

Angelo wrapped an arm around Brianna's shoulders, pulling her close. He murmured something in her ear so low even Noah couldn't hear with his extrasensory hearing.

Brianna stiffened under his hold, seeming uncomfortable with it, and slightly nudged him with her elbow. Whispering, she said, "Just because you're showing me what sexual pleasure is all about does not mean you control me."

Noah choked on air and tried to cover it with a cough, but Angelo glared at him. It was obvious Brianna had meant for her comment to be private, but she didn't have the extrasensory abilities they had and she likely hadn't realized just how loud a whisper was to him.

Making a hasty exit, he hurried toward the front of the house, knowing Erin would be waiting for him. Sure enough her cherry red Challenger idled in the driveway. Instead of heading to the passenger side, he tapped on her window.

Rolling it down, she raised an eyebrow at him. "You're not driving."

"I know where we're going. It's in the swamp." She might have excellent night vision, but driving in the swamp was a pain in the ass even in the daytime. Alligators didn't care about roads and often took naps in the middle of them.

She shrugged. "You can be my navigator."

"Erin—"

"*I'm* driving. You drove practically the whole way here."

"Because you needed to do research."

"Exactly. I don't need your help anymore. We'll get a rental if you want to drive so bad, but you are *not* driving this." She looked away from him now, her hands on the wheel at ten and two, ready to leave.

Despite the reality of what they were on their way to see, a ghost of a smile tugged at the corner of his lips. She was so stubborn. Knowing it was a useless argument, he got in on the passenger side of the car.

"So, you get any sleep?" he asked as she steered away from the house.

Swallowing hard, she gave him a haunted look. It was just for an instant; then her eyes were guarded again as she shook her head. "No, I . . . had a dream about the day you found me."

Holy shit. Erin never talked about that day. Ever. And she rarely showed any weakness. By admitting she'd had a dream—or more likely nightmare—about that dark day, she was basically doing that. "I'm sorry,

Erin." He didn't know what else to say and felt like a jackass with the meaningless apology.

"Don't be," she said quietly, the words almost a sigh. "You were there, right before I woke up. Your face is never clear in my dreams, but your presence is. I'm . . . glad you're here for this case, Noah." It sounded as if it almost pained her to admit that.

But he'd needed to hear the words. Needed to know she actually did want him in her life. Because he sure as hell needed her.

After that the drive was quiet, neither saying much. Under normal circumstances he'd be tempted to flirt with her a little, especially after that kiss a couple of hours ago. Not now. Not when she had shadows under her eyes, which he figured were because of the case and the nightmare she'd had. And soon enough they'd be dealing with the death of one of their own kind.

The Colbys were humans who lived out in the swamp. Their family had owned the property for close to a hundred and fifty years and they'd known about the existence of shifters and vampires long before the rest of the world had. It wasn't deep swamp country so the trip took about twenty minutes from the city. The only lights out that far away from civilization were a brilliant splash of stars and the almost full moon.

Once they'd turned off the highway and onto the dirt road/driveway where he directed her, Erin dimmed the headlights down to the parking lights and didn't stop until they pulled up to a two-story log-cabin-style home. It looked as if it had been recently built—or more likely rebuilt—making Noah guess they'd been hit bad years ago by Hurricane Katrina.

Erin grabbed a small backpack from the backseat and slid the straps over her shoulders after they stepped out of the car. Noah's father was there to meet them with Lionel Colby, a gray-haired former marine who'd been in Vietnam.

Lionel nodded once at Noah, the action curt. "Been a long time. You look good, son."

Noah nodded back. "You too, sir." He was actually older than Lionel by about two, maybe three decades, but he'd always called this human sir. Noah motioned to Erin. "This is Erin Flynn."

Erin held out her hand and shook Lionel's once before looking at Angus. "Where's the female?"

Angus almost looked surprised for a moment, then jerked a thumb behind him. "This way."

Noah knew Erin's question seemed harsh, but he understood her. Understood that she didn't want to make small talk with the human or Angus when she needed to be doing her job. It was just the way she was hardwired.

Lionel stayed back, saying he didn't want to go too far from his sleeping wife, while they trekked down a heavily trodden dirt path. Cypress and cedar trees surrounded them. That cedar scent was so similar to Erin's own natural smell it almost stopped Noah in his tracks. She had a sweet magnolia aroma that always surrounded her, but underneath it was cedar. Just like with Jayce. Noah hadn't asked but he figured it had something to do with her being an enforcer like the other wolf.

About fifty yards down from the house, near the marshy bank, a female body had washed up and was stuck between two logs. The moonlight bathed her body in perfect illumination. Her clothes had been shredded in places, probably getting caught on debris traveling down the river. Her body was bloated, but even so it was obvious she'd been very pregnant when she died. Her distended belly was even more so—Noah hardened his jaw and looked away.

Seeing any female like this made his wolf want to kill. He caught his father's gaze and saw the same rage lurking beneath the surface. As Alpha, it was in his father's blood to protect. That need was a living, breathing thing for good Alphas and right now Noah could see his father's wolf wanted blood.

"We haven't touched the body," Angus said quietly as he turned to look at Erin. "Knew you'd want the scene undisturbed."

"Did you call anyone else? Tell anyone else about this?" she asked.

Angus shook his head. "Not even my mate knows."

"Good, let's keep it that way. Does your friend Lionel know this is to be kept under wraps?"

Angus paused for a moment. "He should, but I'll make sure. Meet me back at the house when you're done."

Erin turned away from him to get to work, then stopped him before he'd taken more than a few steps. "Angus, I don't mean to be a ballbuster or anything, but anytime anything happens in this case I need you to call me first, not Noah. Not anyone. I understand this is your territory and that people will be contacting you with anything out of the ordinary—like tonight— and I'm very grateful you have such a pulse on this community and are willing to help. I just—"

Angus cut her off. "Not a problem."

It was subtle, but Noah watched as Erin breathed out a soft sigh of relief. "Thank you."

Nodding, Angus left and Noah watched as Erin took off her backpack. She pulled out a small kit then handed her pack to him. "Would you mind?"

Shaking his head, he took it. "What are you going to do?"

Bending down, she tucked her pants into her knee-high boots before wading into the thick mud. Hooking her pack over his shoulder, he followed suit. His boots made sucking sounds each step they took toward Kaigen D'Amico.

"Take pictures of the area, check under her fingernails for any DNA, see if there's anything other than her that doesn't belong in this picture. We're going to need to call local law enforcement soon. They'll have more resources and be able to look for more evidence, but it's better if we have the first crack at this scene to check for scent . . . though I don't smell anything other than normal swamp and forest smells . . . and her death." She knelt down by the body and gently took the dead woman's hand.

Yeah, Noah smelled the decaying body too. Had been trying to ignore it from the moment they'd arrived at the scene. "They probably dumped her somewhere upriver, maybe thought the gators would dispose of her body or—"

He stopped when Erin sucked in a sharp breath. "I don't think that's it. I think she was buried just like Meli. Look at this—her clothes and arms are caked with dark soil, as if she was buried. But it looks like someone dug her back up."

Noah frowned, moving closer and bending down next to her. "Why would anyone do that?"

Erin held out the woman's arm and turned it slightly over. She wiped away more of the dirt, leaving streaks along the woman's lifeless limb, but revealing nasty bite marks. "To feed on her like fucking scavengers," she bit out.

After Erin wiped her arm nearly clean, Noah stared at the bite marks covering her exposed arm. He had a feeling they'd find more on her body. "Could be a feral vamp."

Erin looked over her shoulder at him in surprise. "What? Vamps can't go feral . . . can they?"

"Not feral like our kind, but I don't know another word for it. I've seen it happen before to those who shouldn't have been turned in the first place. They feed on anything, including the dead. It's just a guess though. I can't imagine another creature feeding like this."

Shaking her head, Erin looked back at Kaigen's lifeless, bloated body and sighed. She took out her cell phone and began snapping pictures, though he could see it pained her to do so. "I've got a digital camera in my pack, will you grab it too?" she asked as she shoved her phone into her jacket pocket.

As she took more pictures she began talking. "You know, the Rolling Stones were my mom's favorite band."

At first he didn't realize why she was telling him,

then he made out a couple of the letters on the long
black, ripped T-shirt covering most of the woman's
belly. The Rolling Stones.

"She used to sing my baby sister and me their songs
at night before going to sleep. Well, anything by them
or the Beatles. So many of my memories have faded
over the last few decades, but I remember some so
clearly." Her voice broke on the last word as she stared
down at the body. "This never should have happened,"
she whispered almost to herself.

Noah gently grasped her shoulder, knowing she
wouldn't want more and knowing it wasn't the place
to comfort her anyway. Surprising the hell out of him,
Erin reached up and placed her hand over his, but
didn't turn around. The action was so small, but it
touched him that she was accepting his comfort. Finally.

He wanted to say something, anything, but froze
when he sensed intruders. There was a new, foreign
scent in the air that didn't belong. At the same time,
Erin stiffened. Slowly, she withdrew her hand and he
heard the soft buzz of her unzipping her jacket.

As she withdrew her blades whisper quiet, he turned,
scanning the area, but didn't see anyone. Didn't mean
they weren't out there. Moving out of the swampy em-
bankment, he quickly stripped out of his clothes and
shifted form. As a wolf his senses were more attuned to
his surroundings.

He spotted two eyes in the trees to the west. In this
form they almost appeared to be glowing and he could
see the heat signature of the individual was much
lower than his or even a human's. Not all shifters had

the ability to see heat signatures, but it was one of his rare gifts. A familial trait he'd gotten from his father. Right now, he saw a vampire.

Growling low, he took a step forward, knowing Erin was directly next to him. The individual turned and ran deeper into the woods.

Hell no.

He looked up at Erin. Using hand signals, she motioned that they should follow. He nodded and ran ahead of her. He didn't care that it would infuriate her. She might be an enforcer and working this case, but she was still his to protect.

Using his speed and animal grace, he was practically silent as he raced through the woods. Jumping over fallen branches and leaves, he was thankful for his night vision. Behind him, he barely heard Erin moving. Even in her human form she moved so damn fast it was like she was practically flying, her feet barely touching the ground.

A distinctive, almost cinnamon and mango scent teased his nose as they ran right into a small clearing and found themselves surrounded by four vampires. Damn, they were as quiet as he and Erin were.

They all wielded short blades similar to the two Erin always carried and now held expertly in her grip. If he'd been in human form, he'd have cursed.

When one of the vampires sliced his blade through the air in a defensive gesture at them, Noah growled low in his throat and bared his canines to their full, intimidating length. Without having to look at Erin, he knew how they'd do this. He'd fought alongside her before when their now-deceased neighboring pack Alpha thought he could attack their land. Of course then she'd been in wolf form, but the concept was the same.

Turning so that his back was to her, he knew she'd done the same to him as they prepared for an attack. His hackles rose, an almost inaudible growl rumbling from his throat. Whatever happened, these fuckers weren't going to hurt Erin.

Chapter 4

Erin had her back to Noah, but knew he'd provide cover no matter what happened. She could focus solely on the two vamps in front of her. A male and a female. They were both tall, blond, and looked like they might be of Nordic descent. At her brief glimpse of the other two vamps that Noah was facing off with, she'd seen they were both female. One very short, maybe five feet flat, with jet-black hair and bronzed skin. The other female was of average height and had midnight black skin, the whites of her eyes and teeth standing out starkly in the darkness. And they all looked ready to fight. Bodies tensed, they each held blades firmly in their hands.

Erin might be new to her position as enforcer, but she wasn't new to fighting. Some vampires were damn strong, but she was a lupine shifter and growing stronger every day now that she'd fully embraced who she was. Not to mention she'd been training with Jayce, a five-hundred-year-old scary bastard who knew more ways to kill someone than she could probably imagine.

Of course there were only a few ways to kill vamps. But Erin hoped tonight didn't come to that. She didn't need to screw up the balance between supernatural beings in New Orleans by killing some vamps.

"Try not to kill them," she murmured to Noah, who only growled softly.

The blond man to her right laughed, the harsh sound slicing through the eerily quiet night air. All the forest creatures had gone silent, knowing instinctively that bigger and deadlier predators were in their domain.

"Don't kill *us*?" He laughed again and lifted one of his blades higher. When he pulled it back as if to throw at her, she reacted.

It was so instinctual she barely thought about it. Erin whipped one of her blades at his neck lightning quick. It sailed through the air with a swishing sound before embedding itself directly in the middle of his thick neck. There was no way that would kill him—death hadn't been her intent. She just wanted him incapacitated.

The man's bright blue eyes widened, flashing to an amber glow then back to blue, as his knees hit the hard earth. With his free hand, he reached for his neck. He made a gurgling sound as blood spurted everywhere. Even though time seemed to stretch on for minutes, everything happened in milliseconds.

The blond woman who reminded Erin of a Barbie doll let out a vicious shriek and lunged at her, blade raised. Okay then, maybe they'd have to kill them after all. Though she *really* didn't want to.

In her periphery, she watched the blond man slowly pull the knife from his neck and drop it as she dodged to the left. The female sailed past her, letting out another curse.

"If I'd wanted to kill him I'd have nailed him in the heart." A hard thing to do since targets usually didn't stand still. Not to mention she'd have to remove the organ from his body afterward.

The female didn't respond. Just spun around to face Erin, her expression one of rage. Behind the female, Noah took on the other two females. Erin tried not to cringe as the black one sliced a blade across his ribs. He snarled, his head snapping to the right as he tore into the woman's shoulder with his teeth. Yeah, he could definitely take care of himself and she didn't need to be focusing on him. Not if she wanted both of them to survive. If he needed help, he'd let her know. "If you guys would all stop for a moment, we could talk!" she shouted, hoping at least one of them might stop.

No such luck. The blond man got up and both he and the female rushed her. She took a few steps back and realized from their smug expression they thought she was running.

Running backward, she covered a few more yards then jumped up using all the strength in her legs until she latched onto a tree branch. Fighting two vamps one-on-one had disadvantages and she was all about utilizing her surroundings. She'd learned early on that anything could be a weapon and there was no such thing as fighting fair.

Gathering momentum, she swung back once, then let go, flying toward the man first since he was still healing. With her legs, she latched onto his shoulders and stabbed down hard into his back. She didn't aim for the heart, but damn close. His fangs tore into one of her thighs as his claws did the same with her calves.

She let out a hiss as she withdrew her blade then slammed it into the back of his neck this time, severing his C1 and C2 vertebrae—something she'd done in the past. It wouldn't kill him since he was a vamp, but it would incapacitate him long enough to cut off his head if she wanted to. But she didn't. If any of the vamps would stop attacking, maybe they could all talk. Erin wanted to know what the hell they were doing out in the woods near a dead shifter's body and why they'd run from her and Noah. "I don't want to kill you!" she shouted.

Before she could attempt to dislodge from him, strong arms wrapped around her, tackling her to the ground. The blond female screamed nonsensical words at her as she slashed at Erin's neck with her short blade.

Erin lifted her knees, throwing the woman off balance and making her land right in Erin's face. Hauling back, she head-butted her in the nose. A completely human style of fighting she'd picked up and loved. It always took her opponents off guard. It wasn't a lethal move, it usually just pissed people off while simultaneously surprising them.

Using the precious few seconds she had, Erin twisted her entire body to the side, then swiveled back, slamming her elbow across the woman's face. A crack rent the air as she made contact.

The woman didn't roll off her, but as she cried out, her head snapping back once again, Erin thrust her blade into the woman's stomach and twisted. The woman's green eyes widened as she stared down at her body in horror. Her claws unsheathed and she slashed Erin's face, but Erin just twisted deeper then ripped upward. Her entire face felt like it was on fire as the pain exploded but she was so amped up on adrenaline, the agony just fueled her resolve to keep these vamps on the ground.

She wasn't going to kill her, but she was going to keep this female down.

Sliding out from under the now-immobile female, Erin set her booted foot into the woman's stomach and yanked her blade out. As she jumped to her feet, the male on the ground started twitching.

"Son of a bitch," she muttered. She'd hoped she'd have a few more minutes.

Before attacking him again, she turned to find Noah tossing one of the vamps off his back with a snarl while another was running at him with a T-shirt that was almost completely ripped off. They were all covered in blood.

Wanting to help him, she snatched up her other blade, but froze as an unfamiliar male voice tore through the air.

"Enough!" The word sounded like thunder as it ricocheted around them, bouncing off the trees.

The blond female vamp Erin had incapacitated clutched her bloody stomach as she crawled toward the downed male, but she didn't make a move toward Erin again except to spew hatred from her eyes. The other two females Noah had been fighting still held their blades but they'd backed off about five yards each, giving him a wide berth.

Erin raced to his side, both her blades in hand, and didn't let any of the vampires out of her line of sight.

A very tall male with dark auburn slicked-back hair stepped into the clearing wearing a long, black leather coat that rippled in the wind. It matched the rest of his all-black clothing. Seriously? He might as well tattoo I'M A FUCKING VAMPIRE CLICHÉ across his forehead. At least the sword in his left hand was actually pretty bad-ass.

Erin tensed, placing her left foot slightly forward as she braced for an attack. Next to her, Noah growled low in his throat as he prepared to fight too.

When the new vampire twisted his sword back over his head and sheathed it somewhere below his jacket, Erin's shoulders slightly loosened. The blond female— now fully healed—hissed angrily at Erin and made a move to leave the male pushing up off the ground, but the auburn-haired guy stopped her with a deadly look.

Oh yeah, he was definitely the leader.

"I apologize for my friends' actions. We don't wish to fight with you." His voice was deep and there was more than a hint of an Irish brogue in it.

Erin snorted as her gaze flicked around the blood-covered group. "You don't want to fight us, huh?"

Next to her Noah shifted back to his human form, his giant body making her feel dwarfed. She glanced at him to make sure he was okay and she held back a smile when she saw he did the same to her, his eyes quickly tracking over her body.

"Who the hell are you and what were you doing near that dead shifter?" Noah snarled, his voice coming out guttural. His wolf still lurked very close to the surface after his change. No doubt he was still amped up on adrenaline as he tried to tame his beast.

It was one of the reasons she tried not to shift during a fight. Getting control of her wolf was harder for her and she could fight just as well in human form. Erin's eyes narrowed as she eyed the tall vampire. "You like to feed on dead shifters?" *Sick fuck.*

The man let out a sound that sounded a lot like a growl. "No. I'm hunting a group of feral vampires and we tracked the scent here."

Scent? Erin hadn't picked up on anything. She frowned and wiped the blood from her now-healed cheek. "Okay, who are you and why are you hunting ferals?" It wasn't out of the goodness of his heart—that much she was sure of. If he was hunting anyone, it would likely be on someone's orders.

"My name is Ian and we all work for the Brethren. We've been dispatched to hunt and destroy a newly turned group of vampires who have gone feral. They never should have been turned in the first place. I apologize for my team. They are newly formed and should not have gone on the offensive."

Erin eyed him warily, wondering how much truth was in his words. Even if she didn't trust him, she needed to make introductions. "I threw the first blade so no worries. My name is Erin Flynn and this is Noah Campbell." She motioned with her hand.

The blond male grunted rudely as he sized up Noah who was naked. "You let your female speak for you?"

Noah growled and she expected him to snap at the other male, but a slow grin spread over his face. "My female took your ass down in seconds. Could have decapitated you if she wanted. And last time I checked this is the twenty-first century, *dick*. She can do anything she wants."

Erin chose to ignore the "my female" comment, even if his words did make something warm spread throughout her body. And when she noticed the short vamp with black hair checking out Noah's entire, very naked, body with no shame, her inner wolf didn't snap as much as she normally would have at seeing another female eyeing him.

Ignoring the chauvinistic vamp, she focused on the leader. "As I was saying, this is Noah and his father is Alpha in this territory. I'm—"

"The newest enforcer for the North American Council. I recognize your name." Ian watched her thoughtfully for a moment. "Why are you in New Orleans?"

She thought about keeping the information to herself, but now was the perfect time to catch these vamps off guard. Gauging their reaction to her next words should be enlightening. "If you're here you must know that pregnant shifters have been going missing."

Ian's eyebrows slightly drew together as he shook his head. "I haven't heard that."

He didn't stink of lies, but she wanted to be sure. "So you didn't know about it when you arrived in town?"

Ian shook his head again. "We are here for the ferals."

Okay, so maybe he was telling the truth. That didn't mean he didn't know anything about why shifters were being taken. "Why would anyone want shifter blood?" With her question she gave away the fact that she knew *what* was happening to the kidnapped victims, but she had to pursue this avenue. They were vampires and might know something she didn't.

The leader glanced at his people. "Leave us. Now."

The short female looked like she might argue, but they all disappeared into the woods. The vampire reached into his jacket and Noah snarled.

"I'm just getting a card." Ian held up his free hand then pulled out a white card. He covered the distance between them in seconds, earning another growl from Noah who grabbed it from his outstretched fingers.

Resisting the urge to roll her eyes, Erin took it from Noah and glanced at it. It was a simple cream-colored card, made of thick stock, with the name Ian on it—no last name—and a phone number. She tucked it into one of her pants pockets.

"I wasn't lying when I said we're here for the ferals, but I don't like that pregnant shifters are going missing. I'll reach out to my contacts and be in touch if I find out something. And now you have my number if you need me beforehand," Ian said.

"You don't have my number."

"I'll get it from Jayce." The vampire's lips quirked up slightly, then disappeared into the forest.

Wind blew her hair back from his fast departure. So, this guy apparently knew Jayce. That was interesting. Or maybe not. Jayce seemed to know a lot of people. But it wasn't something she could dwell on. She had too many things to do. The first would be calling the local police so they could remove Kaigen D'Amico's body. Then, she'd need to talk to Noah's father about contacting her family. The woman had left two kids behind, something Erin kept trying to forget. The thought of breaking the news to a mate was hard enough, but to children?

She glanced up at Noah to find him watching her intently. He was covered in blood too, but he was practically healed. And he was a warrior. She wouldn't insult him by asking if he was okay. Swallowing hard under his stare, she nodded toward the direction they'd come from. "Let's go."

Brianna flipped open her small spiral notebook full of names, phone numbers, and other random notes she'd jotted down next to her contact list. Despite her recent infiltration of the Antiparanormal League (APL) and her interactions with humans, she still resisted using too much technology if she could avoid it. Her notebook would never freeze or lock up and couldn't be hacked. Unlike computers. Plus she hated those damn things anyway.

At one hundred years old she was an infant compared to the rest of her race. The fae were ancient, brutal, and liked to keep a pulse on any potential trouble in the world. Whether it was between humans and shifters or shifters and vampires, it didn't matter.

That was why she was now in New Orleans, Louisiana, with a very sexy shifter—who she'd recently lost her virginity to—and about to reach out to any and all vampire contacts she had. She might be young but she'd been around long enough to develop her own contacts. Or assets, as her oldest brother Rory liked to call them. Right now trouble was definitely brewing in this colorful city. She would be keeping an eye on the situation for her people. Of course she would also get involved if she felt it necessary. When on a mission she had the right to make executive decisions without checking in with her people. Even if her brothers thought she should check in every hour.

Six pregnant shifters missing in less than a month was bad news. All it would take for a war to erupt between any of the species was a small misunderstanding spiraling out of control. And pregnant shifters being kidnapped wasn't a misunderstanding. This situation had the potential to turn insane fast.

Even the lowest of the low respected pregnant women. It was simple biology and nature to protect females in that state. Even her own people—who were known for their brutality—had the highest respect for them.

Perched on the edge of her bed, she dialed the number of a vampire she hadn't spoken to in decades and hoped she received a warm response. She'd tried calling him when she'd first arrived but the phone had kept ringing. No voice mail or answering machine picked up. Now it was five in the morning but he was a daywalker, a rare breed of vampire who could walk freely under the sun, and she had no idea what his schedule was.

He picked up on the second ring. "Who the hell is this?" he snarled.

Brianna winced. "Hello, Marcus. This is Brianna. I don't know if you remember me, but—"

"Brianna O'Brien?" He sounded surprised.

That was the anglicized version of her family's ancient last name, but it was close enough. "Yes. I'm sorry for calling so early and out of the blue."

"No, it's no problem at all. It's been a long time.

How are you?" He had almost no discernible accent, making it hard to trace his roots, though she knew he was originally from Italy—probably close to six hundred years ago. Maybe even longer.

"I'm well and I'm actually in New Orleans. I was hoping I might be able to convince you to have breakfast with me." She mentally crossed her fingers.

He let out a soft, husky laugh. "You don't have to convince me of anything, sweetheart. And your timing is perfect. I just arrived back in town myself. What time and where would you like to meet?" There was definitely a sexual undertone to his endearment, but that was just the way he acted around females.

Nonetheless, she blinked at how acquiescent he was being. "Don't you want to know why I wish to see you?"

Marcus snorted. "If I get to see your pretty face, I don't give a damn."

She blushed at his words, remembering how he'd previously tried to get her into his bed. But she'd had no interest then and didn't now. He hadn't been too pushy, just persistent. She'd never wanted any man until Angelo. But at least Marcus's sexual interest had made setting up a meeting easier and she wasn't above using that to her advantage. "As soon as possible and I'll let you pick the place since you live here. I would like to try some of this city's famous beignets so if you choose somewhere that has them I would be appreciative."

He chuckled again. "I love the way you talk," he murmured. Then he rattled off the name of a café, gave her the address, and they disconnected.

As she set her phone on the bed next to her, she

smiled. That had gone much easier than she'd expected. Marcus wasn't attached to any coven, which
was good because he didn't report to anyone. He was
old even by vampire standards and powerful, and he
had a lot of contacts in New Orleans. He should be a
valuable source to have. While he was a notorious flirt,
she could handle him if he got out of line.

The door to the bedroom she'd been sharing with
Angelo opened abruptly. He stood in the doorway,
practically glaring at her. She frowned. His hazel eyes
were fierce and angry, which just made him even sex-
ier. But he looked as if something was wrong.

Panic jumped inside her as she rose from the bed.
"What has happened? Does Erin have news on the kidnappings?"

"I haven't talked to her or Noah. Who the hell was
that on the phone and why was he calling you sweetheart?" He softly growled at her, his eyes flashing from
wolf to human so quickly, but she definitely caught the
change.

She'd forgotten how well Angelo could hear, but
she didn't understand why he was so angry. "That was
the vampire I told you I was calling. He's agreed to
meet with me in an hour. This is excellent news so you
have no reason to be upset."

Angelo took a deep breath, accentuating his incredibly broad and muscular chest. As she remembered
how she'd kissed and licked all that expanse only hours
before she felt her cheeks heat up.

A muscle in his jaw twitched. "No one calls you
sweetheart but me."

Brianna watched the rise and fall of his big chest. He

was definitely agitated. The fae could be proprietary
when it came to their mates so she understood the concept and she'd seen shifters act insane regarding their
mates, but she wasn't Angelo's mate. They were simply
lovers. "Is this a shifter thing?"

"Is what?"

"Your possessive behavior."

"You're mine, Brianna." His hazel eyes flashed to a
dark, forest green and before she could respond, he'd
covered the distance between them and wrapped his
hands around her hips, pulling her tight against him.

Yes, this was definitely a shifter thing, she decided.
A thread of alarm spun through her even as it battled
with a slow-spreading heat in her lower abdomen. His
thick length pressed against her, insistent and leaving
no doubt as to how he felt about her no matter the cir-
cumstance. She loved that even though he was clearly
angry, he still wanted her. And she definitely wanted
him. All the time, it seemed.

She smoothed her hands over his chest hoping to
placate him. She didn't like arguing with him when
they could be doing much more interesting things. "I
need to shower before I meet him. I won't be gone
long—"

Angelo laughed, but there was no humor in the
sound. "I'm going with you."

She shook her head and tried to ignore what his very
male presence did to her. It was hard when all she
wanted to do was get naked with him again. He was an
extremely skilled lover and had promised to show her
even more sexual positions. She wasn't sure how that
was possible, but she believed him. "That's not a good

idea. Marcus is attracted to me and while I don't return the sentiment, I will likely garner more information from him if I meet him alone. It is more logical."

Angelo laughed again. "And that's exactly why you're not going alone."

Anger detonated inside her that he could even think that. "I don't mean I'll use my body to get information!"

His expression softened as one of his hands slid up to cup her breast through her top. Her nipples instantly tightened. "I know that, but I don't trust any man, especially a vampire, to be alone with you. Even if he wasn't interested in what's mine, I'd be going with you anyway."

She ignored the "mine" comment again when he lightly pinched her nipple between his forefinger and thumb. All these sexual feelings and experiences were so new to her; she knew that she wasn't thinking logically around him. She could seem to focus only on sex lately. The thought of arguing with him made her stomach twist and she really wanted him to be naked in the next few seconds. She wasn't meeting her contact for another hour—plenty of time to shower with Angelo.

Instead of responding to him, she grasped the bottom of her top and drew it over her head. Pleasure rippled through her as Angelo growled softly at the sight of her breasts. It was a sound she knew she'd never tire of. Even though their time together was limited and she'd eventually have to walk away from him, she wanted to wring all the joy out of their time together.

Chapter 5

Erin sat next to Noah on the iron bench on the D'Amico's front porch. They lived in a double-gallery house in a quiet upper-middle-class neighborhood close to the Garden District.

She could hear Angus inside as he spoke to Bertrand, the deceased Kaigen's mate. She could also hear the two little girls, Ophelia and Marie, sobbing at the news that their mother and unborn brother or sister weren't coming home.

Noah leaned forward and placed his head in his hands. "Fuck," he muttered.

Erin swallowed hard, not responding because she didn't trust her voice. She'd be going inside in a few minutes to speak to Bertrand and didn't want to get emotional beforehand. As shifters they all knew that death was inevitable and most humans considered them lucky because they were able to live so long and spend even more time with their loved ones. The downside for those left behind was the same as it was for humans. Maybe even worse. Being mated to someone for centuries, sometimes longer, and then losing them—unimaginable.

Silence descended on the inside of the house for a brief moment before the front door swung open. Angus stepped outside and nodded at Erin. When Noah rose, the Alpha shook his head. "They're suffering. Let her go in alone."

Noah growled low in his throat, but Erin placed a hand on his forearm and he instantly stilled. "Now's not the time." Whatever was going on with him and his father had no place in this house.

"I'm here if you need me," he said quietly.

"I know." And the knowledge warmed her. More than she wanted to admit. The man had become such an integral part of her life. So much so that she couldn't imagine it without him in it. No matter what she tried to tell herself, if he ever settled down with another female, it would kill her inside.

He pushed out a breath and dropped back onto the bench as she skirted past Angus who watched her curiously.

She didn't have time to figure out what the older wolf's look meant and she really didn't care. Shutting the front door behind her, she was momentarily stunned by the silence. It might be eerily quiet but the grief pulsing through the house was almost tangible. As she stepped farther into the foyer, her boots thudded softly against the hardwood floor. Movement to her left caught her eye. Bertrand D'Amico sat slumped against a red-and-gold-striped settee in the living room. It was early and he wore long checked pajama pants with a plain black T-shirt a shade darker than his skin.

He watched her warily as she stepped into the room. She glanced around and didn't see the girls she'd heard crying. He'd probably sent them to their rooms.

"They're upstairs with my sister," he said, as if he'd read her mind. There was a slight French accent to his voice and he spoke much softer than she'd imagined for such a large feline shifter.

She took a seat on a formal-looking high-backed chair across from the feline and cleared her throat. "I'm so sorry about your mate." The words felt useless, but he gave her a semiappreciative half nod so she continued. "I know this is the worst time to be here, but I want to find out who is taking shifters in this city. If you don't mind, I'd like to ask you some questions." She'd planned to do it before they'd found his mate and as soon as she was done here she planned to speak to the other mates of the missing women. While the timing might suck—that being the biggest understatement ever—she had no choice.

He glanced away from her, staring at the rich gold draperies pulled back from oversized windows. "I'll tell you anything you want." Before she could ask a question he turned toward her, pinning her with his dark gaze full of grief. "Kaigen was fifty years old and she and I were mated for thirty years. Well, mated and married. She wanted the human tradition too." He smiled softly as his eyes glazed over. "She is—was—originally from Chile. Even though she was a beta and I'm an Alpha, she ran this house. She stopped working outside the home eight years ago when our oldest was born."

Erin was silent as he took a deep breath. Glancing around the room in the silence she could see the deceased female's presence in the soft touches around the room. Bright, decorative throw pillows, oversized potted plants, and various pictures of Paris.

While she already knew most of what he was telling her, she realized he needed to be free to talk about his mate. When he didn't continue, she asked, "Can you tell me a little bit about her daily or weekly schedules? Did she drive your girls to school? What days did she do the grocery shopping? Or is that something you do?"

He snorted softly at the last question. "She would never let me buy the food. She would go shopping every Monday morning because that's when the best produce was delivered—or so she told me." He went on to name the store she shopped at regularly, the times she dropped and picked up her kids from school, where she went for Pilates, which friends she regularly had lunch with, and the name of her ob-gyn—even though Erin already knew that one.

After Erin jotted down everything he told her, she asked an obvious question. "What, if anything, about her schedule has changed in the past couple months?" Even though all the women had been taken within the last month they'd likely been stalked beforehand. The fact that they were all pregnant was the biggest link, but it wasn't like shifters wore giant signs around their necks proclaiming them shifters. And as far as she knew, pregnant humans hadn't been kidnapped.

He shrugged, though the action seemed to almost pain him. "Nothing that I know of. We live very quiet, normal lives. We get along with our human and shifter neighbors, have dinners with them, go to neighborhood get-togethers. And we've never had any issues with vampires or any other supernatural beings, *ever*. We just live and let live. Life's too short for . . ." He trailed off as if realizing what he was saying. Clearing his throat, he glanced back at the curtain.

Erin could see tears glistening in his eyes and it tore her up inside. Standing, she made her way to the entryway. "Thank you for speaking with me. I want you to know I'm going to find whoever did this and make them pay." She knew she shouldn't make promises, but watching this man's agony and hearing his children's suffering made her want to rip the city apart until she found anyone involved with the kidnappings and Kaigen D'Amico's death.

Bertrand's head whipped back around to face her. "If you find them, they're mine." His jaguar flashed in his eyes, the feline looking back at her with predatory menace.

Erin didn't respond before stepping out onto the porch. If he wanted justice for his mate's death, she wouldn't stop him, but she didn't have control over how this case would play out so she couldn't make any promises. She didn't blame him for wanting to avenge his mate though. Noah wasn't even her mate and if something happened to him, she'd destroy whoever dared to harm him and feel no guilt. She was completely aware what that said about her feelings toward Noah, but she ignored it as she had to do if she wanted to survive.

The moment she stepped outside, Noah stood and Angus pushed up from where he was leaning against one of the beams of the porch. From the look of things she didn't think they'd said two words to each other since she'd been inside.

"Thanks for talking to the family first," Erin murmured to Angus who just nodded. Then she looked at Noah. "I want to head to the Full Moon Bar and talk to Hector about his sister." The bartender's missing sister was only twenty-four, was an artist, and Erin wanted to see how her schedule and daily habits matched up with Kaigen's. On the outside it didn't seem as if they'd have much reason to cross paths since Kaigen was a stay-at-home mom and Leta didn't have kids, but something had to connect them. Erin just knew it.

Jayce had warned her how tedious investigations could be and while she'd known that on an intellectual level, it hadn't prepared her for the burning need growing inside her to see results faster.

As they headed down the walkway to her car, Noah placed a gentle hand at the small of her back. His spicy, earthy scent enveloped her, and though she knew it would come back to bite her in the ass later, she stepped a few inches closer, leaning into him. Surprising her, he leaned down and kissed the top of her head. "You're not alone right now, Erin," he whispered against her.

For a brief moment she leaned into him, soaking up what he had to offer as if she were a sponge. "Thank you, Noah," she whispered back because she didn't trust her voice. She didn't care that his father could see them. She didn't care if anyone saw her leaning on the tall, strong shifter.

This case had already brought up so many horrific memories and though she wanted to remain stoic and unmoved, she didn't mind his support one bit. He had

no clue about her past and he was still being support-
ive in every way she needed. Her own grief clawed at
her insides, telling her that she could never have a future with this man. She cared too much for him to saddle him with her crap. Especially since in the long run
he'd resent her shortcomings.

Brianna unbuttoned her knee-length wool coat as she and
Angelo entered Café Beignet. The place was charming
with small round café-style tables and matching chairs
with hearts shaping the backs of them. There were also
booths and since the tables looked as if they were made
of iron, she knew where she'd be sitting. Iron and the fae
didn't mix in the same way silver and shifters didn't.

As she slid her coat off, she spotted Marcus sliding
out from one of the booths. Tall, not as pale as most
vampires because he was a daywalker and because of
his Italian heritage, dark brown hair, dark eyes, and a
lean, yet muscular build. With his Roman nose and defined, almost sharp facial features, he was a very strik-
ing male. A few of the female patrons and one of the
male baristas checked him out as he strode toward her.

Marcus's gaze landed on Angelo for a brief moment,
then ignored her shifter as he clasped one of her hands
and held it up to his mouth. He brushed a kiss over her
knuckles, earning a growl from Angelo. Which was
why she hadn't wanted him to come with her. They did
not have time for male posturing. She quickly withdrew her hand.

"You look as beautiful as ever," he murmured, his
voice a seductive whisper.

"She's also taken," Angelo said as he clasped on to Brianna's shoulder and tugged her back.

Marcus sniffed the air—not subtly—then looked at her with a frown. "You're mated?"

Brianna shook her head. "No, we're not mates. And I did not come here to discuss my personal life."

Marcus gave Angelo a look that Brianna could only describe as challenging. Frowning, she looked between the two men to see Angelo staring daggers at the vampire. The fae were much more subtle than these two species. She'd never completely understand them.

Sighing, she stepped forward, ignoring the males and slid into the booth Marcus had come from. She smiled to see a plate of beignets and fig cookies already waiting for them. Angelo immediately slid in next to her, wrapping his arm around her shoulders. She leaned into his embrace, hoping she made it clear to Marcus that she was taken, at least at the moment. She and Angelo might not have a future, but she didn't want him to experience any discomfort or emotional distress because he thought she was interested in another male.

"I'm Marcus," her vampire contact said to Angelo, a smirk on his face. "Who are you?" The question sounded rude, but Angelo simply smiled.

Or more like bared his teeth. "Angelo Medina. I'm a member of the Armstrong pack and I'm here with Brianna as part of my Council and the Tuatha's investigation." The Tuatha were the royal class of fae and they ruled with an iron fist. Something Marcus would know.

He nodded then subtly glanced around the café before focusing on them. "You're here because of the missing pregnant shifters?"

Brianna nodded, but kept her expression blank. "Do you know something?"

His jaw twitched and he shook his head slowly. "As I said on the phone, I've been out of the country, but the topic came up from a contact of mine yesterday. I hadn't realized this is what you wanted to talk about, but since you're here with a shifter I'm guessing it is. . . . If I'd known, I would have been better prepared."

"So you know something about the missing females then?" she asked, watching his facial movements carefully. She might not be able to scent lies in the way shifters could but she could read people.

Frustration clear, he shook his head. "No, but this will not be allowed to go on in the city. As far as I know our leaders are not even aware of this, which tells me my kind haven't informed them. And I find that interesting." The last word came out as an angry snarl.

She frowned and next to her Angelo stiffened, his clasp on her shoulder tightening. "Interesting how?"

He shook his head again. "I don't know, but I intend to find out. I don't know if you understand the hierarchy in this city?"

"Angus seems to run everything here," she said. At least that was her understanding from what Erin had told her and the information she'd received from her own people before coming here.

"He does, for the most part. That Alpha is more or less the law everyone answers to. He also leaves the ancient vampires alone and we leave him alone. Bloodborns don't take orders from anyone easily, especially not a shifter."

Brianna knew a little about bloodborns. They were naturally born vampires, not made. And very rare. They were also powerful. Marcus was definitely one. Something she would have known even if they weren't acquaintances. He emanated a certain power that humans could probably feel, even if they weren't aware what they were experiencing in his presence. "So why is this important?"

He shrugged in a maddening way. "I'm not saying it is. I'm just saying that all the bloodborns in this city would be aware of pregnant shifters being taken, yet the Brethren haven't been informed. At least not that I'm aware of."

The supernatural grapevine was sometimes more active than human social media. In a city where the different supernaturals interacted with each other more than elsewhere, it made sense that bloodborns would be aware. Not to mention those in power often made it their business to know everything that went on in their domains.

The way Marcus said that the Brethren didn't know about what was going on inferred that he would know if they'd been informed. Which told her he had frequent enough contact with them. And she found that interesting. "You have contacts with the Brethren?" Four powerful vampires who more or less ruled all vampires. They didn't have a pulse on their kind the way the fae or shifters did with their own people though. Vampi~ were solitary creatures so it made sense.

Marcus snorted, his eyes flashing to a b

for a moment before returning to their normal brown, but he didn't directly answer. "I'm going to reach out to my contacts around the city, see what I can find out. I'll call you when I know anything." He glanced around again. "I don't like how open this place is. It shouldn't take me long to find out what I need to. If vampires have anything to do with the females being taken, it will end now."

She didn't like the way he was just leaving. Not when she had more questions. "But—"

He shook his head as he slid out of the booth. "I've already paid for the food." When he reached for her hand again, no doubt to kiss her good-bye, she zapped him with a bolt of her energy. A bright blue spark arced between them, slamming right into his outstretched hand. His palm sizzled with smoke.

He jumped back, surprise on his face. "I told you I'll call you as soon as I have something concrete. I'm not brushing you off."

She simply gave him one of her rare, lethal smiles. The one she reserved for those who truly pissed her off. "You'd better. And that wasn't for leaving, it was for being rude to Angelo," she said softly, hoping her show of power reminded him that she might be young, but she was still a powerful member of her race. And Angelo was her partner right now. No matter how helpful this vampire might be in her search for the truth, she wanted him to remember that.

After he'd gone, she looked up at Angelo to find him watching her curiously. She brushed a kiss against his cheek before picking up one of the fig cookies. "Are ·· hungry?"

"Not for food." His hazel eyes flickered between wolf and man for a moment, almost making her lose her grip on her cookie.

Fighting a blush, she cleared her throat. "What did you think about Marcus? What he had to say, not him personally," she clarified when Angelo's face darkened.

His expression slightly relaxed, but she could see the wariness in his gaze. "I couldn't scent any lies but he's an old vampire. I could feel his power. If he wanted to lie, I don't know that I'd be able to tell. Someone like Angus would but . . ." He trailed off, shrugging.

Nodding, she turned away and flagged down a server. They had time for a coffee before she needed to return to her small list of New Orleans contacts. She hated that Angelo couldn't read Marcus any better than she could. She was good at reading people, but she wasn't perfect. For all she knew Marcus was lying about being out of town and was involved with the kidnappings himself. Though she wasn't sure she believed that. From everything she knew about him with her past dealings, he was an honorable vampire. She just hoped he came up with something they could use.

"That bitch is getting antsy," Malcolm growled under his breath.

Chris Tyson glanced at his brother as they crossed over Chartres Street. "She's fine. You need to calm the fuck down." The human female they were using to help locate and kidnap pregnant shifters was acting like she always did. Nothing had changed.

His brother was the one getting edgy. Wanting to pull out of their operation early like they hadn't done this half a dozen times before. If he'd just calm down, he'd be able to see that. But Malcolm had always been that way. Hell, he was barely able to contain his anger issues from people.

"Whatever. You really think there's a female enforcer in town? I didn't even know the Council had one."

Chris shrugged, ignoring the small sliver of fear twining through him. If the Council had sent an enforcer here it meant they needed to be extra careful. He and his brother were raking in so much cash it was sick and he wasn't walking away for anything. Especially not some bitch shifter. But their human contact, Kelly, heard from a vampire she was screwing—not one of their rich patrons thankfully—that there was supposedly an enforcer in town and she'd been spotted at the Full Moon Bar. He and Malcolm stayed away from that place because it was owned by Angus Campbell.

Since this was technically his territory, he and his brother should have announced their presence but there were so many supernatural beings living in New Orleans the normal rules didn't apply. And there was no way in hell they were making an announcement to anyone about their presence. They planned to get shit done, make their money, then get out when the pregnant females had been of enough use to them.

Unfortunately he'd heard on his police scanner earlier this morning that a gnawed-on body of a pregnant shifter matching one of their last victims' description had been found. It didn't make sense since she'd been buried and they certainly hadn't bitten the woman, but he wanted to follow up on that information later.

"This way," Chris murmured as they cut down a

side street. Townhomes and a few businesses lined the quiet road and when they reached the stop sign at the next intersection, he pulled out a cigarette and leaned against the brick wall of a cheese shop that wasn't open yet. He didn't normally smoke, but he and his brother needed an excuse to loiter and peer around the corner toward the bar.

As far as he knew the place was open practically 24/7. They served breakfast to early risers and those who still hadn't gone to bed yet. There was no guarantee they'd even see this supposed enforcer, but it was the only lead they had and he sure as hell wasn't going to start putting out feelers in the city. He could ask some of his vampire patrons, but deep down he knew that would be a mistake. If he tipped them off that someone was in town investigating the pregnant shifters they might stop buying his product. And if word got around that a couple of shifters were asking about the enforcer, he didn't want to chance that this female tortured the shit out of a vampire who actually knew who Chris and Malcolm were. Better to lie low and check things out on their own for the time being.

Half a pack of cigarettes later Chris was ready to give up and come back another time when a very familiar redhead stepped out of the bar with a giant male who was no doubt a shifter too. "Holy fucking shit," he murmured, barely loud enough for his brother to hear. What was that bitch doing in town?

Malcolm, who'd taken to leaning against the building so they could alternate watching the bar from their angled, hidden position pushed up. "What?"

Chris swallowed hard and braced himself for his

brother's wrath. Fuck, fuck, *fuck*. He took a step back behind the building when Erin Flynn and her giant companion started down the sidewalk in their direction. They were on the other side of the road, and would likely pass over this side street, but he wouldn't take the chance that she saw him. "Careful," he murmured.

Malcolm peered around the corner and let out a low curse. Then he moved away and pressed his back against the wall to face Chris. "What the hell is she doing here?"

Chris's heart beat triple time. This was definitely a complication he didn't need. He was already worried about some enforcer. Now he had to worry about Erin. When the male next to her threw his arm around her shoulders, she nudged him and smiled up at the guy. The movement lifted her jacket and showcased the bottom of two crisscrossed sheaths. Yeah, she was usually armed. Some things hadn't changed.

Motioning that they needed to move, he and Malcolm ducked into the entryway of the store. There was a small enclave that kept them hidden as long as Erin and her companion didn't come down their street.

From where they were standing he could see her crossing onto the next street in the opposite direction from them. But then she paused and turned and stared right in his direction. Because of the shadows and the enclave concealing them, there was no way she should be able to see them, but it was possible she scented him. They were downwind of her so they shouldn't have a problem. When her companion frowned and said something to her, she shook her head and they continued.

Only then did Chris let out a low breath he hadn't realized he'd been holding. "Kelly needs to die." He hadn't planned to kill the human until he and Malcolm split town, but now it was necessary. He didn't like that Erin was in town, and he really didn't like the rumor of a female enforcer being in town. It was way too much heat they didn't need right now.

"That's what I've been saying," Malcolm grumbled, shoving a hand through his spiked blond hair. "You don't think . . . she's the enforcer, do you?"

Chris paused at the question, then slowly shook his head. "Nah." But she was incredibly strong. Was it possible? He shut that thought down. No fucking way. "Can you follow Erin and that giant motherfucker without being seen?" he asked quietly.

His brother grunted.

"Good. I'll take care of Kelly. You follow them and don't be seen. Just find out where they're staying and who they're talking to. Whatever you can get on Erin, do it. I want to know what she's up to. I'll call you when Kelly's dead."

Malcolm nodded and took off. Without pause, Chris hurried in the opposite direction. It was time to take care of a loose end.

Chapter 6

Though he wanted to keep his distance as they walked down the sidewalk in the French Quarter, Noah couldn't help himself. He casually slung an arm around Erin and tugged her close. Her magnolia scent twined around him, driving him more than a little insane. While she felt fragile in his embrace he knew that was just an illusion. She nudged him in the side and gave him a half smile that didn't quite reach her eyes. He understood why.

They'd just questioned Hector at the Full Moon Bar and even though the guy was newly mated, he was a wreck over his missing sister. Not on the outside, but the agony rolling off him was almost tangible. Of all people, Noah understood. His younger sister had been killed by vampires many years ago, but the dull edge of his agony still lived inside him. It liked to rear its ugly head every now and then. When that happened he usually took a day away from the pack and roamed the forest in his wolf form.

Fiona had run away because of their father's over-bearing ways and been killed. Then when Angus had gone out to put down the vamps who'd killed her, he'd refused to let Noah partake, even going so far as to have packmates restrain him. Because he would have gone no matter what the old man said. He still hadn't forgiven his father for keeping him away.

But right now other shifters' sisters, daughters, and mates were missing and he wanted to do everything he could to help. It wouldn't ease his own constant guilt over not protecting his sister, but it would help a lot of families.

"I thought for sure Kaigen and Leta might have more in common," Erin muttered as their boots thudded across the sidewalk.

Noah tightened his grip on her hard shoulder. The woman was incredibly lean. "I know. The Pilates class is a start though." Both women had gone to the same studio, but as far as Hector had known, Leta hadn't been friends with the other woman.

That didn't mean they weren't though. Erin had already called information to get the studio's phone number but it was closed at the moment so they were headed back to his father's place to see Meli.

"I hope Meli is up to talking," Erin said, her expression pensive.

Noah just nodded, but alarm jumped in his gut when Erin froze. A haunted look flickered in her mercurial gray eyes for a fraction of a second as she glanced around.

"What is it?"

Blinking, she shook her head as if trying to clear her

thoughts, then looked back up at him, a false smile on her face. "Nothing."

Every time she shut him out like that it was like a dagger through his chest. Sometimes she let him see the part of her she kept hidden from the world but he was tired of those brief glimpses. He wanted all of her and he would have her.

They continued walking and he used one of the many skills he'd learned growing up and pickpocketed her car keys. She was so caught up in her thoughts she didn't notice. This case was only starting and he could see the effect it was having on Erin already. It was a hard case but he didn't want her consumed by it and he just wanted her to smile one time today.

A few blocks later as they reached the car she was obsessed with, she slid her hand into her back pocket and frowned. Then she patted all her pockets and glanced at him. "Noah—"

He dangled the keys from his left hand, swinging them from side to side in a hypnotic motion. "Maybe *I'll* drive your car back to my father's house."

She let out a soft growl and lunged at him. But he was ready for her. Lifting his hand high—way higher than she could reach—he leaned back against the car and kept his hand in the air out of her grasp.

"Damn it, Noah. This isn't funny." Erin grasped his shoulder with one hand and climbed his body. She shimmied up him like a damn feline. With her hand outstretched and her knees clenched around his waist, she was eye level with him.

In that instant she froze and so did he. He'd meant only to play with her but feeling her tight body stretched out on his made him react. He couldn't help it. For decades he'd had control of his body but not around Erin. If she was on him, he was fucking hard.

Dropping her hand, she slid down a few inches and rubbed the juncture between her legs right over his erection. If they didn't have clothes on he'd be inside her tight body right now. Thrusting, taking, and claiming everything that was his.

Her eyes slightly widened and her natural magnolia scent got even stronger. When her eyes dilated and her breathing increased he knew he'd affected her. Part of him wondered if he should let this go, but he couldn't. "You feel what you do to me? What you *always* do to me?"

She swallowed hard. "Noah . . ."

"Cat got your tongue?" he asked, his words low.

Her gaze landed on his lips and she licked her own in an almost subconscious gesture. She moved up a little then back down, as if she wanted to grind against him. His cock jumped at the unexpected reaction from her. She was clearly letting her body take over for an instant, not getting all tangled up in that head of hers.

His inner wolf cheered, but just as quickly she shoved away from his chest and dropped to the sidewalk with a thud.

Turning from him, she crossed her arms over her chest. "You can drive my damn car if you want to," she muttered, sounding like a petulant child.

He didn't miss the way her cheeks were flushed crimson. From embarrassment that she wanted him just as badly as he wanted her—because he knew the sexy woman was still trying to fight her attraction—or just because she was turned on, he didn't know. And he didn't care. He affected her. Plain and simple.

It was all he needed to know at the moment.

One step at a time, he'd break down that protective wall of hers until it was impossible for her to walk away from him.

The drive back to his father's house was short and he took perverse pleasure in taking the turns just a little too sharp. Erin gasped each time he did, as if she thought he'd actually harm her car. Good. He liked that she wasn't in control for once. Since the moment he'd picked her up off that dirty alley pavement his entire world had rolled off its axis and he'd been spiraling out of control ever since. He wanted her to feel the same need and craziness he did every second of every day.

Before he'd even shut off the engine in his father's driveway, Erin was out of the car and striding up the walkway. He quickly fell in step with her, dangling the keys in her face. "Forgetting something? Or are you going to let me start driving your precious baby all the time now?" His voice was taunting.

With incredible reflexes, she snatched them from him but he didn't miss the slight quirk of her lips. "You are nothing but trouble, Noah Campbell. Stay out of my pants."

He let out a bark of laughter at her words and her cheeks flushed pink.

"I meant because of my *keys*, not . . . never mind." She blinked rapidly at him, her embarrassment clear and when a slow grin spread across his face, she turned on her heel and jerked open the front door of the mansion.

The second they stepped inside, all the humor left his body. He could hear a woman crying somewhere upstairs, but other than that the house was eerily silent.

But only for a moment.

Evan, Meli's mate, came storming down the stairs a moment later. He let out a horrific roar and shifted to his wolf form as he reached the bottom stair. Growling at them, he shoved past them and out the front door. The howl that followed made all the hairs on Noah's arms stand up.

Erin shot Noah a worried look and started up the stairs. It was like déjà vu from yesterday as his father and mother quietly strode out of the same room Meli had been in before. His father's face was grim, and his own mother had tears streaming down her cheeks.

Oh no. He knew what had happened before either of them spoke.

"She lost the baby," Angus said quietly. "Now is not the time to question her. She won't even let her own mate comfort her."

When Noah looked at Erin, he was surprised to see that her eyes had filled with tears. He couldn't remember ever seeing her cry. And her next words were like a dagger straight through his chest. "I . . . lost my baby about two weeks before I was due. I could try talking to her to let her know she's not alone if you think it would help." Erin wouldn't look at Noah or Angus as she spoke, but kept her gaze focused on Iris, his mother.

His mother blinked in surprise, then squeezed Angus's forearm. He simply nodded and let Erin pass. Noah couldn't even move as she shut the door behind her. The grief that had flowed off her as she'd spoken in that trembling voice shredded him. Erin had lost a baby? She'd been pregnant? By who? And what had happened? Why hadn't she told him?

"Did you know?" his mother asked quietly.

Unable to formulate words, he shook his head and stumbled down the stairs. Unwanted images from the day he and the warriors of his pack had found Erin in that alley invaded his mind. She'd never spoken of what had happened to her to anyone in the pack. Well, except for Carmen, but she was dead and had never told a soul. Now things clicked into place like puzzle pieces snapping together.

Seeing how strong Erin was, how utterly capable, he'd *never* understood how anyone could have harmed her the way they had. And there'd been so much fucking blood on her thighs he'd just assumed . . . fuck. Growling, he yanked the front door open and blindly walked down the driveway. He needed to get away from the house and didn't trust himself behind the wheel of a car.

As the gears in his mind turned he realized that if she'd been pregnant before they'd found her it would explain how someone was able to hurt her to the extent that she'd almost died. Pregnant shifters were nearly as weak as humans. It would also explain all that damn blood. But nothing could explain why she hadn't told anyone what had happened to her. Noah knew he was making assumptions but his gut told him he was right in this. If he found out who had harmed her while pregnant—there would be hell to pay. He could only hope he was wrong. But he would find out one way or another.

The farther he walked through neighborhoods, the easier it was to breathe. As if the giant weight on his chest had been raised a fraction. Once he finally got his emotions under control, Noah scrubbed a hand over his face and looked around, taking in his surroundings. *Holy hell.* He'd walked—and run—all the way to the Mississippi River. And he wasn't anywhere near Canal Street or shopping or touristy places.

He turned, heading back up the street of hollowed-out businesses. He could hear heartbeats in the vicinity, likely the homeless, but the place was damn near abandoned. Probably due to Hurricane Katrina. He vaguely recognized the area of town but he hadn't been familiar with it even when he lived in New Orleans. But he still knew how to get home. Well, his father's home.

As he came to the end of the street, he was faced with a clearly abandoned industrial warehouse. The reddish coloring on the outside of the three-story building was peeling, the windows looked as if they'd been blown out and the parking lot attached to the east side of it was overgrown with grass and weeds pushing through the cracks. But what caught his eye was a blond-haired man ducking through one of the blown-out doorframes with a speed that was way too fast to be human. There were too many scents in the area for him to discern, but Noah also thought he smelled a shifter. Possibly more than one.

Curious about any shifters that might be in this area of town, he kept his walk casual as he strolled across the street. Then he ducked inside the building through another opening. He didn't need any time to adjust to the semidarkness of the expanse of the interior.

High crisscrossed beams made up the rafters, a moldy stench he'd barely scented outside was now overpowering, and a slew of couches and mattresses were scattered across the football field–sized area. There were also a couple of metal barrels with fire burning inside them. Definitely a place where the homeless lived. But he couldn't *see* any of them. Interesting.

People who lived on the streets had a more honed ability to sense danger or predators. They had to if they wanted to survive. If the blond-haired man he'd seen enter the building was indeed a shifter, then it made sense why everyone had scattered.

Taking a few steps toward one of the dark corners, Noah swiveled as a body dropped from the rafters. Shit. If he hadn't been so damn caught up in his own thoughts he would have sensed it.

The shifter with blond hair and blue eyes stared at him, his eyes flashing darker to show his inner wolf as he lunged with a knife, aiming straight for Noah's heart.

Noah dodged to the side, the blade slicing through his shirt and barely glancing his upper arm. Most shifters preferred to fight in their animal form, though he had no clue why this guy wanted to fight him in the first place. It wasn't as if he knew him or wanted to take his damn territory.

"I'm not trying to take over your warehouse." Noah put a few yards between them and held up his hands in a placating gesture. New Orleans might be Angus's territory, but if someone had carved out a small section in an abandoned warehouse to call their own, the guy would definitely try to defend it.

The male snorted derisively, then wielded the blade around a few times. The quick work with his hand made Noah think he'd seen the action done in a movie or something. It wasn't intimidating, just annoying. As the man began to circle him, Noah stepped to the side, refusing to be cornered.

He didn't relish the idea of being in another fight and something told him this wasn't about the warehouse. The male had seemed to think that idea funny.

"What the hell do you want?" Noah growled, letting his claws unsheathe. He might not decide to turn completely wolf, but he was going to defend himself.

"For you and that slut you're with to leave town." The words were spoken with such hatred Noah realized that something about this was personal.

But that wasn't what registered first. It was the slur against Erin that made him see red. Ducking low, he flew at the other shifter's middle, tackling him with all the force he could.

Taken off guard, the guy grunted as Noah slammed him into a support beam. He could hear the knife clattering to the floor, then the sound of the shifter's own claws unsheathing. The roof above them shook ominously as Noah punched him in the face, the creaking sound eerie in the otherwise silent building.

He took a punch to the kidney, then a slash of claws down his ribs. Gritting his teeth, he held back a howl. After what he'd been through this morning with the vamps, this barely registered on the pain scale.

They were still tangled together, Noah's preferred way to fight. He didn't mind taking a few blows because he could channel the pain before dealing a death blow if it came down to it. Before he killed this guy he was going to get some damn answers.

The blond man hauled back, his fist flying at Noah's face. He dodged to the left and brought his knee up into the guy's stomach.

Clearly amped up on adrenaline, the shifter barely flinched as he swiveled back with his other fist, aiming for Noah's face again. Noah took the blow this time, his head snapping to the left. Instead of fighting it, he let the blow roll through him and lowered his body as he did a three-sixty turn.

Coming back around, Noah kicked out, his boot slamming into the guy's stomach with so much force the shifter flew across the concrete, only stopping when he smashed into another beam. As he took a step toward him, Noah scented another shifter nearby. Not lupine though.

Ambush.

His survival instinct took over as he whirled around. He froze when he saw Hector, the bartender from the Full Moon Bar running across the floor.

The feline shifter raised his hands in the universal symbol for "I come in peace." No weapons and his posture didn't scream aggression or tension. Still unsure about why he was there, Noah half turned at the sound of shuffling. The blond was on his feet and running full speed toward an open window frame.

For a moment Noah contemplated going after him but held off. He needed to return to Erin. He'd been gone too long as it was and they had a hell of a lot to discuss. Chasing after some crazy lupine and creating havoc in the city wasn't the smart move right now. Especially if that wolf wanted to lead him into a trap. Taking a deep breath to get his body under control, his canines and claws retracted as he fully faced Hector. "Why are you here? Don't even *think* about lying to me."

The bartender's jaw clenched. "I saw you leaving Angus's property and you looked rabid. I just wanted to make sure you were okay, but then I realized that lupine was following you and didn't want to be seen so I followed him."

Lies had a distinctive metallic scent and while some could cover their lies Noah believed Hector. His own sister was missing and the agony he'd witnessed from him earlier had been real and haunting. "You know that guy?"

Hector's face darkened as he shook his head. "No, but I didn't like his scent."

Noah nodded, understanding what he meant. It had been subtle, but his nostrils still tingled from the acidic smell. There had been something wrong with the male. He'd seen it in his eyes for a brief flash, as if he had a darkness inside him, but Noah hadn't been paying that much attention to the guy's face in his attempt to stay alive. "Me neither."

Frowning, he looked down at his ripped shirt and bloody side. The skin covering his ribs was already knitting together but after being so injured that morning it might take a little longer for him to heal. Shifter bodies could take only so much abuse.

"You drive here?" Noah asked.

Hector nodded. "And I've got some extra clothes. Might be tight but it's better than you running around the city all bloody in the middle of the afternoon."

Afternoon? Shit, how long had he been gone? As they headed toward one of the doors, another thought hit Noah. "Why were you on your way to Angus's?" Hector had been working when he and Erin had left him earlier.

"Heard about Meli. Wanted to check on Evan. We bonded when his mate and my . . . sister were taken." There was a catch in Hector's voice so Noah remained silent.

He was still trying to wrap his mind around the fact that Erin had once been pregnant and lost her baby. It was clearer now why this case was so important to her. Why she seemed so personally invested in it. While she might want to keep him out he'd be damned if she didn't open up to him. They were a team and he wanted to help and comfort her any way he could. Whether she wanted it or not.

Chapter 7

Erin opened her eyes, blinking in the dim room. She was still on the bed with Meli, her arm around the long-legged shifter's shoulders. She'd cried right along with Meli until they were both exhausted and must have dozed for a moment. They'd been talking for hours—well, crying and talking. It was clear Meli needed to express her anger and bitterness and Erin figured it was easier to do so with her because she'd been through something similar and because she was a relative stranger.

Sometimes telling your life's problems to a stranger was easier than confiding in those you knew and loved. "You awake?" she asked quietly.

"Unfortunately. I keep thinking this is all a nightmare I'll wake up from." Meli's voice had lost that bitter edge and now she sounded sad and tired.

Erin cleared her throat and hoped she didn't cross a boundary with her next words. "You're lucky to have a mate who loves and cares about you. He's hurting too and while he'll never fully understand what you went through, he's trying. Keeping him out will only hurt your relationship and make things worse. Let him grieve with you. If not he's going to feel like he lost both of you." God, it was so much easier to give advice than to do the things she knew would be beneficial for her own healing.

Noah might not be her mate but Erin knew she could open up to him. Too bad she was too terrified at the prospect of completely laying herself bare like that. The thought of him feeling sorry for her, pitying her, was something she didn't want to deal with.

Meli sniffled and picked up one of her fallen tissues. She dabbed at her red-rimmed eyes. "I know. Will you send him in?"

Erin nodded and slowly slid from the bed.

As she headed toward the door, Meli stopped her. "Thank you for staying in here with me and I'm sorry for everything you lost."

Erin couldn't find any words and before she'd even opened the door it flew open and Evan strode in. His face was drawn and haggard, his gaze sweeping over his mate. "I was listening outside," he said to Meli. "I . . . can come in?"

On a sob, Meli nodded and started murmuring apologies about kicking him out. Wanting to give them privacy and needing to put more distance between Meli's fresh agony and herself, Erin hurried out and shut the door behind her. If she wanted to keep it together for this case she'd have to be stronger and a little more detached.

Of course she knew the latter wasn't going to happen. She was already invested. So much so that she'd gone and admitted her darkest secret in front of Noah and his parents. But she hadn't been able to stand idly by with another female suffering through something similar to what she'd gone through and not try to help.

Erin wrapped her arms around herself as she descended the stairs. She wasn't sure where Noah was and she'd turned her phone to silent while she'd been in with Meli. She'd figured if any emergencies had come up, Noah or Angus would have retrieved her. Right now she missed him so much her arms ached to hold him. At the same time she was scared of a confrontation.

She passed a couple of female shifters in the foyer and nodded politely, but didn't attempt to make any conversation as she left. The second she stepped onto the porch she scented Noah.

His spicy scent tickled her senses and ripped open whatever control she thought she'd had on herself. He was either going to be pissed at her or look at her with pity. Or maybe a combination of both. She couldn't handle any of that now.

As she stepped down the few stairs onto the walkway, Noah appeared as if out of nowhere. He strode across the expansive yard, his walk steady and sure as he stared at her with those dark, smoldering eyes. His handsome face was expressionless. Well, hell. Normally she could get a read on him, but his jet-black hair was pushed back and damp as if he'd just had a shower. The sharp planes of his face and full mouth just begged her eyes to trace over him. He was wearing a different sweater than he had been earlier. Frowning, she started to ask him what had happened when he let out a growl.

Standing on the driveway a foot in front of her, his expression was soft, almost pitying. The sight was a jolt to her system. She didn't want anyone's pity.

He swallowed hard. "I get one question right now; then I'll leave this alone for today only. Did you lose . . . your baby the day I found you?" His voice was hoarse.

The words shattered through her like shards of glass, cutting and slicing. He certainly wasn't pulling his punches. "Yes." And that was all she would say. All she *could* say without having a breakdown. Her throat tightened with emotions threatening to spill over as unshed tears burned her eyes. She blinked rapidly, refusing to let them fall.

His eyes narrowed with some emotion she couldn't define. Noah was so hard to read right now yet she felt as if he was ripping open old wounds. "Who hurt you?"

She wasn't ready to talk about that yet. It was too damn hard. "You said one question," she whispered.

Even the thought of admitting what she'd been through was flaying her alive. She simply couldn't tell him the truth. Not yet.

His jaw clenched, his fury potent, but eventually his expression softened as he asked, "Why didn't you tell me?" Underneath the anger she could feel rolling off him, was a whole lot of pain.

She'd hurt him by keeping something so huge from him. She knew that and wanted to reconcile it but didn't know how. Didn't know if she could. But she wanted to try because Noah meant so much to her. While she wasn't ready to tell him the whole truth, she stepped forward and opened her arms. Before she'd fully embraced him, he crushed her body to his.

Noah buried his face against the top of her head, the feel of his hold almost brutal with its intensity. She could feel his heart beating out of control, the tempo matching her own. She always felt that way when he was touching her.

"I want to tell you everything Noah, I just . . . can't. Not yet. Okay?" Her voice cracked on the last word and his grip finally loosened.

Sighing, he dropped a soft kiss on her forehead but she couldn't meet his gaze. She felt too exposed.

"If you want to hold back stuff from me, fine. Okay, it's not fucking fine but I'll deal with it *for now*. But you will eventually tell me everything. You need to get this off your chest and I deserve to know. I'm not walking away from us, Erin. Not until you make me. And I don't see that happening anytime soon." There was a challenge in his last words.

Damn. Yeah, he definitely wasn't pulling his punches. She wasn't pushing him out of her life and he knew it. It didn't matter how much she wanted to, she couldn't *force* him. Doing so would be like ripping out her own heart and trying to function without it. He deserved better. Even though it was instinctive for her to hold anyone's gaze, she dropped her eyes and looked down at the ground. Shame overwhelmed her. She hated that he'd just called her on her bullshit. She wanted to tell him everything, to explain how he was too good for someone so broken, but the stupid words wouldn't come.

Maybe he sensed her inability to communicate because finally he spoke, cutting through the tension. "While you were in with Meli I went for a run and was attacked by a lupine shifter. I didn't recognize him, but I'm going to send a description to Ryan, see what he can come up with."

Her head snapped up. "Are you okay?"

He nodded. "Yeah, I would have followed him, but Hector showed up and took me off guard. Without much backup I didn't want to follow someone into a trap. Now . . . I wish I'd gone after the fucker. He said something along the lines that he wanted you and me to leave town, which leads me to believe he doesn't want an enforcer around. That could be for any number of reasons but this guy might be involved in the kidnappings."

"What did the guy look like?"

He shrugged, but the tension rolling off him was palpable, taking away the casual action. "Blond hair, blue eyes—dead, like he had no soul. He smelled wrong too."

She frowned. That wasn't exactly a detailed description, but if he'd been fighting for his life, there was no way Noah would have noticed much more. She hated that some unknown shifter had attacked him, especially if the male was involved with the kidnappings. If someone thought they could run her out of town, they were out of their mind. "I want to hit up that warehouse and see if I can pick up any scents." She was still waiting for that vampire from earlier to call her and she needed to check in with Brianna and Angelo. But first, she hoped she might be able to pick up a lead with a scent. It was a long shot, but one she had to try.

Twenty minutes later she fought her disappointment as she and Noah left the warehouse. There had been too many damn scents inside the building—many of them gross—to pick up on anything solid, let alone a scent trail.

"We need to grab some food." Even if the thought wasn't exactly appealing she had to eat. They both did. As a shifter her metabolism was off the charts and she needed to be in prime fighting form at all times.

Noah just nodded and fell in step with her. He was silent as they got in her car. For a moment she contemplated opening up to him, but shoved that fantasy away. After today she was too raw and would give in to almost anything Noah demanded. She scrubbed a hand over her face as if that could somehow wipe away her memories. When she went to put on her seat belt, she found herself being tugged across the center console.

Yelping in surprise, she tried to find balance as Noah firmly pulled her into his lap. He twisted her so that she had no choice but to straddle him. Not that she actually fought him. Her knees slid around his outer thighs, the tight confines of the car pushing her even closer to him. "What are you doing?" Her windows might be tinted but if anyone walked by they'd be able to see them and she'd never thought Noah was an exhibitionist. He was much too possessive for that.

Noah didn't respond. Just grasped the front of her pants, unsnapped the button, then tugged her zipper down. The spicy scent rolling off him was potent and delicious.

A very small part of her wondered what he was doing. Okay, not *what*, but what had brought this on. He'd told her he wouldn't do anything with her unless she gave him everything. Yet he'd initiated this and she hadn't indicated things had changed between them. She couldn't find the energy to stop him. There was no way she wanted to either. She was so damn needy for his touch it scared her.

"Noah . . . things haven't changed between us." Or had they and she was just too stubborn to admit it?

He surprised her when he just slid his large hand down the front of her panties and cupped her mound possessively. "They have, but that's not what this is about. You need this right now."

Heat flooded between her legs, but he didn't enter her even though her inner walls clenched convulsively, desperate to be filled by him. As he just sat there, watching her with that heated gaze, her nipples tightened as she imagined what it would feel like when he finally pushed into her.

A slight tremble rolled through him and she felt it only because of how close they were. His wolf flared in his eyes for a second, letting her know how little control he had at the moment.

She felt light-headed as she inhaled his scent. The man smelled like the earth. All spicy and masculine and all hers. At least for the moment. Whatever the scent was, it surrounded her. If she could bottle it up, she would. He leaned forward, brushing his lips softly against her cheek. His hot breath only added to the spreading heat in her belly and her tightening nipples. She couldn't seem to find her voice.

"You're going to come for me," he ordered, his deep growl making her shiver.

With his hand remaining still, he repositioned his head and sucked her earlobe between his teeth. He gently tugged and another tremor raced through her.

Every instinct she possessed told her to push him away. Told her to shove at his chest and make him let her go. But she couldn't find the energy. Hell, she didn't want to. Right now she was terrified she'd screw up this case, that she wouldn't be able to bring the missing females home safely. All she wanted to do was *not think* for just a little while. It would be so easy to let go and do everything with Noah that she'd fantasized about on a nightly basis.

From the moment she'd met him, even broken and bloody, she'd intrinsically known he was a decent, good man. The kind of man she wished she'd met when she was younger. He'd have never taken advantage of her naïveté.

Erin clutched his broad shoulders, digging her fingers into his unforgiving muscles. As soon as she did it, she realized it was a mistake. Or maybe not, considering he took it as an invitation.

Before she could blink, his mouth was no longer on her earlobe, but directly on hers. His lips were warm and demanding and his tongue was probing her mouth with insistency. There was a hunger raging inside him. But he was restraining himself. She could feel it as sure as she could her own heartbeat.

For some reason, the knowledge touched her. Though

he was demanding she give in, he was holding himself back *for her*.

His tongue stroked over hers in erotic little flicks that sent waves of pleasure curling through her. She knew she shouldn't be doing this, but couldn't stop herself. It had been so long since she'd let a man touch her and she was tired of getting herself off to fantasies of Noah. She wanted to experience the real thing.

Almost as if he read her mind, he slid one of his fingers inside her wet sheath. The action was so unexpected and abrupt that she froze for a moment. She thought he might work up to it, tease her a little.

Unable to stop herself, she rolled her hips against him, wanting more.

Wanting everything.

Letting her head fall back, she let out a low moan as he plunged another finger into her. She sucked in a breath at the intrusion.

"Let go, Erin." He nipped her jaw. "Let me give this to you."

God, the way he said her name was enough to make her come. His deep voice rolled over her as her inner walls clenched around his thick fingers. She tried to move, to grind herself against him, but he grabbed her hip and held her firmly in place.

It was maddening, yet hot as hell.

As he continued kissing and nipping her jaw, trailing a path of hot kisses in his wake, she buried her face against his neck and inhaled his scent.

She knew it wouldn't take her long to climax and that scared her. Her entire body was primed for him and had been for far too long. Her inner wolf instinctively trusted him.

Pressing a thumb to her clit, he began rubbing her sensitive bundle of nerves as he moved his fingers in and out of her in an almost frantic rhythm. She tried once again to move against him but he just flexed his hand against her hip.

His show of dominance pushed her over the edge. She didn't like to be restrained but she was on top and he still held all the power. It was an erotic sensation. As her climax ripped through her, she bit his shoulder, not wanting to scream out his name. The second she did it, she realized her mistake. Pure instinct took over and she let her canines descend to pierce his skin. She screamed at herself to stop but the most selfish part of her didn't care. She wanted to mark him because she wanted the entire world to know he belonged to her. It wasn't like his cock was inside her while she was doing it. If it had been then she'd have been marking him as her mate.

Erin bit him, breaking the skin as wave after wave slammed into her. She simply couldn't pull back.

Noah sucked in a sharp breath, arching against her bite and grabbing the back of her neck to hold her tight to his body.

Her orgasm was sharp and intense, flowing through her like a fast-breaking wave. The pleasure punched through her system, hitting all her nerve endings until she loosened her grip on his biceps and slowly pulled her head back.

Noah's fingers were still buried inside her, her slick release coating him. He remained still, though his breathing was just as erratic and unsteady as hers. And he hadn't made a move to take off his clothes or push things further.

Her gaze tracked to his neck where the puncture marks were healed but two faint bruises remained. "I'm so— "

Noah's fingers curled inside her, the action making her hips jerk against him. "Don't you dare apologize for that. Not when my fingers are still inside you," he growled, anger in his voice and on his face.

She cringed, realizing what she'd been about to say. "I just meant I'm sorry I didn't ask." Not exactly true, but she wouldn't say the other words. Wouldn't tell him that she was horrified she'd shown so little control around him. This is why kissing him got her into trouble. He'd used only his hand on her and she'd marked him. "Thank you for . . . that." She could feel the blush creeping up her neck and cheeks and Noah's expression instantly softened.

Slowly and with a wicked grin, he withdrew his hand and brought one of his fingers to his mouth. When he licked her off him, her face flamed even brighter, but she couldn't look away. They'd just crossed a serious line and she knew there was no going back for her. She wouldn't stop until she'd experienced everything Noah had to offer. Well, just short of mating. She refused to saddle him with someone as fucked-up as she was. Not when he deserved so much better. But there was no way to put the brakes on what he'd just started in this car.

She had a feeling he knew it. It was probably why he'd come at her like this when she was raw and vulnerable. Noah was a damn sneaky wolf when he wanted to be. And when he wanted something, there wasn't much he'd let get in his way. It was something she'd always loved about him.

Chris sat low in the front seat of the four-door sedan he and his brother had bought with cash when they'd arrived in New Orleans. It had been cheap and they would leave it when they moved again. Which would likely be sooner than he'd originally planned. His brother's last text had him seething, but he managed to keep his beast at bay.

At least killing their human contact had been easy enough. After he'd slit her throat, her vamp lover had arrived so he'd had to kill him too. That kill had been harder, but he'd done what he had to. One less vamp in the world was fine with him.

Movement from the rearview mirror caught his attention. Without turning around, he watched as his brother hurried down the sidewalk toward him. He'd parked down a side street a few blocks from Decatur Street where their next target was.

Of course Malcolm didn't realize that yet.

Seconds later his brother slid into the passenger seat. Chris tossed him a plain dark blue ball cap. Not much of a disguise but it would still cover part of their features. And they had to move fast right now because of his brother's monumental fuckup.

"What's this for?" Malcolm asked but still put it on.

"Thanks to you, dumb ass, we have to do some damage control," he said very quietly in case anyone with supernatural hearing was nearby.

"What was I supposed to do—let that guy kill me?"

They still didn't know who the male with Erin was or even why she was in town. They couldn't afford to get on her radar or that of someone even more powerful. Chris hated the unknown, especially if it affected his money. "You didn't have to attack him. From what it sounds like, you could have just run."

"He might have come after me."

Sometimes Chris wondered if his brother being dead might be a good thing. But their operation was too hard to do alone and he couldn't trust anyone like he could Malcolm. His brother had no problem killing anyone or crossing any line. Just like Chris. To be successful and get ahead, that was how they needed to be. He wasn't going to live under any Alpha's rules again and he and his brother were going to have their own money. Boatloads of it by the time they were done in New Orleans. Since he wasn't physically strong enough to be an Alpha, he'd be damned sure he had enough money to buy him all the protection he could ever want.

"So what's the deal with the ball cap?" Malcolm finally asked again, motioning to it on his head.

Chris eyed the mirrors and when he was sure the side street was deserted he looked at his brother. "We're going to throw a few Molotov cocktails through Screamers and make it clear we're part of Angus Campbell's pack."

"Why?"

"Because we need a distraction." Screamers was a vamp nightclub and since dusk had just fallen it wouldn't be too crowded. He and his brother were strong, but they couldn't take on an army of pissed-off vampires. However, there would be enough vamps there that word would get around. "This should cause enough of a divide in the city to keep the Campbell pack busy with angry vamps looking for retaliation and not worry about the pregnant shifters. And it might distract the enforcer enough to split focus from their job." They already had enough to worry about with Angus Campbell, the enforcer, and Erin's presence in the city. He had no problem raising the stakes. Hell, he'd set the entire city on fire and raze it to the ground if it meant he got what he wanted. They needed the attention off of them long enough to complete their job and rake in enough cash to live well the rest of their very long lives.

Chapter 8

Brianna wanted to toss her cell phone out the window, but instead she held it up to her ear, listening as her oldest brother, Rory, spoke to her as if she was a child and not a one-hundred-year-old woman perfectly capable of taking care of herself.

"I don't like the thought of you interacting with that vampire, Marcus." Rory spoke as if his opinion in this mattered.

Next to her in the driver's seat of their parked vehicle where they were waiting for Marcus to arrive, Angelo snorted in agreement. Which infuriated her more. He didn't like Marcus for stupid, male reasons that had no bearing on what they were doing at the moment.

"Why does it even matter to you?" she asked her brother. When she'd checked in with her mother—who was not only royalty, but also a fae warrior—to fill her in on what she'd found out in New Orleans so far, she'd received a call from Rory minutes later. Sadly, she knew she'd be getting a call from her other brother soon too.

While her mother trusted her to call for backup if she required it, Brianna's two big brothers thought she needed to hear their opinion on everything. All the time.

"Because he is a man whore. He screws anything that moves." Rory sounded frustrated as he spoke.

"Yes, I know. Who cares? It does not affect the information I receive from him!" For just a moment she lost her temper and raised her voice. It was better than breaking her phone, which is what she wanted to do so she wouldn't hear the phone ring if he called back. But she knew she would regret it the second she did.

"He will try to sleep with you."

"He wants to, but it doesn't matter. I'm hanging up now. This is ridiculous and if it's all you have to say, then—"

"Marcus lost his mate about five hundred years ago. His female was killed by a shifter. If he's helping you it's for his own gain. Why should he care if shifters are being taken? The answer is, he *wouldn't*. Don't trust this male. Find someone else to help you. Better yet, come home. You've been away too long." The pain in her brother's voice was real enough that it made Brianna's heart soften.

But her resolve didn't. She was tired of being coddled. Closing her eyes, she leaned her head back against the headrest. "What I'm doing is important and you know I'm more than capable of taking care of myself. What's this really about?"

He paused for a long moment. "What about that fucking shifter?"

Without opening her eyes she could feel the tension

rolling off Angelo, who had definitely heard the question. Her brother knew she was with him, but maybe he'd forgotten about shifter hearing. "His name is Angelo and he's sitting right next to me and can hear every word you're saying."

"Good. That fucker better not think about touching you." His words were an angry order.

"We're through; good-bye, Rory."

"I'm serious, Brianna. Has he touched you?"

"No. Now good-bye." She hung up before he could continue his stupid tirade. Turning to Angelo she grimaced. "I'm sorry. I wouldn't have answered if I'd known how pointless that conversation would be. He's normally very . . ." Well, he wasn't polite or civilized so that would be a lie. "I'm just sorry."

Angelo watched her with that steady gaze, but there was something lingering in the depths of those sexy eyes that confused her. He looked almost hurt. "Are you ashamed to be with me?" he asked, his question taking her completely off guard.

"Why would you ask that? Is it because of what I said to my brother?"

He just shrugged.

Which made her sigh. "He's my brother, I'm not going to tell him anything about my . . . our . . . things that are none of his business. That doesn't mean I'm ashamed of us."

His lips pulled into a thin line, but he didn't respond. Just turned to look out his window. "Your brother had a point about Marcus. It's curious that he's helping you when he has every right to hate shifters."

"If what Rory said was true and his mate was killed

five hundred years ago, that's a very long time ago. There's nothing *curious* about it. And it doesn't mean he hates all shifters. I've never known him to be prejudiced." The way she saw it, Marcus had agreed to help them because what was happening was wrong. She wasn't going to see motives that weren't there.

Angelo didn't say anything, just grunted. She was about to respond when she saw Marcus appear from the shadows along the sidewalk of the quiet neighborhood. Without informing Angelo, she slid from the vehicle and heard him curse as she shut the door.

Her boots clicked softly against the concrete curb as she stepped out. Without turning, she could hear Angelo get out on his side, but he was much quieter than she was, moving like the lethal predator she knew him to be. She wasn't sure which direction Marcus had come from as she hadn't seen him walking up or down either direction of the sidewalk. He'd picked the area and the neighborhood was in the Garden District with most homes protected by gates or walls. While it had annoyed Angelo that they hadn't picked the meeting location, she'd agreed to meet here. Marcus had nothing to gain by hurting either of them.

She smiled at Marcus and ignored Angelo's soft growl as she stepped toward the vampire. "Where did you come from?"

His mouth quirked slightly as he pointed up with a long, elegant finger.

Her eyebrows rose. She'd forgotten some vampires could fly. Now it made sense why he'd picked the area. It was secluded enough, but he would have had an aerial view if he'd come through the air.

"Why did you insist on meeting in person? You could have spoken to Brianna over the phone." Though low, Angelo's voice had a deadly edge to it. He stood next to her, his stance protective and slightly aggressive.

These males were going to give her an aneurism.

Marcus's own gaze was filled with annoyance as he flicked a glance at Angelo. "I could have, but then I wouldn't have been able to see her lovely face."

She cleared her throat as she placed a hand on Angelo's forearm. This was ridiculous. "What have you found for us?"

"It's not much, but one of my contacts gave me the name Kelly Bridges. She's human and runs a Pilates studio not far from here. I have her work and home address." He pulled a slim envelope from the inner pocket of his leather jacket and gave it to her. "This is all the information I have on her. It's not much."

"What's her involvement with the pregnant shifters?"

"They've all attended her studio and it sounds as if she's handpicking them. For who, I don't know. *Yet.*" There was a wealth of rage in that one word.

"Who's your contact?" This time Angelo spoke.

Marcus didn't even look at him as he replied. "None of your business."

"Then how do we know your information is even good?"

"The male I got it from has a lot to lose if I find out he's lying. And his maker is involved with the human female."

"Your contact betrayed his maker?" She found that hard to believe.

Marcus shook his head. "He betrayed no one because I am not giving you his maker's name. Or my contact's name. A human female who hasn't been claimed, mated, or protected means nothing."

Technically Marcus was correct, but no one would betray their maker unless they were weak. So he had likely threatened this male. Probably even hurt him. She didn't push because she knew it would be pointless. And she didn't care so much about his identity, but why the shifters were being kidnapped.

"Why are the females being chosen by her? Why are they being taken?" The important question none of them could figure out.

Marcus shut down, his expression becoming unreadable. "I've given you what I know and that is all I am telling you. Find the woman and you might get answers."

Brianna looked at Angelo. "Will you wait in the car?" She squeezed his arm slightly and hoped he understood why she wanted to be alone with Marcus. Her shifter would do whatever he damn well pleased, so she just waited while he clenched his jaw and gave her this unreadable look until finally he did as she asked.

Angelo could still hear them, something Marcus knew, but she wanted to be alone with him for just a few moments. Even the illusion of privacy mattered. "Rory told me something I was not aware of. You had a mate?"

It was as if she was looking at a stranger for how stony his expression turned. He simply nodded.

When it was clear he wouldn't respond, she decided

to be blunt. "She was killed by a shifter so why are you helping us?"

Marcus's dark eyes flashed amber quickly before returning to their dark brown. "I don't owe you or anyone else an answer to that, but this is my city and I don't like those who prey on females. I won't tolerate it here."

"Why are they being taken?" Marcus had to know. If he knew this human female's name, he would know why the shifters were being kidnapped.

He glanced at their quiet surroundings as a car cruised past. Once it was gone, he looked back at her. "There is much I would do to help you, but I won't betray the secrets of my kind. Not directly."

Then he was gone so fast she didn't see him leave, but he left a big gust of wind in his wake. She wasn't even sure if he'd flown into the air or down the sidewalk.

Fighting frustration, she slid back into the passenger seat. As she started to thank Angelo for giving her privacy, he leaned across the console, his mouth crushing over hers.

His big hand slid through her hair, his hand cupping the back of her head in a dominating grip as his tongue danced with hers. He was always a bit wild, but she had the feeling he'd been holding back until now. The way he kissed her, it was like a claiming, raw and hungry.

Her fingers dug into his shoulders as she tried to gain her balance, but just as suddenly he pulled back. Breathing hard, his normally hazel eyes had darkened to a forest green, showing his wolf. "You ready?"

Feeling dazed, she blinked. "For what?"

"To head to the human's house?"

Right. The human. How was he even thinking clearly after that kiss? "Yes. You're not angry?"

His half grin was wry as he shook his head. "No. I understood what you were doing. I just needed to re-assure myself and my wolf that you are mine. It's an animal thing, sweetheart."

She sucked in a breath at his erotic words. She wasn't his—or maybe she was. Being with him had disrupted her perfectly ordered world and she knew things would never be the same once she let him go. Except . . . she didn't want to let him go. Wasn't even sure if she could. She pushed those thoughts away. They had someplace to be and she needed to keep her focus. "Let's go."

Erin tried to shift against her seat inconspicuously as she tore down LaSalle Street in her Challenger. The ache between her legs was growing and becoming more uncomfortable. Even though Noah had brought her to orgasm a few minutes earlier, it wasn't enough. Not even close. She wanted all of him and now that her inner wolf had been woken up, she refused to be locked down again. Her animal wanted out to play and she couldn't understand why Erin was still clothed and not riding the insanely sexy shifter only inches away until they were both sweaty and sated. An edginess had taken root inside her and it was all his fault.

"How are you feeling?" Noah's words were practi-cally a purr. No doubt he could scent her growing hun-ger for him.

The scent of her need was almost suffocating her in the enclosed space of her car so there was no way he could miss it either. The only thing that made her feel a little better was that his spicy arousal was just as potent as hers. "Don't be smug. It's not attractive."

"Oh, I think you find me *very* attractive. And right now you're wondering how much better my cock will feel than my fingers as I'm thrusting into you." Erin nearly choked at his words. Damn him, it was true. He would feel amazing. She just knew it.

She and Noah joked around all the time and despite that he'd just brought her to orgasm he'd never talked to her like that. It was arousing and erotic and completely disconcerting. Her face—and much lower places—warmed instantly, but she didn't respond. Doing so would be insanity and just encourage him. And since she'd already met her quota of crazy actions for the day, *no, thank you.*

"Nothing to say?" he purred again, sounding so smug he might as well be feline.

She bit back a response, knowing anything she said would bite her in the ass later. What had happened to Noah? It was like a switch had been flipped and he was . . . oh no. No, no, no. He might have made that first move but she'd let him in and now he'd be pursuing her like there was no tomorrow. She might as well have hung a neon sign around her neck that said CLAIM ME.

It was his inner wolf taking over, she knew that. The beast had been let out, much like her own inner wolf, and it wouldn't stop until it claimed her as his mate. And double damn him, she knew he'd never settle for just a mate. He would want to eventually bond and have kids and the whole package. "Noah, I'm not good for you so keep your wolf leashed."

He laughed, the seductive sound wrapping around her and sending more heat to the pulsing ache between her legs. God, he was so fucking alpha, but she sometimes forgot just how much. Ever since he'd found her near death he'd been walking around on eggshells, being extra sensitive with her. Until roughly a couple of months when he'd seen her fight, and then they'd shared their first kiss. Then he'd started to get more aggressive in his pursuit of her and now he'd apparently taken off the gloves and was coming after her hard. Not that she blamed him.

The heat and attraction between them was combustible. He was so strong and competent and unlike any man she'd ever known. Her inner wolf always wanted to preen and strut around for him. Noah just brought out her most basic, primal side. While she could never be with anyone weak or submissive, something told her that Noah would eventually come to crave someone softer. When she'd been found she'd been just that. Well, not submissive—never that—but she'd been weak and in need of care and nurturing and he'd been there. Every day she grew stronger and there was no way in hell she'd ever be that person again. What happened when Noah realized he wanted someone more feminine and not broken? Someone who could give him everything he deserved, including cubs. Lord knew, Noah deserved the whole damn package, including a big family.

When he didn't respond further, she slightly relaxed

and took another sharp turn. Now wasn't the time to hash out anything anyway. The warehouse had been a bust, but they'd grabbed a quick bite to eat and she was ready to go.

She had a job to do and right now she planned to break into a Pilates studio while she waited on Ryan to get the home address of a woman named Kelly Bridges. She'd discovered that the human female had also taught classes that Meli had gone to during her pregnancy. That was three shifters with one solid link and Erin didn't believe in coincidence. She still planned to follow up with the other families, but she had a feeling the missing females had all taken Pilates at CC Pilates. She assumed the CC stood for Crescent City. Not particularly clever, but easy to remember.

They slowly drove past the two-story building of the studio. It was encased on either side with restaurants. One was a bistro that was closed and the other a place that sold gourmet cupcakes. Also closed. Good. Erin didn't want to risk any nosy neighbors. They parked a few blocks down. After tucking her hair under her cap to hide the vivid color, she and Noah got out. Since darkness had just fallen it would be much easier to blend in to their surroundings.

"I say we go in from the back," she murmured as she and Noah strode down the sidewalk.

"I'd like to take you from behind." Noah's voice was sin and sex.

"Noah! I can't— Tone it down until later, okay?" She shot him a pleading look.

His dark eyes flared with heat for a moment, but his teasing grin faded and he nodded. "Fair enough. I know we have work to do, but don't think I'm letting you put me back in some designated box again. You let me out and I'm not stopping until I get what I want."

She swallowed hard at those words. "Noah, I will *never* be what you want. *Ever.*" How could he not understand that? They were both going to get hurt and while she'd come to terms with the fact that once Noah found the right female for him she'd get burned—okay, flayed alive—she didn't want to cause *him* pain.

"How about you don't make decisions for me?" Noah snapped in a tone she'd never heard from him before.

Before she could respond he made a sharp turn down the alley between the bistro and the Pilates studio. Gritting her teeth, she kept pace, her boots quietly thudding against the gravelly ground. When they reached the end of the alley, they both slowed. At the exit she found a small parking lot that was clearly designated for the three shops. It was also empty.

The rancid stench of decaying food wafted from the bistro's Dumpster next door. Erin breathed through her mouth. Definitely one of the downsides to their oversensitive noses.

"Stay here," Noah said quietly before darting around the edge of the building.

She stayed put but peeked around the corner and watched him crouch by the door. He pulled out his lockpick kit and made fast work of it. She'd seen him do it before but it never ceased to amaze her how quick he was. He'd once told her this was a leftover skill from his misspent youth. Mere seconds later she heard the snick of a lock popping free.

He shot her a quick glance and nodded as he stepped inside. After glancing around the darkened parking lot again, she darted in after him. No alarm had gone off and even if it had, they didn't plan to be inside longer than two to three minutes. They didn't turn on the lights but with their night vision they didn't need to. After a quick visual scan she was almost certain there weren't any video cameras around either. Normally she would have done a hell of a lot more recon and been prepared with anything and everything on this female, but the situation didn't allow it and she had to adapt. Pregnant shifters were missing so she had to jump on this lead *now*. Erin had come here for one thing—to check the human's computer. If she needed to come back, she'd do a better sweep next time.

The studio was a decent size but there were no heartbeats in the direct vicinity so no chance of pregnant shifters being held captive inside. Not that Erin had ever considered that a viable possibility. It was more likely the women were being held somewhere isolated. Hiding that many females would require privacy. She figured the offices must be upstairs as they moved into the room with hardwood floors and weird-looking equipment. Erin was all about staying in shape but this stuff looked too complicated. "I'll take the upstairs," she said quietly.

Noah nodded and she hurried toward the front of the building where she guessed the stairs were. Seconds later she was in a sparse office on the second floor. Instead of a chair, there was a big yellow exercise ball under the desk. And the desk had a laptop on it. After slipping on her gloves, Erin fired up the computer and waited. Once it was on, she pulled out one of the flash drives she'd been keeping stored in the center console of her car—according to Jayce she needed to always carry at least three with her—and downloaded everything from the hard drive. By the time she reached the stairs, Noah was waiting at the bottom for her.

"I didn't find anything interesting, but we'd have to do a full sweep to know for sure," Noah said as they hurried toward the back door.

"I got whatever's on her computer, but it could be useless." Erin wasn't getting her hopes up that they'd find anything interesting, but she'd still had to try nonetheless. She had to look at every angle until the missing women were found.

As they reached her car, she received a text from Ryan with the human female's home address. *Perfect timing.* She handed her phone to Noah as she started the engine. "You know that street?" She could easily plug the address into her car's GPS, but Noah was familiar with the city and the layout of the streets in New Orleans was odd. She'd discovered that the GPS didn't always match the correct route. She had a feeling he'd know how to get somewhere quicker than a computer.

He nodded. "Yeah, I know the neighborhood. It's barely five minutes from here. Finding the address will be easy. Head south."

Following his directive, she pulled out into the street, then did a U-turn. Her phone buzzed again and Noah looked at it since he was still holding it. "You have a text from Brianna."

Erin had been wondering when she'd hear from the blond fae. "What's up?"

"She just texted you the same address Ryan did. She and Angelo are on their way there now. Said they might have a lead." Noah's frown matched how Erin felt.

That was very interesting. "Text her that we're on the way."

Erin gunned the engine and took the next turn Noah directed her to. If this place was less than five minutes away, she'd just see them when they arrived.

Erin made it in three minutes flat. As they drove past the group of townhomes sitting side by side with barely a sliver of space to separate the buildings, Erin mock shuddered. "I could never live in such an enclosed area." It was one thing to live in a city, but not to have a back-yard or a place to roam free—her wolf would go mad.

"For real," Noah murmured as his gaze constantly roamed the quiet residential street. Magnolia and oak trees lined it and even in the dark she could see sparkly beads hanging from most of the trees. And each home had a purple and green wreath on the front door. Some were in the form of masks and others were more intri-cate, but it was clear this street celebrated Mardi Gras, which was barely a month away.

"Park here." Noah motioned to a giant oak tree in the middle of the sidewalk. It had a wrought iron fence around it as a protective barrier and the sidewalk was cracking where roots were pushing up.

She parked next to the curb behind an extended cab truck she was surprised had even managed to maneu-ver a parking spot. As she killed the engine she looked at Noah. "When we get out . . ." She held up a finger to her lips and he grinned almost wickedly.

Yep, he understood. They were going hunting and

there was no guarantee this human was alone—if she was involved at all. But the signs were pointing in that direction. And according to Meli, shifters had been behind this so she could have backup.

When they passed the house, she shot Noah a sharp look. He frowned and nodded at her unspoken question. He smelled it too.

Blood.

It was fresh. Keeping their pace steady, they continued down the sidewalk until they reached the end of the townhomes. It wasn't the end of the street though. More houses—shotgun-style and cottages—continued on, but this was the opening they needed.

After making sure they weren't being watched, Erin and Noah sprinted between the last townhome and a pastel blue and yellow cottage. There was a metal fence surrounding the small backyard of the townhome. From the looks of it, each one had a fence separating the backyards.

By the time she'd looked at Noah, he'd jumped the first fence in one bound. Okay then. Following suit, she used all the strength in her legs and jumped. She raced across the yard, avoiding a kid's bicycle and toys and continued jumping and sprinting until they reached the backyard they needed to be in.

There was a small table with a mosaic-tiled top on the back porch and two matching chairs, a few hanging plants, but not much else. And that stench of blood was unmistakable and even stronger from the back porch. Creeping along it, she peered into a window with light streaming out. Noah was right behind her.

A lacy white curtain did nothing to hide the horror

inside that kitchen. A male and female were on the floor, blood pooled all around their bodies, covering the black-and-white-checkered tile in a river of red. The female's throat was slit and the male's heart had been ripped from his chest.

But the worst thing about the scene was the fucking vampires feeding on the bodies. There were three of them and they were so engrossed in their feeding they hadn't even realized they were being watched. Any vampire over the age of five would have sensed her and Noah by now. This had to be the ferals that vamp Ian was hunting.

Quietly, she crept back across the porch toward the back door. With her hands, she signaled that they should storm the kitchen. Noah nodded, that warrior's glint in his eyes. He was ready for a fight and more than capable of unleashing hell if needed.

On the count of two she lifted her right booted foot while he lifted his left and they kicked the door in. It splintered under the impact as if it was made of cardboard, flying off the hinges and slamming against one of the vampires biting into the dead male's wrist.

"We're not hurting anyone! They were dead when we got here," the only male out of the three whined as he shoved the door off him. He had stringy black hair that hung down to his shoulders and she couldn't begin to guess when he'd last showered.

His eyes glowed red, much like a wolf who had turned feral. Yep, these were definitely feral vamps. Before she could respond, one of the female vamps feeding on the dead human lunged at Noah with claws unsheathed. She let out a high-pitched shriek as she aimed for his throat. Did she really think she could take down Noah?

At the same time, the male who'd been whining lunged at Erin. Without pause and with incredible speed borne of her abilities, she unzipped her jacket and whipped out a blade. Before he'd even made contact with her, she sliced hard and fast through his neck.

Because of the angle, blood sprayed to the left, bathing the stainless steel refrigerator in a shower of crimson. The vamp's head rolled to the floor with a thud the same time Noah dropped the female vamp's body to the floor—without her heart. Damn. She'd seen Noah fight before and she knew he was strong, but to realize he'd done that in human form still awed her.

By the time both bodies made contact with the tile, the third female vamp who'd been too busy feeding to even pay attention to them before, looked up.

Her curly brown hair was matted against her pale, ivory face and her red eyes were wilder than the male who had just tried to attack Erin. This one was so far gone there was barely a flicker of awareness in her glowing gaze. She wiped her bloody mouth with the back of her wrist and stared at them. Blinking, she looked back and forth between Erin and Noah, looked at the fallen bodies, then went back to feeding.

"Holy shit," Erin breathed out, horrified beyond belief.

Noah's dark eyes widened, mirroring her own shock. Erin didn't want to attack and kill someone who wasn't attacking her, but this creature clearly needed to be put down. Before she could ask Noah what his opinion was, she scented intruders.

Noah did too. Backing up, they moved away from

where the door had once been, tensing for an attack. A moment later Ian filled the doorway.

His gaze swept the kitchen, taking in the carnage, without a flicker of emotion. Then without a word he withdrew his sword, strode over to the female who was still feeding, and sliced her head off. One clean stroke.

The dark-haired female turned to dust. Under other circumstances that might have surprised Erin but she knew that Jayce's blades could do the same thing to vampires since they'd been blessed by the fae. And her own Alpha's mate had a blade that could dust feral shifters. She guessed Ian's sword had a similar blessing.

"I take it these are the ferals you've been hunting?" Erin asked. She could see the outlines of his team out on the back porch but they didn't make a move to enter the kitchen.

That soothed Erin's wolf. She didn't want to be cooped up with a bunch of strangers she'd recently battled against.

Ian nodded as he slammed his blade into the other dead bodies. They also turned to dust and when Erin glanced at the refrigerator, where the blood spray had once been was a coating of the same colored dust. Very cool.

"Yes," he said quietly. "There are still more out there though. Someone has been turning vampires who are not emotionally stable enough and far too young. I didn't tell you earlier but we are hunting their maker and any of those who have turned feral. These three"—he motioned with his head to the scattering of ash—"we followed from the morgue where they'd attempted to break in."

"They didn't kill this female or the male." Erin motioned to the two bodies still on the kitchen floor. One human female, one male vamp.

Ian nodded and sheathed his sword. She was fascinated that such a large weapon could be concealed so nicely beneath that coat. "I didn't think so. Other than the fact that ferals are inherently lazy and want quick food no matter how disgusting, these vampires are much too young to take on a strong vampire. Who are the dead? Is that why you're here?"

Erin flicked a look at Noah who simply clenched his jaw. Yeah, she didn't have to be a mind reader to realize he didn't want to tell Ian anything either. Erin didn't know much about this vamp—though she had received a quick text from Jayce earlier telling her that he knew the guy and he wasn't a liar, but that she still shouldn't trust him or anyone—and she didn't plan on telling Ian anything until he gave her something in return.

"Why would any vampires want pregnant shifters? And why haven't you called yet? You've had an entire day."

"The majority of my team *sleeps* during the day so my time and resources are limited." Ian scrubbed a hand over his face, the action taking Erin off guard. He looked weary. As he opened his mouth to continue, Erin scented others nearby. Brianna and Angelo.

At the same time she smelled them, the vamps outside must have seen them.

"Who the hell are they?" one of them muttered. Then, "Stop!"

Erin hurried outside, elbowing past them into the backyard. Noah wasn't far behind.

Angelo and Brianna had jumped the fence and were striding toward them. It looked like they'd come in the same way she and Noah had. Erin watched as Brianna's left hand glowed that eerie blue she'd seen only once before. That woman might be small and almost angelic looking but Erin had seen her take off a guy's head with a blast of energy. It had been freakishly cool but also a little terrifying since the fae's powers had evidently been drained when she'd done it. Erin would love to see the woman at full capacity—only if that particular skill wasn't directed at her.

"I don't know if it's her for sure, but a human female is dead inside," Erin directed to them.

Brianna frowned, but her expression quickly turned to surprise as she looked past Erin. "Ian?"

Erin turned to see Ian striding out after them, his face just as surprised. "Brianna? What are you doing in town?"

The small blond fae smiled genuinely and rushed at the tall vampire. She hugged him fiercely, earning an angry growl from Angelo. Brianna shot him an annoyed look, then turned back to Ian, Erin, and Noah. "I don't have time to catch up, Ian, but we will talk later. I'm working with Erin, her two packmates, and the Campbell pack to find out what is happening with missing pregnant shifters. I didn't realize you were in town or I would have called you." Then she glanced at Erin and Noah, all business. "This was our only lead, but I think if I press my contact I might be able to find out why the shifters are being taken."

Though she was desperate for an answer, Erin didn't let her frustration show. If she knew the reason why maybe she could figure out *who* was doing it. That one piece to the puzzle was screwing everything up.

"I might know why they're being taken," Ian muttered, making it clear he didn't want to reveal the truth.

Brianna's sharp gaze turned, narrowed on him, the blue of her hands glowing brighter. Oh yeah, she was ready to battle if need be. Erin liked her even more. "You're part of this?" the fae demanded.

"No! I just think it's related to an ancient, sick practice by fucking bloodborns. When Erin told me about the missing women I mentioned it to the Brethren and found out that . . . *some* bloodborn vampires like to drink the blood of pregnant shifters in an attempt to increase their own fertility. Bloodborn births are so rare and it is extremely hard for vampires to conceive so they do *this*."

Erin's stomach turned over at the vampire's words. "I've *never* heard of that." She might be young, but this was the kind of thing that would get around.

Ian's expression remained grim. "The practice goes back millennia, but it is not common knowledge even among my people. When I say it's a rare practice, an elite few know of it and even fewer practice it. Apparently it is a dark, well-kept secret among my kind. The Brethren are pissed."

"You know what this will do between our people if word of this gets out?" Erin asked quietly, not expecting a response. Of course the vampire knew.

He nodded anyway. "My leaders and I are disgusted by this and want it clear to you that we are not involved. No one wants a war between our people and I'm willing to share information that might assist you."

She glanced around at the other vamps who were standing a few yards behind Ian, their expressions carefully guarded. Then she looked at Ian again. "You trust them?" If this was as secretive as he said—and considering neither she nor Ryan had been able to find even a mention of the practice in their research, she believed him—she needed to know that all those present would keep their mouths shut.

One sharp nod. Good enough for her. Hell, it would have to be. At this point she had to trust someone. Working in a vacuum was impossible if both species were involved. "Lupine shifters are behind the kidnappings. That much we know. What we don't know is their identities and who they're selling to. Well, who specifically, because obviously it's fucking bloodborns." The rare vampires that were actually born, not made. They were harder to kill, lived a hell of a long time, and after centuries their powers could manifest into true greatness. To have a bloodborn among your line was to have power. Something all species respected and desired.

"I know of at least one bloodborn in the area," Angelo drawled, an angry bite to his words.

Brianna shot him a sharp look. "My contact who gave us this female's address is a bloodborn but he would not be involved in any of this." There was truth in the fae's statement, but that just meant she believed what she was saying.

Not that it was actually the truth.

"Who is your contact?" Erin demanded.

Brianna shot Angelo a beseeching look, then shook

her head at Erin. "I cannot tell you. He gave me this information on the condition of anonymity."

Erin glared at Angelo who looked torn, but he eventually shook his head. "I won't betray Brianna's trust, even for you. We gave this guy our word."

Okay then. Erin concealed her surprise and frustration and nodded instead. "Fair enough." She wasn't going to push her own packmate to betray a woman he clearly intended to claim as his mate. If he didn't, there was no way in hell he'd have kept this information from Erin. As enforcer she could demand it, but that wasn't something she planned on. Not with a male she'd fought side by side with and not over the name of someone whose identity she could get on her own and would very shortly. Once she discovered the buyers, she'd be able to ferret out the sellers—then hopefully find the captive women.

She had no issues torturing some pathetic vampires who were part of this practice, but knew she'd probably be better off if her group worked with Ian. She gave him a thoughtful look. "You work for the Brethren and my mentor tells me that you're an admirable warrior."

"Jayce said that?"

She nodded. "He also said not to trust you."

Ian smiled, revealing a dimple that seemed out of place on his harsh face. "That bastard doesn't trust anyone."

He was almost correct. Since taking a mate Jayce had loosened up. Well, sort of. "Do the Brethren approve of this practice?"

Ian's eyes flashed a glowing amber as he shook his

head. "Fuck no. And neither do I nor my team. We'll help you in any way we can, but our priority is to hunt down these ferals and their maker. No matter what, they *have* to be stopped. This problem could quickly grow out of control and we cannot allow that."

"That's fine. I want names and introductions to all the bloodborns in the area."

"Introductions?"

"I want *you* to take me to their homes." She wasn't looking for a damn phone call. She wanted face-to-face time with them.

Ian's eyes flared with surprise, though she wasn't sure why. What did he think, she was going to call them and simply ask if they were buying pregnant shifter blood? Oh yeah, genius idea.

"I'll be able to scent their lies and if shifters have actually been there or are currently there, I'll scent them too." Then there would be hell to pay. Something she was kind of looking forward to. The people behind this needed to be stopped and she had a hell of a lot of tension building inside her over this case and . . . other stuff.

"Bloodborns are all wealthy and very well protected." His statement made her want to roll her eyes.

Clearly they'd be rich and guarded. It didn't change a thing. She shrugged and as she did, her cell phone buzzed in her jacket pocket. She planned to ignore it, but then Noah's buzzed and Ian's rang. What the hell? After a glance at the caller ID, she frowned. It was Angus Campbell. "Is everything okay?"

"Hell if I know. There are a dozen vampires outside the compound right now looking to start a fight. We

can easily take them but I don't think this has to esca-
late if I can defuse the situation. Unfortunately my pack
is pissed after Meli lost her baby and half of them are
looking for blood—anyone's. Just thought you'd want
to know what was going on." Angus sounded just as
tired as she felt. It had been a long freaking day and
now this?

"I'm with some vamps who work for the Brethren
right now. We're on our way." She hung up and looked
at Ian questioningly.

"I just got a call from the owner of Screamers. Seems
a couple guys claiming to be members of the Campbell
pack firebombed the place right as it opened. Now a
bunch of young vampires are on their way to the
Campbell compound. Great way to start our night," he
said, his voice laced with annoyance.

Noah immediately shook his head. "No way in hell
would anyone from my father's pack do that. They're
too terrified of him."

Ian slipped his phone back into his pocket. "I didn't
say they did. I just said they claimed to be members."

"We're leaving now and you're coming with us,"
Erin said. She glanced at Brianna and Angelo. "Will
you guys sweep this house and look for anything po-
tentially helpful? If she has a laptop, anything elec-
tronic, any photographs or phone records—I want
everything. As soon as you've cleared the place, call
the cops anonymously." They could deal with the bodies.

Angelo nodded once. "I'll text you when we're
done." He and Brianna strode past them.

Ian's expression was one of tightly controlled fury

when she looked back at him. She raised her eyebrows in silent question. What now?

"I don't take orders from anyone." His voice was a razor-sharp blade.

Seriously? She fought a sigh. If Jayce had been here in her place this guy probably wouldn't have balked. On second thought, he probably would have. Maybe even more so if Jayce had told him what to do. Ian did carry a sword after all. Before she could respond, Noah took a slight step forward, his entire body tense and his expression menacing as he glared at Ian. His claws had unsheathed again and Erin could feel the anger pulsing off him. She placed a gentling hand on Noah's forearm, but he didn't acknowledge her. She could deal with only one pigheaded male now, not two amped up on testosterone. Noah tensed even more when she squeezed.

Oh crap. She tightened her grip but focused on the vampire again. "Will you pretty please with a cherry on top come with us to the Campbell compound?" She didn't hide her sarcasm, which earned her a ghost of a smile. "Your presence will no doubt help defuse the other vamps there."

The anger melted out of Ian's expression as he nodded and stepped back. "I planned to go over there anyway."

"Good." There was nothing left to say then. Some of the heat rolling off of Noah eased. But he still didn't step back. Her wolf side appreciated his protective tendencies, but her completely female, human side didn't need him to fight her battles. She could damn well do that herself.

When he looked down at her she could see his wolf

lurking in the depths of his eyes as he fought for control. It took her a moment to realize that what they'd shared in her car earlier was directly responsible for this change in him. He might have felt proprietary toward her before, but the look he was giving her now and his behavior was positively possessive.

Both her wolf and human side liked the possessive bit.

Erin had no idea what to do with either her feelings about that or her feelings toward him. Giving her head a mental shake, Erin turned on her heel. "Let's move."

Chapter 9

Noah fought to keep his wolf in check as he and Erin pulled up to his father's palatial home. Instead of pulling through the wrought iron gates that were surprisingly still open considering the six vampires loitering and shouting outside the fence, Erin parked by the curb. Ian and his team were right behind them.

He and Erin quickly exited the vehicle and she stripped off her jacket before tossing it into her seat and slamming her door shut. He figured she wanted her blades exposed for everyone to see. Nice show of force without having to say a word.

Keeping an eye on the vampires wanting to cause trouble and the ones getting out of the SUV behind them, Noah didn't know who posed more of a threat. He didn't like the way that vamp, Ian, kept looking at Erin. As if he wondered what she looked like naked and could see if he just squinted hard enough.

Noah's inner wolf was going crazy right now. Erin had *bitten* him as she'd been climaxing. It had been light, but she'd broken his skin, marking him with her teeth and it was like his wolf had been set free to pursue her. No more restraint.

Rolling his shoulders once, he locked down those thoughts. Later tonight, if they ever got a couple of hours of downtime, he planned to pick up right where they'd left off in her car. He wanted to give her even more pleasure. So much so that she passed out with his name on her lips.

The six vampires near the outside of the gate all turned and immediately glared at them. Fangs and claws descended as they took menacing steps toward Erin and him.

Instinctively, he stepped forward, partially blocking her with his body. He knew it would piss her off, but his inner wolf was feeling wildly protective at the moment. It kept screaming at him to mark and mate her. To fuck until neither of them could walk. To keep her safe from anyone and everything. He had no doubt how capable she was and part of him wondered if one day soon she'd be able to kick his ass into the ground. Her strength was growing by leaps and bounds, and it was sexy as hell thinking he could be mated to someone so strong and capable. None of that mattered now, though, and he wasn't questioning her ability to protect herself. Just the thought of her being harmed killed him inside and his wolf didn't always listen to human reasoning.

A male vampire with mocha skin and long dreads, dressed in all black leather, stepped forward first. He hissed at them, fury rolling off him in waves. Next a female with long black hair, ivory skin, bloodred lips, and wearing a black corset top, black leather pants, and five-inch-heeled boots stepped forward. "Who the fuck are you?" She eyed Erin first, then Noah, then glanced past them to the other vampires. "Are you with these shifters?" the female snarled again, her voice deeper than he'd expected.

Before either he or Erin could answer, Ian flew past them. A light breeze rolled over Noah's skin as Ian jerked to a halt a foot in front of the six vamps.

"I'm Ian and I work for the Brethren. Who the fuck are *you*?" His voice was so low Noah almost didn't hear the question.

But it was clear the others did. The six quickly scrambled back a few feet and the female with the Goth-inspired looks who was clearly the spokesperson for the vamps held up a hand in a surrendering gesture. "These bastards tried to kill us. They firebombed Screamers barely an hour ago." She jerked a thumb in the direction of Noah's father's compound where Noah could see at least two dozen males and females patrolling the grounds. Yeah, they were ready for a fight with these young vamps should it come to it. And these vamps would *lose*. No doubt about it.

"And how do you know it was anyone from the Campbell pack?"

The Goth chick shifted nervously. "Well, the two guys who did it shouted that they were doing this for their pack, the Campbell pack."

Ian let out a long string of creative curses that had Erin glancing at Noah with an almost scandalized expression. If it was any other time he'd have laughed.

Ian sighed and withdrew his sword. Everyone went

deathly quiet. "For one second, did it cross your tiny brain that it wasn't someone from this pack? That someone might be setting up the Campbells for whatever reason? Shifters are hunters, just like us. They're not going to start something out in the open like that and they sure as hell wouldn't use firebombs. How old are you?"

The female glanced back at her group as if for support but they were all quiet and wide-eyed. When she looked back at Ian she wrapped her arms around herself. "I'm four," she said quietly, hesitantly. Vampires considered their ages by the day they were made and this female was definitely young. Had probably been changed when she was roughly twenty-three.

So damn young. Noah shook his head at her stupidity and clear lack of training. If the others with her were just as young they'd have been slaughtered by his pack in seconds. And all over a misunderstanding.

"How many shifters bombed the club?" Erin asked, stepping forward.

Noah moved with her, keeping pace, watching her back.

The vampires eyed them warily but the female answered. "Two. Both males."

"What did they look like?" Noah asked, wondering if the shifter who had attacked him earlier was one of the ones behind the fire.

She shrugged. "They wore plain blue ball caps but I'm pretty sure they both had blond hair. I saw some sticking out from one of the guys' caps. They were tall, sort of rugged looking, and one wore a wolf ring. They *were* shifters. They threw the Molotov cocktails through the windows of Screamers, then threw a bunch at us and they were *fast*. Once they'd unloaded on us, they ran."

"Did anyone go after them? Tail them anywhere?" Erin asked, hope in her voice.

The female shook her head. "No. We were too busy trying to put out the fire in the club and on ourselves."

Noah silently watched as both Ian and Erin questioned the six vampires. They pretty much went around in circles with no helpful information. But at least they'd clearly calmed down. The other vamps working with Ian looked almost bored as they waited several yards behind them, but he knew better. They were on alert, scanning the neighborhood for any possible threats.

As the conversation started to die down, Noah turned back to the young vamps. He eyed the designated speaker. "Do you guys belong to a coven?" he asked.

She shook her head and wrapped her arms tighter around herself. In that moment she looked impossibly young. Even though she was strong since she was a vampire, she couldn't have had much training to come over to his father's compound tonight. It was a suicide mission.

Noah glanced at the compound, eyeing the wolves lurking in the darkness. Some had already shifted forms and he was surprised his father hadn't come outside yet. That was interesting and he wanted to know why. "I'm not part of the Campbell pack, but Angus Campbell is my father. He's fair but he's also vicious if you cross him or anyone he considers his own. If you had attacked tonight, you'd all be dead right now."

He expected some sort of denial but when none was forthcoming, he continued, softening his voice. "I have no idea what's going on in the city or why someone would want to set up the local pack, but spread the word to any young vamps you know about what happened tonight. Right now this entire pack is mourning the loss of a cub so emotions are high, yet none of them attacked you when in all fairness they could have. You arriving on their doorstep ready to fight was reason enough. And they'd have been justified. Instead, they called us. Those aren't the actions of a pack who wants to go to war with vampires." Noah's mother had called him and he knew his father had called Erin. And he was still wondering where the hell his father was.

Almost as if he read his mind, Angus appeared on the long driveway, his strides steady and sure as he stalked toward them, power pulsing off him.

Next to him, the vampires looked at one another nervously, but remained in place. After a sharp nod at Ian and Erin, Angus clasped Noah's shoulder in a tight grip, taking him by surprise. He squeezed as he faced the vamps. "My son is right. The majority of my pack is over a century old and we've all seen enough war and death to last a lifetime. Vampires killed my own daughter, but I don't hold a grudge against your entire kind. That kind of thinking is ignorant." Noah went still at his father's words, but remained silent as Angus continued. "You need to think before you act and if any of you set foot on my property again or attack any shifters in this city—lupine or feline—I'll gut you and remove all your organs before I kill you."

Noah might have issues with his father, but he understood and respected the threat. If he appeared weak in front of anyone, including his own pack, it could have long-lasting effects on the stability of the entire city.

Ian spoke next, drawing Angus's attention away from the young vampires, though Noah knew the Alpha was aware of everything. "If you're done with them, I need to take them with me."

Angus nodded, and then Ian motioned to his own people to round up the vampires. Noah couldn't be sure but he had a feeling Ian was going to use these vamps to help him track down the ferals and their maker.

Before they left, however, Ian turned back to them, his gaze roaming appreciatively over Erin's tight body before meeting her eyes.

"Look at her like that again and lose your fucking head. I don't care who you work for," Noah snarled before he could stop himself. His inner wolf was clawing at him, needing to assert dominance over everyone, but especially the prick who was checking out his female.

Ian looked at him, surprise on his face. "I meant no disrespect. She's beautiful and strong."

"I know. And she's mine." Erin let out a huff of annoyance, but Noah didn't glance at her, not wanting to see denial on her face.

The vamp nodded once, his expression turning blank as he focused on Erin again. "I'm hoping these young ones can help us track down the ferals but I'll be in touch about the bloodborns. I'll e-mail you a list of names and addresses. Don't go see any of them without a vampire escort though. These vamps are ancient and arrogant and wouldn't care that killing an enforcer would incite a war in their region."

Erin snorted, but nodded. Once they were gone and out of earshot, Angus spoke, his words surprising Noah. "If you need the addresses of bloodborns, I know every one that lives in the surrounding area."

"Why . . ." Erin trailed off as understanding hit Noah at the same time.

Of course his father knew them. Probably had detailed dossiers on them since they lived in his region. If Noah had been thinking clearly he'd have likely thought of that.

Before either of them could ask, Angus spoke again. "You can have everything you want on the bloodborns. Why do you want to know about them, though?"

Noah glanced at Erin who slightly shook her head. Yeah, she was thinking the same thing he was. "Not here." There were too many shifters nearby with exceptional hearing. If they got even a whiff that bloodborns were involved with the kidnappings, some of them— like Evan—might do something stupid. If he got himself killed . . . Noah didn't even want to imagine how Meli would cope. She'd already been kidnapped and lost her unborn cub. Losing a mate would destroy her. Not to mention the fallout would be a fucking war between the supernaturals in this area and it would inevitably spill into the human realm, then into other parts of the country. He could actually imagine how horrific the spillover effect would be. There'd be no damn winner in a war like that. Just death and pain.

Angus flicked a glance around him, then nodded in understanding. "Everything you need is in my office."

Noah risked a look at Erin as they strode up the driveway. The energy rolling off her was wild and unsteady and he understood exactly why. Getting this information could change everything they knew about this case.

Unfortunately, he also knew Erin well enough to realize there was no way in hell she'd wait for a vampire escort to visit any of the locations they received. Which meant they'd be walking right into a viper's nest.

Chapter 10

Noah's eyes were gritty and tired after the last couple of hours of going through the laptop Angelo and Brianna had retrieved for them from the dead human's house. And the body of the female was indeed Kelly Bridges. They still weren't sure about the vampire's identity but luckily Angelo had taken pictures. Noah had e-mailed them to his father in the hopes that the Alpha recognized him. He'd thought about calling but his father had enough to deal with and it was two in the morning. He and Erin had enough paperwork and information to sift through as it was. Getting the guy's name could wait until they'd gotten some sleep. Brianna had also sent a picture to her mystery contact to see if he knew the guy.

Closing the laptop, he slid it away from him on the desk in Erin's room. She looked up from her own laptop where she was going through the information she'd downloaded onto a flash drive. Her gray eyes were red-rimmed and she looked ready to pass out.

They'd been in multiple fights since before dawn, changed bloody clothes more .than a few times, and right now he realized they'd be more apt to miss something important if they didn't get some sleep. There was no way in hell they could even contemplate going to any of the bloodborns' homes this late. Or early, as it was. All vampires were more powerful at night and he and Erin were operating on fumes right now.

"You done for the night?" she asked, her voice husky.

Stripping off his sweater, Noah nodded and stood. "And so are you."

Erin's eyes widened as she raked her hot gaze over his body. Her look alone had his lower abdomen tightening with need. Unfortunately he wouldn't be getting any release tonight—well, this morning—but he planned to make sure she did.

"Is that right?" she asked dryly.

She didn't make a move to close her computer so he covered the distance between them in a flash and snapped it shut. Those gray eyes blinked once in surprise before she made a grab for it. Though she was fast, her movements were slower than usual. Which just proved his point that they both needed to recharge. "What the hell are you doing? Give that back."

He held it out of her reach, then set it on the desk with the other laptop. When she didn't struggle or try to get it back he knew he'd already won any forthcoming argument. "We're both tired and need a few hours of sleep before dawn if you want to hit up those bloodborns' houses." Most of them would be sleeping then and weakest. She planned to disturb their rest and hopefully take them off guard. He wasn't a huge fan of the plan, but they had to do something. And it was better than going in at night.

She opened her mouth as if to argue, but then nodded and fell back against her pillow. "I don't know how Jayce does all these investigations alone. Having you with me is . . . well, I appreciate it more than you know. I was excited when he told me it was time for my first case, but when I realized what was going on here, I was glad you were coming with me."

Her candidness surprised him. It must have shown on his face because she half smiled and propped herself up on her elbows as she watched him. "Yes, that's me saying thank you for being you in case you missed it. Just don't get smug about it."

He half smiled in return but didn't respond as his gaze drifted down her stretched-out form. She wore black yoga-style shorts and a loose T-shirt with a fleur-de-lis and the word SAINTS on it she'd stolen from his suitcase. Seeing her in his clothes did something primal to him. It always had. Practically from the moment she'd joined Connor's pack, long before they'd joined with the Cordona females, Erin and Noah had been close. He'd looked out for her and she'd kept his inner wolf calm without even trying. She'd always taken his shirts to sleep in at night, clearly having no idea what it did to him to scent himself on her. Now, however . . . "Did you wear that shirt to drive me crazy?" he murmured, stalking closer to the bed.

Her mouth pulled into a thin line as she looked down at herself. She snorted. "You're telling me this is sexy?"

He nodded, continuing until he reached the foot of

the bed. "I want to bury my face between your legs and taste you."

Erin's cheeks flamed, but that magnolia scent of hers intensified a hundredfold. Yeah, she was turned on. "You can't just *say* stuff like that."

"Why not? I want to and I'm not playing games."

"You said you wouldn't have sex with me until I give you everything you want and there's no way that's happening. I care about you—"

He couldn't listen to her say she fucking *cared* about him, like she was trying to let him down. Fuck that. "Who said anything about sex? I just want to taste you and I want you naked right now." Okay, that was a half-truth. He did want to taste her but he also wanted to fuck her desperately. It would be more than fucking though. He understood that on every level but he wouldn't allow himself to think of those words yet. Not until she agreed to surrender to him in every way.

Her gray eyes narrowed dangerously, flashing to almost black, then back again. "So if I was naked right now you wouldn't want to have sex?"

Of course he'd *want* to have sex. He wanted it now and she was clothed. Hell, he always wanted it. Shrugging, he crossed his arms over his chest. "You think I have so little restraint?"

Surprising him, she grasped the edge of her T-shirt and tore it off. Her bra followed quickly after. Then went those damn shorts and a black thong that shouldn't even be considered underwear. That's what she'd had on underneath her clothes? His cock jumped.

"Fuck." His entire body tensed, primed as she laid back completely naked against the pillows.

She was nervous, he could see it in every taut line of her toned body, but she was still laying herself out like an offering for him. And she was definitely turned on. That scent filled the room and wrapped around him.

He had restraint. Maybe. Her skin was ivory and a smattering of freckles covered her in the cutest places. He'd seen her naked before, after their pack had fought with their former neighboring pack and she'd shifted back to human form, before runs through the woods, and of course the night he'd found her. But he wouldn't let himself think about that. Not now.

So he knew her nipples were a pale pink, but it didn't stop his hunger as he devoured her with his gaze. Seeing them hardening right before his eyes sent a jolt of electricity through him. What he wouldn't give to run his tongue over the hard peaks.

Restraint. He repeated it again.

"Are you going to stare all night?" The way her voice shook with arousal was so un-Erin-like he would have smiled if he could have made those muscles work.

But right now it was taking everything he had not to throw his plan out the window. "Spread your legs," he demanded softly as he kneeled on the bed.

She paused for a moment, but let her thighs fall apart slowly. Seeing that soft patch of dark auburn hair covering her mound and scenting her sweet need made his wolf claw even harder. But he had more control than his animal and he'd be damned if he screwed things up with Erin. He planned to do things right between them, and until she was ready for a relationship with him, no sex.

That didn't mean he couldn't taste her though.

Reaching out, he cursed his shaking hand. He'd already stroked her to orgasm, but seeing her so open to him like this was messing with his head.

Slowly, he stroked a finger down her slit, testing her slickness. God, she was already wet. He'd scented her need, but actually feeling it . . . he shuddered. Pushing a finger inside her, he kept his gaze on her face as he slid deeper.

Her eyes grew heavy lidded and her breathing increased as her inner walls tightened around him. Keeping his finger buried in her, he didn't move. He wanted to make her shout his name, but he also wanted to tease her.

Leaning down, he pressed a kiss to her inner knee. Definitely not an erogenous zone, but she clenched around his finger when his lips brushed against her skin.

He lightly raked his teeth over her, then followed up with a soft kiss. A tremor rolled through her and she started to clench her legs together, but he lifted his head. "No."

She froze at that one word, then practically scowled. "You're getting off on teasing me."

Hell yeah he was. Even if he was simultaneously torturing himself. Continuing the path where he alternated between using his teeth, then following up with kisses, he finally settled where his finger was still inside her.

Her breathing had grown even more unsteady the closer he got to that soft thatch of hair covering everything he wanted to taste. Her clit peeked out from her lips, swollen and begging for his touch. Instead of continuing to tease her, he zeroed in on it and sucked on the swollen nub.

She jerked under him, rolling her hips up but he grasped her hip with his free hand and held tight. He didn't want her to be able to move as he pleasured her—he wanted to intensify it as much as possible and force her to let go of her control. She could be wound as tight as she needed any other time, but not now. Not when it was just the two of them completely laid bare to each other.

He inserted another finger as he licked and teased her. She tasted sweeter than he'd imagined. Hell, nothing he'd fantasized came close to the reality. Keeping his pressure steady as he stroked between her folds, he savored the sounds of her moans and sighs of pleasure. She fisted the cover beneath her and a soft tearing sound filled the air as she shredded the bedclothes. It didn't stop her from writhing against the bed.

"Noah," she breathed out, the word a pant. Hearing her cry out beneath him was almost too much. He wanted to be inside her when she came again, but he would wait as long as it took to break down that wall she'd built around herself. He loved sex as much as any male and having a near-permanent hard-on was damn painful, but making Erin his mate was all that mattered.

When her breathing became more erratic and her inner walls tensed harder around his fingers he knew she was close. Arching her back, she let go and for the second time in so many hours he felt that hot release around his fingers again. The way she tightened around him was like nothing else. His cock strained painfully, jealous of his fingers. It wouldn't take much to release himself and push deep in her tight body.

As her climax began to ebb, he withdrew his fingers and licked the length of her slit. He wanted to taste her release more than he wanted his next breath. She jerked against him, but he refused to let her go.

"Too sensitive," she panted.

Noah flexed his hand on her hip, keeping her in place as he continued stroking the length of her before settling on her clit again. He had no doubt it was sensitive and he planned to wring one more orgasm from her. Erin needed sleep and she needed a few moments of fucking peace.

This, he could give to her.

"Oh . . . Noah." She threw one of her legs over his shoulder and dug her foot into his back. When she shouted out a surprisingly dirty curse, telling him what she wanted him to do to her in explicit detail and came *again*, he let her hip go.

Now she arched fully off the bed, but didn't move away from his face. Just ground against him until she fell back limp and out of breath.

Though he didn't want to, he lifted his head, then shimmied up her body, crawling until he caged her in his arms. Her legs wrapped around his waist and she pulled him flush against her body. As she slid her hands down his chest, he savored the feel of her touching him so intimately. How many times had he thought about this very moment, with no barriers between them? When she stopped at the top of his pants though, he stilled her hands.

"No."

Her half-lidded eyes flew fully open then, her gray gaze clear but confused. "What?"

"I wasn't kidding about no sex." Though he was starting to question his own sanity.

She swallowed hard and he fought against the hurt he saw in her eyes. "So you won't even let me pleasure you? It doesn't have to be—"

He shook his head. If his pants came off, he knew himself well enough that his control would shred and he'd be buried deep inside her in moments.

"You fight dirty," she whispered as she wrapped her arms around his neck.

At least she wasn't pulling away from him, which was what he'd feared. "According to that mouth of yours, you like it a little dirty."

Her face flamed crimson, but she smiled wickedly. Almost instantly, however, that smile faded. He could practically see the wheels turning in her head. "Noah—"

"You need sleep and I'm not in the mood to hear how this will never work out." Because he refused to believe it. He slid off her body, but instead of leaving he pulled the covers down, then up around both of them. Holding her back tight against his chest, he closed his eyes, hoping his erection would go down soon and that Erin would get some much-needed sleep.

They had a lot do to in a few hours and something told him that today would be even worse than yesterday.

After ten minutes ticked by he was surprised when Erin spoke. Her voice was soft and lilting. "You know that my parents and sister died when I was ten."

He nodded against her, his chin rubbing against the top of her head. They'd been killed by vampires, just like his younger sister had been.

"It's how I ended up with the Murphy pack. The pack was good to me, provided for all my needs and when it was clear that I had the makings of a warrior despite my smaller size, Adam—that was my Alpha's name—never balked. I always held myself back just a little bit from everyone because I was afraid to let anyone too close."

Noah thought that wasn't much different from now, but it was clear she was opening up and he didn't want to say or do anything to stop her so he remained completely still.

"One of the warriors started courting me. . . ."

Noah stilled when she trailed off and he realized he'd been growling. "Sorry," he muttered, embarrassed.

Even though she was turned away from him, Noah swore he could feel Erin smile. "Anyway, he was well liked by everyone in the pack and a lot of the females had had their eye on him, but he picked me. I cared for him, or thought I did, but I knew I'd never love him. Not the way my parents had loved each other. I'd heard about the mating call and that it's like something inside you just wakes up and takes over when you're near your true mate, but I never felt that with him. And I was glad."

Noah frowned, not understanding. "Why?"

"I thought it would be a hell of a lot easier—safer for my heart—to be with someone like that. At the same time I still looked up to him, thought it was flattering that he'd 'chosen' me out of all the females of the pack." She snorted before continuing. "I didn't realize it at the time but later it was obvious that he thought I'd be easy to manipulate. We weren't mated, but I got pregnant with his cub despite the fact that we'd used protection during my heat. During my pregnancy I discovered that he and some other males from the pack were selling vampire blood, and I was disgusted. I . . . I should have just gone straight to Adam, but I didn't want to betray the father of my child. So I told him to come clean to our Alpha and stop what he was doing or I'd tell Adam for him."

Noah's entire body went cold as it registered what she was about to tell him. Even though he'd known she'd recently been pregnant when he'd found her he'd never imagined . . . *fuck*. He tightened his grip around her bare waist. "You don't have to go on," he rasped out, not wanting to hear the words.

She swallowed hard. "He told me he would, but then he ambushed me, beat me within an inch of my life and left me for dead. The baby didn't make it. Even though I hated him, I still wanted the baby. I would have loved—" Her voice broke off and he felt her hot tears on the arm he had underneath her head.

He tried to think of a response, but there was none. He wanted to rip that bastard apart limb from limb and watch him writhing on the ground as he suffered. He wanted to torture the guy until all he knew was pain. But telling her all that wouldn't do a damn thing.

"What's his name?" he rasped out, surprised his voice even worked. Whoever he was, he was a dead man walking.

"No, Noah. Just . . . no." Her voice was soft and tired and even though he wanted to demand she tell him, he knew it wasn't the time to push.

As he tried to think of suitable, comforting words, Erin turned to face him and buried her face against his chest. His grip on her tightened. He'd do anything to protect this amazing woman and he hated that someone had hurt her so badly. So deeply. No matter what, he would find out who hurt her.

"Just hold me, Noah," she murmured against his skin.

So he did. Stroking his hand down the length of her spine, he kept his movements soothing and steady until her breathing evened out and it was clear she was asleep.

Too many conflicting emotions raged inside him. The need for vengeance and the need to take care of Erin. Whether she wanted to admit it or not, they were fated to be mates. What she'd described about something waking up for mates was exactly how he'd felt the instant he'd met her. Something had been missing in him until her and no matter what happened here in New Orleans or in the future, he would protect her from anything.

Chapter 11

Chris had his elbow propped up on the interior of the driver's-side door of the new truck he and his brother had stolen a few hours earlier. After throwing those Molotov cocktails into Screamers they'd had to pick up a new ride. They would have to exchange it for something with an extended cab soon to accommodate the next female they took, but for now it would do.

"We should cut our losses and go." Malcolm had been unusually quiet since they'd attacked that club.

"No way." The rich vamp bloodborns in New Orleans had more money than sense. He and his brother worked off recommendations and other vamps from California had recommended them to the ones living here. They couldn't just pull out and leave. That was a fast way to make powerful, wealthy enemies who had all sorts of resources.

"We can easily set up shop somewhere else." Something foreign trickled off his brother—raw, unadulterated fear.

The bitter scent lingered in the air, nauseating him.

"What's the matter with you?" he asked, not bothering to hide his disgust. He didn't take his eyes off the two-story townhome across the street though.

"You saw those vampires," Malcolm murmured.

Yeah, Chris had. He wouldn't admit it aloud but he was terrified of them too. After firebombing Screamers, they'd run, then doubled back after stealing a truck. Then they'd waited to see if anyone leaving looked like they planned to start trouble. Sure enough a handful of vampires had run straight to the Campbell compound. He and his brother had been forced to hide a street over on top of another mansion's roof and they hadn't seen everything, but they'd seen enough. There were some powerful-looking vampires and it seemed as if they'd been working with Erin and that giant male who was her partner. Whoever those vamps were could definitely be a complication, but Chris and his brother had the wealthy vamps on their side so it eased his lingering fear. Unfortunately Erin was another problem he hadn't counted on. He'd discovered she was the enforcer they'd been worried about so her presence in addition to those vampires was disconcerting. Not enough to make him leave though.

Ignoring his brother's worries, he glanced at his watch. Three a.m. Like clockwork, sixty seconds later a light in one of the upstairs bedrooms came on. He watched as they continued to flick on, making a trail through various rooms until the kitchen light illuminated the downstairs left window. Curtains covered the window but he'd scoped out the house before. Well, he'd hired a human criminal to break in and take pictures and get the layout so neither he nor his brother would leave a scent behind. Then he'd killed the thug.

"We still have four women," Malcolm continued.

"Exactly and they're all too weak. We need another source." And the female shifter in the townhome they were watching was their next victim. Their human Kelly had picked her out so they knew a little about her. Young feline shifter, forty-five years old, first pregnancy, and only two months along. Still lots of time to drain her of plenty of blood. If they didn't want to lose any more females until they were ready to kill them, they had to conserve their resources.

Unfortunately this female had a very protective mate. Well, all the previous mates of the females they'd taken had been protective too, but now that word of the kidnappings had spread through the city, everyone was being more vigilant. Chris wouldn't let that stop him though. They were slowly learning this female's schedule and soon enough they'd find an opening in it and take her when the time was right.

Malcolm shifted nervously in his seat. "Come on, let's get the hell out of here. I feel like we're targets sitting on a main street in a stolen truck. Plus we need to make that delivery soon."

Gritting his teeth, Chris conceded that his brother was actually right. They needed to just buy a new vehicle with cash so they wouldn't have to worry about being stopped by the human police. He didn't want to have to be forced into killing a cop. That would bring more trouble their way and they couldn't afford that right now.

They still had to make an unplanned delivery before

dawn. He'd received a text right after they'd bombed Screamers that one of his best-paying customers was running low on product. Unfortunately he and his brother were too. Their demand was growing, yet they hadn't managed to take another shifter yet. He'd almost said no to his customer, but had decided against it. They'd get this female soon enough and if they had to drain her or one of the others, so be it.

Erin moved against the soft sheets, her heart racing out of control. Sweat blossomed across her face and covered her neck and had started to drip between her breasts despite the chill in the room. The flames in the fireplace had dwindled to almost nothing and it was snowing outside, the wind battering her window. The eerie howls of the wind felt like a reminder that she couldn't let her guard down.

It didn't matter that this small band of male shifters had taken her in and had been kind to her. What if they turned on her? What if . . .

She tensed and pulled the sheet up to her neck as the door to her bedroom opened. Immediately the tension fled her body. It was just Noah.

He was one of the biggest, most intimidating shifters she'd ever met, but deep down she knew this male would die to protect her. His mere presence dispersed the stupid fears she'd latched onto about this pack. Connor and his wolves would never hurt her.

Hell, even her wolf knew that, but when she was left alone she let her mind wander and sometimes worked herself up. The wind had woken her up a few minutes ago and she'd started internally freaking out for no reason. Only a month had passed since they'd found her in that disgusting alley but it seemed like a lifetime ago. As if that was some other female who'd almost died.

Now she was in upstate New York on her new pack's secluded land trying to get her shit together. Connor, his brother Liam, and the rest of the Armstrong pack had taken her in with no question. They'd been so kind to her and asked for nothing in return.

"You okay?" Noah asked softly as he stepped into the room. The way he walked was as if he was literally moving over eggshells.

He was like that with her and though she hadn't seen him interact with many other females, something in her gut told her that he wasn't like this with everyone. Just her. He was so protective, almost like a mother hen. After what she'd been through, she was soaking up his caring nature like a sponge.

"Yeah, I'm fine. Just . . . restless." She still didn't know him well enough to open up to him about her past, but she was honest enough. The thought of lying to him did something strange to her insides. Okay, his presence did something strange to her. She just wasn't sure what it was.

He stepped farther into the room until he was at the edge of her bed. She was wearing a thin tank top and pajama pants but she held the sheet up to her as a small barrier. "You can sit."

He did, but on the edge of the bed and he perched so close to the end it looked as if he might fall off. "I thought I heard . . ." He cleared his throat and continued. "I just wanted to check on you. Feel like going for a run?"

She didn't think she'd made any noises in her sleep loud enough to draw anyone from another room so she wondered if he'd been sleeping outside her door again. She'd caught him once in wolf form dozing out there and had told him it *was unnecessary. He hadn't exactly agreed though. He'd just grunted a nonresponse and walked away.*

Erin glanced at the clock. It was five o'clock in the morning. The sun wouldn't be up for another hour or so, but her wolf could definitely stretch her legs. And the thought of going running with Noah before anyone else had risen was exhilarating. "Just me and you?"

He nodded, his dark eyes glinting with something he quickly covered. It looked a lot like lust. "Yeah," he rasped out before quickly standing and turning away from her. "I'll wait on the front porch for you."

So he'd already be shifted and waiting for her, which sadly meant she wouldn't get to see him naked. Something she shouldn't even be thinking about. All the males had been so careful about shifting in front of her, especially Noah. But the more days that passed, she became more and more curious about what he would look like without any clothes. And she never wondered about the other pack members.

Just him.

Erin's eyes flew open as she jerked against a tight hold . . . Noah. It was just Noah. And they were in New Orleans, not New York. Without turning over to look at the clock, she knew it was still too early to get up. The room was way too dark and if she was being honest, she wanted to snag just a little more time in Noah's embrace.

Half asleep, he murmured something soothing to her and nuzzled the side of her neck with his face. Even in human form, he sometimes acted like a wolf. Sighing, she closed her eyes and decided to steal just a bit more of this precious time with him because she knew it wouldn't last forever.

Chapter 12

Brianna poured herself a cup of coffee before sitting down at the small, round kitchen table to reread the list of bloodborn names Erin had given her and Angelo. After scouring the house of the dead human female last night, she and Angelo had met up with two more of her vampire contacts. They had been neither helpful nor particularly polite to Angelo. That alone angered her beyond belief.

And now Marcus wasn't answering her calls. If he was somehow involved in this, she would destroy him. But deep down, she knew he wasn't.

She'd been extremely surprised to see Ian in New Orleans and working with such an obviously young group of vampires no less. Last she'd heard he'd been in Europe somewhere and was being groomed to eventually join the Brethren. She was sure there was a story about why he was here now, but she didn't have time to worry about it. Not until these females were found.

As she lifted her mug to her lips she felt more than

heard Angelo enter the room. His big hands settled on her shoulders and he dropped a kiss on the top of her head. Her sense of smell wasn't nearly as strong as his, but he reminded her of the forest with his wild and clean scent. "Why didn't you wake me?" he murmured sleepily.

She tilted her head up to look at him. His dark hair was mussed sexily and she knew there was no way he'd done it intentionally. The slight curve of his normally hard mouth made her shiver as she remembered how he'd taken her hard and fast from behind last night. She'd climaxed so quickly it surprised her. Then he'd held her with such gentleness until they'd both fallen asleep. The thought of waking up in his arms every morning was so appealing. Okay, more than just appealing. She wanted it so bad she ached for it. This sexy shifter had gotten under her skin so quickly that her entire world was off-kilter. He made her want things she knew she had no business dreaming about. Not when they came from such vastly different worlds. She squashed the thought as she smiled at him. "You looked so peaceful, like a big feline, I didn't want to disturb you."

He growled softly and leaned down to nip her ear-lobe. "I told you not to compare me to a freaking cat."

Brianna couldn't hold back her grin. She wasn't used to teasing or playing, but this big lupine shifter made it so easy. "Why not? You're as pretty as one." It drove him insane when she called him pretty, which made it that much more fun to do. When he got worked up, they usually ended up in bed. Or on the floor. Or on the kitchen table. She didn't care where as long as she was with him.

Those hazel eyes of his narrowed. "Damn, you're good. I know what you're doing."

"And what would that be?" She widened her eyes, trying to look innocent.

"Goading me into taking you right on the kitchen table." He stood and headed for the full coffeepot on the counter, but she didn't miss his erection before he turned from her.

"Do I truly have to goad you into anything?" She struggled to hide her laugh.

He turned back to her and she could tell he was fighting a smile. "You know you don't. What are you looking at?"

All thoughts of teasing fled her as she slid the list of names to the side. Angelo picked it up and was silent for a moment. He'd already looked at it the night before. They had also scanned the laptop they'd retrieved before handing it over to Erin. Neither of them had found much of interest. There had been a lot of pictures, some downloaded bank statements—the recent ones showing very large deposits that didn't fit with a Pilates instructor's salary. Brianna knew her way around computers well enough even if she did hate the damn things and something she'd noticed last night kept bugging her. The storage space on the computer was almost completely full, but she couldn't figure out why. Not with the simple amount of files on it.

"What are you thinking?" Angelo asked as he took a seat next to her.

The man seemed to dwarf everything in the room, especially when he was this close. She shrugged. "Nothing important." Well, nothing she could pinpoint at the moment so it wasn't worth bringing up.

Watching her, he was silent for a long moment before he said, "What time are we meeting your contact again?"

"An hour."

His hazel eyes glinted almost wickedly at her answer and before she could even think about saying more, he'd scooped her off her seat and had her straddling him. Her thighs stretched around him as he pushed the long T-shirt she was wearing up to her waist. She'd snagged it off the floor this morning. It was his and she liked the way his scent wrapped around her. Of course he would prefer she walked around naked, but she couldn't do it. Shifters were so unabashed in their nudity and maybe one day she would adjust, but she doubted it.

"I like my scent on you," he said before dipping his head to her neck where he gently nuzzled her. He growled softly as he did, a sound that made her shiver in a very good way.

Last night when he had refused to tell Erin Marcus's name it had surprised her. The cynical part of her had briefly wondered if he planned to tell the red-headed shifter later when Brianna wasn't around, but she'd quickly dismissed that. Angelo was a man of his word and he had promised her and Marcus. Even if he did not care for the vampire—at all—or even trust him at this point, Angelo would not betray him. In the fae world, her people often said one thing, but did another. Not the warriors, but the majority of the royalty had no problem lying and playing politics. Human politicians had nothing on the fae royalty.

That was why it was refreshing to be with someone like Angelo. He was so honest and raw that she didn't want to go back to Ireland without him. Not because she didn't love her country or her people. She definitely did. But she'd come to realize in the short time they'd spent together that location didn't matter to her. Just him. She would live on the Armstrong ranch where he lived with his pack if they allowed her.

She sucked in a sharp breath when one of his hands found her breast. He cupped it, teasing her nipple with his thumb in erotic little flicks. Closing her eyes, she held on to his shoulders and let her head fall back. God, what she wouldn't give to take him home with her. Before she left she was going to have someone take a picture of them. So she would at least have something to hold on to—*picture*.

"Pictures!" Her eyes snapped open and her head jerked back up.

Angelo's hand froze on her breast, the other working its way beneath her panties. "What?"

She slid off him and tugged her shirt down. "Those damn pictures," she muttered.

Angelo blinked at her. "Did you just say damn?"

"Ha-ha." She rolled her eyes and hurried toward the door that led to a utility room housing a new washer and dryer. It led right into another kitchen. Clearly this home had once been two separate places, but for whatever reason the owner had combined them.

"Brianna," Angelo's voice was heated as he followed after her.

She looked over her shoulder as she stepped into the other kitchen. "What?"

"You're not dressed." His eyes darkened to almost midnight as his gaze raked over her.

She glanced down. His T-shirt fell almost to her knees. "I have dresses shorter than this."

Interest, then something else much darker flashed in his eyes. "You wear them in public?"

Shaking her head at the ridiculous question—of course she wore her dresses in public, she wouldn't have purchased them otherwise—she turned away from him. His shifter possessiveness was something she would have to get used to. Right now was not the time to explain that she was perfectly covered and even if she was wearing nothing at all, it was unlikely Noah would even notice. He had eyes only for a petite red-headed shifter. She knocked quietly on Erin's door, hoping she was already awake.

The door opened a moment later and she found herself face-to-face with Noah. He had on jeans and no shirt, but he looked wide-awake. She hadn't realized Erin and Noah were sleeping together, but hadn't doubted that it would happen soon.

"Is Erin . . ." She trailed off as the redhead strode out of the bathroom with a blue robe cinched tightly around her waist and her wet hair brushed back from her face. "Did you find anything last night on the human's computer?"

Erin scowled, frustration clear on her face. "No."

"Check the pictures for hidden files. I can't believe I didn't think of it last night but I was so tired. If there is anything in the pictures, they likely won't be encrypted. You'll just have to extract them." They wouldn't be encrypted without specific software and she hadn't seen anything like that downloaded. The amount of space being utilized on the computer had been bugging her last night and then this morning. Hidden files might account for it.

The shifter's gray eyes widened with hope. "Good idea, thank you. I'll let you know if I find anything."

Brianna returned to the kitchen with Angelo. Silently, he scooped her up into his arms. "We have time for a quickie before we leave and I can't go another second without being inside you."

Heat bloomed inside her at his words. He was so honest about what he wanted that it floored her. The more time she spent with him, the more she realized that walking away wasn't going to be a simple thing. If she even could at all. But how would they make things work between them? They were so different and came from wildly different worlds.

When he stripped her shirt off and laid her on their bed, all thoughts of the future disappeared. Right now she simply wanted to enjoy being with Angelo.

Chapter 13

Once Brianna left the bedroom, Erin dressed, then turned on the dead human's laptop. She sat on the bed and as she waited for it to power up, she ran a towel through her damp hair—and tried to keep her gaze off Noah's broad chest. He'd showered but he'd put on only pants. Nudity to shifters was no big deal and she preferred to wear as little as possible when she could, but seeing all of his bare, muscular body had her tense and more than a little sexually frustrated.

After the way he'd pleasured then comforted her last night—well, technically this morning—she was on edge and unsure of herself. She'd been convinced she could compartmentalize Noah into a certain part of her life just like before. Now she knew that to be impossible. He wouldn't go willingly back into that "box" and she couldn't even try to put him back there. Things would never be the same between them again.

"How'd you sleep?" Noah asked quietly, forcing her to look at him. He'd flipped the desk chair around and sat on it backward like he normally did. The way he leaned his arms on it only accentuated the muscles and striations. She wondered if he was aware of how crazy he drove her.

Blinking, she mentally shook herself. "Good. Thank you." God, she felt so awkward. Like a teenager with a ridiculous crush. Of course nothing about their relationship was ridiculous. Just complicated. She'd basically laid herself bare to him when she'd admitted everything she'd lost and she didn't worry he'd judge or even feel sorry for her, but it didn't negate her discomfort.

"I liked holding you last night." Noah watched her intently.

Part of her enjoyed that he was so blunt, but right now she was barely hanging on. "I liked it too." Way too much. Looking away, she crossed her legs and pulled the computer into her lap, determined to block him out.

She pulled up the file labeled PICTURES, then right clicked on the first one to check the properties. The first ten were of the human and the dead vampire she and Noah had found in her kitchen. Their sizes ranged from nine hundred kilobytes to three megabytes. When she got to one that was almost eight megabytes she made a note of it and continued checking the rest. Only two were bigger than normal so she e-mailed them to Ryan, then texted him to let him know so he'd check the e-mail immediately. It was early but she knew he'd be up. That man never slept.

Sure enough, five minutes later she received a message with a bunch of text documents extracted from the photos. The first document listed names and addresses of not only the women who'd been taken so far, but half a dozen other shifters who were also pregnant.

In addition it had other stats like how far along they were in their pregnancy and in some cases the names of their doctors. It made sense that the human would have known this if she'd been their Pilates instructor. Women talked about this kind of stuff without any thought, especially to someone they assumed they could trust. Even though Erin wished the woman was alive just so she could question her, she sure as hell wasn't sorry the woman was dead. What kind of monster could betray women she saw all the time? Women who in all likelihood considered her a friend or were at least friendly with.

Erin turned the computer so Noah could see. While he read she grabbed the printer she'd brought, plugged it in, then attached the USB cord to it and her laptop. She wanted to print out a copy for herself. Technology had a lot of uses, but it was easier for her to read this way and she could carry the list with her. She also forwarded the information to Brianna and Angus and copied Jayce just so he'd know what was going on. They'd kept in touch with texting but they'd both been too damn busy to talk much otherwise. As she was printing it out, another e-mail popped up from Ryan.

"Holy shit." She turned the computer screen to Noah again and let him read the laundry list of crimes committed by Kelly Bridges. Also known as Bridgette James and Janice Bright. She probably had more pseudonyms they'd never know about. Her crimes ranged from petty larceny, solicitation, check fraud, driving without insurance, and a bunch of scams she was never convicted of but arrested for. About two years ago it looked as if she'd cleaned up her act and settled down in New Orleans. Apparently the lure of a lot of cash was too much to resist and she'd gone back to her criminal ways. Or more likely, she'd never stopped and just happened to be caught this time.

"What do you want to do?" Noah asked as he looked up from the screen.

"Will you call your father and ask him if he has enough people to shadow the women on the list?" Erin could call Angus herself but she'd seen the way Angus was subtly reaching out to Noah. When he'd come outside the compound last night he'd squeezed Noah's shoulder in that typical fatherly manner and the look of raw longing on his face had taken Erin by surprise. He wanted to be in his son's life. Maybe more than Noah realized.

Seeing that had made Erin ache. Like a punch to her bruised, scarred heart, she'd suddenly remembered the agony she'd experienced the night she'd been told her parents and little sister were dead. She thought she'd buried her grief years ago and for the most part she'd learned to live with it, but Noah hadn't lost his parents. Just his sister. That was sad and she understood his pain, but it didn't negate the fact that his father was *alive* and clearly wanted a relationship with him.

Noah's eyes narrowed. "I thought you wanted to be his contact for everything. You made that pretty clear."

She shrugged. "I need to finish scanning the rest of the documents and he's *your* father."

"Don't push something like this," he growled in an

angry tone she'd never heard from him before. He was coming out of his shell with her now, not afraid to hold anything back.

"I'll push whatever I want," she snapped. She'd opened up to him and he supposedly wanted everything from her. If that was the case, then he'd have to give her all of himself too. The second *that* thought entered her mind, she cursed herself. No, no, no. She shouldn't even be thinking in these terms. But damn her, she was.

His eyebrows rose and he started to say something, but unable to stop herself, she cut him off. "My parents are dead, Noah. Yours are right here in front of you and they're pretty freaking nice. You might talk to your mom all the time but how long since you've seen her because of your stupid pride?" He tried to interrupt but she was on a roll and the edgy way she was feeling this morning had killed her filter. Not that she had much of one to begin with. "Your dad hasn't given me any grief about being in his territory. He's completely given me the reins for this case, which I know is my absolute right, but I didn't expect it. He cares deeply about his pack, felines who aren't even his responsibility, and it's clear he cares about you. You're pissed because he wouldn't let you kill the vampires who killed your sister? Did you ever think that maybe he was doing it for your own good? That he was trying to be a good father?"

"He pushed Fiona away! It's his fault she left." It was one of the few times Noah had said his sister's name.

Erin didn't back down. "You don't think he lives

with that grief every second of every day? You think you're punishing him more than he probably does every damn day?"

"I'm not trying to punish him." Noah's jaw clenched tight and she knew she'd crossed a line, but she didn't care.

"Whatever you want to tell yourself. You've got a family that loves you and you've turned your back on them for no good reason. If I were in your shoes . . ." She trailed off, realizing she couldn't finish that thought. If she was in his shoes she'd hug her family every damn day. She'd tell them she loved them as much as she could.

"You fight fucking dirty," he snarled and stormed from the room.

Yeah, she guessed she did. The problem was, she and Noah had never argued before. Not truly and not over anything that mattered. Little spats about who got to control the television remote—and she'd always won that one—didn't count. Things between them had been full of sexual tension for the past year but they'd always been friends. *Buddies.* And Noah had been very careful around her. She could see that now with twenty-twenty vision. Now that they'd veered into dangerous territory the gloves had come off in too many ways. If he got to push her until she was about to snap, she got to do the same. He deserved a family who loved him and he had one. She just wanted to see him make up with his father even if he was pissed at her in the short-term. Hell, if he was annoyed with her maybe he'd lay off on pursuing her.

Sighing, she turned back to her computer and pulled

up the rest of the files. Somehow she shut down thoughts of Noah. She had work to do.

Most of the files were old records of people the human had scammed before. Their names, addresses, and money she'd stolen. Even bank account numbers. Lord, it was like the woman had kept a journal of all her misdeeds. Maybe it turned the shitty human on or something.

Nothing else was tied to Erin's case so she forwarded the rest of the pictures to Ryan. As she did, an e-mail from Ian popped up. His screen handle, *biteme*, made her laugh despite her mood. He sent her the same list Angus had already given her, but he'd made notes next to each name. After making notes in the margins of the list she'd already printed, she turned off the laptop.

Noah strode back in, fully dressed in a black sweater and jeans. He wore a knit skullcap and some dark strands of his hair peeked out. Underneath his sweater she could see the outline of a few weapons. Guns mostly, she assumed. Well, they were going to visit the houses of six different bloodborn families. Definitely made sense. She was certainly strapping on more armor than normal.

Before she could ask anything, he said, "My father can spare enough for all the females except two. He's keeping the compound on lockdown with everything going on and won't put his pack at risk."

Erin nodded. She understood that. "I'll ask Brianna and Angelo to take the other females until we're done. Then we can take over for them?"

Noah's expression remained dark, but he nodded. "My father also talked to the rest of the families with missing women. I know we have enough info for a connection, but they all confirmed the women were taking Pilates at the same place."

"Thanks." She didn't expect a response, yet when he turned on his heel and left her alone she fought the sadness welling up inside her. He was dealing with stuff in his own way. Even if she disagreed, maybe she shouldn't have pushed him so hard. Hell, she'd been in denial about her own issues for an entire year.

She'd just been freaked out after the night they'd shared and she'd pushed his buttons. God, he was right. She did fight dirty. She still thought he needed to work things out with his father but that wasn't her place. They weren't mates.

After calling Brianna—who told her as soon as she and Angelo met up with one of her vampire contacts they'd be splitting up and shadowing two of the pregnant shifters on that list—she found Noah outside leaning against the passenger side of her car with his arms crossed over his chest.

He still wore that dark expression and it killed her. Before she could change her mind, she tossed him her keys.

Eyebrows raised, Noah caught them. "What's this?"

"You can drive to the first address." In other words, *I'm sorry*.

He paused for a long moment and the tension in his shoulders loosened. "Damn, you don't fight *that* dirty, short stuff." A hint of a smile played at the corner of his mouth.

She rolled her eyes at the nickname. "Fine, give me the keys back then."

He just shook his head so she got into the passenger seat before she could change her mind.

Noah slid into the driver's seat, making a sound of overexaggerated appreciation as he grasped the steering wheel and basically stroked it. Taking her off guard, he leaned over and brushed his lips over hers before starting the car.

That small action had butterflies taking flight in her belly. Sighing, she looked out the window. She was so screwed when it came to him.

Noah slowed Erin's car as they pulled down the long, winding road that couldn't really be called a driveway because it was two miles long. Live oak trees covered in Spanish moss lined the paved road and covered much of the surrounding acres. Even though the gate hadn't been closed, Noah knew they were being watched.

His innate wolf sense was going crazy, clawing at him to be set free. There were definitely more than two vampires in the vicinity. Probably worked for François LaPomeret, the vamp they were visiting. Or maybe he had guests. It was late afternoon and after visiting six other bloodborn households in and around New Orleans Noah was ready for a break from interacting with vamps. The first two they'd visited had been unattached males who'd had no interest in continuing their line at the moment. They'd been relatively young bloodborns born into this century living off their family money, and while they'd been annoyed to have had their sleep disturbed, they'd seemed so human compared to many of the vamps Noah had interacted with. And they'd both checked out Erin blatantly in the way

Noah imagined human college boys would have done. Under other circumstances it would have pissed him off, but they'd been harmless. Well, as harmless as a vampire could be, but no threat to either him or Erin. And Erin was hot. Other males would notice and it was something he was trying to deal with.

"Ian made an interesting note next to LaPomeret's name." There was a touch of humor in Erin's voice that made Noah turn toward her.

"Ian?"

She nodded, her lips quirking slightly. "He sent the same list your father gave me but he added anecdotes next to each name. The others have been professional but apparently this guy is a goat-fucking-piece-of-shit and if I killed him the Brethren would probably give me a medal or make me an honorary vampire."

Despite his feelings toward Ian, Noah laughed. "Damn."

She chuckled quietly, then sobered as they neared the antebellum home. "Just because Ian hates him doesn't mean he's involved. The first places we visited also had notes from him that those individuals were highly suspect."

Yet neither he nor Erin had sensed any deceit from the vamps. Of course the vampires could have been lying, but Erin's senses were finely honed when it came to scenting lies and he was even older and had an innate ability as well.

Noah had wondered how she'd chosen the houses to visit and had considered asking, but things were still tense between them. Not hostile, just edgy. He hadn't said much as he'd driven to each address and she definitely hadn't opened up the lines of communication. That kiss had seemed to relax her as they'd left their place, but since the first vamp's house she'd been focused and tuning him out.

It might have bugged him more if he wasn't so caught up in replaying the words she'd flung at him. Until seeing his father in person after so many years he'd never thought that his father was punishing himself. Now he felt like a dick for not realizing it. Angus had lost a daughter and inevitably a son when Noah had left. While he spoke to his mother often she always tiptoed around the topic of Angus.

Noah didn't want to feel guilty about that but it had been growing inside him like kudzu since the moment they arrived. Erin's words had only fanned the fire.

"Think they knew we were coming?" Erin asked as he put the car in park directly in front of the house. The rose bushes were immaculate as was the two-story manor. The entire house was a bright white with dark blue shutters closed over the windows.

Though he couldn't see them, Noah sensed probably a dozen individuals on the grounds. Humans, probably, considering they were all out in the sun and daywalkers were rare.

As they exited the car the front door opened and a tall, elegant-looking man walked out wearing a high-waist coat, a vest underneath, and a pocket watch. His eyes were bright amber like most vampires when their emotions were high. The color was startling against his café au lait skin.

Erin shot Noah a covert look and he could see the laughter in her eyes. They were both dressed to match in almost all black with similar-looking knit skullcaps and they were strapped down with weapons. It was cold, not that it bothered them much, but the caps would keep their hair out of the way if a fight broke out. He and Erin were all about practicality like that. It was something he loved about her. To this guy they probably looked like thugs.

The way he raked gazes over both their bodies with absolute disdain confirmed it.

"Mr. LaPomeret?" Erin asked, even though they both realized this was the vampire they'd come to see.

"At your service, Ms. Flynn." There was a mocking undertone in his cultured, slightly French accent.

Oh yeah, he'd known they were coming and he didn't like it.

His bright gaze turned toward Noah. "Who are you?"

"Noah."

The other man gritted his teeth, probably pissed he hadn't given his last name. But Noah wasn't telling this guy shit. He hadn't introduced himself at the other homes and those vamps hadn't asked. They'd just looked at him curiously as he maintained silence.

"You're her bodyguard?" It was clearly a baiting question.

Erin simply unzipped her jacket and Noah remained silent. This guy meant nothing to him and he wasn't eyeing Erin as if he'd like to see her naked. It would be a piece of cake to keep his cool around him.

"I take it you're a daywalker." Erin spoke, drawing the vamp's attention back to her.

"Clearly," he said, not bothering to mask his sarcasm

now. "Why are you here? I could kill you for trespassing."

Considering LaPomeret had expected them, he had an idea why they were there. And he could *try* to kill them. It would be stupid though.

Erin snorted softly, mirroring Noah's feelings. "First, you can't kill us." She said the words as if the concept was ridiculous.

Not won't, *can't*. Fuck yeah, Erin. He loved it when she got tough.

"Second, not only does my Council know I'm here—and that includes Jayce Kazan—so do Angus Campbell and your own Brethren."

The vampire had paled at the mention of Noah's father. Noah inwardly smiled.

"Fine. Ask your questions."

"Have you had illegal dealings with shifters in the past year?"

"No." The answer was instant.

An acidic scent rolled off the vampire. It was subtle, but Noah smelled it.

"Has your mate?" Erin asked.

"No." The scent was gone this time.

Interesting. Maybe the mate didn't know about her male's actions. It might spare her life later because there was one thing Noah was sure of. This guy was going to die. Maybe not today, but soon.

"Have you ever kidnapped pregnant shifters?"

"No." No stench this time. Because he hadn't done the actual dirty work.

Erin didn't react, but Noah realized that this guy had basically just given them a baseline for his lies.

They'd expected him to say no and the lack of metallic scent confirmed what his lies smelled like.

"Have you ever paid for or procured pregnant shifter blood in the hopes of continuing your bloodline with bloodborns?" Erin's voice was monotone as she spoke.

He was impressed with her stoic, deceivingly casual stance when he knew she was ready to attack at any moment.

The acidic scent now overpowered both of them as the vampire said, "No."

"Have you ever fucked a goat because I heard that you liked it that way." Noah's crass statement rent through the air with the subtlety of an atomic bomb. Which is exactly what he intended. He wanted to piss this liar off.

LaPomeret snarled, his civilized demeanor falling away as his fangs and claws descended. Murder was in his eyes as he lunged at Noah, his arm pulled back lightning fast as he prepared to strike.

Noah dodged to the side, but moved slow enough that the vamp could slice through his shoulder. Pain ripped through him, splintering his nerve endings, but Noah channeled his pain. Erin's eyes widened as she watched him, no doubt wondering what was wrong with him for not moving faster. The attack from the vampire hadn't been very well thought out, but they'd both *known* it was coming after the question about the goat. The confusion bled from her eyes as quickly as the understanding crept in.

LaPomeret had just attacked Noah in broad daylight in front of the enforcer. Erin was the perfect witness and Noah was Angus Campbell's son. It was all the provocation his father would need to attack this vampire and torture the information out of him. Sure, Erin could have done it herself, but this place was heavily guarded and if the two of them had decided to go up against an unknown number of threats—well, that was just stupid.

The vampire straightened his coat as he continued to snarl. "Get off my property." His voice was deeper than it had been before.

Noah smiled widely, which he knew pissed the guy off. Palming the keys, he strode toward the car alongside Erin. He tossed her the keys and as she slid into the driver's seat, he said, "By the way, my last name is Campbell, you stupid fuck."

Noah jumped into the car to the sound of LaPomeret shouting. It sounded a lot like "kill them" but Noah couldn't be sure above the explosion of gunfire surrounding them. He pulled out one of the guns he'd strapped on, but so far nothing was penetrating the car.

"Way to be subtle!" Erin revved the engine, burning rubber as she screeched away.

Bullets pinged the back of the car and the window. Thank God she'd had bullet-resistant windows installed before their trip.

"What the hell were you thinking?" she snapped as she increased the speed. The needle on the car hit sixty-five in seconds and kept climbing.

Out of the corner of his eye he saw a vamp dressed in something that mimicked riot gear racing toward them from across the land. Damn male was *fast*. Noah ignored her question, his focus on their attackers. "I'm rolling down the window so brace yourself for possible gunfire."

Raising his weapon with one hand, he depressed the window button with his other while he took aim. The guy was running closer, closer—Noah pulled the trigger.

The guy's head exploded in a crimson mess as his body jerked to a sudden halt. Erin was driving so fast Noah barely got a good glimpse of him. Seconds later they reached the end of the driveway.

Hardly slowing, she took a sharp turn onto the desolate highway and gunned the engine again as they headed back to New Orleans proper.

When he was sure they weren't being followed, he semirelaxed against the seat and laid his weapon in his lap instead of sheathing it completely. He looked at his wounded shoulder. The adrenaline that had surged through him minutes ago was ebbing and a dull ache remained where he'd been injured. His skin was already knitting back together and he'd be healed by the time they reached his father's compound. "I wanted to piss that guy off."

"Yeah. I figured that out," she muttered. "You're gonna pay for the damages to my car. . . . Are you okay?" The note of worry in her voice surprised him.

"This is just a scratch." He motioned to his arm, then glanced behind them again. In minutes they'd be on a main road far enough away that LaPomeret wouldn't think about touching them. Not that it would matter. There was nowhere the vamp could hide now that he'd attacked Angus Campbell's son.

"You gonna call your father and tell him or should I?" Erin sounded positively smug.

Which is exactly how Noah felt. "I'll call." By the time anyone from the Campbell pack got to LaPomeret's home Noah worried the vamp might be long gone. But he wouldn't have gone far. Not if he was buying pregnant shifter blood. And if his mate wasn't a daywalker they wouldn't be able to go far anyway. His father would catch up to this guy soon enough and when he did it would be only a matter of time before the vamp confessed what he knew about who was behind the kidnappings.

Noah wanted these fuckers stopped. Females were to be protected at all costs. It was simple nature, but especially for shifters. They protected their own. Yet shifters were kidnapping and hurting their own females. There was no way anyone was letting whoever was behind this walk away alive.

More than that, Noah wasn't letting Erin walk away from him. She was his to protect and take care of and vice versa. He wanted to make a home with her and to spend every damn day of his life making her happy. Even when they were arguing there was no place else he'd rather be.

Chapter 14

Brianna tapped her finger against the center console of the car Angus Campbell had let her borrow. She hated driving, especially in the States, but she and Angelo had needed to split up today. It had surprised her how much she missed him. She was used to working solo and preferred it that way. Until him.

The sexy shifter had completely worked his way under her defenses and what was worse, she had a feeling he knew it. Originally she'd thought he'd be the perfect man to have a sexual relationship with since she'd be returning home after this job and he had no ties to her people, but now .... well, things changed. She didn't want to go home anymore. Her phone buzzed in her pocket and she smiled when she saw Angelo's name on the caller ID. *Speak of the devil.*

She answered immediately. "Hello."

"Hey, sweetheart. How's everything over there?" Angelo's voice wrapped around her, the endearment meaning much more coming from him than Marcus.

"No one is home and I have no way to track them so I'm sitting across the street. The neighbors probably think I'm casing their house." After she and Angelo met with the last contact on her list, which had been a complete waste of time, she'd picked up the car and made her way to Paige and Carlton Moreau's house. Paige was a feline shifter and two months pregnant according to the file Erin had found. As soon as Brianna made contact with her she planned to let the feline know about the threat and that she would be provided extra security whether it was from Brianna, Angelo, Erin, or any of Angus Campbell's pack. Maybe the woman would even leave town for a few weeks. That would be the best thing.

Angelo laughed. "Somehow I doubt that. . . . I wish I was with you."

Heat bloomed inside her at the way he said that. "I wish you were too." Part of her wanted to refrain from telling him that, but she didn't know how to play the games humans did. She didn't want to anyway. Not with Angelo. She'd been up front that she would likely be leaving the country after this job.

"You know what I would do if I was there?" His voice had a wicked quality to it.

She knew without a doubt she would like the answer. "What—oh, hold on. Marcus is on the other line. I need to take this."

Angelo growled. "I can't stand that guy."

She laughed softly. "I know and he knows. I'll call you back."

"Okay."

She clicked over. "Hello, Marcus."

"Hey, sweetheart," he purred, all sin and seduction.

She'd let it go before because the endearment hadn't bothered her. But it bothered Angelo and even if he wasn't here, she felt as if she needed to make something clear. "Don't call me that anymore."

A pause. "Damn. It's serious with that shifter?"

"That shifter has a name and . . . I don't know." It was serious for the moment. And more serious than any relationship she'd had previously. But how could things ever work between them? That question had been plaguing her since she'd realized just how much Angelo meant to her.

"Well, it's serious for him," Marcus said quietly.

Yeah, she was well aware of that. He hadn't said the actual words but she knew it in a bone-deep sort of way she couldn't explain to herself that he wanted to mate with her. Angelo made it clear every second they were in the same vicinity. Shifter-fae matings were rare but they'd happened in the past so she wasn't worried about their compatibility. They definitely had it in the bedroom. But there was more to a relationship than sex. Originally from Spain, Angelo's pack had long since passed away and he'd been with Connor Armstrong's newly formed pack for only a year. Before that he'd roamed all over the world pretty much aimlessly. At least that's what he'd told her. He'd also told her that he felt as if he'd been searching his entire life to fit in somewhere but that need had disappeared the moment he'd met her. Those words still rattled her because she felt the same. Growing up as royalty and then working harder to prove herself because of her small stature among the Fianna, her warrior brethren, she'd never felt as if she fit in anywhere. Except with a bunch of wolves. Or at least one wolf in particular. Sighing, Brianna mentally shook herself. She couldn't think about having this conversation with anyone, let alone Marcus. "It's taken you a while to get back to me." Okay, it hadn't been that long, but it had felt as if he was avoiding her calls.

He paused for a long moment. "Loyalty to my kind is important."

Brianna knew that and she thought she understood what he was saying. He'd told her what he was comfortable with earlier, but he'd still held back the reasoning of the pregnant females' kidnappings out of some sense of honor to his people.

Before she could respond, he continued. "Some things are more important than loyalty, however. I got a call from a human contact of mine a few minutes ago. The shifter enforcer has been making the rounds today. She came by my place and spoke to some of my employees since I wasn't home. Did you tell her anything about me?"

"No. I swore I wouldn't and I don't lie." It rankled her that he had to even ask. Her word was her solid vow.

"What about Angelo?" he snapped.

She bristled at his tone. "No."

"And I should believe that?" There was a bite to Marcus's words.

"I relayed some of the information you gave us and Angelo refused to tell her your name." Brianna hadn't been sure if he would stand by her. She had hoped but in that moment last night she had realized just how much Angelo meant to her even if she couldn't admit the truth out loud.

"Good. I learned something very interesting today and since you kept your word I will tell you. François LaPomeret is one of the wealthiest bloodborns in the area. He's a total dick and today it seems he attacked Noah Campbell and the enforcer. Unfortunately for him they made it off his property alive so he's scrambling as we speak to evacuate his property. He's leaving a few humans behind to care for the place—including my contact—but LaPomeret is going to be in the wind soon. He'll leave town and relocate somewhere else. Probably Europe."

"Did Erin and Noah find a connection between him and the missing shifters?" Erin didn't need to check in with Brianna, but she wanted to know what had spooked the vampire and what the vamp was guilty of that made him attack Noah.

"That, I don't know. I just know that LaPomeret is shitting-his-pants terrified of Angus Campbell, but yes, I think he's involved. He's skeezy enough."

She frowned. "Skeezy?"

"Uh, a sleazeball. Just thought you might want to know."

"Thank you. You must know that we're aware why the females are being taken by now."

"I knew you would figure it out."

"You should have told me."

He grunted softly. "If I discover any others involved in the disgusting practice, I'll send you their names. I cannot be loyal to those who don't deserve it." Without giving her a chance to respond, he hung up.

She started to call Angelo back but stopped when she saw a white SUV pull into the Moreau's driveway. According to the information Erin had given her, that's what the Moreaus drove. A tall, lean male with bronze skin got out of the driver's side and a moment later a tall, ethereal-looking woman with ivory skin stepped from the passenger side. She had a small baby bump and even though she was only two months along it made sense that she was showing. Shifter pregnancies were shorter so their young developed faster.

The male opened the back hatch of the vehicle and they began pulling out plastic bags. Groceries, she guessed. Sitting back against the seat she decided to wait until they'd unloaded everything before she let them know what was going on. She would be laying a lot on them at once and wanted them somewhat comfortable when she did.

Scanning the neighborhood, she zeroed in on an older-model dark van slowly driving down the road. As it slowed even more in front of the Moreau house, Brianna got out of her car. Before she'd taken two steps, the van jerked to a halt and two men wearing black masks jumped out.

Panicked, Brianna raced across the street, ready to intervene. She didn't make a sound because she didn't want them to notice her yet.

With a raised gun, one of the men started shooting at Carlton Moreau. There was no warning. There was a silencer on the weapon, muting what would have disturbed the entire neighborhood.

The feline cried out in agony as he slammed back against the pavement. The bags in his hand fell, sending apples rolling down the driveway. His mate, Paige, screamed and tried to run to him but the other male grabbed her by the arm and yanked her back to his chest.

Brianna was sprinting toward them but she didn't have the speed of shifters or vampires. Calling on the power she did have, she took a calming breath and harnessed her energy in her left hand. Her palm tingled as warmth spread through her body. The one with the gun noticed her right as she raised her arm.

As if she was throwing a ball, she hauled back and let her energy loose. The arc of blue lightning slammed into the middle of his chest, sending him flying through the air, across the length of their yard. He hit a tree that bordered the sidewalk but before he'd made contact with the ground his shoes and clothes had shredded as his wolf took over.

Brianna could easily kill humans but supernatural beings were trickier. Especially with shifters. Their animal took over instinctively when under this kind of threat from her. She shot a blast of energy at him again, but he dodged it, running farther away. She did manage to strike his tail. He howled in pain as the scent of burning fur reached her nostrils.

After releasing a couple of bolts like that she normally felt the drain of her energy but she was completely amped up and she was fairly certain it had something to do with all the sex she'd been having. She'd heard from other fae that sex could increase powers. She really hoped that was the case because she didn't want to fail.

As she started to blast him again, the other shifter shouted, "Stop!"

She'd been keeping him in her peripheral vision since he had the feline female pulled against him, but she needed to get one of the attackers down first. They were physically stronger and they clearly weren't afraid to use weapons, so she couldn't let them get too close.

As she turned to the shifter holding the pregnant shifter, she saw the male she'd blasted stagger, then collapse in a heap of fur on the sidewalk, not moving. Good. She narrowed her gaze as the other male brandished a knife and pressed it to the female's belly.

The woman whimpered, but Brianna ignored her. She needed to eliminate the threats first. Then she could focus on saving the female's wounded mate. "How do you possibly think this will end?" she snapped to the still-masked shifter.

"I'm going to leave with her and you're not going to do a damn thing about it unless you want to watch her bleed out," the male snarled.

"You're not going anywhere." Without taking her gaze off him, she turned her hand in the direction of the van and sent out a blast of energy. A muted boom ricocheted around the previously quiet neighborhood as the vehicle lifted a couple feet into the air, then slammed back to the ground. Smoke billowed out from the hood where she'd fried all the circuits. No matter what, she couldn't let them leave with the pregnant female.

Disabling the van was a risk, but there wasn't an alternative. Now the males had limited options. "Your partner is badly hurt so if you're smart, you'll leave with him. Leave the female and run. I can't catch you. You must know that." That didn't mean she wouldn't blast him apart the second she got the chance. He might not know exactly what she was, but he could guess by her coloring and her abilities. Unfortunately he was using the pregnant female as a shield, stopping her from attacking him.

He glanced over his shoulder where his brother was attempting to stand on wobbly feet. The animal let out a yowl and stumbled farther down the sidewalk out of her blast range. "Yeah, but you'll blast me the second I let her go." Without warning he slammed the blade into the female's upper thigh.

The woman screamed and fell to the ground. Brianna aimed and fired as the male shifted forms. Her blast of energy skimmed over him, hitting a tree instead. It creaked and splintered straight up the middle. As it did, half of it toppled over onto the smoking van. She blasted at him again, barely missing and hitting another tree before he was out of range.

Fighting her urge to chase after the shifters since she knew she'd never catch them, she knelt in between the fallen male and female. They were both stretched out on their driveway right behind their vehicle, side by side. The dinging sound from the SUV caused by the open back door rang out insistently.

The pregnant shifter moaned softly as her eyes closed and she laid her head against the driveway. "Knife . . . hurts."

Hating to do it, Brianna gripped the blade and pulled it out in one tug. The woman screamed again and in the distance Brianna heard sirens wailing. She only hoped they were coming for them. Normally she wouldn't remove a blade, but she had to for what she intended next.

Using her healing powers, she placed one palm over the female's gushing wound and spread her other palm over the unmoving male's chest. After a few long moments the woman opened her eyes again. She looked at her mate, then at what Brianna was doing to both of them.

The soft green glow of Brianna's healing energy illuminated both of them. This was more draining than her blasts of destructive energy had been. She was trying to heal not destroy and that took more concentration.

"You're fae?" Her question was a bare whisper.

She nodded. "My name is Brianna and I'm here to help you." The sirens were growing louder, sending a bolt of adrenaline through Brianna. She really hoped they were coming for them and she didn't dare take her hands off either of the wounded shifters to call the police herself. The male was incredibly weak and while she could do a lot to repair the damage or at least slow the bleeding, the bullets needed to come out.

"Use . . . all your energy on him. Not me." Paige's voice was a little stronger now and Brianna could feel the life force pulsing stronger around the female, but she couldn't stop what she was doing. As a pregnant shifter, the female was much weaker than normal.

"Keep your eyes closed and take deep breaths. An ambulance is on its way." Or she hoped it was.

When the screaming siren tore down the street, Brianna finally let out a breath of relief. Help was here.

Moments later four men in police uniforms and three in paramedics' uniforms spilled out of vehicles. She also saw a fire truck out of the corner of her eye, but kept her energy focused on the downed couple.

As the three paramedics knelt down next to them, she started firing information at them. "The female is a feline shifter and has been stabbed with that knife." She nodded her head to the jagged hunting-style knife lying in the driveway. "She's two months pregnant and incredibly weak. She can still heal at faster than normal rates, but her pregnancy is draining her energy. The male has been shot multiple times and he's also a feline shifter. If you get the bullets out of him, he should heal quickly."

The paramedics nodded briskly, the action telling her this wasn't the first time they'd dealt with paranormal beings.

Though she didn't want to move away, she knew the humans had a job to do. She stood while they took over and started talking in a medical language she didn't understand. She hadn't taken one step away before two men in black police uniforms were right in front of her. They were both at least half a foot taller than she was and their expressions were wary. Probably because whoever had called the cops had told them what she'd done. Either that or they'd seen the green glow coming from her healing energy when they'd walked up. It was different from the energy when she was in battle mode, but probably no less freaky to humans.

As the man on her left opened his mouth, a man behind them shouted, "Harmon, Cardenas, stand down. She's my witness." He raced up the driveway.

The two officers shot each other an almost relieved look and immediately strode away as a gorgeous man with mocha skin and bright green eyes stopped in front of her. His suit was rumpled and his tie had been loos-

ened. He held out a hand and though his expression
was stressed, she could tell it wasn't directed at her.
"Are you Brianna?"

Surprised, she nodded and shook his extended
hand. "How did you know that?"

"Angus Campbell keeps me and a few of my superiors informed about what goes on in the supernatural
community. Gave me a bunch of addresses that were
being watched by his pack and when I heard a call
come through that there was an incident at one of them,
I called him. He told me who I should talk to. I'm Detective McCarty but you can call me Colt." His brief
smile was genuine.

She was grateful to be speaking with someone who
wasn't completely clueless about the situation. Fishing
her buzzing phone out of her pocket, she looked at the
caller ID. She had ten missed calls. Some from Angus
and the others from Angelo. The Alpha had probably
called Angelo when he couldn't get through to her.
"Would you mind if I sent a quick text before we
speak?" She didn't want Angelo to worry.

He nodded though she could tell he didn't want to
say yes. After letting Angelo know she was okay, she
tucked her phone back into her pocket and faced the
detective.

As he fired questions at her, she answered all the ones
she could. There was no need to lie to the police, especially since she knew there had been witnesses. Someone had called the cops, after all. Either way, the police
wouldn't find the masked men before the shifter community would so it didn't matter what she told them.

Once caught, the men behind this would face shifter justice and it would be swift, brutal, and final.

Erin would have preferred to work with her own pack, but when she went back to LaPomeret's house she wasn't going without backup. Unless she made a sneak attack in the middle of the day, invading a completely unknown territory was just plain stupid. And Angus's warriors were more than willing to back her up.

The Alpha had been beyond livid about Noah being scratched. Because in truth, that's all the attack had been. Something told Erin that Angus just wanted an excuse to kill LaPomeret. Whenever anyone said that guy's name it was followed with a curse.

As she started to pace the foyer of Angus's home, Noah put a hand on her shoulder to still her. They were waiting for two more warriors to finish gearing up with extra weapons. For the most part shifters didn't need them, but with this vampire they all wanted to be prepared.

Even if she knew in her gut that LaPomeret would be gone by the time they got back to his home, she still had to follow up. There might be a lead or something that could point her to where the missing shifters were being stashed.

At this point she wanted the females safe and home with their families. While she'd love nothing more than to bring their kidnappers to justice and stop them from doing this ever again, she desperately wanted to save these women. Being pregnant was stressful enough but to be used as blood donors for some sickos, to be ripped away from their mates and in some cases, their children—it made Erin see red.

"Let's wait outside with the others." Erin nodded toward the front door and Noah opened it.

They stepped out together to be met with six warrior shifters. Four males and two females. Plus Angus. Including the two she could hear barreling down the stairs at the moment, and her and Noah—that made eleven. She wished it was more, but right now Angus's pack was already stretched thin. And a handful of them were watching the homes of pregnant feline shifters. There was no way she'd ask him to call those guards off.

Angus ended his phone call when he saw them. "There was a possible sighting of the two shifters who are taking the women."

As Erin listened to him relay what two masked men had done and how Brianna had nearly stopped them, Erin wanted to rip something apart. If only she'd been there. They would finally have been within her grasp.

Clenching her fists, she glanced at Noah, then Angus. She hated making this decision, but if she didn't follow up on this possible lead it would be unforgivably stupid. "I need to see if I can pick up a scent. Can you—"

Angus nodded, cutting her off. "We're more than capable of ripping LaPomeret's house apart. If we find anything useful, I'll call you."

"Noah, you should go with your father. I can track alone." She looked him square in the eyes as she said it. She knew he'd fight her, but as far as hunting skills went, they were evenly paired in tracking. "You can help them more than me."

Noah snorted. "No fucking way." Then he palmed her car keys and strode down the driveway toward *her* car. She watched as he slid into the driver's seat like he owned it. Gritting her teeth, she looked back at Angus. "Thank you for helping with this. Keep me informed of what you find and I'll do the same."

He nodded, then started barking orders to his people while she jogged to her car. Getting in, she slammed the door a second before Noah tore out of the driveway.

"You know where you're going?"

"No, but I'm sure you'll give me the address," he said smoothly, as if he had no idea how pissed she was.

She rattled off the address and barely managed to keep the lid on her temper. The rage rolling off her right now was a combination of a whole mess of shit including his blatant show of disrespect for her in front of the Alpha of New Orleans. Didn't matter that it was his father, she was so angry she wanted to punch him.

After a solid minute of driving she forced her jaw to work. "I can't believe you did that in front of your father and all those other warriors. If you'd tried that shit with Jayce he would have flattened you."

"I don't want to protect Jayce so that's a nonissue," he snarled.

She let out a brief scream of rage. Her inner wolf howled so badly right now. All she wanted to do was be set free and kick someone's ass. Namely the annoying shifter right next to her. "You put me in a bad position and made me look as if I have no authority. It's hard enough being the enforcer. Add to that I'm also a female . . . damn it, Noah. You embarrassed me."

He swallowed hard, but didn't respond. As they pulled up to a stoplight, he looked at her and she glared back. His dark eyes were filled with something she'd never seen before. Shame. "I'm sorry, Erin," he said so softly she could barely hear him. "Right now I'm . . . confused about us. My wolf is going insane wanting to know why I can't claim or protect you all the time. The need to mate with you is making me crazy. I should have let you track alone and I know that. I have no doubt about how capable you are. Part of me is afraid that if I let you out of my sight I'll lose that chance to claim you. And that thought is worth all your anger. I'd rather be fighting with you and have you pissed at me than have something happen to you and know I could have been there to protect you."

Well, damn. Noah had just taken all the steam out of her rage. How could she stay angry at him when he was doing what came naturally? Her wolf wanted him too. With a vengeance that was hard to deny. If the roles had been reversed she'd have done the same thing. She didn't know what to say though.

A horn blasted behind them and Noah turned back to the road. She could see flashing red and blue lights a street over and guessed they were close to the sight of the attack. They turned down the street and despite her residual anger, she reached out and squeezed his forearm. "I shouldn't have said you embarrassed me. Everyone there knows why you did what you did." Because he was a male crazed by the mating need. This was about as close as she could get to letting him off the hook at the moment. And only because his words had been so freaking heartfelt and out of character. Damn him for that.

Noah parked along the curb, barely squeezing her car in between a Volkswagen Beetle and an extended-cab F-150. When she got out she grimaced at the bullet holes in the body of her car. It was a miracle they hadn't hit her tires. Soon enough she'd get her baby fixed, but for now it didn't top her priorities. Without looking at Noah, she got out and scanned for Brianna.

The fae warrior was talking to a man in a suit behind a line of yellow tape. As she and Noah hurried down the sidewalk she spotted a worried-looking Angelo hauling ass along the same sidewalk but on the other side of the crime scene. A man in uniform tried to stop him, but as soon as Brianna said something, the guy in the suit let him through.

Erin breathed a sigh of relief. Maybe this was the detective Angus was friendly with. Would make her job a lot easier. Not that she planned to stick around for very long. Just enough to pick up a scent trail. If they'd even left one behind. Shifters could mask their scents various ways, though most didn't. But most weren't psychopaths who kidnapped and abused their own kind either. She didn't smell anything yet, but there were a lot of people around and she hadn't acclimated enough to sift through everything.

Brianna saw them as they reached the yellow tape. Men and women in uniform were milling around and before a woman wearing a black, standard-looking police uniform could tell them to stop, the man with Brianna shouted to let them through also.

Hell yeah, agency cooperation. Ducking under, she and Noah nodded at Angelo who had slung his arm around Brianna's shoulders and was holding her tight. Erin held out her hand to the man in the suit. "I'm Erin Flynn. Enforcer for the North American Council of lupine shifters. I'm sure you know why I'm in town since you've been in contact with Angus."

He nodded once, the handsome man's full lips quirking up. "I do indeed. It's nice to meet you. I'm Detective McCarty."

Erin quickly shook his hand. "I need to clear the crime scene and entire front yard so I can attempt to pick up the scent of the perpetrators." And she wasn't asking.

The detective nodded and started shouting orders at everyone to move.

She glanced at Noah to find her sexy wolf watching her without a flicker of emotion in his gaze. She hated that she was likely the reason for that. He was trying to keep his wolf on lockdown. What happened between them last night had probably only exacerbated his need. God knew it had for her. She was agitated, sexually frustrated, and her own wolf wanted to know what the hell was wrong with her for denying him. Too bad her human side knew better.

As soon as the area was free of humans, Erin made her way across the driveway, but jerked to a halt as she reached where the concrete met the grassy lawn. Shifter blood was on the ground below her, the scent strong, but that wasn't what made her blood run cold.

She could scent two males she'd never wanted to scent again. Never wanted to see again either, unless she was shoving blades through their black hearts. For just a second the other day when she and Noah had been leaving the Full Moon Bar she'd thought she scented them but had convinced herself she was crazy. This case had been making her insane so she'd chalked it up to frayed nerves. Now she knew she was wrong. She scented *them* clearly.

Chris and Malcolm Tyson. Chris, her former lover, the male who'd tried to murder her and left her for dead. His psychopathic brother had taken part in trying to kill her and was just as evil. Their strong scents nearly overwhelmed her now, making her take an involuntary step back as if just the smell of them could taint her.

It had taken her almost an entire year to get back on her feet, to admit what she'd lost, to admit she was still a warrior at heart and could survive anything. But now she felt like that wounded shifter again as she struggled to drag in a breath. It was as if her lungs refused to expand, making it difficult for her to breathe. Chris and Malcolm were *here*, in New Orleans. And were likely behind the kidnappings and murder.

Erin wasn't sure how long she stood there frozen, but she eventually felt more than heard Noah behind her, his strong hands settling on her shoulders as he turned her around.

"What is it?" he asked softly.

"I think I know who's behind the kidnappings." While she wanted to break down and tell him everything, she had to act fast. Now that she had their scents, she was going to track them down.

Ignoring Noah's surprised expression she whipped

her phone out and called Ryan. Now that she had names, Mr. Computer Genius should be able to work a miracle.

Or she really hoped he could. Either way, she was hunting down these monsters and ending them for good. If she had to chase them across the entire globe, so be it. She didn't care how long it took either.

Chapter 15

Chris and his brother raced through neighborhoods as if hellhounds were after them. He'd never seen a fae before but he had no doubt that's what that blond bitch had been. Malcolm was limping, moaning, and barely keeping up as they darted down a quiet backstreet. There wasn't much on this road. Just two long, brick walls lining it and blocking the homes behind them.

The walls also blocked him and his brother from curious eyes. He scented some spicy kind of food nearby. It mingled with raw meat—steak maybe—and he also smelled marijuana and laundry detergent. The mix of scents was even stronger now that his adrenaline was pumping overtime.

The gravel dug into his paws as they ran. As scents grew stronger, he slowed then stopped. His brother did the same but collapsed. His tail was completely fried and if he changed to his human form it would accelerate the healing. Which is exactly what they needed right now. First Chris had to find them some clothes though. Grabbing his brother by the scruff of the neck with his jaws, he dragged him into an arched alcove carved right into the wall.

He'd never understand the jumbled architecture in New Orleans, but this was a decent hiding spot for the moment. Even if someone drove down this desolate road they wouldn't see his brother unless they were looking. There were voices, a few female and one male, nearby. Talking about the weather and supper.

Concentrating harder than normal, he let the change overtake him as he shifted back to his human form. The brick wall was only about five feet tall so he remained crouching until he could gain his bearings.

Going after that feline shifter had clearly been a mistake, but the lure of extra cash from LaPomeret had been too much. The vamp wanted someone in the early stages of her pregnancy and who hadn't been used yet. Someone he could keep himself. Normally Chris would have balked but when he'd talked to him on the phone the vampire had been desperate. Now he wondered why.

Peeking over the brick wall he saw the back of a townhome. The rain gutter was rusted and dangerously close to falling off and the small yard looked like a jungle. Scanning the rest of the townhomes, he saw that they looked basically the same. About a foot of space between each one. Two homes down to his left was where the source of the food and voices were coming from. A sheet and a few shirts stretched out over a clothesline covered most of his view, but he could see the male and females he'd heard talking earlier. They were all old humans, probably in their sixties, and he was pretty sure they were the ones smoking marijuana too. He just hoped they were distracted enough because to the right of the house he was behind was another clothesline with shirts, sheets, and pants. Even if they didn't fit, he and his brother needed some damn clothes to blend in.

His phone had been in the van and though they hadn't brought any identification with them, their wallets and cash had been left behind when they'd shifted forms. Whoever that blond bitch was, she was going to pay. Not that she was at the top of his list of problems now. He hadn't realized the fae were after them too. Or at least involved. He'd heard enough horror stories to know they could be scary motherfuckers when they wanted. Seeing that female shoot lightning out of her freaking hands was all the proof he needed to know it was true.

Glancing at his brother, he frowned. Malcolm was barely moving, but he was awake. "I'll be right back," he whispered.

Crouching down again, he kept low as he hurried to the next home. After another scan of the surrounding area, he jumped the brick wall. His bare foot slammed onto a broken beer bottle and it sliced deep into the arch. Biting back a groan, he yanked the piece of glass out. Blood trickled off his foot but he was already healing as he limped toward the clothesline. Luckily the clothes from the other yard a few houses down blocked what he was doing from the humans he could still hear laughing. As someone cranked up the music, he pulled off two button-down flannel shirts

that had seen better days. They were clearly work
shirts. He also grabbed a pair of jeans and one pair of
work pants that would definitely be too short. Better
than nothing.

He found his brother still huddled in the small alcove, but at least his eyes were open and Chris could see
awareness in them. "Shift, Malcolm. We need to get the
hell out of here." Chris kept his voice low, not wanting
to disturb the humans. He wanted to leave before anyone noticed the missing clothes and started raising hell.

His brother growled low in his throat as he shifted
back to his human form, but the music drowned it
out. Or even if it didn't, the humans didn't seem to
notice.

Malcolm's teeth were chattering and his entire body
shook as he grabbed the clothes Chris gave him. Outwardly he didn't look as bad as Chris had expected. A
large bruise the size of a baseball had formed in the
middle of his chest. The ugly black and purple coloring
was sharp against his skin.

As soon as they were dressed, they slowly made
their way to the end of the road. Right now Chris had
no idea if they were being tracked. His senses were all
screwed up and even though he could smell, he was
rattled beyond belief. This hadn't been part of their
plan. Too many people were involved and his brother
was no use at all. He could barely talk after what that
fae had done to him. If he'd been pure human, Malcolm would be dead.

The street ran right into a four-lane road lined with
closed businesses, where at least a dozen people were

loitering. Some he guessed were prostitutes, others drug dealers, and there was a string of vehicles parked along the curb for the next three blocks. Some of them looked as if they hadn't been moved for a decade.

"Stay here," he murmured to his brother, who crouched low and leaned against the brick wall.

Malcolm wrapped his arms around his knees as he brought them up to his chest. If anyone saw him they'd assume he was a homeless person. Just as well.

Keeping his head low, Chris stepped out onto the cracked sidewalk and headed east. With no shoes and pants that were too short, he looked ridiculous but the few people he passed didn't notice or even glance at him. When he passed an older-model Datsun with yellow peeling paint and the keys still in the ignition, he didn't even pause. He glanced around, didn't see anyone in the immediate vicinity—though the front door to a brick townhome with busted-out windows was open—and jumped in.

Pulling away, he flipped a U-turn and picked up his brother. Malcolm curled on his side as he collapsed against the passenger seat. Just great. Now he had to take care of him too. As Chris drove, he opened the center console and was surprised to find three cell phones inside. Whoever owned the car was probably a drug dealer or into something illegal to have that many phones.

Whatever. At least he didn't have to find a pay phone now. He dialed LaPomeret's cell phone.

Bastard finally picked up on the fourth ring. His voice was hesitant. "Hello?"

"I couldn't get the female and I think we might have a problem."

"Oh, we most certainly have a problem. Angus Campbell is now after me and the enforcer knows that I'm somehow involved in all this."

Chris wanted to snort at the way he said "this" as if he was somehow detached from it. Vamp didn't want to get his hands dirty, but he had no problem paying for the product. "How the hell do they know you're involved? Did you give them my name?"

"No, but I unknowingly attacked his only son. He was with that enforcer bitch and he angered me."

The giant with Erin was Angus Campbell's son? Fucking great. Like he didn't have enough problems already. "My brother and I are leaving town and I suggest you do the same if Campbell knows who you are." Chris didn't actually care about the vamp, but the guy was a paying customer. Maybe they'd be able to do business again. While he'd planned to kill Erin, things were way too hot now. And his own brother couldn't even back him up—and he had no clue how long these effects would last. He would still get her though. In time. He was patient and had no problem waiting to end her life.

"What are you going to do with the females?" LaPomeret asked.

He snorted. "What do you think?" Chris took a sharp left, but kept to the speed limit. No need to draw any undue attention.

"Sell them to me and my partners." There was an underlying note of desperation in his voice he couldn't disguise.

"You know what kind of risk I'd be taking? Besides, I don't have a way to transport them anymore." Not after he'd lost their van. Killing them would be easiest. He just needed to get to their place on the outskirts of town, kill the females, kill his assistant, and disappear. Things might not have worked out the way he'd planned but they had a lot of money and he could still make more.

"I have an SUV you can use."

Chris gritted his teeth and glanced over at his shaking brother. They could make so much money, then retire for good. Live the way they wanted with no Alpha or pack breathing down their necks. People respected money. "It'll cost you for the women."

LaPomeret sighed. "I *know*. Meet me at Barrett's house. We are all hiding out here until we know more about this enforcer. Campbell has nothing against Barrett and I have no tie to him so we will be safe. Pick up the vehicle here and use it to bring the females to us. He has a dungeon where we can keep them."

Chris wanted to say no, but that kind of money . . . "I'll want half up front. Cash. I'm taking a huge risk."

There was a short pause. "Fine. Half up front."

He had no doubt that LaPomeret was good for it. The vamp had more money than God. "Good. And get some clothes together for me and Malcolm. I'll be there in an hour." He wanted to drive around for a while and if possible switch vehicles. He needed to make sure they weren't being followed. Leading a tracker back to the vamps he dealt with would be almost as bad as leading them back to his hideout where the pregnant females were.

When he pulled up to another stoplight, he texted his assistant to start packing up the house. Chris would be killing the guy soon but he might as well get some labor out of him before then. It would save him some extra steps when he and Malcolm split town.

Chapter 16

Feeling nauseous, Erin motioned to the others to follow her down the sidewalk as she waited for Ryan to answer her call. The police had moved back in, taking over the crime scene once again. Considering what she'd just discovered, she didn't need anything from the scene anymore.

Her mind was working overtime as she tried to come to terms with the reality that her ex was behind the kidnappings. And likely the bombing at Screamers. Two blond-haired lupine shifters, one who wore a wolf ring—just like Meli and that vamp from Screamers had described. Yeah, that was definitely them. And shit . . . probably one of the blond wolves who'd attacked Noah too. She'd have to get a picture from Ryan.

As soon as he picked up, she didn't give him a chance to speak. "I think I know who's behind the kidnappings. Their names are Chris and Malcolm Tyson. They used to belong to Adam Murphy's pack." Just like she had.

After almost a year of being terrified of her own fucking shadow she'd finally worked up the courage to ask Jayce to look into the Murphy pack for her a couple of months ago and he'd come through with some information. Which wasn't as much as she'd have liked.

The first time Jayce and she had met he'd thought she was dead because Murphy had reported her as such. Knowing how she'd been found—so close to death behind that damn Dumpster—Jayce had thought her Alpha might have had something to do with it. But he hadn't. No, just Chris and Malcolm Tyson.

According to Jayce's report, the brothers had split town as soon as they'd told Adam Murphy a bullshit story about her being killed by vamps. Of course, Murphy hadn't actually believed them and had tried to hunt them down himself, but he hadn't had any luck. It was a big damn world and he had only so many resources. Maybe if he'd reported them to the Council back then the bastards would have been hunted down, but Murphy had only had suspicions, no proof—she knew all this only because of Jayce. And in reality, without real proof, there was little the Council could have done back then.

Right about now Erin wished she'd been strong enough to report them for dealing vampire blood and for trying to kill her. Maybe then they wouldn't have come to New Orleans. But she'd been so damn afraid of everything and even though she'd healed physically fairly quickly, her emotional scars were *still* there. They hurt worse than the physical ones had because they simply wouldn't go away. The only time they seemed to fade was around Noah.

"Those their real names?" Ryan asked.

"Yeah." She loved that he didn't even ask if she was sure they were involved. Ryan trusted her and now she prayed he could work his magic.

"You know their socials?"

Her file on them was in her laptop, but . . . "Is Jayce at the ranch?"

"Yeah."

"He's got them both—from a different investigation." Okay, not exactly an investigation but she didn't have time for semantics. "Send me their pictures too when you get a chance."

"Fuck yeah," Ryan muttered. "That's all I need. Give me twenty minutes and I'll see what I can come up with." Then he disconnected.

Erin leaned against her car, wrapping her arms around herself as she looked at three questioning pairs of eyes.

"You know the identities of the shifters behind this?" Brianna asked.

Erin nodded, but kept her gaze on Noah who was watching her intently. "Remember what I told you about . . . who hurt me?"

Noah's eyes went pure wolf, his entire body going impossibly still. "Yeah." That one word was guttural and deep.

"His name is Chris and his brother is Malcolm. I guess selling vampire blood wasn't enough for them. I scented them at the scene." Her voice cracked on the last word but she held Noah's gaze. "They're here. No doubt about it. They're afraid too—probably because of what Brianna did to them. Considering what they used to be into, kidnapping shifters for their blood isn't a stretch for them." Because they clearly didn't give a shit about anyone or anything. Chris had tried to kill her, someone he'd supposedly loved.

A myriad of emotions flashed through Noah's beautiful eyes before he suddenly turned away from her. Letting out an eerie howl, he let his claws extend and slashed through the nearest tree, tearing away the bark like it was paper. Then he went still again, but kept his back to her. His breathing was erratic and unsteady and she couldn't decide if she should reach out for him or not.

"These guys are the ones who hurt you?" Angelo's deep voice and question took her by surprise.

She didn't know him as well as Noah and some of the others from her pack, but he'd been there the day she'd been found. And clearly hadn't forgotten. Nodding, she faced them. Brianna just looked confused, but Angelo looked ready to murder.

"They're dead. No matter what happens with this investigation, they will die," Noah said as he turned back toward them, his wolf right at the surface. Then he hauled her into his arms, pulling her close, practically crushing her.

She didn't care if she appeared weak. The realization that the monsters from her past were not only in the same city, but were the ones behind the terrible kidnappings and murder, had stunned her. She didn't know how to compartmentalize her feelings now. It felt as if a year of pushing down that pain and agony had finally rushed to the surface and was taking over. All because of two bastards who deserved to die.

Who would die. But by her hand. Not Noah's or Angelo's. She was going to end this.

She wasn't sure how much time passed, but Noah eventually let her go. Turning her face away from Brianna and Angelo, she wiped away the tears that had welled up. She'd cried enough to last a lifetime over everything she'd lost. Now wasn't the time.

Clearing her throat, she faced everyone. As she did, her phone buzzed, signaling she had a text. It was a picture from Ryan. She pulled it up and her throat tightened, making it hard to breathe. There in color were photos of Chris and Malcolm. Both so handsome and charming-looking that it made her want to scream and claw their faces off. She held her phone out to Noah. "You recognize either of them?"

He instantly nodded, a growl building low in his throat. "That one."

He pointed to Malcolm. Erin forced her own wolf back down. For daring to attempt to hurt Noah, Erin would kill them both and enjoy it. The darkness that pushed up inside her at the thought surprised her, but she didn't deny the truth, even to herself. Ending these two would be doing the world a favor.

She glanced back down the street to where the cops were. They were talking to some of the neighbors, but it looked as if they'd be pulling out soon. Erin didn't want to just wait here while they waited for Ryan. It might take him longer than he thought. She started to suggest they all leave when her phone rang.

Seeing his name on the screen, she answered immediately. "Tell me you have good news."

His half laugh was arrogant. "I am a fucking genius,

which you already know. I'm pretty sure I have their address."

Hope burst inside her, the feeling overwhelming. "Their address?"

"Maybe. With their socials it was easy to dig into their financials. I linked a transfer to their bank account from a company—which turned out to be a shell company—to some real estate purchases. The purchases aren't bogus though. In the past year a company called Aude Toys has bought three residential places, but they went to a lot of trouble to hide those purchases."

Erin liked where this was going. "And?"

"And, each purchase has coincided with a rash of pregnant shifters going missing in that particular city. The last purchase was a home right on the outskirts of New Orleans and—"

"Give me the address." She was more than appreciative of Ryan's hard work, but didn't have time to hear anything else. More important, the missing females didn't have the time. Chris could be on his way to kill them right now.

Ryan rattled it off. When he was done she asked him to hold on and relayed it to Angelo and Brianna though she was sure Angelo had already heard everything. Then she looked at Brianna pointedly. "We need you as backup, especially if these females are barely hanging on. Do you have enough energy to help heal them if necessary?"

She nodded. "More than enough."

Erin frowned and glanced over her shoulder at the detective coming toward them. He might be a problem if he wanted to keep Brianna around. As if she read her mind, Brianna smiled. "I can take care of him with a little mental persuasion."

Angelo nodded. "We'll be right behind you."

"Good." She looked at Noah whose expression was intense. "You ready?"

"Hell yeah."

"You find anything else?" she asked Ryan as she tossed her keys to Noah. Right now she was too edgy and he was more familiar with the city and outlying areas. She could give up control if it helped her get centered.

Noah looked surprised, but didn't argue as he slid into the driver's seat and she hurried to the passenger side.

"Just that all the shifters taken in the past had no Alphas or packs or anyone to look out for them. Something we already knew." Ryan's voice was tight and angry.

She sighed and prayed this would be the end of the Tyson brothers' reign of terror. "Thanks, Ryan. I'll contact you later and let you know what happens."

"Get those bastards," he growled.

After a few minutes of driving in silence, Noah spoke. "Are you going to be able to handle this?"

She wanted to be offended by the question, but it was valid. A chill snaked through her as she thought of facing off with Chris. Of looking into the eyes of the man who had taken so much from her. "Yeah, it's just . . . the thought of seeing him again. It's hard." That being the understatement of the century. But she would do it. For herself and all the females and families he'd ripped apart with his evil and greed.

Noah's claws unsheathed and he tore through the leather of her steering wheel. He cursed, then muttered, "Sorry."

Erin didn't care about the damage. Especially not now. "If we can take him down I want to, but if it comes down to the females' safety or getting him, I'm willing to let him go. For now." Something she'd never thought she'd say, much less truly mean. But it was true. Yes, she desperately wanted to stop him so that no one else could suffer because of him, but she wouldn't let any more innocents get hurt in the process.

"If I get the chance, I'm killing him." Noah's voice was so resolute, it stunned her.

"Noah . . ." Erin didn't know what to say to that. She wouldn't order him not to. By Council law she had the authority to make the decision how things should be handled. There would be no trial for the Tyson brothers. They'd be eliminated for their crimes when they were caught. She didn't know if she wanted that blood on Noah's hands though.

When she didn't continue, Noah didn't push. There was nothing left to say anyway. They had weapons and two megasized first aid kits she'd been carrying since they left North Carolina. A gift courtesy of Jayce. She wasn't sure if they'd sustained any damage from the gunfire because she hadn't checked them after LaPomeret's men had opened fire on her car. Hopefully they wouldn't need the kits, not with Brianna's presence. But what she really hoped was that the women were at the address alive and healthy.

Chapter 17

Noah steered down the long, dirt path surrounded by the forest. When Ryan had given them the address Noah had recognized the name of the area. He'd lived in New Orleans a hell of a long time and while some things changed, a lot didn't. There were only three homes along Clear Wood Bayou Road. And it wasn't exactly a road. Especially when it rained heavy.

Tonight was dry, windy, and getting colder. The cold didn't bother him but it felt like an omen or something. Especially with the near-full moon gleaming high in the sky. The chill in the air was downright icy and foreboding. Erin had been tense and quiet the majority of the drive, but the bitter scent she exuded was killing his inner wolf.

He just wanted to gather her in his arms and do something for her, but knew that was impossible at the moment. Bringing the Tyson brothers down was the only thing that would give Erin any sort of lasting peace. She may be willing to let them go if necessary but Noah wasn't so sure he could. They'd tried to kill the woman he loved—and loving her was something he could finally admit to himself. He'd feared that if he put the thought out into the universe it would somehow curse his chance with Erin. Paranoid? Absolutely. But shifters were a superstitious bunch and he was no different, especially when it came to his female. The more he thought about everything that had been done to her, the more restless his inner wolf grew.

Yeah, these bastards were dying.

When he neared the turnoff to the next dirt path that would lead to their final destination he pulled off the road into a cluster of gnarled cypress trees. He pulled up far enough so that Brianna could move in behind him. She'd apparently made fast work of convincing that detective to let them go because she and Angelo had caught up to them within minutes.

Erin patted her coat, her subconscious act of checking her blades, then tugged on her black knit skullcap to cover her head. Her short red braid peeked out the back, secured by a black elastic hair band.

She glanced at Noah, her gray eyes a mercurial storm. "You think we should strap on more weapons?"

"Maybe we can give some to Brianna just in case but I'm probably going wolf if we're attacked." He understood that Erin likely wouldn't unless things got too insane. She had a tight grasp on her inner wolf. So much so that it impressed the hell out of him. He'd seen her fight in animal form only once and it had been beautiful and terrifying at the same time. Compared to other warriors she was smaller in animal form but damn vicious. And he found that incredibly hot. He could never be with a beta or . . . anyone who wasn't Erin.

She nodded and exited the vehicle. Brianna and Angelo were both already out of theirs and Angelo looked pumped and ready for a fight. The bronze-skinned shifter's hazel eyes had gone completely wolf, his animal lurking right at the surface.

Noah rolled his shoulders once, trying to ease some of the tension out, but it was useless. He glanced at Erin. "What's the plan?"

She eyed Brianna. "Do you need any weapons?"

The blond female smiled and her blue eyes flashed darkly, mirroring the brief spark of energy from her hands. "No." Damn, even her voice was a little deeper.

All right then.

Erin looked between them and Noah. "When we come up on the house we need to surround it. I'm going to take the back, Noah will take a window on the east side, Angelo the west, and, Brianna, you either go in the front door, but a front window will be preferable. If we can't breach it quietly, we'll storm it all at once."

Ryan had sent them a satellite photo using Google Earth and an architectural layout of the house, though God only knew where he'd gotten *that*. Not for the first time was Noah thankful Ryan was on their side. The man could be an absolute menace with his skills.

Next Erin held out her hand so they could all take earpieces. "These are for us to communicate with. Keep them in at all times. Don't use them if you don't have to."

Technically, three of them wouldn't even need these in such a contained area, but if they got separated or one of them ended up in a chase, these would come in handy. And Brianna didn't have any of their extrasensory abilities so they would be useful for her.

Angelo took his with a grin. "Getting fancy, short stuff."

Erin smiled back, though her expression was tight as she put her own piece in. "Remember. Silence from this point on unless you absolutely have to break it."

Noah understood why. This was her first mission and a lot was riding on this besides her reputation. Add in the personal issues. . . . Noah took his own earpiece. It was time to go to work.

Putting in his own piece, he fell in step with Erin as they trekked through the woods. They had maybe forty or fifty yards until they would reach a clearing that would lead to the front of the house. When the woods began to thin, Noah concentrated but couldn't hear any heartbeats. At the clearing, they all remained hidden in the shadows of the trees. It was a brick, two-story home that had probably been repaired or completely rebuilt since Katrina. There wasn't a vehicle in the driveway but there could be one in the garage. Noah couldn't see any movement inside, but that didn't mean no one was in there. According to Meli, she and the other pregnant shifters had been kept in a dungeon/prisonlike area in cages. They could be underground or something.

Erin made a hand signal and they all spread out. Brianna was the only one who remained in place. Because she wasn't as fast as the shifters, she would be entering from the front. It was closer to the clearing and wouldn't be as much ground for her to cover.

Noah raced along the edge of the woods, moving in

a circular pattern until he was on the east side of the home. A few long moments later he barely heard Erin's "Now" command through his earpiece.

He flew toward the house, a blur of motion, and crouched right under one of the curtain-covered windows. Under other circumstances they would have done a lot more recon but women's lives were at stake. There was no time and working on the fly was what had to happen. While the hunter in him hated that they weren't being as thorough as possible, his human side understood. Before attempting to break in, he tried pushing on it and was surprised when the pane slid open.

Shaking his head, Noah checked for a tripwire or any other kind of trap. When he was certain it was safe, he eased the curtain fully back. He could scent that at least three, maybe four shifters had been in the room, but none of the smells were recent.

The room was completely empty except for an unused stone fireplace in the corner. His shoes barely made a sound as they touched the hardwood floor. There were two exits. One open entryway that looked as if it led to the front of the house. Maybe a dining room. The other was on the opposite side and the two French doors appeared as if they opened into the back part of the house. A porch. As he cautiously took a couple of steps, three familiar scents surrounded him. Erin and Brianna came in from the front open entry and Angelo followed a moment later.

Erin's face was tense, but there was an eager quality about her. She pointed behind herself and he could tell she was barely containing her excitement. It was rolling off of her in waves.

Tensing, he let his claws unsheathe. If he had to go wolf, it would be quick. They quietly moved through the house, passing first through what would have been a dining room. There was a card table with three chairs around it and three stacked plastic bins he guessed were being used for moving. One of the lids was half off revealing folded clothes. The shifter scent coming from it was unmistakable.

As they moved into the kitchen in single file, Erin pointed toward a door. That's when he scented it. Other shifters. Not his kind, but feline. It was so faint that if someone had been cooking in the kitchen, it would have overpowered the scent.

Erin tried the door but it was locked. He'd showed her how to jimmy a lock before, but he could do it a lot faster. When she looked at him with raised eyebrows, he retrieved his slim kit from one of his cargo pockets and bent down. It was a dead bolt, but not a problem for him. A few seconds later, the lock sprung free.

The sound seemed to reverberate like a gong in the mostly bare kitchen. Tensing, they all froze and waited. No one came barreling out from behind the door. There was no scuffling sound, just silence.

Easing the door open, he peered in to find a set of stairs. At the bottom a dim lightbulb cast an eerie glow. The scent of the felines hit him stronger now.

Erin hurried past him, one of her blades gripped tightly in her hand as she descended the stairs. She wielded it like it was an extension of her.

Noah hated going in blind anywhere but more than that, he hated that Erin was going first. It was ingrained in him to protect anyone weaker. Of course, she wasn't weaker. Not even a little bit. But she was still his to claim and protect as far as his wolf was concerned. Reining in those urges, he kept his wolf in check and let her do her job.

Behind him, he barely heard Angelo and Brianna moving. The fae might not have their extrasensory abilities but she was stealth personified too.

Erin reached the end, then peered around the corner. First to the left, then the right. She sucked in a breath, then let out a curse as she sheathed her blades. Glancing back at them, she nodded. "They're here. Come on."

As Noah followed, his eyes widened when he saw the row of cages along one wall in the basement. They were barely large enough for the females to stand up in, but it didn't appear as if the females had been beaten or abused in any other way. Looks could be deceiving but they were all clothed and he could hear heartbeats. Two steady, two not so much. The females hadn't moved or said a word though. They were all almost preternaturally silent and they all had blindfolds on.

They were probably hoping whoever had come down here would leave them alone. Noah bit back a growl. Yeah, he'd take pleasure in hurting those who had taken these females.

Erin hurried to one of the cages and ripped the door off. He did the same, as did Angelo. The female in the cage Noah had taken apart stirred against her cot.

"I'm not going to hurt you," he said as gently as he could.

The female on the cot whimpered but still didn't move.

Instead of stepping into the cage, he remained where he was. Her hands weren't bound so clearly she'd been convinced that taking off her blindfold wasn't a good idea. "Your name is Lorena, right?" Noah recognized her from one of Erin's photos. She was about five months along in her pregnancy, the furthest out of all the females.

She shifted positions and sat up but still didn't remove her blindfold.

"You can take off the blindfold. We've been sent by the Council and the Campbell pack to save you."

"It's true, Lorena." A soft, unfamiliar voice cut through the air.

He turned to find that Erin had her arms around a tall, lean Hispanic shifter he recognized as Leta—the bartender Hector's sister. On her other side was a female he recognized as Concha. An artist originally from Cuba, according to her file.

At those words, the woman took off her blindfold and blinked. Her midnight blue eyes flashed with hope. Noah held out an arm to her and she started bawling. Collapsing against him, she sobbed into his chest. Afraid to hold her too tight, he stepped back so they were completely free of the cage and held her close.

Erin gave him a soft look but frowned when Angelo couldn't get the last woman up. Noah tensed too, but didn't move because he didn't want to disturb Lorena. Before either of them could say anything, Brianna was kneeling next to the cot, placing her hand on the woman's chest. A green glow emanated from her, spreading across the pregnant shifter's body, engulfing it completely.

"We need to get them out of here," Noah said quietly, his gaze on Erin.

"I know." She looked at Leta who seemed to be the steadiest of them all. "Who watches you normally?"

"A human male. He's creepy but he doesn't say much to us. Just feeds us, drugs us, and tells us to shut up if one of us is crying too much." There was a note of venom in her voice.

"Where is he?"

She shrugged. "I'm not sure. He received a call from one of those shifter bastards who took us. Told him that they'd be leaving soon and to pack up. I guess he went out for supplies or something."

As if on cue, they all heard a scuffling sound upstairs. Though Noah hated to let go of Lorena, he didn't pause. He raced up the stairs and eased the door open. A man was mumbling to himself about wanting more compensation. Inhaling, Noah scented only one person. A human. He stank of tobacco and alcohol. Whiskey, to be specific. His shoes thudded loudly against the hardwood floor.

Noah sensed Erin come up behind him. He turned a fraction. "Want to play good cop, bad cop?" he whispered, so low that no one but her could hear without earpieces. When her eyes lit up with understanding he was glad he didn't have to explain what he meant.

Not that he'd worried much about that. He and Erin were almost always on the same wavelength.

Her grin was wicked as she clutched her blade. Too bad he planned to play bad cop. She might be the enforcer but to this human she was still a petite female.

He plucked the knit skullcap off her head. Without it she looked less threatening.

Though she scowled at him, he didn't have time to explain as he tucked it into his back pocket. Noah could hear the human moving through the house, his loud steps practically a homing beacon for his exact location. Turning from Erin, Noah silently crept through the kitchen.

The footsteps were coming closer, closer. . . . Noah jumped out from the entryway.

A dark-haired male about six feet tall with two grocery bags in his hands stared at him. His head snapped back, his green eyes wide with surprise. Noah didn't give him a chance to let his body catch up with his mind. Grabbing him around the throat, he slammed him against the nearest wall. His claws extended farther, digging into the man's flesh. The two bags thudded to the floor.

"What do you want?" the man whispered, the acrid stench of fear pulsing off him. He grabbed at Noah's wrist, so Noah tightened his hold.

"Let go or I'll rip out your jugular."

The man slackened his hold but his entire body was tense, his fear growing even stronger.

"Where are the two shifters you're working for?" Noah growled, his voice more animal than man.

"Don't . . . know," he gasped out.

"Let him go so he can talk." Erin's voice was soothing and melodic, but Noah didn't miss the underlying steel edge. She placed a soft hand on his forearm. "Come on. He's not important. We just need the names of his bosses."

She looked at the human, her eyes big and guileless. Damn she was good. Noah loosened his grip, letting the man slide down the wall. He collapsed on the floor, huffing and trying to drag air into his lungs.

Erin knelt in front of him. "I'm really sorry about my friend. We just want to know where Chris and Malcolm Tyson are and we'll let you go." She sounded so earnest, as if she really meant it.

The guy glared at her, then spit in her face. Before Noah could think about moving, Erin slammed a fist into his stomach before wiping it off. Already on the floor, he coughed and sputtered and fell to his back. Moving fast, Erin was on her feet. She placed her booted foot over the guy's crotch. "Guess this is going to be 'bad cop, bad cop,'" she said to Noah, her attention still on the male. "I don't give a shit who you are or why you're helping out the Tyson brothers. My guess is money."

The man's eyes flared in acknowledgment.

"I'll take that as a yes," she continued. Pressing her boot down on his balls, she grinned wickedly at him while he yelped in pain. "I don't want to know a damn thing about you. Not your name, where you come from. Nothing. Just tell me where the brothers are and I swear I won't hurt or kill you. I give you my word as one of the enforcers for the North American Council of lupine shifters."

His eyes widened at that. "You work for the Council?"

She nodded once.

"You swear you won't hurt me? What about him?" the human gasped out, strain clear on his face.

She sighed, as if it pained her to agree. "I swear Noah won't hurt or kill you either. We only care about information. If you don't have any, you're useless and I'll kill you where you lie. I have the females downstairs. They're safe and I'll be taking them home soon. I don't need the Tyson brothers right now. I want them brought to justice, but I don't need them to close this case. As a matter of fact, it will be easier to kill you since you don't know shit. Trust me, I'm doing you a favor. The Tyson brothers have a habit of killing anyone they work with when they leave town. And I know from experience they don't like to make it quick."

Noah inwardly grinned at how smoothly she lied to the guy. They had no idea whether or not the brothers killed those they worked with—though she was probably right.

Erin pointedly glanced around the bare room as she pulled out her other blade. The moonlight from one of the windows gleamed off both her weapons.

"No! I . . . I might know where they are. They sell to some really rich vamps and I don't know if that's where they're going but . . . one of 'em texted me and told me to get the women ready. Said they'd be leaving in a couple hours but had to stop by a customer's house first."

"Whose house?" Erin growled.

"I'm not sure but they've done business with François LaPomeret and Gervais Barrett. Both scary as shit and richer than God. I heard the brothers talking a few times and put two and two together when I heard the vampires' names. I've lived here all my life and I know who both of them vamps are . . . and where they live," he rushed on.

Erin sheathed one blade but kept the other in her hand. She pointed it at the human's neck and pressed down harder on his crotch with her boot as she looked at Noah. She didn't say anything, but she raised her eyebrows.

The guy did know the name of LaPomeret and Noah couldn't smell the metallic scent common with lies over the guy's blatant fear so maybe he was telling the truth. Noah looked at the human. "What's Barrett's address?"

"No way." He swallowed hard as his gaze flicked back and forth between them. "I'll take you there and then leave. His place is in the Garden District."

In other words, this human didn't trust them and thought he had a better chance of getting away once they reached their destination. Maybe he thought in a semi-public place he'd be safer.

Erin pulled back her blade. "Fine." She looked at Noah again. "Search him and strip him of his phone. I'll meet you out front in a minute."

Noah yanked him to his feet as soon as Erin removed her boot. Erin might have promised this guy that neither she nor Noah would harm him, but he didn't believe for one second that she was letting this guy walk away unscathed. The human had been part of this operation and would undoubtedly pay.

Chapter 18

Erin drove down the cobblestone street, eyeing the giant stone wall covered in ivy surrounding a palatial home in the Garden District. She couldn't see any of the house thanks to the wall, but she could scent vampires. Noah had already told her he saw the heat signature of one crouching in one of the oak trees. She'd always thought that was a cool ability he had. So whoever was in there, they definitely cared about security. Instead of stopping, she kept driving and only when she was three blocks away and out of sight did she park on the curb in front of a historic landmark home. One of the former presidents had lived in it. Not that any of that concerned her. She just knew that no one was living there now.

She and Noah both got out and left the human, whose name they'd learned was Ray Gans, in the car. They'd restrained his wrists behind his back and shoved him onto the floorboards. He couldn't overpower them but they hadn't wanted to worry about him trying to flag someone down. Her windows were tinted anyway, but she'd wanted to be careful. He'd been vague about where to go until they were actually in the Garden District. He was being pretty smart, but nothing would save him. She'd had Ryan run his records while they were driving and the guy had a long criminal record. More proof that the human court systems were utterly broken. This guy never should have been let out of jail.

As she rounded the car to meet Noah, he tensed, glancing up and down the cracked sidewalk. Erin knew that he scented Hector because she did too, but she'd expected the feline. "Chill, it's just Hector."

Noah's gaze narrowed at her as he looked around again. "Why?"

"I texted him to pick up Ray and my car." She didn't need to leave her bullet-riddled vehicle out in public view for long, but her main concern was Ray.

"Hector will kill him." Noah's words were a fact.

"I know." She glanced up at a sudden sound and saw Hector drop from one of the oak trees. Damn felines were always climbing stuff.

He landed on the sidewalk with a grace only found in feline shifters. Hector nodded once at Noah, then looked at Erin. "My sister is truly okay?" His voice shook even though his question was quiet.

Erin nodded and glanced around. She didn't see anyone but that didn't mean they were alone. She looked at Noah questioningly.

Reading her expression, Noah shook his head. "I can't see any heat signatures other than some humans through open windows."

Her focus returned to Hector. "Brianna is transporting them back to Angus's compound as we speak and Angelo is waiting at the house in case the brothers return. Wait until the females are at the compound before contacting the other families. I don't want anyone getting wind that they're gone yet." She still had no clue if the brothers were even at the house they'd just driven by. Their scent had been damn strong, but they could have left recently. She and Noah were about to find out.

Hector's eyes burned with the need for vengeance. "What do you need from me?"

She patted the hood of the car. "The human male who's been helping the Tyson brothers keep the pregnant females captive is in here. I swore to him that neither me nor Noah would harm him. And since I always keep my word, I thought I'd hand him over to you."

Hector's eyes went pure jaguar. "Where are your keys?" he asked, his voice rough and animalistic.

She held them out to him but didn't ask any questions. What he and the other families did to the kidnapper was their business and she had too much to do. "Leave my car at Angus's place and don't get any blood in it."

After he nodded and started purposefully around the hood, she looked at Noah. "Ready?"

His expression grim, he said, "Yep."

Without a backward glance they headed down the sidewalk. There wasn't time to wait for backup. Not when they could be closing in on the people responsible for these heinous acts.

"You sure that was the right choice?" Noah asked quietly as they jogged down the sidewalk.

"No." She wasn't sure at all, but she wasn't turning this guy over to the humans. They'd had enough chances to keep this monster locked up. And she wasn't dragging any of the females into a trial. Besides, humans were happy enough letting shifters deal with shifter crimes. This case was odd in that a human had been helping shifters commit crimes. He could claim the brothers coerced or threatened him or a bunch of other things. He hadn't actually harmed the females. Hell, he'd been the one to feed them. Any defense attorney could make enough reasonable doubt and if there were antiparanormal people on the jury, this guy would walk easy.

Noah didn't respond and she was grateful. She didn't need to second-guess her decision right now. Not in the middle of a mission. Maybe it had been wrong, maybe not, but the choice was made.

When they were a block away, he spoke again. "My father said he could be here in twenty minutes with his warriors." Noah had texted Angus five minutes before.

"We're not waiting." She couldn't. She was too damn close to bringing the Tyson brothers down. It didn't matter that she'd told that human male she could close the case without them.

She wouldn't.

If the Tyson boys escaped now she'd end up hunting them down later. And how many more innocents would be hurt in the meantime? She wasn't willing to sacrifice other lives.

"Good." Noah's response surprised her, but she was glad for it.

Instead of heading directly down the sidewalk toward the mansion owned by Gervais Barrett, they cut down another street and came around the back. They darted through the yard of another mansion clearly owned by humans. There was a wrought iron fence around the yard that shifters would consider pure decoration. Even at seven feet, she and Noah scaled it with ease. There weren't any lights on in the two-story home or surrounding the expansive yard so she and Noah stuck to the shadows and crept around back. An Olympic-sized pool with a light gleaming below the turquoise surface and a pool house took up most of the yard that was bordered by the high stone wall of Barrett's backyard.

She and Noah paused in the shadows, using the pool house as cover. Erin could see well in the dark, but Noah could see heat signatures. Right now she spotted one individual on top of the wall to the far west end of it. The man was crouched low and visually scanning. When he turned in their direction they ducked back behind the pool house. She'd also spotted a man in one of the trees. It looked as if his back was turned to them, but she couldn't be sure and there was no guarantee he'd stay turned around.

She nudged Noah who held up two fingers, then a V symbol. Two vampires. Then he held up his fist indicating zero other individuals were visible.

Visible being the key word. They knew there had to be more vamps behind that wall. They just couldn't see them yet.

Erin nodded, then pointed at herself and made hand signals indicating she'd take the one in the tree. She'd have to double back and come at him from another angle. Noah shook his head and leaned in close so that his breath was hot against her ear. She fought the shiver that rolled over her.

"I'm a better climber," he whispered so low she almost didn't make out the words.

Though she wanted to argue, he was right. Whereas she was fast with a blade and fast in general, he could scale a tree like a damn feline.

She nodded and held up one finger, then tapped her watch. Their signal that he had one minute to backtrack, then come hard at the other vamp. This way they'd move on both individuals at the same time. They needed to take out any outside guards before infiltrating the house.

He was gone in an instant, blending into the shadows like a ghost. Erin ticked off the seconds and when a minute passed, she peeked out from the pool house. The vamp was turned to the side, showing her his profile.

Instead of her blade, she withdrew one of the tranquilizer guns she'd strapped to her ankle earlier. Since they didn't know the situation yet or if this vamp was even involved, she and Noah had decided to use tranqs unless given no choice. She had enough of the weapons stored in her trunk for such an occasion. It was sick how many weapons Jayce had provided her with. *Always be prepared* was one of his mottos and she found she agreed.

Considering she'd scented the Tyson brothers when she'd driven by, something told her the vamp who owned the house was up to his neck in the plot.

When the guard turned and made another visual

scan, she used her small window of opportunity. Racing at him in complete silence, she used all her lower-body strength as she jumped onto a wooden patio table.

As her boots hit the table he turned, but it was too late. She used the flat surface as a springboard and launched at him. Gun raised, she fired two shots right into his neck.

His eyes flashed amber, and then the color fizzled to black as he toppled off the wall. If Jayce was right, he'd be down for half an hour. Should give them enough time to get in and out. If not, well, she'd deal with that later.

Catching the wall with her free hand, she tucked the weapon into the front of her pants, latched on with both hands and swung herself to the top. Crouching much like the downed vamp had done, she quickly scanned the yard. One man was down by the tree.

Quick work, Noah, she thought with approval.

There were two more that she could see patrolling. Only one had seen her. He didn't say a word though. Just hissed and ran at her. He was almost completely silent as he flew across the grass. Without pause, she jumped down and fired at him.

His head jerked back as if he'd run into a brick wall when the tranq hit his neck. Damn, that one worked fast. She landed with a thud and stayed in her crouch. The vampire's hand flew to his neck as he stumbled back. His eyes lit up like a freaking Christmas tree, then did the same thing the first vamp's had done. The color faded to black and down he went.

She couldn't see Noah and as she looked around the

yard with overgrown trees and bushes, panic slid through her veins. What if he'd been hurt?

As she started creeping toward the tree where the vamp he'd taken out still lay motionless, Noah appeared out of the shadows, all darkness and stealth. She almost jumped at his presence.

He held up three fingers, then made a motion like he was cutting his throat. Three down. She nodded and held up two fingers.

Five vampires patrolling was normal for someone wealthy so she could only guess how many more were inside. She still had a few darts loaded and another gun strapped to her other ankle.

She and Noah made their way through a kitchen—clearly unused—and into a long hallway adorned with a lot of expensive-looking art. The lighting was dim, not that it mattered with her and Noah's eyesight.

Creeping along the Persian runner, they didn't make a sound. When they neared the end of the hallway, they both paused. She could scent an array of vampires and shifters. The Tyson brothers. Coldness seeped into her veins at the familiar, nauseating smell.

She heard male voices nearby. To the east of them. Maybe two rooms over. Straining, Erin tried to listen but heard only bits and pieces because of so many angry voices trying to talk over each other.

"Better come back with the females . . ." A voice she didn't recognize. Then something garbled but angry sounding. Then . . . "Nowhere you can hide . . . double-cross us."

"I'm taking a big risk! You should be thanking me." That was definitely Chris's voice. And the only confirmation she needed that the owner of this house was in on it.

That meant all the people who worked for him were liable for his actions. Vampire law. She might not be as well versed as she'd like on vamp rules and regulations but this one she knew well.

She immediately sheathed her tranq gun and pulled out her blades. Noah did the same, except for blades, and let his claws unsheathe. She knew she shouldn't be noticing, but dressed in all black, including his inky black hair, with his dark expression he looked like a fallen angel ready to kick ass. He'd never looked hotter.

Yeah, definitely not the time for her to be thinking about that.

Peering around the corner she spotted two guards standing outside a door. Two doors down. Her calculations were right.

They wore black suits that were probably custom-made and they weren't bothering to hide the fact that they were vamps since their fangs were showing. Though she was within her rights to kill these vamps she decided on the tranq gun again.

Looking at Noah, she made a motion letting him know what she planned so he retrieved his again too. On the count of two they both rounded the corner, weapons raised. They fired at almost the same time. She hit the one on the right, he took down the one on the left. Part of her hated to get used to working with Noah, but damn, the man was so capable it was hard not to get a rush that this male would always have her back.

The giant vamps fell so quickly and the sound of

their bodies hitting the floor might as well have been a bomb going off. It would have been the same as if Erin had gotten on a loudspeaker and announced their presence.

"What the hell?" a muted male voice said from behind the door.

Erin dropped her gun and whipped out her other blade as she and Noah covered the last couple of yards to the door. Before she blinked, Noah slammed the door in with his booted foot. It was definitely a thick, quality door but it splintered under the force.

Noah let out a growl as he and Erin swept into the room. She took everything in without blinking. Six vamps, dressed in clothes that screamed wealth. And two shifters. Malcolm looked as if he could barely stand, but Chris was there looking just as she remembered him.

He was a handsome man and knew how to pull off charm. Too bad a coldhearted monster lay beneath that thin veneer. Instead of fear as she'd expected, the only emotion that rolled through her was white-hot rage. She wanted to take off his head like she'd never wanted anything before. To watch him bleed out on the ground as he'd done to her. The darkness rising up in her scared the hell out of her, but she embraced it. She needed to be strong to take down the nest of vamps and shifters they'd just jumped into.

The vampires remained preternaturally still, eyeing her and Noah as they slowly separated and spread out. The room was elegant and lined with wall-to-wall bookshelves. Erin kept her back to one of the shelves while Noah did the same. While these vamps weren't visibly armed, she knew that each and every one of them was damn dangerous. If her assumptions were correct, they were all bloodborns. At least two of them were. She knew that from her files. The others she'd never seen before. If they were bloodborns, they were stronger and faster than made vamps. When they struck it wouldn't be with man-made weapons, but fangs and claws. For the first time in a long time she had to leash her wolf who desperately wanted to come out and fight.

"Why are you in my home?" one of the vamps demanded, clearly Gervais Barrett.

She flicked a glance at LaPomeret whose face was a furious red, then back to Barrett. "Don't ask stupid questions. We've taken out your guards and we'll give you *one* chance to surrender. Your own people can deal with you. I just want the Tyson brothers." Not exactly true, she'd deal with these monsters too. But first she wanted to see if their mates had been involved and if this ring was bigger than just the six of them.

Chris laughed, the harsh quality of it grating over her senses. His expression was dark and filled with unbridled hatred. "You stupid cunt. Why can't you just die?"

Before Erin could respond to his vicious words or even move, Noah flew across the room with a quickness that stunned her. Air brushed over her face as he tackled and slammed Chris's body into one of the bookshelves.

Then, all hell broke loose.

Chapter 19

One of the bookshelves splintered and cracked under the force of Noah slamming Chris into it. Erin wanted to jump into the fight and protect Noah, but as two vamps rushed at her with fangs gleaming and deadly claws flashing, she went into battle mode. Noah could take care of himself. She had to believe that if she wanted to stay focused. He was older and had been alive a long damn time. He hadn't gotten that way by sheer luck. Not in this violent world.

Dodging to the side, she avoided the sudden rush from the vamps. Without pause, she ran at one of the bookshelves and scaled it. The two males who'd originally come at her must have thought she was running because they gleefully cackled.

They sounded like something out of a bad horror flick. She resisted snorting in disgust at them. The framed leaf vintage lights that spanned out in a display similar to the ivy on Barrett's outer walls appeared sturdy. At least the base did. She sure hoped it was as she jumped from her high perch and grabbed on to one of the three lighting fixtures on the ceiling.

She grasped the mounted part, swung back, and used the momentum to turn her body into a weapon. Throwing herself at three vampires, she prepared to get ripped to shreds, knowing it would be worth it if she could pull off her plan.

Spreading her arms out wide, she angled her blades down on the two vamps flanking the middle one. With one vicious stroke she sliced off the head of the one on the right and nearly decapitated the one on the left. Warm wetness splashed her face but she ignored it. The sweet scent of vamp blood filled the air, adding to the horror of the battle.

As she tackled LaPomeret, the vamp in the middle, he sliced his claws into her. One hand grabbed her thigh and tore at her like she was paper. The other ripped into her waist.

Fire and agony erupted all over her body as she gritted her teeth and brought her knife down in the center of his chest. LaPomeret's eyes flickered to bright amber, but he stopped moving at least.

"Behind you!" Noah's shout rent the air.

Without looking, she rolled off him as one of the bloodborns sliced down with his claws, barely missing her and cutting across LaPomeret's jugular instead. Blood spurted everywhere.

Fighting through the burning pain in her wounds, Erin jumped to her feet and brought her blade down on the vamp she'd only partially decapitated and finished the job. Two down. Out of the corner of her eye she saw that Noah had taken down one too.

Okay, three dead.

He was still fighting with Chris and another vamp. As the vamp who'd accidently wounded LaPomeret jumped over his friend's twitching, but unfortunately still-alive body, Erin leaped over him and landed on LaPomeret's body.

Her boots slammed into his chest, pinning him as she finished what the other vamp had started with one clean sweep of her blade.

Now there were only two left. Erin swiveled and faced off with the other vampire. Barrett. He jumped back about ten feet and latched onto one of the bookshelves. "You're going to pay for this!" As he flew at her, she jumped over one of the tipped-over settees. His claws barely missed grazing her throat.

She was vaguely aware of the agony coursing through her from LaPomeret's earlier attack but adrenaline had taken over, drowning out everything else. Out of the corner of her eye, she saw Chris attack Noah from behind, slicing his claws down his side. Erin started to cry out, but Noah roared, the sound eerie and all-consuming as he shifted to his wolf form.

He shook off Chris, then lunged at the remaining vamp he'd almost decapitated. He finished the job as his jaws clenched around the vamp's neck.

In that moment, Chris raced toward a curtain-covered window. He dove through as if he was jumping into a pool. Glass shattered, flying everywhere but before she could chase after him, the last remaining vamp launched at her again. She let out a growl of frustration. She wanted to hunt down Chris before he got too far away.

As he flew through the air, she used a broken piece of what had once been a table as a springboard to propel herself at him. Slashing out with both blades, she brought them down fast and hard on his neck from both sides.

His head hit the ground before she did. Noah had already started for the window to run after Chris and she was a step behind him. But she froze when three more vampires raced into the room. One she recognized as the vamp she'd tranquilized on the wall. Guess half an hour sleep time was a bit of an exaggeration. She'd have to thank Jayce for that later.

The vamps took in the room, murder in their gazes. Furniture was busted apart and covered with blood and body parts.

Panic exploded inside her at these newcomers. Not because she didn't think she could take them, but because Chris was getting away. Malcolm still huddled in the corner, looking like a scared bunny. Whatever Brianna had done to him had some serious lasting effects. Now his own brother had abandoned him, but Erin took no pity. He'd get what was coming to him soon enough. More time she spent fighting was more time Chris had to increase the distance between them. She held in a scream of frustration.

Noah dove at one of the vamps, his all-black coat gleaming under the lighting—even if it was a little bloody. In that instant, Ian sailed through the broken window with his sword and a shorter blade drawn. His crew was close behind, leaping through the window with a lethal grace that was beautiful to behold.

Everyone froze, including Erin and Noah, who'd

stopped a foot in front of the vamp he'd been about to rip apart. The vampire watched Noah and Ian, looking between them warily and she saw a bit of hope in his gaze. Maybe because Ian was a vampire. She hoped Ian would be on their side, but she truly didn't know enough about him to make any assumption that could get her and Noah killed.

With inhuman quickness he threw the short blade at the closest vamp. It drove right through the middle of his chest, pinning him to one of the built-in shelves. The vampire cried out briefly but slumped against the blade a moment later. Then Ian wielded his bigger, scarier sword, like he was showing off that he knew how to use it.

Damn. Okay, Ian was definitely on their side.

And she needed to haul ass. "I need to hunt down a shifter that got away. He's involved in this mess, but I'll be back. No one leaves this house and try to keep at least one of them alive." At that, she sprinted toward the window, ignoring Ian's crew. She glanced at Noah who was a step behind her. "You all right?"

He let out a yip and kept running. She inwardly smiled. As long as he was okay, she could deal with anything. Noah was a giant black wolf and would probably scare the shit out of any humans that saw them—and her blades and blood-covered self probably looked awful too—but Erin didn't care. She was catching Chris once and for all.

Heart racing, she jumped through the broken window and plunged into the semidarkness. As she sprinted across the lawn she nearly stumbled when Chris dropped down from one of the low-hanging branches of a live oak, his canines bared, eyes glittering with hatred. What the hell? Before she could formulate anything audibly, he answered her unspoken question.

"I know you'll keep coming after me and I'm not spending the rest of my life looking over my shoulder," he growled, circling warily.

His clothes were shredded and his face was covered in bruises. Blood was also smeared all over his body, some of it his, some Noah's if she scented right. She could kill him for that. The thought that he'd even scratched Noah let alone done worse made Erin's claws ache. But she kept her cool.

Noah had come up next to her and he made a move to go after Chris but she held out her blade in Noah's direction. Without looking at him, she said, "No. This is between me and him. I don't care what happens, stay out of it, Noah. I'm declaring a *nex pugna*." Technically that was a death match between Alphas but Chris would understand the sentiment. She wasn't stopping until one of them was dead.

Chris glanced at Noah and practically smirked when he focused on her again. "You really want to take me on by yourself, little wolf?"

She snarled and took a step forward with a calm she didn't feel. "You're so fucking pathetic you couldn't even kill me when I was *pregnant*. I was as weak as a human and I still had enough strength to withstand your beating." Erin couldn't believe it when her words came out calm and steady. Inside she was shaking like a leaf, though her wolf was just plain pissed. She wanted blood.

His eyes spewed rage and hatred. "I made a mistake, but I won't again. I'm just glad I killed the baby. The thought of having a kid with you . . ." He shuddered as if the idea repulsed him.

Erin wanted to remain in control. She fought so fucking hard, but she couldn't hold back anymore. This monster had not only taken her unborn child, but her chance to ever have children again. His words set her inner wolf free. With a rage she didn't know she was capable of, her inner wolf took over, ripping aside the human veneer with razor-sharp claws until her animal was the one in control.

Erin was vaguely aware of Noah creeping up close to her. She briefly turned her head and snapped her jaws at him, ordering him to back up. When he didn't move she swatted her paw at him. She was so damn close to giving in to her animal instinct completely that she didn't want to hurt him if he jumped into the middle of this.

He moved back.

As she turned to face her enemy, Chris had shifted too. He was big, a brown-and-gray wolf that stood maybe five feet tall on all fours. She was a little smaller and though she couldn't see herself knew her coat was a shade darker than her auburn hair.

They started circling each other, slowly moving around. She was aware that some of the vamps in Ian's crew had come outside, but they were standing back. Noah was still nearby but he'd given her a wide berth.

Blood and tears.

That's all she could see in her mind for a moment. Her own blood. So much of it. And blinding tears when the doctor had told her the depth of what she'd lost.

She could even smell the garbage and days'-old food from that alley Chris had dumped her in when he'd thought she was dead.

She wanted to attack outright, but her wolf was having none of that. A born predator, she knew more than Erin. Doing what she hated most, Erin let her animal take even more control until all she saw was the enemy.

Prey.

The wolf in front of her might be big, but she was faster and deadlier. Drawing on her speed, she stepped back and ran toward the back wall.

Her prey howled, taking chase. Picking up speed, she darted around the back corner of the house. The yard was big, with a surprising amount of open land and trees. Her paws pounded the earth as she pulled even farther away from the other wolf.

He thought she was afraid. That she was running.

He should be so lucky.

On a burst of energy, she quickly rounded the other side of the house and made a beeline for another giant live oak. The branches swooped out low, some touching the earth. But others were much higher, running parallel to the wall.

That's where she wanted to be. Racing up one of the low-hanging branches, she jumped from branch to branch until she reached the wall. Launching herself, she landed on all fours. As she skimmed the top of the west wall, she crouched, using the tree as cover. She'd have only seconds now.

When her prey rounded the corner, snarling and clearly agitated, she went completely still. It raced past the tree and her, running for the front of the house once again.

She jumped from her perch, wondering how long it would take him to figure it out. Silently, deadly, she ate up the distance between them in seconds. He was weak and he would soon be dead.

She was so close she could taste her victory. Could feel her jaws snapping around his neck. Her hackles rose, tail puffing up in preparation for the attack.

Chris raced on, his legs stretching and straining as he foolishly tried to catch her. Up ahead Noah and the vamps waited still, watching. That's when her prey realized his mistake.

He slowed and turned his head, his actions a fraction faster than she'd anticipated. She was already in the air, pouncing with her claws at the ready, jaws open wide. Instead of landing on his back like she'd planned, she tackled his big form and sank her canines into his side instead of his neck.

He yowled in pain and thrashed against her as she dug deeper. Her prey was going to feel her wrath in a way he'd never imagined, he was going to pay for all of his sins here and now. She ripped through fur, skin, and bone as she connected with his rib cage. A crack rent the air as bones broke and blood filled her mouth.

He shrieked more than howled at the pain she knew he must be feeling. Suddenly, sharp claws pierced her sensitive underbelly as he twisted their bodies and gained more purchase. He was thrashing around, not fighting like a true predator, but his adrenaline would be raging now.

Releasing her grip, she rolled to all fours and he did

the same, facing off with her, his jaw open wide as he snarled at her.

Slowly, she started backing up and stupid wolf that he was, thought she was running again. Or at least afraid.

Not of him. Never again. The pain was still there though, lurking right under the surface, spurring her on. This bastard had taken so much from her. Too much.

Yelping as if she was scared, she turned, tucked tail and ran toward the wall. She could hear his yowl of victory and the sound of his paws slamming against the ground as he gave chase.

She couldn't wait to end him.

Instead of racing toward the wall, she aimed for one of the ancient oaks and with her unsheathed claws she scaled the bottom half before releasing and turning on her would-be attacker.

Her timing was perfect as she landed on his back. It was a dirty move, but she wanted him to suffer before she finished him off. Her wolf was bloodthirsty. Ripping through his tail, she sliced through it until he screeched in agony and twisted, throwing her off.

The scent of his blood teased her nostrils as he tried to run away. He made sad little mewling noises that sounded almost feline.

Pathetic.

But she was done playing with her prey. Her paws had barely hit the ground before she leapt onto his back again. This time she was at the perfect angle to destroy him. Her teeth shredded through tendons as she sliced into his neck, completely taking his head. His blood was warm, and though she'd won, it tasted bitter as it coated her tongue.

It was over too fast. She hadn't wanted him to run any longer, hadn't wanted him breathing the same air as her, but it was like someone had sliced right through her middle. The pain at having her vengeance cut so short was brutal. Agonizing. Why didn't she feel better? Wasn't she supposed to feel more of a victory?

Her wolf howled, loud and long. She'd wanted him to suffer more. Just like she had.

Tossing his head to the side with a growl, she wanted to feel something, anything, as she stared down at his lifeless body. It didn't matter what she did. Nothing could change the past. Nothing could bring back her former dreams.

He truly was pathetic. The monster who had haunted her nightmares for a year was dead. She couldn't believe this piece of shit had kept her living in a state of fear for so long. That she'd been afraid to tell anyone what he'd done to her, what he'd taken.

She let out another howl, her cry of agony filling the night air. She didn't care who heard her. Didn't care what anyone thought.

"He can't hurt anyone else." Noah's voice sounded a few feet behind her, but it was like he was at the end of a tunnel.

He must have shifted to his human form. She found him standing there, naked, his hands hanging at his sides. Turning away from him, she ran deeper into the darkness, away from him and the others. She could clearly see them with her night vision, but she used one of the trees as cover and flopped down on her belly.

Chris was dead. So what? It didn't change anything. The ache was still there. Hollow and painful. She'd thought it might go away if he was finally gone. Nope. She'd still lost so much and no one could ever give it back to her.

"Erin?" Noah's voice was soft, soothing as he made his way to her, slow and steady.

She ignored him.

"Are you hurt?" he asked again in that soft voice.

She wanted to be annoyed with him, but she couldn't muster anything. Just sadness and hollowness. It welled up inside her like a geyser, taking over everything in its path. If she'd been human, she'd be bawling right now and she refused to let anyone see her like that. All weak and pathetic.

She'd just remain a wolf. She liked it better like this anyway. No decisions to make, no one to worry about.

Eat, sleep, and hunt. That's all she needed in life.

Closing her eyes, she ignored Noah as he examined her body with his hands. His touch was gentle, but clinical as he searched for wounds. She wasn't hurt physically. Her one wound had already healed. Chris hadn't been a skilled fighter. Not like her. Not even close. Yet he'd taken so much from her and countless others because of his treachery and greed.

"Erin, shift back now," Noah demanded, anger and worry in his voice.

Still, she ignored him. Her wolf was in control and she was fine exactly where she was. If she shut down her human side, maybe this hurt would vanish completely. . . .

Chapter 20

Noah took the pants Ian handed him gratefully. He didn't care about nudity but he didn't like his goods hanging out around so many vampires. Especially when one of the females was eyeing him like she'd like to lick him from head to toe. He wanted only Erin looking at him like that. Unfortunately she'd completely shut down and refused to move from her spot on the grass.

"What's wrong with her?" Ian asked, keeping a fair distance between them after he'd given him the clothes.

Noah winced as he wiped his arms and torso with the cloth Ian had also given him. He tried to clean the blood off. The gash in his left arm was already knitting back together as were the slices along his back. He still ached all over though. Not that he gave a shit about any of that.

Not with Erin lying on the ground anywhere near the treacherous shifter she'd just killed. For a while she'd closed her eyes. Now she just stared at Noah with those gray eyes and all he saw was wolf. Not Erin. Usually he could see human awareness and intelligence looking back at him, but not this time. He understood why. "She shifted in a highly emotional state. Her wolf is more powerful than mine or most of my kind and it took over. My guess is, she's happy right where she is and doesn't want to become human again."

"You mean . . . ever?"

Noah would never let that happen. "No." Or he hoped not. "I think once the adrenaline wears off, her human side will take over again." Man, he hoped so. He was just guessing at this point and had no clue what to do. He wanted to call Jayce but didn't know if that would be a mistake. Erin was a new enforcer and he didn't want to mess up anything for her with Jayce or the Council. The last thing he wanted to do was cause her pain. She'd suffered enough for one lifetime.

"You *think*? As in, this has never happened before." Ian sounded incredulous.

What the hell was Ian trying to do to him? Noah grunted. He wasn't going to get into this with a vamp he barely knew. He started to ask him about the vamps inside when Ian spoke again.

"I heard some of what that guy said. Did he really try to kill her when she was pregnant?" There was a note of horror in Ian's voice.

Noah didn't blame him, but he also didn't respond. He didn't want to talk about Erin with anyone. He just wanted her back in her human form. Damn it, why wouldn't she shift? "What's up with the vampires inside?" he asked, his gaze still on Erin. Her reddish coat was slightly matted, but she was unharmed. Physically at least. Her blades lay on the ground ten feet from her. Frustration punched through him that she was just lying there.

"They're talking to my people. Seems Barrett and the dead vampires inside were all involved in this blood ring. The vamps working for them knew about it, but weren't directly involved. None of them are mated or bloodborns anyway, but they knew and said nothing. My bosses are *pissed*." Ian shook his head.

"What about the mates of the dead vamps?" Noah didn't care that much since he had a feeling vamps would be handing out the punishments for anyone remotely involved.

Ian shrugged. "That's still up for debate. They're sequestered away at one of the other's homes. They'll all be interrogated."

Yeah, Noah really didn't want to know about all that.

"Hope you guys didn't need the shifter inside for anything."

Noah finally turned away from Erin at that. His eyebrows rose. "You killed him?"

"Not me personally, but he went after Sekani—one of my warriors." There wasn't a flicker of emotion in his words.

Good. Erin's other attacker was dead too. All Noah cared about was her, though. *Shift, shift, shift.* He tried to silently order her to change forms. He hated that they had a fucking audience for this. "Can you clear everyone out of the yard?"

Ian sighed, then nodded. "Yeah, we've got a ton of cleaning to do inside anyway."

As he started to leave, Noah stopped him. "Can I use your phone?"

With a flicker of surprise, Ian handed him his cell. Noah texted his father and told him to stay away from Barrett's house. They didn't need any more people drawing attention to this place. The vamps could be in charge of cleanup duty. He was sure Erin wouldn't mind and he definitely didn't.

Once the yard was clear, he knelt down next to Erin, then laid down. He stayed on his back and turned so that their faces were side by side. She sniffed him a couple times, then nudged him with her nose, as if telling him to give her space.

Yeah, not gonna happen. Ever. "I'm not going anywhere, short stuff. I'll stay here all night and all day or all freaking year if that's what it takes."

She sniffed in what he could only describe as a sound of disdain.

He continued. "Maybe I'll even buy this place. You can be my pet wolf. My guard wolf. You can keep intruders out."

She let out a snarl and shoved her nose into his shoulder. Now he could see a flicker of Erin looking back at him, not her wolf. She was agitated.

"I'll get you a pink collar and take you on walks around the neighborhood. I bet all the neighborhood kids will love you. You can give them rides like a pony. I could even charge admission—"

With a yowl of indignation she shifted back to her human form in a flurry of breaking bones. Breathing hard, she crouched on the grass, naked and glaring at him. Her gray eyes were so dark they were almost black. "Pink? You'd get me a *pink* collar?"

"I say I'm going to collar you and let little kids ride you like a circus animal and that's what you focus on." He let out a bark of laughter, almost light-headed with relief.

Sighing, she wrapped her arms around her chest but remained kneeling. She was silent for a long moment, then said, "Thank you. My wolf didn't want to give me control back."

"I figured." Thank God that was all it had been. He'd been terrified she'd *stay* that way, but somehow he kept his words nonchalant as if he hadn't been *dying* inside. "Good to know all I have to do is threaten to collar you in the future."

She rolled her eyes, but then her gaze strayed to Chris's body. She took in a ragged breath. Sadness rolled off of her in potent waves. "I thought he'd be a better opponent. Harder to kill. I thought I'd feel better about killing him, that I'd feel relief or something. Instead I'm just . . . sad and exhausted."

He wanted to reach out and hold her but he was afraid she'd push him away. Since she'd shifted back, he didn't want to make any moves to freak her out. Especially since her control had to be fragile right now. He couldn't risk her wolfing out on him again. But he could give her words. "You faced your demons in a way most people never get to. And you saved countless future victims. The world is a better place because of you. The females you saved and their families will be forever grateful. You reunited females with their mates and in some cases, their children. This is your first job and you kicked ass, Erin." Noah stared at her and couldn't stop the feeling of pride welling up inside him. He hated what had been done to her, but . . . "Chris Tyson might have hurt you once, but you beat him and you're stronger for it. Don't let him take away all the good that's been done. All the good *you've* done."

"I couldn't have done any of this without you." When he started to protest, she shook her head and just said, "Don't."

She started to say more, but the sound of his father's voice startled them both. He was stalking across the lawn from the direction of the main entrance. Three pack members were behind him, but Noah scented more nearby hiding in the shadows.

"What's going on?" Angus demanded. He tugged his shirt off as he reached them and handed it to Erin without looking at her.

Noah stood, frowning. "Didn't you get my text?"

"It wasn't your number. Didn't know if it was a trap." He glanced at the headless body on the ground. "Damn, son, nice work."

"I didn't do that."

Angus's gaze flicked to Erin who was now covered with his shirt.

It hung to her knees and even though it was irrational, something territorial flared deep inside Noah at the thought of any other male's scent on her. Even his own father who'd been happily mated for centuries. Damn his inner wolf.

Erin's soothing hand on his forearm stilled him. "I'll change as soon as possible."

He blinked, surprised she'd read him so easily. He

was also surprised by the speculative look in her gray eyes. She was watching him intently and there was something in her gaze he was trying to put his finger on, but just couldn't. It was as if something had changed between them. He grappled with whatever it was, trying to figure it out, but couldn't. Whatever was going on with Erin, her words had their intended effect. His animal immediately calmed.

She gave him a soft smile, then turned toward his father. "We've eliminated the two shifters responsible for taking the pregnant women. They're dead and their only partner is likely dead by now too."

"He is," Noah's father said.

That didn't take long.

"Ian and his vampires are inside cleaning up the mess," Noah said to his father.

Angus was silent for a long moment as he looked at the dead body then back at him and Erin. "Now that your job is done how long will you be in town?" he spoke to Erin, but Noah was under the impression he was asking him.

Erin looked at Noah with raised eyebrows. He could read exactly what she was thinking too. He gritted his teeth and looked at his father. "We'll have loose ends to tie up, so maybe a few more days."

Angus nodded, but didn't respond.

Noah took a deep breath and forced himself to extend the olive branch he really didn't want to. But Erin had been right. His own pride was no reason to lose a relationship with his father. He cleared his throat. "Maybe Erin and I can come over for dinner with you and Mom before we go."

"And maybe you guys can plan a trip to North Carolina to visit us," Erin interjected smoothly.

Surprise flashed in Angus's eyes but it didn't last long. He just nodded once, abruptly. "Sounds good. I'll talk to you later. If you guys don't need us, I want to check on the females brought in."

"How are Brianna and Angelo?" Erin realized Angelo was still waiting at the house the Tyson brothers had used as their prison.

Angus pulled out his phone as he spoke. "Once Brianna got all the females to safety she headed back to wait with Angelo. I'll call her and let them know they can come back now."

Noah nodded and once his father was gone, he pushed out a long breath. He looked at Erin. "So what now?"

She shrugged. "We help clean up this mess, then head back to our place. I'm tired, hungry, and dirty. I just want to shower and sleep for two days."

Noah was all those things, but sleeping was the last thing on his mind. He might be tired, but his brain was also going into overdrive where Erin was concerned. She'd fought and killed vampires and a shifter tonight. And she'd done it lethally and with an impressive amount of skill. He might not have officially claimed her, but that was his female that had done that and he was so damn proud of her.

He still wanted to hold her, though, if only to convince himself that she was okay.

Erin sat on the edge of her bed, completely naked. After helping Ian and his crew clean up everything, she'd decided to let him take the remaining vampires who had worked for Barrett into their custody. Her only job had been to stop any more pregnant shifters from going missing and to find and eliminate the culprits. She'd done that. The vampires would dole out worse punishment than she or her Council ever would. Shifters just killed wrongdoers. If you were guilty and deserved it, you died. Simple. Vampires . . . tortured. And probably relished it just a little bit too much.

There were still a few more things to iron out with Ian and even the Brethren, but that could wait a couple of days. Once Ian had gotten all the information he needed from the vamps they'd taken, he'd be information sharing with not only her, but Jayce and their Council. They wanted to know if this was widespread. Their current intel didn't suggest it was, but now that they knew what pregnant shifter blood could be used for, they planned to keep a much more vigilant eye on things.

None of that was her concern at the moment. Right now she was trying to figure out how to face Noah the way she needed to. No, the way she *wanted* to. She desperately needed to explain some things to him, but the thought of his rejection when she admitted everything she'd been holding in . . .

Screw it.

Pushing up, she didn't bother with clothes. He'd told her that he was going to take a shower when they'd arrived back at their place and she could still hear the faint sound of water running. She knew he wouldn't reject her physically, but when she told him all that other stuff. . . . *Stop thinking*, she ordered herself.

She opened her door and headed across the common area with the combined kitchen and living room. No surprise, his door was unlocked. The bathroom door was open a fraction. She could see steam rolling out of the opening. Taking a deep breath, she pushed it open and stepped inside.

He had to have scented her, but he didn't say anything. He was probably waiting and letting her make up her mind about whether she wanted to do this or not. The shower had a glass-and-stone enclosure just like the one in her room. She could see his powerful outline as he stood under the rushing water. His body was distorted though and she wanted the real thing.

Her strides were silent as she crossed the tile. When she stepped into the shower behind him, his entire body tensed. All his muscles pulled tight and taut, begging her to run her fingers and mouth over every inch of him. First, they needed to talk.

Stepping forward, she wrapped her arms around him from behind, pressing her breasts and the side of her face against his back. He shuddered under her touch. Immediately his hands covered hers, strong and reassuring.

"I thought I'd lost you when you wouldn't turn back to your human form." His quietly spoken words surprised her.

For a little while, she thought she'd lost herself. "I'm glad you didn't."

"Me too." She knew the guttural words came from a place deep inside him. He was practically shaking as he spoke them.

Okay, now or never. "I need to talk to you, Noah. It's

important." The most important thing she'd ever tell him.

His fingers tightened over hers at her words. In an instant, he turned and looked down at her. Rivulets of water ran down his face and chest, creating little rivers over all that gorgeous expanse of skin. "No talking."

Then his mouth was on hers. Hungry and needy. Grabbing her hips, he hoisted her up against the wall. The tile chilled her back, but did nothing to douse her own hunger. Her legs were wrapped around his waist and if she slipped down just a bit farther he'd be inside her. Her inner walls clenched greedily at the thought.

Just as his tongue started to part her lips, he pulled back. His breathing was ragged as he stared at her. He swallowed once, convulsively, as if he needed a moment. She totally understood.

"Condoms," he gasped out.

"We don't need 'em." She went to kiss him again, but he pulled his head back.

His chest rose and fell in rapid breaths. "Heat . . . you're close, don't want to chance it."

Just like that his words doused most of her desire. Her fingers loosened on his shoulders and she let her legs go lax. But he wouldn't let her go. He'd said he didn't want to talk so she'd thought she could have him just once before he rejected her. Before he tried to let her down easy with words that he'd *try* to make soothing, but would cut her to shreds just the same.

He pinned her to the wall harder. "What did I say? I didn't mean I don't want kids with you. You just started your new job and it would be fucked up of me to . . . fuck, don't look at me like that, baby."

To her horror, Erin started crying. Like seriously, big fat tears rolling down her cheeks as sobs racked her body. Oh my God, she wanted to die. She buried her face against his chest because she couldn't look at him. She was too embarrassed by the spectacle she was making, blubbering all over him. She was just making things a thousand times worse but she couldn't stop.

Noah pulled her tight to him, pulling her away from the wall and hugging her close. Water rushed around them, but he didn't move. He just held her and murmured soothing sounds as he stroked a gentle hand down her spine.

She wasn't sure how much time had passed. It felt like forever but eventually her tears dried up, though she was pretty sure she'd start crying again once she told Noah what she needed to. She tilted her head to the side so that she could breathe better and talk without sounding like a garbled mess. "I'm sorry," she murmured, her throat raw.

"You don't have anything to be sorry for." He finally moved then, taking a seat on the built-in bench.

She spread her legs wider but didn't change position as she remained straddling him. Instead of looking at his face, she rested her chin on his shoulder. If she wanted to get the words out, it was now or never. "I can't have kids. Ever. I might have survived but the damage I sustained was too severe. My ovaries . . . well, the details don't matter." She sniffled once, dragging in a ragged breath.

His hand never stopped stroking down her back. Combined with the rhythmic beating of the water against the tile floor, she found herself being soothed despite her internal warfare. When he didn't say anything, she sat back and looked at him.

He stared at her with soft, dark eyes.

"Aren't you going to say anything?" she snapped, hating that her voice came out harsher than she'd intended.

His eyes widened, then softened. "I'm sorry. I didn't know if you were finished. I'm so damn sorry you can't have kids, sweetheart. It kills me what that bastard took from you."

She frowned, watching him carefully, waiting to see the pity in his gaze before he slammed her with his rejection. "And?"

Now it was his turn to look confused. "And, what?"

She sputtered for a moment, trying to formulate words. "Don't you care?"

"Of course I care! I care about what was done to you, taken from you. I want to kill that bastard all over again." He let out a menacing growl but not once did he loosen his grip on her.

Erin slapped a fist down on his chest. Not hard, but enough to make a point. "What's wrong with you? I can't have cubs. Ever. Don't you want to tell me something, like how you don't want me as your mate now? I'll never be able to give you what you want. There's not even a one percent chance, Noah. I physically can't!"

He blinked at her, then let out a sharp bark of laughter. Actually laughed as he shook his head. "You're so fucking arrogant, woman."

"Excuse me?" She struggled against him, but he just tightened his hold, his cock pressing harder against her stomach where it was caught between them.

"I want to make sure I get this straight before I fuck you senseless." She gasped at his words, but he barreled right on as if she hadn't made a sound. "You thought because you couldn't have cubs that I'd what, not want to be with you? And you decided that since I must be so desperate to continue my line that I'd all of a sudden decide that I don't want to mate with you? Like I'm *that* pathetic." He shook his head, his eyes glittering with anger and passion. "I love you, Erin. I love your physical and emotional strength, your fucking *arrogance*, and yeah, I love your hot body. I don't care about kids. They're great and I love the cubs running around the ranch as if they were my own, but I don't care about having my own. I never have. And even if I did, it *still* wouldn't make a difference in how I feel about you. If you want to adopt, fine. I'm on board with it. All I care about is your happiness. Every second we spend together I love you more. The fact that you actually think I'd turn my back on you because of something so small, hurts."

She sat there, stunned and feeling guilty as she stared at his dejected expression. "But . . . you deserve to be with someone sweet, soft, like Esperanze. You deserve a family."

"First, I adore Esperanze and so does her *mate*."

"I didn't mean her specifically, I meant someone *like* her. A nice, sweet beta," she snapped.

He continued as if she hadn't spoken. "Second, while I have nothing against betas—they're the backbone of our pack, in fact—I don't want someone like her or even another Alpha. I want you. Only you. Sweet and soft is fucking overrated and boring." He reached out to stroke a strand of wet hair from her face. "You're so strong and smart and *you* deserve happiness. Hell, I do too. And you make me damn happy, even when we're fighting. What makes you think you don't deserve to be with the man you love?" His question came out hesitantly, as if he was unsure about the love part.

She almost snorted. As if she didn't love him. She'd been in love with him for much longer than she cared to admit. "You're pretty arrogant yourself, making assumptions that I love you," she said through another sniffle. It made her feel excruciatingly vulnerable to lay her soul bare to him like this.

He grinned then, wickedly, seeing right through her. She wanted to say the words and tell him she loved him too but what he did next stopped her.

"So, if we have all this bullshit and your assumptions out of the way . . ." His hands tightened on her hips then he lifted her up so quickly she hadn't realized what he intended until he slid into her tight sheath. Her inner walls stretched and molded around him, a perfect fit.

"Oh . . . God." She'd been wet earlier but she'd lost some of her arousal during their talk. Having him stretch her so fully like this was heaven. She swallowed hard as she adjusted to his size. Being with him was different from anything she'd ever experienced. Not that she had a ton of experience in the first place but this was *Noah*.

Her best friend. Now he knew everything about her and accepted the bad with the good.

A low growl emanated from him, making her clench her toes in anticipation for whatever was next. His hips rolled once, pushing even deeper inside her. She let out a gasp and tightened her fingers on him. Carefully watching her, he slowly leaned down and grasped her hardening nipple between his teeth. Closing her eyes, she let her head fall back as she moaned. This was almost too good to be true. She was so afraid she'd wake up and find out this was a dream. But it wasn't. Noah loved her and wanted her as his mate. He didn't care about things she'd assumed were important.

Ugh, he was *right*. She was arrogant. But, in her defense cubs were so important to shifter life and . . . *oh*, his teeth tightened on her nipple, the sensation bordering on pain, but so pleasurable it was sending tiny little messages to her clit, which was pulsing and swollen with arousal. Keeping his teeth pressed down, he lazily licked over the tip of her nipple, slowly and erotically. Sweet Lord, she could come from those strokes alone.

Holding on to his shoulders, she started moving over him, up and down in a very slow rhythm. Her inner walls clenched around him tighter with each stroke. It wouldn't take her long and even though she desperately wanted to prolong this, she wanted to come even more. She was so greedy for him and everything he had to offer, it scared her.

It had been way too long and having Noah inside her right now was almost surreal. His mouth and hands were amazing, but having his cock inside her was pure bliss.

As she started to ride him faster, Noah chuckled

against her breast. The action tingled, making shivers
skitter over her sensitive skin. He tightened his hands
on her hips and tugged her down so that she was completely impaled by him, but he refused to let her move
as he oh so slowly kissed a path toward her other
breast. His wicked tongue flicked over her other nipple. Then he feathered the softest kisses around her
areola, teasing her relentlessly.

She tried to rise up, but he held fast. "Tease," she
growled. It was one of the things she loved most about
him. He was so damn strong and had no problem taking charge in the bedroom, but he was strong enough
to let her do her job without being intimidated. If anything, he seemed to get off on her strength. But right
now he was getting off on keeping her immobile. And
so was she. She grew wetter by the second as he held
her in place. Being unable to move like this was incredibly erotic.

He just chuckled against her breast. The sensation
sent a shiver rolling through her. "Touch yourself," he
ordered, his voice raspy.

He didn't have to tell her twice. Reaching between
her legs, she started rubbing her clit. She'd done this so
many times to thoughts of Noah it was kind of embar-
rassing. "You know how many times I've touched myself thinking about you?" she whispered.

He froze, his tongue on the underside of her breast.
His breath was hot against her body. Then she could
feel more than see him smile. "You thought about me?"

"Uh-huh." She continued moving her finger over
herself, the friction pushing her closer and closer to cli-

max. It felt amazing, especially combined with what he was doing with his mouth but it wasn't enough. She needed more movement inside her.

He completely stilled. "What kinds of things did you think about?"

"Later." She could barely think, let alone talk dirty right now. She just wanted to come. So bad her body was trembling with the need.

"We're revisiting this conversation later." He sucked on her breast then, the action sharp and hungry. She arched into him, needing more.

"Move, damn it." She was on the verge, if he'd just let her . . .

His hands loosened on her hips but instead of letting her ride him, he moved quickly and pinned her back against the wall. His mouth covered hers again as he thrust into her in long, hard strokes.

That was exactly what she needed. Everything about his movements was frantic and unsteady. Noah rarely lost control so as he pounded into her as if he might actually die if he didn't get to come inside her, she couldn't have stopped herself from climaxing if she'd wanted. Which she didn't.

Her orgasm was sharp as it punched through her entire system. Her breasts, still reeling from his kisses, felt heavy and sensitive as she rubbed against his chest. She tightened her legs around his waist as he continued slamming into her. Her heels dug into his tight backside. She savored the feel of those muscles clenching as he completely lost himself.

Noah tore his lips from hers, his mouth latching onto where her neck and shoulder met. His canines pierced her skin as his climax overtook him. Pain didn't even register, just pure pleasure. She sucked in a sharp gasp. The feel of being marked by him was like nothing she'd experienced. To have someone completely accept her for who she was, to not want to change or manipulate her was amazing.

And not just anyone, but Noah. Warmth rippled through her sated body as he completely filled her. Part of her wondered what the hell he was thinking by loving her, but she didn't care. He did and he was all hers now. There was no way she could ever let this man go. "I love you," she managed to get out as his thrusts slowed, then subsided.

A stillness came over him, as though her words had just registered. Breathing hard, he still had her pinned up against the wall. The tile was cool against her back, but she felt as if her body was on fire. His cock had gone down a little, but not much. He was still half hard inside her and something told her it wouldn't be long before he was ready to go again. That was fine with her. She could do this with Noah all night long and never tire. Months and months of pent-up sexual frustration— yeah, they were going to make up for all that lost time starting now.

He lifted his head and let his canines retract. The gleam in his eyes was positively smug. "I knew you loved me."

She grinned at his tone before nipping his bottom lip with her teeth. Yeah, she loved him. More than anything. And she was going to show him every day for the rest of their lives together. She hadn't brought it up, but she wanted to be more than just mates. More

than the way he'd just marked her so that every supernatural being would know they were together. She
wanted to be bondmates, to be forever linked to this
incredibly sweet, sexy, and patient man for the rest of
her life.

Chapter 21

Brianna zipped up her suitcase as she fought the dread welling up inside her. Finding those women in time and reuniting them with their families was the best possible outcome for this mission. She knew that wasn't what her mission had been about, though. The fae were all about information gathering and keeping themselves strong, not saving shifters. But for her, it was what the mission had become and she was so grateful things had turned out for the best. Her joy was overshadowed by her recent orders from her mother. Not just because she'd be leaving Angelo, though that was the main reason for her distress.

Collapsing on the sheets that still smelled of Angelo, her sexy, strong shifter, she stretched out on her back and covered her face with her arm. She was supposed to be getting on a plane in three hours to head to Dublin. Her mother had decided that since Brianna had done so well in America, she was being called home to teach the newer warriors about interacting with and infiltrating human hate groups. While she appreciated that her mother was so proud of her, especially when the woman had loudly voiced her doubt about Brianna coming to America in the first place, she didn't want to leave Angelo.

As the bed dipped, she dropped her arm to find that Angelo had stretched out next to her. Damn, he was quiet. Sometimes she really wished she had his extra-sensory abilities. Lying on his side, his elbow bent as he propped his head up, his expression was dark. "I see you're all packed." He sounded angry and hurt.

"I don't *want* to leave you." He had to know that.

"Then don't," he said simply. As if it was a simple thing.

"I—"

"You're a grown woman, you make your own decisions. You can stay or ask me to go with you." There wasn't a flicker of doubt in his hazel eyes. He absolutely would come with her. Before she could respond, he continued. "And if you don't ask, I'm going anyway. I've never been to Ireland, but I always wanted to."

"You . . . what? Do you mean in a permanent sense or . . ." She couldn't keep going. What if he didn't mean what she thought? Sometimes she had a hard time with cues or exact meaning, especially with shifters who were so much more passionate.

"I'll move anywhere for you. I love my pack, but I want to be with you more. A lot more."

"How can you make things sound so simple?"

He shrugged in that maddening way of his. "Because they are. I didn't plan to fall for you, but I did and nothing will change that. I'm not a complicated man, Brianna. I want you as my mate and I love you. How is that hard?"

She sucked in a sharp breath. It wasn't even the words "I love you" that stunned her—which, okay, those did too. All her focus was on the word *mate*. Even if she sometimes struggled with exact meaning, she definitely knew what that meant for shifters. Every supernatural being did. "Mate?"

His dark eyebrows drew together. "How could you not realize that's what I want? God, from practically the moment Connor assigned me to you. You stuck that pert little nose in the air and acted all haughty—"

She shoved at his shoulder. "I did not act haughty!" She'd been so nervous around him back in North Carolina. And he'd been so darkly sensual and sexy. He'd kept making those not-quite-subtle sexual comments and she hadn't known how to react. So she'd given him the cold shoulder in an effort to protect herself when she thought he'd been making fun of her. But then he'd gone and kissed her and she'd realized he was just as consumed with lust as she was.

"I know that now. You got me so hot the first time I saw you. I thought you got off on teasing me, and then I realized you weren't teasing. And when Connor told me you compared me to a feline . . ." He growled low in his throat and quickly closed the distance between them. He tugged her bottom lip between his teeth, nipping and kissing her in that playful way he liked to do.

Unable to stop herself, she smiled as she pulled back a fraction. "I can't believe he told you." She paused, her grin widening. "I also called you pretty."

His eyes flashed to wolf for a fraction of an instant. "I'm going to pretend I didn't hear that."

"But you're so very pretty," she whispered. *And you could be all mine if I take that leap.*

They were both silent for a long moment as they watched each other. *Mate, mate, mate.* She kept saying the word over in her head and really liked the way it sounded. Okay, loved the sound of it. She wanted to say it out loud just to taste it on her lips, but held off for the moment. "I don't want to go back to Ireland. Not to live."

He shook his head, misunderstanding her. "I'm not taking you away from your family. I'm adaptable, honey. I can live anywhere and as long as I'm with you, I'll be happy."

No, he wouldn't be happy with her people, but she didn't explain all that to him. He didn't need to know how cold and unfeeling the majority of the fae were. How they would never accept a shifter into their ranks, even if she was royalty. To them, he would always be an outsider. She didn't want to drag him to a place he'd grow to hate. It would be the worst way to start off their relationship. Not to mention, she loved living in the United States and yes, she'd found she really liked shifters. One in particular. "I'd rather stay and live on the ranch. Only if you think Connor will allow me to." She couldn't believe she'd just said those words. Speaking them aloud made her decision real. Her insides quivered as she thought about the mess this would cause with her family. Well, that's what they got for sending her out into the world. Of course no one could have predicted she'd fall for a shifter, least of all her. She was so glad she had.

Connor Armstrong was a good Alpha—a bit overbearing and protective sometimes—but he was fair and she wouldn't mind living in his territory if he let her. Especially if she got to wake up next to Angelo every morning. Even thinking about the many ways he'd woken her up using his mouth since they'd arrived in New Orleans had her shivering.

Angelo shook his head. "Honey, I don't want to take you away from everything you've known."

"I know that. I *want* to live in North Carolina. I might be called away for work more than half the time, which means I'll be traveling a lot, but I want to stay. With you. I . . . I love you too." She'd never told another man those words before and while it was foreign on her lips, it also felt right.

"Looks like you'll be missing that flight," Angelo growled before covering her mouth with his.

Yes, she would be.

Chapter 22

Noah clasped Erin's hand and slid his fingers through hers, intertwining them as they walked out of the parking structure at the ranch. A light layer of snow covered the ground, crunching under their boots. It was also about twenty degrees colder than where they'd been the past week. Three days had passed since the first time he'd finally made love to Erin and marked her as his mate and it still felt surreal. Her scent covered him and vice versa. It was an all-consuming thing. The more he had of her, the more he wanted.

It didn't matter that they'd had sex every chance they got until they'd finally left New Orleans early this morning. Erin had wanted to visit with all the rescued women, and her car had needed to be repaired. Luckily Noah's father knew a guy who owed him a favor so the repair was fast and flawless.

After twelve hours of practically straight driving and being teased by Erin's erotic scent in the enclosure of her car, Noah was ready to get naked with her and he hoped she felt the same. Even though they were connected as mates, much the same way humans married, they hadn't bonded yet and part of him wondered if things would be different now that they were back with their pack. If she would be different about their relationship.

"It feels weird being back," Erin said quietly.

He squeezed her hand. "I know." All the houses were quiet, though a few lights were on in all of them. No cubs out playing and while he had no doubt some of the warriors were out patrolling, it almost felt as if they were the only people on the ranch. It was dark, but it wasn't that late. What the heck was going on?

"It's dinnertime," Erin said suddenly, as if she'd sensed what he was thinking.

That's why it was so silent. He let out a breath he hadn't realized he'd been holding. The past few months their pack had been under scrutiny by humans and outright attacks by some crazies. For a moment he'd been worried something else had happened.

As they walked, Kat strode out of the barn looking slightly flushed. Bits of hay were sticking out of her dark hair and she actually blushed when she saw them. "Oh, uh, hey, guys. Didn't know anyone was, uh . . . welcome back."

A second later Jayce walked out looking supremely proud of himself. Noah's eyes widened, not that he was exactly surprised. They were newly mated after all. "Dude, you guys have a house now."

Jayce just grinned and slung an arm around Kat's shoulders. It was the first time since Noah had met the enforcer that he actually looked relaxed. And . . . happy.

"Our new house isn't complete yet and Leila's at our place right now." Kat pulled a piece of hay out of her hair and tossed it to the icy ground.

"Why isn't your house done yet?" Noah asked, his breath curling in front of him like winding smoke. Connor had hired a construction crew to expedite all the new construction and their house had been next on the list.

Kat shrugged. "We had the construction workers focus on the newcomers' houses first. They hired an additional crew, though, so ours will be done in a few days. We just dropped by for dinner with December and Liam. Leila has a new human friend over and they were having a girls' night. We wanted to give them some space."

"That's right. Are the new shifters here? Are the houses done?" Erin and Noah both looked to the west but the new homes were blocked by the ones that had been there for decades.

The pack owned God only knew how many acres of land, but all the homes were centralized, spread out in a circle like a village. When Connor had approved letting six new members join—two who were pregnant, one with twins—they'd started building right away, creating another circle of houses around the current one.

Jayce nodded. "Yeah, they're getting settled in. Connor had the construction team start on a new house for you guys, too. Should be ready in a few weeks."

Noah glanced at Erin in surprise. He hadn't told anyone they'd mated. Not because he was ashamed, but there hadn't been time and he wasn't going to call up any of his packmates and tell them when they'd know the second he and Erin returned. For a moment he wondered if she had but her gray eyes mirrored his own surprise.

She turned back to Jayce, a calculating expression on her face. "When exactly did he start construction on it?"

"The day you two left," Kat said matter-of-factly, a big grin on her face.

"That sneaky bastard." Erin frowned, but Noah inwardly grinned. Yeah, that sounded like his Alpha. The man had a sense about stuff.

"What are the new shifters like?" Noah asked.

Kat smiled enthusiastically. "They all seem pretty nice. The males are a little reserved but the females sure can bake. They're both pregnant and are as crazed as December in the kitchen. If you stop by and say hi, they'll definitely give you a pie or something."

Jayce snorted. "Kat's been stopping by twice a day looking for a handout."

They all chuckled and were silent until Jayce cleared his throat. "I heard from Ian a few hours ago." His words made both of them pause.

Erin's hand tightened in Noah's and he found himself pleased she was still holding it. "And?"

"They've interrogated all the mates of the vampires involved in the ring. Two are actually pregnant now, but it doesn't seem as if they knew anything about what their mates were doing. They're horrified according to Ian. Out of the six, only one female knew and she's being eliminated if she hasn't been already."

"What about our Council; anything new?" Erin asked.

Noah knew she'd talked to one of the members a handful of times and everything seemed to be settled, but he hadn't pressed her for details about her job or interactions with her superiors. He was glad he'd been able to help in New Orleans but he understood that might not always be the case. That he might not always be able to go with her on assignments. Though he could hope.

Jayce shook his head. "Everything's settled as far as they're concerned. The perpetrators were eliminated and the problem is now over. Well, not the problem with the ferals, but that's the vamps' job to deal with, not ours."

Noah almost relaxed when Jayce continued.

"We've got our own shit to deal with here though. Neither you nor I will be going on any other assignments until it's taken care of."

Noah was glad to hear Erin wouldn't be going anywhere for the time being, but Jayce's tone got his hackles up. Their pack had been through enough.

Erin frowned, a thread of annoyance rolling off her. "Why didn't you say anything before?"

"I wanted you focusing solely on your case, but now that you're back we have a lot to talk about. There's something fucking weird going on in and around all the surrounding counties, but specifically in Winston-Salem."

"What is it?" she persisted.

Jayce shook his head. "We'll talk in the morning." He flicked a glance at Noah. "You guys have been traveling all day and it's a full moon, so . . ." Trailing off, he strode away with his arm snuggly around Kat's shoulders.

Well, damn. Noah had planned to broach the subject later, but not during *this* full moon. He'd planned to wait until next month at least. Not because he didn't want to bond with Erin more than he wanted his next breath, but because he didn't want to push her too soon. He knew his stubborn, sexy female better than that.

Turning, he held her hips and pulled her flush against his body. He needed to hold her so bad his wolf cried out for it. Her eyes had turned a mercurial gray storm of emotions. She cleared her throat and the nervousness rolling off her stilled him.

"It *is* a full moon," she said, stating the obvious.

Though it killed him, he didn't say what he really wanted. "I know, but forget what Jayce said. We'll wait."

She looked at him as if he'd slapped her. "Oh."

That's when understanding slammed into his chest. "You want to bond tonight?" he barely managed to rasp the words out. It was almost too much to hope for. Once they bonded it would be forever. Mates could walk away if they chose and that mated scent would eventually fade. Nothing but death would separate bondmates. Which was exactly what he wanted. He and Erin deserved some damn happiness.

Erin paused for a moment, but nodded. "I didn't want to pressure you or anything, but there will never be anyone else for me, Noah. I've been fighting my feelings for too long. Since you were dumb enough to fall in love with me, I'm not letting you go. I want to bond."

That was all he needed to hear. As he scooped her up in his arms, she let out a yelp, but wrapped her arm around his neck. "What are you doing?"

"We're doing this now." His entire body hummed with energy, his wolf clawing at him in excitement. Yeah, his human and animal sides were in complete agreement. They were doing this before she changed her mind. The rational, human part of his brain knew she wouldn't, that she was completely serious, but his wolf side wasn't taking any chances. This was his female and he was making her his right now.

Noah stomped up the few stairs to the porch of the cabin where he lived with the rest of the warriors. After he practically kicked the door in, he paused in the entrance. Aiden was stretched out on one of the couches, a half-eaten sandwich in his hand. Nathan was reading a book on firearms by the fire and Ryan was at the kitchen table in front of his laptop looking pissed off as anything. Nothing new there.

"Where's Lucas?" Noah demanded, looking at Ryan, the cub's adoptive father.

Ryan looked at them, sniffed in surprise, then grinned because he could no doubt scent that they were mated. "He's over at Ana and Connor's playing with Vivian."

"Good. Tell him to stay the night. The rest of you get the hell out and don't come back all night. Tell everyone else to stay away from here too," he growled, barely holding on to his restraint. He couldn't wait until they had a house of their own and he and Erin could be naked all the time. He'd never want to leave the house.

Erin nudged his chest with her elbow. "Noah, you can't just kick everyone—"

Ryan snapped his laptop shut with a click and without a word the males got up and filed out, though of course Aiden had a shit-eating grin on his face. Not that Noah cared.

He was beyond caring about anything other than pushing deep inside Erin and claiming her forever. Looking around the place, he was relieved to see that it wasn't the usual pigsty. No dirty clothes or boxers anywhere. No food or dirty dishes lying around in weird places. There was even a fire blazing in the giant stone fireplace. He could move the coffee table out of the way and lay out some blankets.

He looked down at Erin to find her watching him with lust and curiosity. "What are you thinking about, Noah?"

"Are you sure you don't want to wait a month? I can do something special." With candles, flowers, and other romantic shit.

She snorted. "If you say you'll do something cheesy with flowers or candles, I'm going to punch you."

God, how did she read him so well?

"Have I ever indicated any of that crap is important to me? We could go find a private place in the woods right now and I'd be happy. I've never been more sure of anything in my entire life. I want this *now*."

Okay, that was all he needed to hear. He set her on her feet, then hurried to shove the table out of the way. "I'll be back in a minute." Without waiting for her response, he flew out of the room and up the stairs. They could have done this in his room, but he wanted space and the fire was kind of romantic. Not that he'd utter those words to anyone.

He scooped up a bunch of soft blankets he found in one of the linen closets and practically sprinted back down the stairs. He felt like an eager cub with his first crush. This was so much more than a crush though. Erin was his everything. He couldn't imagine life without her. While he hated how dangerous her job was, he loved that she was strong enough to take anything life threw at her.

Soon she was going to be completely linked to him. They'd be telepathically connected, strengthening their bond even more. Striding into the giant open living room he stumbled, then froze in midstep. Erin was completely naked, on her knees in front of the fire. Her profile was to him but she turned as she heard him.

The firelight illuminated her, making her look like some kind of an angel. She'd taken the braid out of her hair so that it fell around her face in soft waves. Her gray eyes glittered with lust as she raked them over him. "Why are you still dressed?" she asked softly.

His cock jumped to attention at that. It was a good question. In a second he was in front of her. With trembling hands, he tossed the blankets out next to them, layering them for added softness. By the time he was done and had turned back to her, Erin had grabbed the bottom of his sweater and was tugging it upward.

She was so eager, which only spurred him on. She yanked it over his head then shoved at his chest, sending him sprawling back against the blankets. Her hands shook too, which soothed his inner wolf. She was just as turned on as he was. Not that he had any doubts. Her magnolia scent had spiked and wrapped around him like a sweet embrace.

Practically ripping at them, she managed to yank his jeans off in seconds. His cock sprung free and all he could think about was sinking into her.

Until she took him in her mouth. His brain almost short-circuited. All his muscles pulled taut as her lips circled the crown of his erection. He closed his eyes, struggling to breathe for a moment, it felt so good. She teased him as she flicked her tongue down his length, then back up again. Sliding a hand through her silky hair, he cupped her head, but didn't press down, letting her set the pace. He just needed to be touching her, especially now. They might be mated, but this would change everything.

Groaning, he rolled his hips, unable to stay still. She was going excruciatingly slow—on purpose, he was sure. He'd teased her enough to know exactly what she was doing. Over the past couple of days they'd had sex every way imaginable and she'd done this more than a few times, and while he loved it, he didn't want to come in her mouth. Not tonight.

Tonight was all about the bonding.

"You taste amazing," she murmured against him, the vibration of her voice slamming through him.

"No talking," he gasped out.

She looked up at him in confusion. "What?"

"You can't say stuff that gets me even hotter when your mouth is on me. In fact . . ." He pulled her on top of him so that she straddled him. He savored the feel of her completely naked body pressed against his, wanting to stretch the moment out, but he was too impatient. Rolling over, he stopped only when she was pinned beneath him. One of his hands clasped her hip possessively and he slid the other under her nape and threaded his fingers through her hair. "No touching either."

A slow, wicked grin covered her face as she splayed her hands over his shoulders and squeezed. "You don't trust yourself?"

"Hell no." And he wasn't afraid to admit it. Not to her. With Erin he could completely be himself and never worry about her judging him. Being with her was freeing on every level and in a way he'd never imagined. Hell, never even hoped for with a female.

She reached around him and clutched his back. When she slid her hands down lower and dug her fingernails into his ass, he jerked against her. He could feel the tips of her claws extend, not piercing his skin, just enough to claim him. "Can I touch *this*?" she asked, her voice a seductive whisper.

He couldn't respond when she rolled her hips against his.

On a moan, she met his mouth, stroking against his tongue hungrily. He wanted to spend some time teasing her and getting her worked up before they bonded. But if she kept this up, he might throw his good intentions away.

Reaching between them, he cupped her mound, placing his thumb right over her clit. The little bud was swollen and begging for his touch. Satisfaction rolled through him when she let out a strangled sound. Using more pressure, he began circling right over her sensitive bundle of nerves with no reprieve.

When she began panting and grinding against his

hand, he slid two fingers inside her instead of one. He'd planned to tease her a little, but he was so damn worked up it was all he could do to give her just one orgasm before thrusting into her. But he'd give her another during and plenty after.

God, he just wanted inside her.

Her inner walls tightened around his fingers with each stroke. She was so wet he knew exactly how tight and slick she'd be when he slid his cock into her.

The past year Erin had come so far, from being so reserved and introverted to this sensual, amazing woman about to come apart in his arms. The fact that she not only loved him, but trusted him so much meant everything.

Erin surprised him by wrenching her head back and tearing her lips from his. "I want you in me when I come." A sharp demand.

One he was more than willing to carry out. Noah knew everything about the bonding process. Every shifter did. The male took the female from behind and sank his teeth into her neck during the full moon. It would solidify their bond and link them telepathically forever. But he didn't want to take her from behind. Not that they hadn't already had sex in that position and two dozen others, but right now it didn't feel right to him.

Something primal in him told him that wasn't for them. Pulling back so that he was sitting up, he drew Erin with him. Without having to say a word, she straddled him, sinking down onto his cock in one stroke.

He hissed in a breath at how good she felt. Grabbing her ass, he clutched on to her as she began to ride him.

Meeting her stroke for stroke, he thrust his hips up and into her tight body. Out of pure instinct, his canines descended. He knew what was coming. Her inner walls were convulsing around him so quickly he knew she was about to come.

A second later her climax hit fast and hard. Finally, he let go of his own control, letting the orgasm tear through him and pierce all his nerve endings. His entire body shook from the pleasure.

Burying his head against her neck, he sank his canines into her soft flesh. The moment he pierced her, she did the same to him.

He jerked even harder against her, emptying everything he had into her. It still blew his mind that she'd been ready to walk away because she assumed he wouldn't want her. God, how could anyone not want this brave, strong woman? As his canines retracted, so did hers. Instantly he felt the loss.

As his orgasm fled his body, he didn't move. Neither did Erin. She was plastered against him, her legs wrapped around his waist, her head still on his shoulder as she nuzzled his neck.

He did the same to her, kissing where he'd bitten her. Though he'd just climaxed, he was still rock hard and would be ready to go in another minute. Hell, he wanted to stay inside her all night if she'd let him.

Testing, testing. He heard Erin's words loud and clear in his head.

Pulling back, he stared into her wide gray eyes. "Did

it work?" she whispered, even though they were the only two people in the house.

Grinning he nodded. *I think you and I can cause a lot of mischief with this new gift.*

Erin laughed, the sound so rich and real it hit him square in the chest. She tackled him back against the blankets, still straddling him. "I love you more than anything."

I love you too, he projected, loving this new link between them. *What does my bonding symbol look like?* he asked.

"Holy crap, I forgot about that!" She scrambled off him and practically shoved him face-first into the blankets as she got a look at his back.

Noah stretched out on the soft fur blanket, resting his chin on his hands. "Was that really necessary?" he asked, chuckling.

She straddled his back and traced her finger over where he guessed his new tattoolike symbol was. When she didn't respond, he turned his head to see her. That's when he realized tears were streaking down her face. Immediately his stomach dropped. Had the bonding not been completed correctly? Did he not have a symbol? He clawed against the panic bubbling up inside him. "What's wrong?" he barely squeezed the words out.

She just shook her head. "Not a damn thing. You have two blades crisscrossed right on your upper left shoulder blade. . . . How do they, the gods or magic or whoever is responsible for this linking, *know* what the right symbol should be?" Her voice was impossibly thick with tears.

His own throat tightened at the knowledge that his

mark was a direct representation of her. His strong enforcer. Now his bondmate.

He twisted so that she was straddling his stomach. She swiped away her tears and he could see the joy shining in her stormy gray eyes as she looked down at him.

"I have no idea, but it's perfect. You're perfect." All he could do was stare at his lean mate as she sat there. The firelight created dancing shadows, playing off her beautiful features and naked body.

"I've never been more happy in my entire life," Erin murmured before she leaned down and kissed him.

Me neither, he projected to her.

Chapter 23

Erin leaned back against the couch in Ana and Connor's home. With her legs crossed and arms folded over her chest, she knew she probably looked defensive, but she wasn't at all. This new energy was pulsing through her and she could barely contain it. She and Noah were actually *bonded*. He loved her for exactly who she was. No stipulations. He accepted her. Period. That knowledge made her giddy and she could only imagine how goofy she'd look if she wasn't controlling all her energy. She wanted to tell everyone how amazing it was. Fucking shout it out to the world like a maniac.

After Noah had left to patrol this morning she'd been amped up. Even a seven-mile run hadn't taken the edge off and she'd ended up being the first one to arrive at the house.

Ana and Connor were in the kitchen and Jayce was on his way. Well, Vivian was sitting on the ground in front of her with Transformer action figures and talking about something. The jaguar cub Ana and Connor had adopted raised her dark eyebrows. Erin knew they might not be related by blood, but when Vivian got into a snit, she looked so much like Ana sometimes it stunned Erin.

Erin blinked. "What did you say?"

Vivian scowled at her in the way only a ten-year-old could. "Were you listening to *anything* I said?"

Completely chastised, she shook her head. "Sorry, hon."

Vivian sighed heavily. "I asked if you were back to stay for good. Lucas told me that Noah kicked every-one out of the guys' cabin last night and that it was now yours and Noah's."

Erin felt her face flush. At least Lucas didn't know the real reason they'd taken over the cabin. "No, it's still the guys' cabin. But, yes, I'm back for good. Mostly. I'll still have to leave for assignments but this will al-ways be my home."

Vivian put a hand to her forehead dramatically. "Good! I thought Lucas was going to move in here."

"I thought he was your best friend." The blond wolf cub was adorable and would definitely be a heart-breaker in a few years.

"He *is* my best friend, but he always tries to steal my toys."

"Uh, aren't those his Transformers?" Erin nodded pointedly at the little plastic toys in Vivian's hands.

Vivian's grin widened. "Not anymore." Then she jumped up and ran from the room, carrying the bundle of action figures with her.

As she left, Jayce strode into the room, his expression grim. Any humor she'd felt, left Erin in an instant.

Jayce gave her a tight smile as he collapsed on the couch across from her. "Where's your man?"

"On patrol." Even though she wished she and Noah could stay holed up for weeks engaging in nothing but sex, eating, and sleeping, the real world would never allow that. Especially not since she was an enforcer now. She had a feeling that taking an actual vacation was something she wouldn't be doing for decades. Not that she minded. And more important, Noah didn't either. "What's up? You look like you want to murder someone."

He glanced at the doorway. "Let's wait 'til Connor and Liam get here."

She nodded, the stone in her stomach growing heavier by the moment.

"Congrats," Jayce said, breaking the growing silence.

Now she did smile. No matter what she was about to hear from Jayce and no matter how bad it would inevitably be, she was now officially mated to Noah. Nothing and no one could ever change that. "Thanks. It's kind of awesome."

He snorted. "I know."

"How's Leila?" The young teenager whose parents had recently been murdered by vampires had come to live with Jayce and Kat. They were pretty sure that Leila had the makings of an enforcer too, though only time would tell.

Jayce's lips twitched. "She's a teenager full of hormones and she just met a human boy in town who rides a motorcycle." He said the last word in disgust.

Erin's eyebrows pulled together. "*You* ride a motorcycle."

"Exactly. I don't trust the little shit."

She snorted. "Is there anyone you'd trust with her?"

His lips pulled into a thin line, but he didn't respond.

She decided to change the subject. "So you really think she's like us?"

He nodded. "Definitely. I gave her some sparring sticks to practice with and she's almost as good as you. I'm almost afraid to put actual blades in her hands."

Erin's eyebrows rose at that. She was decades older than the young girl and had been fighting a lot longer. Erin couldn't wait to see the young shifter in action. "Damn."

Jayce just nodded again.

The front door opened, slammed, and Liam stomped in, scowling. He smiled as soon as he saw her though. "Congrats, short stuff! I heard the good news. Plus you stink like Noah now."

She rolled her eyes but stood and hugged him anyway. Seconds later Connor and Ana entered, carrying a tray of coffee mugs for everyone. Her eyes lit up and she snatched one from Connor's tray before he'd even set it down on the table.

After congratulations for her new bonding, they all settled around the table, Liam the only one standing by the fireplace. That wolf could never sit still.

"So what's going on?" Erin asked.

Jayce and Connor exchanged worried looks. Uh-oh. That was definitely not good.

"Strange things have been happening all over the state, but it seems as if the majority of the cases are centralized near Winston-Salem," Connor said darkly.

That was only a couple of hours from them. "What do you mean, strange things? This sounds like more than just vamp blood dealings."

"It is. Or we think it is. Everyone involved in the past couple weeks has been hopped up on vamp blood."

"Involved with what?"

Jayce's gray eyes went almost completely black for a moment. "There have been cases of older vamps committing suicide, humans hopped up on vamp blood robbing banks but once they come down from their high they don't remember any of it. That could just be something they're saying as a lame defense, but it's the same with all the humans committing crimes on vamp blood. Amnesia, or whatever, is not a side effect of taking vamp blood. In each case the humans said they felt as if they were in a fog, almost as if someone else was in control of their bodies."

"What about with the vamps acting strangely?"

Jayce shrugged. "None of them are alive to question."

Oh, right. "So what's the link? If there is any?"

"The humans bought vamp blood from different suppliers, but those suppliers all have a source in Winston-Salem. Right now I've managed to follow a trail to a well-known club that caters to supernatural beings."

The way Jayce said club was odd. "What kind of club?"

"Not exactly a strip club, but most of the employees

don't wear much clothing and they cater to every need a vampire or shifter or whoever could want."

"You've been there, huh?"

Jayce rolled his eyes. "It's all part of recon."

She lifted an eyebrow. "Is that what you told Kat?"

Ana stifled a laugh and Liam just growled in annoyance. Surprised, Erin turned to look at him. "What's wrong with you?"

"Jayce didn't get in trouble, *I* did." By his pained expression she could imagine he actually had.

Erin shut her mouth. Liam's mate was pregnant and probably a little hormonal. What female would want their male at a place with a bunch of naked women? Not Erin. "Okay, then. What's the plan?"

"Infiltrate the club, see what we can dig up," Connor said immediately.

As Jayce started talking about different ideas they had, Erin listened and tried not to focus on images of Noah completely naked and waiting for her back in his room. She couldn't wait until their house was built. Until then she figured they'd have to get creative about finding privacy. Realizing she'd zoned out, Erin quickly refocused on the conversation at hand.

The more Jayce and Connor talked, the clearer it became that this was going to be a big job for them all. As in the entire pack. If whatever was going on became widespread it could affect vampires everywhere—which would spill over to shifters and fae. Whether she liked it or not, what affected one supernatural being would inevitably affect them all. But she knew the real reason they were getting involved now was because of how close this was to Connor's territory. The Alpha had a right to be protective and he took his duties seriously. "When do we start?"

She realized she probably sounded too eager, especially when Jayce's lips quirked up. "I think I've created a monster."

After what she'd just dealt with in New Orleans she figured she was ready for anything. She'd killed the monster who'd stolen something huge from her and for the first time in forever, she felt whole. As long as she had Noah at her side, she could handle whatever nastiness life threw at them.

Epilogue

Ned Hartwig tossed another log onto the fire he'd recently made. It was damn cold out here, but there wasn't a soul hiking the Appalachian Trail this time of year. Too fucking cold. And right now he needed to stay hidden and away from everyone.

Ever since Jayce Kazan had forced him to blow up all his product a few weeks ago he'd been in hiding. Ned still mourned losing all that vamp blood. He'd had close to half a mil of unsold goods. People paid so much shit for vamp blood it was ridiculous. Good for his bottom line though. But that wasn't his real problem right now.

His problem was the scary motherfucker he'd gotten the stuff from in the first place. Ned wasn't sure what that guy was—vamp, shifter, or some scary-ass thing he'd never heard of—but the man's eyes turned a wicked red when he was angry and he'd seen his teeth descend before. But he wasn't sure if they were canines or fangs and he sure as hell wasn't brave enough to ask.

And those fucking eyes were the kind of red that made
him think of brimstone and hellfire. Growing up in the
Bible belt probably helped his imagination along, but
damn, that guy scared him more than *anyone*. Even
more than the feared enforcer for the North American
Council.

At least out in the woods Ned was safe. Well, safe
enough. There was no way anyone would find him out
in this cave. He'd been here only a few times before and
he'd never told anyone about it. It had the perfect ven-
tilation so he could build fires to keep warm, but the
structure also kept the actual fire hidden from outsid-
ers' eyes. If someone wanted to get to him they would
have to venture deep into his cave and he'd set up half
a dozen traps to ensure that didn't happen.

Satisfied the fire wouldn't die out before daybreak,
he lay back against his travel pillow and tucked his
sleeping bag around him. The second he closed his eyes,
a strange almost hollow feeling settled in his bones. As
if someone was sucking the life force from him.

Sitting up, he glanced around the dimly lit cave. His
heart had started beating overtime and he felt as if he
was being watched. But that was impossible. No one
would be getting past his traps.

Feeling foolish, he started to lie back down when a
shadow stepped from the darkness. The figure came
from the direction of the mouth of the cave. Ned instinctively reached for the gun he kept tucked under
his pillow but didn't pull it out yet. His fingers wrapped
around the cold steel. He savored the feel as he watched
the figure move with a lethal, supernatural grace that
told him this was no fucking human coming to see him.

Which raised the question—how the fuck had anyone gotten past his trip wires?

"Are you attempting to hide from me?" The low, male—and unfortunately familiar—voice ricocheted through him like shards of glass.

As the figure came closer, Ned could make out a long, black coat and a hood pulled up over the man's head. The guy often wore a hood, obscuring most of his face. But there was no doubt that this was *him*.

The man from Ned's worst nightmares. Once Ned had watched him stare a human down until that very human scratched and stabbed his own eyes out. It had been the freakiest thing he'd ever seen.

He cleared his throat, never taking his hand off his weapon. "I'm not hiding from anyone."

"That's not what it looks like. It looks like you stopped selling my product, then ran away instead of coming to me." The quiet note in the man's voice was a hell of lot more intimidating than if he'd started screaming threats.

He was like a predator, going all quiet right before the final strike of death. Ned tried to think of a lie, but then opted for the truth. Sometimes that really was the best policy. At this point, he didn't have anything to lose. Well, except his life. "I didn't stop intentionally. My bus was blown up." Technically true. It had been blown up. Of course, Ned had been the one to throw that grenade in it, triggering all the other explosives that sent that yellow rusted piece of junk sky high.

"I *know*." He said it with an air of absolute certainty, making Ned glad he'd told the truth.

Ned swallowed again. "You do?"

"Your silly human news stations do have some purposes." He laughed, the harsh sound grating against Ned's entire body.

The way the man with no name said "human" freaked him out, but he managed not to move a muscle. Ned wanted to remain as still as possible. Some small part of his brain hoped it would make the guy forget he was here. *Right*. Like that was possible. "Then you know it wasn't intentional."

"I know no such thing. Why did your bus blow up and who did it?"

Here came the tricky part. Ned felt like he was tap-dancing on a high beam a thousand yards up in the air with no safety net. He should be so lucky. A fall like that would just kill him. This guy . . . he fought off a shudder. "Jayce Kazan was sniffing around my trailer and bus. He'd heard from someone that I was selling vamp blood and wanted to know why."

A sharp intake of breath. "What did you tell him?"

"I didn't tell him shit. I did the only thing I could. I tossed a grenade into the bus and hauled ass. I don't know if he survived or not but—"

The man laughed again and this time it sounded real. "Of course he survived, you fool. Sometimes I wonder if even taking off that shifter's head would kill him. That's beside the point. You ran and you didn't reach out to me."

There he went again, sounding like he wanted to flay him alive. "I didn't know what else to do. I thought about coming to Winston-Salem but I worried I'd lead someone back to you." There, that actually sounded like a good reason.

The eerie silence that descended on the cave cut through Ned bone deep. He wasn't taking vampire blood anymore so he didn't have that extra dose of strength he'd grown accustomed to. Of course, something told him that no matter how much vamp blood he took, nothing would matter against this guy.

"Jayce Kazan knowing your identity is a problem I cannot overlook." Hoodie still pulled down over his face, the man stepped a few feet closer, though he was still several yards away. The flames in the fire danced so high they almost licked the ceiling of the cave.

Fuck.

Ned's hand tightened around his gun, though he had no control over it. Blinking, he looked away from the horrible flames and watched as his own hand brought the gun up. What the hell was going on? He tried to stop himself, but his body wouldn't listen to him. Panic punched through him, sweat pouring off his face in waves.

Suddenly the barrel was in his mouth. Ned wanted to scream, but the sound stuck in his throat. *No, no, no,* he silently shouted.

Then he pulled the trigger.

Acknowledgments

I owe a huge thank-you to my wonderful editor, Danielle Perez, for her guidance with this story. I'm also incredibly grateful to the New American Library art department for the gorgeous cover. You all never disappoint. Thank you to my agent, Jill Marsal, for her continuous support. For my readers, words fall short, but thank you for loving the Moon Shifter world as much as I do. You guys are amazing and I'm so appreciative of your kind e-mails. Kari Walker, thank you for reading the early version of this story and being the biggest cheerleader anyone could ask for. Cynthia Eden, thank you for that first research trip we took to New Orleans! I can't wait for our next trip back. For my husband and son, who put up with my insane writer's schedule, thank you a billion times over. And as always, thank you to God for His never-ending support.

Don't miss the first novel in the exciting
Deadly Ops series by Katie Reus,

TARGETED

Available now.

Prologue

Marine Corps Scout Sniper motto: one shot, one kill.

Sam Kelly could see his GP tent fifty yards away. He was practically salivating at the thought of a shower and a clean bed. But he'd settle for the fucking bed at this point. He didn't even care that he was sharing that tent with twenty other men. Showers were almost pointless at this dusty military base in hellish sub-Saharan Africa anyway. By the time he got back to his tent from the showers, he'd be covered in a film of grime again.

Four weeks behind enemy lines with limited supplies and he was also starving. Even an MRE sounded good about now. As he trekked across the dry, cracked ground, he crossed his fingers that the beef jerky he'd stashed in his locker was still there, but he doubted it. His bunkmate had likely gotten to it weeks ago. Greedy fucker.

"There a reason you haven't shaved, Marine?"

Sam paused and turned at the sound of the condescending, unfamiliar voice. An officer—a lieutenant—he didn't recognize stood a few feet away, his pale face flushed and his skin already burning under the hot sun. With one look Sam knew he was new in-country. Why the hell wasn't the idiot wearing a boonie hat to protect his face? Hell, it had to be a hundred and thirty degrees right now. Yeah, this dick was definitely new. Otherwise, he wouldn't be hassling Sam.

Sam gave him a blank stare and kept his stance relaxed. "Yes, sir, there is. Relaxed grooming standards." *Dumbass.*

The blond man's head tilted to the side just a fraction, as if he didn't understand the concept. God, could this guy be any greener? The man opened his mouth again and Sam could practically hear the stupid shit he was about to spout off by the arrogant look on his face.

"Lieutenant! There a reason you're bothering my boy?" Colonel Seamus Myers was barreling toward them, dust kicking up under his feet with each step.

The man reminded Sam of an angry bull, and when he got pissed, everyone suffered. He was a good battalion commander, though. Right now Sam was just happy the colonel wasn't directing that rage at him. Guy could be a scary fucker when he wanted.

"No, sir. I was just inquiring about his lack of grooming." The officer's face flushed even darker under his spreading sunburn. Yeah, that was going to itch something fierce when it started peeling. Sam smiled inwardly at the thought.

"You're here one week and you think you know more than me?"

"N-no, sir! Of course not, sir."

The colonel leaned closer and spoke so low that Sam couldn't hear him. But he could guess what he was saying because he'd heard it before. *Stay the fuck away from Sam Kelly and the rest of my snipers or I'll send you home.* Rank definitely mattered, but to the colonel, his few snipers were his boys, and the man had been in more wars than Sam ever wanted to think about. Sam had seen and caused enough death himself to want to get out when his enlistment was up. That wasn't too far off either. He'd been to Iraq, Afghanistan, a few places in South America that weren't even on his official record, and now he was stationed in Djibouti, Africa. Or hell, as he liked to think of it. He loved his job and he loved his country, but enough was enough. Sam just wished he could figure out what the hell he wanted to do if he got out of the military.

He watched as the colonel started talking—loudly—to the new guy. Getting right in his face as only a pissed-off Marine could. Sam almost felt sorry for the guy, but what kind of stupid fucker didn't know that since the environment here was so dirty that staph infections were rampant, grooming standards were *different*? That was one of the reasons he and a thousand other guys his age had relaxed grooming standards in the bowels of this hellish place. But they also cut him slack because he was a sniper. Sometimes he had to blend in with the populace, among other things. He might be stationed in Africa, but he'd just gotten back from—where else?—Afghanistan. He'd stayed holed up for days in that dank cave just waiting—

"Sergeant, in my tent. Now."

Sam blinked and realized Colonel Myers was talking to him. He nodded. "Yes, sir."

The colonel was still reaming out whoever the newbie was, but Sam always followed orders. Looked as though that shower was going to wait. The walk to the big tent in the middle of the base was short.

As he drew the flap back and stepped into the colonel's tent, he stilled when he spotted a dark-haired man leaning against a table with maps on it. He looked as if he thought he had every right to be there too. Interesting. A fly landed on Sam's face, but he didn't move. Just watched the man, ready to go for one of his weapons if need be. He didn't recognize him and he wasn't wearing a uniform.

Just simple fatigues and a T-shirt that stretched across a clearly fit body even though the guy had to be pushing fifty. There was something about the man that put Sam on edge. He was like a tiger, coiled and waiting to rip your head off. The man's eyes weren't cold, exactly, but they were calculating.

Carefully the man reached for a manila folder next to him and flipped it open. He glanced down at it. "Sam Kelly. Originally from Miami, Florida. Grew up in foster care. No known family. One of the best damn snipers Myers has ever seen. Sniper school honor grad, aptitude for languages, takes orders well, possibly a lifer." He glanced up then, his green eyes focusing on Sam like a laser. "But I don't think you're a lifer. You want a change, don't you?" The man's gaze was shrewd, assessing. Sam didn't like being analyzed, especially by a stranger. And the guy didn't even have an accent, so he couldn't place where he might be from. Nothing in his speech stood out.

Who the hell was this guy? And how the fuck did he know Sam wanted a change? It wasn't as if he'd told anyone. Sam ran through the list of possibilities. He'd been on different operations before, sometimes working for the CIA for solo things, and he'd been attached to various SEAL teams for larger-scale missions, but he'd never worked with this guy before. He did have Sam's file, though—or Sam guessed that was his file in the man's hand. He could just be bluffing. But what would the point of that be? He dropped all semblance of protocol since this guy clearly wasn't a Marine. "Who are you and what do you want?"

"You did some good work in Cartagena a few years ago." He snapped the file shut and set it back on the table.

Sam just stared at him. His statement said a lot all by itself. That mission wasn't in his official jacket, so this guy knew classified shit and was letting Sam know it. But since he hadn't asked a question or introduced himself, Sam wasn't inclined to respond.

The man's lips quirked up a fraction. As they did, the tent flap opened and the colonel strode in. He glared at the man, cursed, then looked at Sam, his expression almost speculative. He jerked a thumb at the stranger. "Whatever this guy tells you is the truth and he's got top secret clearance." He snorted, as if something was funny about that, then sobered. "And whatever you decide . . . Hell, I know what you'll decide.

Good luck, son. I'll miss you." He shook Sam's hand, then strode out of the tent.

Miss him? What the hell was he talking about? Sam glared at the man in front of him. "I asked you once who you were. Answer or I'm out of here."

The stranger crossed the short distance and held out his hand.

Sam ignored it.

The man cleared his throat and looked as if he was fighting a smile, which just pissed Sam off. "I'm Lieutenant General Wesley Burkhart, head of—"

"The NSA. I know the name." Sam didn't react outwardly, but the gears in his head were turning. "What do you want with me? I thought you guys were into cryptography and cyber stuff."

"We are, but I'm putting together a team of men and women with a different skill set. Black ops stuff, similar to the CIA, but with less . . . rules. I want to offer you a job, but before I go any further, you need to know that if you come to work for me, Sam Kelly will cease to exist. You will leave your past and everything in it behind."

Sam stared at the man, overwhelmed by too many feelings. Relief being one of them. Leaving his identity behind didn't seem like such a bad thing at all. Finishing the rest of his enlistment in shitholes like this wasn't something he looked forward to. He'd seen and caused so much death that sometimes he wondered if God would ever forgive him. The idea of wiping his record clean was so damn appealing. Maybe this was the fresh start he'd been looking for. Except . . . he touched the hog's tooth hanging from his neck. He'd bled, sweated, and starved for this thing. For what it represented. It was part of him now. "I'm not taking this off. Ever."

The other man's eyes flicked to the bullet around his neck, and the corners of his mouth pulled up slightly. "Unless the op calls for it, I wouldn't expect you to."

Okay, then. Heart thudding, Sam dropped his rucksack to the ground. "Tell me everything I need to know."

Chapter 1

Black Death 9 Agent: member of an elite group of men and women employed by the NSA for covert, off-the-books operations. A member's purpose is to gain the trust of targeted individuals in order to gather information or evidence by any means necessary.

Five years later

Jack Stone opened and quietly shut the door behind him as he slipped into the conference room. A few analysts and field agents were already seated around the long rectangular table. One empty chair remained.

A few of the new guys looked up as he entered, but the NSA's security was tighter than Langley's. Since he was the only one missing from this meeting, the senior members pored over the briefs in front of them without even giving him a cursory glance.

Wesley Burkhart, his boss, handler, and recruiter all

rolled into one, stuck his head in the room just as Jack started to sit. "Jack, my office. Now."

He inwardly cringed because he knew that tone well. At least his bags were still packed. Once he was out in the hall, heading toward Wesley's office, his boss briefly clapped him on the back. "Sorry to drag you out of there, but I've got something bigger for you. Have you had a chance to relax since you've been back?"

Jack shrugged, knowing his boss didn't expect an answer. After working two years undercover to bring down a human trafficking ring that had also been linked to a terrorist group in Southern California, he was still decompressing. He'd been back only a week and the majority of his time had been spent debriefing. It would take longer than a few days to wash the grime and memories off him. If he ever did. "You've got another mission for me already?"

Wesley nodded as he opened the door to his office. "I hate sending you back into the field so soon, but once you read the report, you'll understand why I don't want anyone else."

As the door closed behind them, Jack took a seat in front of his boss's oversized solid oak desk. "Lay it on me."

"Two of our senior analysts have been hearing a lot chatter lately linking the Vargas cartel and Abu al-Ramaan's terrorist faction. At this point, the only solid connection we have is South Beach Medical Supply."

"SBMS is involved?" The medical company delivered supplies and much-needed drugs to third-world countries across the globe. Ronald Weller, the owner, was such a straight arrow it didn't seem possible.

"Looks that way." His boss handed him an inch-thick manila folder.

Jack picked up the packet and looked over the first document. As he skimmed the report, his chest tightened painfully as long-buried memories clawed at him with razor-sharp talons. After reading the key sections, he looked up. "Is there a chance Sophie is involved?" Her name rolled off his tongue so naturally, as if he'd spoken to her yesterday and not thirteen years ago. As if saying it was no big deal. As if he didn't dream about her all the damn time.

Wesley shook his head. "We don't know. Personally, I don't think so, but it looks like her boss is."

"Ronald Weller? Where are you getting this information?" Jack had been on the West Coast for the last two years, dealing with his own bullshit. A lot could have changed in that time, but SBMS involved with terrorists—he didn't buy it.

"Multiple sources have confirmed his involvement, including Paul Keane, the owner of Keane Flight. We've got Mr. Keane on charges of treason, among other things. He rolled over on SBMS without too much persuasion, but we still need actual proof that SBMS is involved, not just a traitor's word."

"How is Keane Flight involved?"

"Instead of just flying medical supplies, they've been picking up extra cargo."

Jack's mind immediately went to the human trafficking he'd recently dealt with, and he gritted his teeth. "Cargo?"

"Drugs, guns . . . possibly biological weapons."

The first two were typical cargo of most smugglers,

but biological shit put Keane right on the NSA's hit list. "What do you want from me?"

His boss rubbed a hand over his face. "I've already built a cover for you. You're a silent partner with Keane Flight. Now that Paul Keane is incapacitated, you'll be taking over the reins for a while, giving you full access to all his dealings."

"Incapacitated, huh?"

The corners of Wesley's mouth pulled up slightly. "He was in a car accident. Bad one."

"Right." Jack flipped through the pages of information. "Where's Keane really at right now?"

"In federal protection until we can bring this whole operation down, but publicly he's in a coma after a serious accident—one that left him scarred beyond recognition and the top half of his body in bandages."

Jack didn't even want to know where they'd gotten the body. Probably a John Doe no one would miss. "So what's the deal with my role?"

"Paul Keane has already made contact with Weller about you—days before his accident. Told him he was taking a vacation and you'd be helping out until he got back. Weller was cautious on the phone, careful not to give up anything. Now that Keane is 'injured,' no one can ask him any questions. Keane's assistant is completely in the dark about everything and thinks you're really a silent partner. You've been e-mailing with her the past week to strengthen your cover, but you won't need to meet her in person. You're supposed to meet with Weller in two days. We want you to completely infiltrate the day-to-day workings of SBMS. We need to know if Weller is working with anyone else, if he has more contacts we're not privy to. Everything."

"Why can't you tap his phone?" That should be child's play for the NSA.

His boss's expression darkened. "So far we've been unable to hack his line. I've got two of my top analysts, Thomas Chadwick and Steven Williams—I don't think you've met either of them." When Jack shook his head, Wesley continued. "The fact that's he's got a filter that *we* can't bust through on his phone means he's probably into some dirty stuff."

Maybe. Or maybe the guy was just paranoid. Jack glanced at the report again, but didn't get that same rush he'd always gotten from his work. The last two years he'd seen mothers and fathers sell their children into slavery for less than a hundred dollars. And that wasn't even the worst of it. In the past he hadn't been on a job for more than six months at a time and he'd never been tasked with anything so brutal before, but in addition to human trafficking, they'd been selling people to scientists—under the direction of Albanian terrorists—who had loved having an endless supply of illegals to experiment on. He rolled his shoulders and shoved those thoughts out of his head. "What am I meeting him about?" *And how the hell will I handle seeing Sophie?* he thought.

"You supposedly want to go over flight schedules and the books and you want to talk about the possibility of investing in his company."

Jack was silent for a long beat. Then he asked the only question that mattered. The question that would burn him alive from the inside out until he actually voiced it. The question that made him feel as if he'd swallowed glass shards as he asked, "Will I be working with Sophie?"

Wesley's jaw clenched. "She *is* Weller's assistant."

"So yes."

Those knowing green eyes narrowed. "Is that going to be a problem?"

Yes. "No."

"She won't recognize you. What're you worried about?" Wesley folded his hands on top of the desk.

Jack wasn't worried about *her*. He was worried he couldn't stay objective around her. Sophie thought he was dead. And thanks to expensive facial reconstruction— all part of the deal in killing off his former identity when he'd joined Wesley's team with the NSA—she'd never know his true identity. Still, the thought of being in the same zip code as her sent flashes of heat racing down his spine. With a petite, curvy body made for string bikinis and wet T-shirt contests, Sophie was the kind of woman to make a man do a double take. He'd spent too many hours dreaming about running his hands through that thick dark hair again as she rode him. When they were seventeen, she'd been his ultimate fantasy and once they'd finally crossed that line from friends to lovers, there had been no keeping their hands off each other. They'd had sex three or four times a day whenever they'd been able to sneak away and get a little privacy. And it had never been enough with Sophie. She'd consumed him then. Now his boss wanted him to voluntarily work with her. "Why not send another agent?"

"I don't *want* anyone else. In fact, no one else here knows you're going in as Keane's partner except me."

Jack frowned. It wasn't the first time he'd gone undercover with only Wesley as his sole contact, but if his boss had people already working on the connection between Vargas and SBMS, it would be protocol for the direct team to know he was going in undercover. "Why?"

"I don't want to risk a leak. If I'm the only one who knows you're not who you say you are, there's no chance of that."

There was more to it than that, but Jack didn't question him. He had that blank expression Jack recognized all too well that meant he wouldn't be getting any more, not even under torture.

Wesley continued. "You know more about Sophie than most people. I want you to use that knowledge to get close to her. I don't think I need to remind you that this is a matter of national security."

"I haven't seen her since I was eighteen." And not a day went by that he didn't think of the ways he'd failed her. What the hell was Wesley thinking?

"It's time for you to face your past, Jack." His boss suddenly straightened and took on that professorial/fatherly look Jack was accustomed to.

"Is that what this is about? Me, facing my past?" he ground out. Fuck that. If he wanted to keep his memories buried, he damn well would.

Wesley shrugged noncommittally. "You *will* complete this mission."

As Jack stood, he clenched his jaw so he wouldn't say something he'd regret. Part of him wanted to tell Wesley to take his order and shove it, but another part—his most primal side—hummed with anticipation at the thought of seeing Sophie. She'd always brought out his protective side. Probably because she'd been his entire fucking world at one time and looking out for her had been his number-one priority.

He'd noticed Sophie long before she'd been aware of his existence, but once he was placed in the same foster house as her, they'd quickly become best friends. Probably because he hadn't given her a choice in being his friend. He'd just pushed right past her shy exterior until she came to him about anything and everything. Then one day she'd kissed him. He shoved *that* thought right out of his mind.

"There's a car waiting to take you to the flight strip. Once you land in Miami, there will be another car waiting for you. There's a full wardrobe, and anything else you'll need at the condo we've arranged."

"What about my laptop?"

"It's in the car."

When he was halfway to the door, his boss stopped him again. "You need to face your demons, Jack. Seeing Sophie is the only way you'll ever exorcise them. Maybe you can settle down and start a family once you do. I want to see you happy, son."

Son. If only he'd had a father like Wesley growing up. But if he had, he wouldn't have ended up where he was today. And he'd probably never have met Sophie. That alone made his shitty childhood worth every punch and bruise he'd endured. Jack swallowed hard, but didn't turn around before exiting. His chest loosened a little when he was out from under Wesley's scrutiny. The older man might be in his early fifties, but with his skill set, Jack had no doubt his boss could take out any one of the men within their covert organization. That's why he was the deputy director of the NSA and the unidentified head of the covert group Jack worked for.

Officially, Black Death 9 didn't exist. Unofficially, the name was whispered in back rooms and among other similar black ops outfits within the government. Their faction was just another classified group of men and women working to keep their country safe. At times like this Jack wished the NSA didn't have a thick file detailing every minute detail of his past. If they didn't, another agent would be heading for Miami right now and he'd be on his way to a four-star hotel or on another mission.

Jack mentally shook himself as he placed his hand on the elevator scanner. Why was Wesley trying to get under his skin? Now, of all times? The man was too damn intuitive for his own good. He'd been after him for years to see Sophie in person, "to find closure" as he put it, but Jack couldn't bring himself to do it. He had no problem facing down the barrel of a loaded gun, but seeing the woman with the big brown eyes and the soft curves he so often dreamed about—*no, thank you.*

As the elevator opened into the aboveground parking garage, he shoved those thoughts away. He'd be seeing Sophie in two days. Didn't matter what he wanted.

Sophie Moreno took a deep, steadying breath and eased open the side door to one of Keane Flight's hangars. She had a key, so it wasn't as though she was technically breaking in. She was just coming by on a Sunday night when no one was here. And the place was empty. And she just happened to be wearing a black cap to hide her hair.

Oh yeah, she was completely acting like a normal, law-abiding citizen. Cringing at her stupid rationalization, she pushed any fears of getting caught she had to the side. What she was doing wasn't about her.

She loved her job at South Beach Medical Supply, but lately her boss had been acting weird and the flight logs from Keane Flight for SBMS's recent deliveries didn't make sense. They hadn't for the past few months.

And no one—meaning her boss, Ronald Weller—would answer her questions when she brought up anything about Keane Flight.

Considering Ronald hadn't asked her over to dinner in the past few months either as he normally did, she had a feeling he and his wife must be having problems. They'd treated her like a daughter for almost as long as she'd been with SBMS, so if he was too distracted to look into things because of personal issues, she was going to take care of this herself. SBMS provided much-needed medical supplies to third-world countries, and she wasn't going to let anything jeopardize that. People needed them. And if she could help out Ronald, she wanted to.

She didn't even know what she was looking for, but she'd decided to trust her gut and come here. Wearing all black, she felt a little stupid, like a cat burglar or something, but she wanted to be careful. Hell, she'd even parked outside the hangar and sneaked in through an opening in the giant fence surrounding the private airport. The security here should have been tighter—

something she would address later. After she'd done her little B&E. God, she was so going to get in trouble if she was caught. She could tell herself that she wasn't "technically" doing anything wrong, but her palms were sweaty as she stole down the short hallway to where it opened up into a large hangar.

Two twin-engine planes sat there, and the overhead lights from the warehouselike building were dim. But they were bright enough for her to make out a lot of cargo boxes and crates at the foot of one of the planes. The back hatch was open and it looked as if someone had started loading the stuff, then stopped.

Sophie glanced around the hangar as she stepped fully into it just to make sure she was alone. Normally Paul Keane had standard security here. She'd actually been here a couple of weeks ago under the guise of needing paperwork and there had been two Hispanic guys hovering near the planes as if they belonged there. She'd never seen them before and they'd given her the creeps. They'd also killed her chance of trying to sneak in and see what kind of cargo was on the planes.

When she'd asked Paul about them, he'd just waved off her question by telling her he'd hired new security.

One thing she knew for sure. He'd lied straight to her face. Those guys were sure as hell *not* security. One of them had had a MAC-10 tucked into the front of his pants. She might not know everything about weapons, but she'd grown up in shitty neighborhoods all over Miami, so she knew enough. And no respectable security guy carried a MAC-10 with a freaking *suppressor*. That alone was incredibly shady. The only people she'd known to carry that type of gun were gangbangers and other thugs.

So even if she felt a little crazy for sneaking down here, she couldn't go to her boss about any illegal activities—if there even were any—without proof. SBMS was Ronald's heart. He loved the company and she did too. No one was going to mess with it if she had anything to say about it.

Since the place was empty, she hurried across the wide expanse, her black ballet-slipper-type shoes virtually silent. When she neared the back of the plane, she braced herself for someone to be waiting inside.

It was empty except for some crates. Bypassing the crates on the outside, she ran up inside the plane and took half a dozen pictures of the crates with the SBMS logo on the outside. Then she started opening them.

By the time she opened the fifth crate, she was starting to feel completely insane, but as she popped the next lid, ice chilled her veins. She blinked once and struggled to draw in a breath, sure she was seeing things.

A black grenade peeked through the yellow-colored stuffing at the top. Carefully she lifted a bundle of it. There were more grenades lining the smaller crate, packed tight with the fluffy material. Her heart hammered wildly as it registered that Keane was likely running arms and weapons using SBMS supplies as cover, but she forced herself to stay calm. Pulling out her cell phone, she started snapping pictures of the inside of the crate, then pictures that showed the logo on the outside. In the next crate she found actual guns. AK-47s, she was pretty sure. She'd never actually seen one in real life before, but it looked like what she'd seen in movies. After taking pictures of those, she hurried out of the back of the plane toward the crates sitting behind it.

Before she could decide which one to open first, a loud rolling sound rent the air—the hangar door!

Ducking down, she peered under the plane and saw the main door the planes entered and exited through starting to open. Panic detonated inside her. She had no time to do anything but run. Without pause, she raced back toward the darkened hallway. She'd go out the back, the same way she'd come in. All she had to do was get to that hallway before whoever—

"Hey!" a male voice shouted.

Crap, someone had seen her. She shoved her phone in her back pocket and sprinted even faster as she cleared the hallway. Fear ripped through her, threatening to pull her apart at the seams. She wouldn't risk turning around and letting anyone see her face.

The exit door clanged against the wall as she slammed it open. Male voices shouted behind her, ordering her to stop in Spanish.

Her lungs burned and her legs strained with each pounding step against the pavement. She really wished she'd worn sneakers. As she reached the edge of the fence that thankfully had no lighting and was lined with bushes and foliage behind it, she dove for the opening. If she hadn't known where it was, it would be almost impossible to find without the aid of light.

Crawling on her hands and knees, she risked a quick glance behind her. Two men were running across the pavement toward the fence, weapons silhouetted in their hands. She couldn't see their faces because the light from the back of the hangar was behind them, but they were far enough away that she should be able to escape. They slowed as they reached the fence, both looking around in confusion.

"*Adonde se fue?*" one of them snarled.

Sophie snorted inwardly as she shoved up from the ground and disappeared behind the bushes. They'd never catch her now. Not unless they could jump fences in single bounds. Twenty yards down, her car was still parked on the side of the back road where she'd left it.

The dome light came on when she opened the door, so she shut it as quickly as possible. She started her car but immediately turned off the automatic lights and kicked the vehicle into drive. Her tires made a squealing sound and she cringed. She needed to get out of there before those men figured out how to get through the fence. She couldn't risk them seeing her license plate. Only law enforcement should be able to track plates, but people who were clearly running weapons wouldn't care about breaking laws to find out who she was.

She glanced in the rearview mirror as her car disappeared down the dark road, and didn't see anyone in the road or by the side of it. Didn't mean they weren't there, though. Pure adrenaline pumped through her as she sped away, tearing through her like jagged glass, but her hands remained steady on the wheel.

What the hell was she supposed to do now? If she called the cops, this could incriminate SBMS and that could ruin all the good work their company had done over the past decade. And what if by the time the cops got there all the weapons were gone? Then she'd look crazy and would have admitted to breaking into a private airport hangar, which was against the law. Okay, the cops were out. For now. First she needed to talk to her boss. He'd know what to do and they could figure out this mess together.

ALSO AVAILABLE FROM

NEW YORK TIMES BESTSELLING AUTHOR

Katie Reus

The first book in the Moon Shifter series

Alpha Instinct

Ana Cordona has been a strong leader for the few
remaining lupine shifters in her pack. But with no Alpha
male, the pack is vulnerable to the devious shifter Taggart,
who wants to claim both their ranch and Ana as his own.
When Connor Armstrong comes back into her life,
promising protection, it's *almost* enough to make Ana
forget how he walked out on her before—and she
reluctantly accepts his offer to mate.

Taggart and his rival pack are not the only enemies.
A human element in town is targeting shifters. Their plan
not only threatens Ana and Connor's future—but the
lives of the entire pack.

"A wild, hot ride."
—*New York Times* bestselling author Cynthia Eden

Available wherever books are sold or at
penguin.com

facebook.com/ProjectParanormalBooks

ALSO AVAILABLE FROM

NEW YORK TIMES BESTSELLING AUTHOR

Katie Reus

The second book in the Moon Shifter series

Primal Possession

As his pack's second-in-command, lupine shifter Liam
Armstrong is used to giving orders—not taking them.
That works fine until he meets December McIntyre.
Liam knows the human is his intended mate the moment
he sees her, but December is too strong-willed to accept
his protection. December has every reason to mistrust
shifters after one killed her youngest sibling.

Things get even more complicated when a radical hate
group targets all humans known to sympathize with
paranormal beings. When December is attacked in the
bookstore she owns, she reluctantly turns to the only
person who can help her: Liam.

"You'll look forward to visiting this world again soon!"
—*RT Book Reviews*

Available wherever books are sold or at
penguin.com

facebook.com/ProjectParanormalBooks

ALSO AVAILABLE FROM

NEW YORK TIMES BESTSELLING AUTHOR

Katie Reus

The third book in the Moon Shifter series

Mating Instinct

For centuries, powerful lupine shifter Jayce Kazan has
managed to stay away from humans...until he meets
Kat Saburova. While Jayce shares his passion with the
human seer, he refuses to make her his bondmate—
a refusal that causes the end of their relationship.
A year later, an attack that left Kat near death has
resulted in another lupine shifter turning her. Furious
that he wasn't the one to save her, Jayce is determined
to show Kat that he is the one she should rely on...

**"Reus has an instinct for what wows in this
perfect blend of shifter, suspense, and sexiness."
—*New York Times* bestselling author Caridad Piñeiro**

Available wherever books are sold or at
penguin.com

facebook.com/ProjectParanormalBooks